LADY BERESFORD'S LOVER

Vivian hesitated. "The dance floor is the other way."

"I know." The last few days of being in her presence, and always with others, had decided him. She was his, and this evening he would not share her. It was past time she was made to realize how he felt, how much he wanted her.

Rupert placed his lips close to her ear. "I wish to be alone with you."

Her eyes widened in surprise. "You do?"

She was so beautiful, his heart ached with wanting. The pulse at the base of her throat throbbed, as his must be doing as well. "More than anything."

He guided her around the edges of the rapidly filling ballroom, onto the balcony. It was blessedly empty. The music began, and he took her in his arms. For a moment she was stiff, then she relaxed and allowed him to pull her close. "You are intoxicatingly beautiful."

Behind her mask, her lashes lowered. "I have to say, I've never seen a more handsome Mark Antony."

"Nor I a more lovely Cleopatra. Stay with me."

"But I can only dance with you twice."

"Not tonight. That is one purpose of a masquerade. Who is to know who we are?"

"Oh, I see." She pulled her full lower lip between her teeth. "I—I—"

Twirling her into the shadows, he brought them to a halt. With one finger, he raised her chin. "Be with me."

He lowered his lips to hers. Touching softly, tasting, allowing her to grow used to his attentions . . .

Books by Ella Quinn

THE SEDUCTION OF LADY PHOEBE

THE SECRET LIFE OF MISS ANNA MARSH

THE TEMPTATION OF LADY SERENA

DESIRING LADY CARO

ENTICING MISS EUGÉNIE VILLARET

A KISS FOR LADY MARY

LADY BERESFORD'S LOVER

Novellas

MADELEINE'S CHRISTMAS WISH

Published by Kensington Publishing Corporation

Lady Beresford's Lover

ELLA QUINN

LYRICAL PRESS
Kensington Publishing Corp.
www.kensingtonbooks.com

LYRICAL PRESS BOOKS are published by

Kensington Publishing Corp.
119 West 40th Street
New York, NY 10018

All Kensington titles, imprints, and distributed lines are available at special quantity discounts for bulk purchases for sales promotion, premiums, fund-raising, educational, or institutional use.

Special book excerpts or customized printings can also be created to fit specific needs. For details, write or phone the office of the Kensington Sales Manager: Kensington Publishing Corp., 119 West 40th Street, New York, NY 10018. Attn. Sales Department. Phone: 1-800-221-2647.

Lyrical and the L logo are trademarks of Kensington Publishing Corp.

First Electronic Edition: July 2015
eISBN-13: 978-1-60183-458-4
eISBN-10: 1-60183-458-6

First Print Edition: July 2015
ISBN-13: 978-1-60183-459-1
ISBN-10: 1-60183-459-4

Printed in the United States of America

When I originally set out to write this book, I had intended it to be Rupert's story. Then I met Vivian, a young, beautiful woman with horrible body issues. Which is, sadly, a problem that many women suffer from today. So this book is dedicated to every woman who has trouble believing she is beautiful just the way she is. And to my granddaughter, Josephine, who I hope always thinks she is beautiful.

ACKNOWLEDGMENTS

As always, I want to thank the following people: My critique partners. They push me to make the book better. My wonderful agent Elizabeth Pomada, for taking a chance on a very new writer. My fabulous editor John Scognamiglio, for the support he has given me, particularly recently as I've been going through some major life changes. Rebecca Cremonese, for the great job she does correcting my mistakes, and the rest of the Kensington staff for the great job they do in making my books possible. And my readers. You are the best!

CHAPTER ONE

End of August 1817, Beresford Abbey, England

Vivian, the widowed Countess of Beresford, sat at her desk in the morning room of the dower house in which she'd been living for the past year, plotting her escape. A beam of bright afternoon sunshine shot along the gold and blue Turkey carpet, interrupted only by the supine form of her gray cat, Gisila.

In truth, plotting was probably too strong a word, though Vivian liked how it sounded. And she did feel as if she was escaping not only the dower house but Beresford Abbey itself. In a few short days her period of mourning would end.

Her hand clenched as if she could strike her dead husband and everyone else in this hellish place. Once gone, she vowed never to return to this estate and the market town where everyone had known of her late husband's deceit and had pitied her, but had said nothing. Not that Vivian had ever been given the opportunity to be a real wife. Soon after her marriage, Edgar, who at the time was still the heir, couldn't stand the sight of her, in or out of the bedchamber. Mrs. Raeford had that honor, if it could be called such, absent the ring and title, of course.

Vivian should not have had such great expectations of her marriage, but while their fathers arranged the union, Edgar had been attentive and charming. Father had assured her this was a good match and a dutiful daughter would trust her papa, like the good puss she was. After all, he had said in a kind tone, Vivian was no great beauty, too blond when the fashion was for dark hair, slender to the point of skinny when men preferred voluptuous ladies, and too bookish.

Although, if someone, anyone, would have told her about her future husband's lover, Vivian was sure she could have brought herself to refuse the match, for among her many failures was too much pride.

She waited for the familiar rage to rise, but after a year of waiting to be released from her duty to her husband, there were no more tears, and the pains in her stomach had finally ceased.

She would never again allow herself to be so naïve, or so trusting. Giving herself a shake, she opened the weekly letter from her mother.

> *My darling Vivian,*
>
> *I am so pleased to hear you are going to Town with Cousin Clara. As you are aware, your father and I had not planned to arrive for another several weeks. However, there has been a new development. Your father has taken it into his head that he needs a new hunting bitch, and nothing will do but he must have it immediately. All else has been forgot in his search. You may well imagine my frustration, but Papa will have his way. Consequently, it appears we will not attend the Little Season at all.*
>
> *Have a wonderful time. I look forward to your letters concerning the entertainments.*
>
> *Give Clara my best.*
>
> *With much love,*
>
> *Mama*
>
> *VB*

Poor Mama. Did reasonable men even exist?

"My lady—" Hal, who'd been her personal footman since her come out, hovered in the open door. "The new Lord Beresford asks if you'll receive him."

What could he possibly want? Since the reading of the will, Vivian hadn't had much to do with her husband's cousin and best friend who'd come into the title.

Well, whatever it was, she would not allow it to stop her from leaving.

"I'll see him. Please bring tea and ask Miss Corbet to join me." Silvia Corbet, the vicar's eldest daughter, had been Vivian's companion for the past year, and during that time Vivian had come to love Silvia like a sister.

"Yes, my lady. I'll get her first."

"Thank you. That would be best."

Vivian was not completely conversant concerning the rules of being a widow, but she could not think they would allow her to be in the same room with a gentleman who was not a close relation. Or perhaps that was incorrect. She had heard that some widows took lovers. Still, she did not want to be alone with the man. In any event, he could have nothing to say that would interest her.

A few moments later, Silvia entered the room. "Hal said we have a visitor."

"Indeed, the new Lord Beresford." Vivian moved to the sofa. "Thank you for coming so quickly."

"I was on my way to you in any event." Silvia's demeanor had changed from her normal friendliness to barely suppressed anger upon hearing his lordship had come. She chose a chair in the corner of the room near one of the windows, took out her embroidery, and gave a short nod.

As soon as Vivian's companion had settled, his lordship was announced. At the same time, Hal brought in the tea tray, setting it in front of her and obviating the need for her to stand and greet the man. "Good afternoon, my lord."

Lord Beresford glanced at her, bowed, and smiled, apparently not even noticing that Silvia was in the corner. "Good day. I hope I find you well."

"Yes, thank you, quite well." And she'd be even better when she left this place. What she did not understand was how the man could fail to notice Silvia; however, he hadn't glanced her way. What could he want that had him so focused on Vivian? "Would you like some tea?"

"Please. Two sugars and milk, if you would."

The Queen Anne sofa opposite her groaned as he lowered his large, muscular frame onto the delicate piece. Vivian winced, expecting it to splinter at any moment. Nothing in this parlor was made for persons of his size and weight. Finally satisfied the sofa would not break, Vivian handed him the cup.

He took a sip, focusing his solemn brown gaze on her. "Have you made plans for what you will do after your year of mourning is over?"

Vivian glanced up, then lowered her eyes. By any standards, he was a handsome man with thick sable hair, a straight nose, and well above medium height. However, his resemblance to her late husband was too strong for her to be comfortable in his presence, and she had no intention of telling him of her cousin Clara's invitation. "Have you need of the dower house?"

"Of course not," he assured Vivian hastily. "You are naturally welcome to remain as long as you wish." He set his cup down, clearing his throat. "There is, however, a proposition I'd like to place before you, if I may?"

He probably wanted her to act as his hostess until he married. She would tell him she was not interested. Vivian wanted no more dealings with anyone by the name of Beresford. Unfortunately, curiosity had always been another one of her faults. She raised her brows and returned his gaze, praying she presented the image of a calm, composed widow, when in fact her stomach churned as it had when facing her husband. "Go on."

"I'd like to propose a marriage between us."

Marriage!

In the year Lord Beresford had been at the abbey, he hadn't once sought her out, and now he proposed marriage? Did he think she was simply to be a piece of property to be traded at will? Fury pierced her like lightning during a summer storm. After what his cousin had put her through, he must be mad. It was all she could do to maintain her countenance. How could he think she would exchange one Lord Beresford for a newer version? She would never even consider such a suggestion. And if she did, she'd be made a laughingstock among the servants and the villagers. If his expression weren't so serious, she would have thought he was playing a sick joke.

When she didn't respond, he continued. "You are, after all, familiar with the abbey and the area. It would not be a love match, but neither was your union with my cousin. I believe I can promise I will never embarrass you or cause you any distress."

As her husband had done when she'd discovered his long-standing affair with a local farmer's wife. She took a few shallow breaths, attempting to gather her wits and find a way to end this conversation civilly. "We barely know one another."

For some reason, that seemed to hearten Lord Beresford. "A state which may be easily remedied. The fact remains that I am in need of a wife, and you fit the bill. I can give you children."

Vivian's cup rattled. She was that close to throwing cup, saucer, and pot at him all at once. The next thing she knew, the delicate china was taken from her hands. Silvia put her arm around Vivian's shoulders and sat next to her.

Beresford jumped to his feet as if a bee had stung him. "What are *you* doing here?"

"Why am I not surprised?" Silvia replied in a voice of icy disdain. "Apparently you have forgot I am Lady Beresford's companion. Now, *my lord*"—her tone took on the manner of a queen—"I believe you've said quite enough, and it is time to take your leave."

He flushed as he stood, strode to the door, opened it, and fixed his fierce look on Silvia. "You may leave. I wish to speak with her ladyship alone."

"Over my dead body," Silvia mumbled just loudly enough for him to hear.

He opened his mouth, and Vivian decided to step in before all-out war could ensue. She knew nothing about his lordship's manner, but, as much as she appreciated her companion's championship, she'd never seen Silvia so exercised or rude.

In a calm but unapologetic tone, Vivian said, "I asked Miss Corbet to remain with me."

He glared at Silvia as if he'd argue.

"However," Vivian continued firmly, "I do not believe I need to hear any more of your proposition, my lord. My answer is no. I have no desire to wed you. In fact, I have no desire to marry anyone ever again. Once was quite enough, thank you."

As he stalked out of the parlor, he glanced over his shoulder. "I'll speak to you again when you are in a better frame of mind, my lady."

"Not if I have anything to say about it," Silvia hurled at his retreating form.

His shoulders hunched, then the door snapped shut behind him.

"What gall!" Vivian picked up her tea-cup and took a sip of the now tepid liquid. "That was as unexpected as it was unwanted."

"He's an impossible, arrogant man." Silvia fumed. "And always has been. He hasn't changed at all. Having inherited the earldom has probably made him worse."

"I'd forgot you and he were acquainted."

"Unfortunately." She scowled at the door. "He spent much of his childhood at the abbey, and was always trying to tell my sisters and me what to do. How dare he stroll in here and think he could make a proposal like that!"

Vivian's lips twitched. Suddenly the whole preposterous situation was humorous. After all, he couldn't make her marry him. "I do recall that he did not call it a proposal, but a proposition."

"Who made whom a proposal?"

Standing just inside the room was a tall woman past middle age, with bright red curls, dressed in a gown the same color as her hair. Her large bonnet appeared to hold a nest of birds. Although her clothing was in the latest fashion, the hat, although new, was clearly from the style of the previous century.

"Cousin Clara!" Vivian jumped up and rushed to hug her relative, almost tripping over the Italian greyhound hovering next to her cousin's skirts. "I didn't expect to see you until next week. We didn't even hear you arrive."

"It's all right, Perdita." Clara picked up the dog and soothed it, petting and cuddling it. "I told your footman not to announce me." Setting Perdita down, Clara returned Vivian's hug. "I assume this has something to do with the young man I saw stalking out of the house in a rage."

"The new Lord Beresford apparently thought I'd make a good wife for him as I'm used to being Lady Beresford. Silvia sent him away with a flea in his ear. Oh, pray forgive my manners." Not that Vivian had had much of a chance to use them in the past six years. "Cousin Clara, this is Miss Corbet, who has been acting as my companion. Silvia, my cousin, the Dowager Marchioness of Telford."

Silvia curtseyed. "I'm so glad to have finally met you. Vivian tells me you have great plans for her for the Little Season."

"And for you as well." Lines fanned out from Clara's eyes as she smiled. "I understand that without your company, this past year would have been unbearable for Vivian."

"I don't know about that." Silvia glanced at Vivian. "We've always got along well, and I was happy to help her. Since my father's remarriage, he was pleased I was out of the house." Silvia's fine dark brown brows furrowed. "Yet, I cannot accompany you to Town."

Clara's eyes opened wide. "Why ever not? I sincerely hope it is not because of your father. I already have his permission, and now that Vivian's year of mourning is completed, you are no longer acting as a companion. Therefore there is no reason you should not have a come out." She waited a moment for the news to sink in. "Besides which, I've made all the arrangements. We shall have such fun. I've never had the opportunity to bring a young lady out. Sons are not at all the same." She removed her bonnet and sat down on the same sofa recently vacated by Lord Beresford. "I wish to leave in two days' time."

"That soon?" Silvia gasped. "I don't even know what to bring with me. I'll require new gowns—"

"There is nothing to worry about." Clara picked up her dog, placing the small animal on her lap only for the dog to jump down and duck under her skirts. "From what I see, both you and Vivian need new wardrobes. In fact, I think we shall leave in the morning. There is no need to waste time. Besides, Perdita is ready to be home. All this traveling has upset her nerves."

Or, Vivian thought ruefully, no need to give her former companion time to find an excuse not to go. She, on the other hand, was more than happy to quit Beresford as soon as possible.

Vivian didn't know how her cousin had arranged everything or why, but she was happy Silvia would finally have the Season she'd never had. Her younger sisters were already married. One to a wealthy young man of good lineage and the other to his friend, the heir of a viscount. Although Silvia's sisters had offered to sponsor her for a Season, she had declined, stating that someone must remain with Papa and take care of him. An excuse she no longer had.

More tea arrived, and she busied herself fixing a cup for Clara. Vivian's thoughts turned to Lord Beresford's reaction to her companion and Silvia's behavior in response. Sparks had definitely flown, and he had seemed not only angry but embarrassed that she was present. Was there something between them other than childhood animosity? If so, why had he proposed to Vivian?

Perdita remained close to Clara, peeking out every once in a while from under her skirts. "Cousin Clara, when did you get a dog? I've never known you to have one before."

Clara stroked the small animal. "We always had hunting dogs, but one of my nephews brought her back from the Peninsula and asked me if I wouldn't mind keeping her until he found a new owner. They stayed with me for a few weeks while he sorted out his business. She and I just took to each other. I don't know why I never had a house dog before. She's an excellent companion."

"I hope she likes cats. You know I've had my Gisila for years and cannot go anywhere without her." Speaking of her cat, Vivian glanced around and found Gisila under the desk.

"I'm sure they'll be fine. Perdita normally remains under my skirts. It's amazing I don't trip over her." She turned her attention to Silvia. "Miss Corbet, as you will be residing with me, I believe I would prefer to address you as Silvia, and you may call me Cousin Clara."

Silvia appeared slightly startled, not a state that happened often or easily. "Yes, ma'am."

"You may think this is a strange start on my part." Clara smiled gently. "But I knew your mother when she was a child and your grandmother was a close friend of mine."

"I had no idea there was even that much of a connection."

"There is no reason you would have known. Your grandmother died many years ago."

While her cousin and Silvia chatted, Vivian strolled to the window seat. For the past few months, just the idea of going to Town again had occupied her mind. She had not attended a Season since her first one, and was both excited and frightened. It had been much too long since she'd been around the *haut ton*. At first, she thought merely to attend the smaller entertainments and the theater; now, with Silvia coming out, Clara would insist on their being present at the large balls. Perhaps Vivian would be better served by remaining with the chaperones and older matrons. That would be easier and less fearsome than worrying about dance partners.

The other business she must be about was finding a small estate. Her mother had offered to bring Vivian home after her husband died, but she'd had a feeling then that she could not go back to her parents, and nothing had occurred to change her mind. It was time to strike out on her own.

To have a home where what she said was the law, and the sooner the better. After all, that was the most she could expect from her life.

Departing on the morrow was easily done and for the best. She stepped into the corridor and found one of the maids. "Please tell my maid and Miss Corbet's maid that we shall require our trunks packed immediately. Also, have Lady Telford's bags placed in the green room, and inform Cook we'll have a guest at dinner."

The maid bobbed a curtsey and hurried off.

Vivian slipped back into the morning room.

If only she was the type of widow who could take a lover, but what sane man would want a lady with a deformed body? Her husband's cousin could not possibly know about her problem; otherwise he would never have suggested marriage. She supposed she should be glad Edgar had not discussed it. Thankfully, her clothing covered the worst defect. No, other than as dancing partners, gentlemen had no place in her life; or, rather, they would not want her in theirs.

CHAPTER TWO

September 1817, Palace of Westminster, London

"**R**upert."

Rupert, Earl of Stanstead, turned as his cousin Robert, Viscount Beaumont, caught up with him. "I thought you were coming home with me. Elizabeth has been asking for you."

"Elizabeth is only six months old," Rupert pointed out. "She is much too young to ask for anyone."

"Nonsense, she's extremely advanced for her age." Robert's whole demeanor changed when he talked about his family. It was as if he had entered a land where nothing could make him sad or angry.

"Sorry. I was waylaid by Lord Banks." Rupert ran his palm down his face. "I'll go with you now." Before Robert had met his wife, Serena, he'd been the worst rake in England. Now his world revolved around his wife and baby daughter. Rupert had never before seen such a sudden and permanent transformation.

His cousin's gaze sharpened. "What did Banks say to you to put you in such a foul mood?"

"He warned me away from his daughter." Not that Rupert had any clear idea who the girl was, but apparently she'd been part of a bevy of young ladies walking in the Park yesterday. "I am too young to have serious intentions, and he'd thank me not to raise her hopes. He has five other daughters and needs to marry this one off as soon as may be." Robert's lips tightened, and Rupert went on. "He did say that the girl he has coming out in about six years might do. By then, I'd be of sufficient age and maturity."

"Damn," Robert swore softly.

"My thoughts precisely, even if I can't remember her. I expect to hear similar warnings from other fathers. He suggested I find a mistress."

"You have one already." Robert linked his arm with Rupert's as they strolled down the street toward St. James's Park.

"I *had* one." Rupert paused, selecting his words. "It is not what I want. After seeing the arrangements my mother and father and you and Serena have, as well as our other friends, I desire nothing more than a wife."

His cousin was quiet for a few moments as they strode through Green Park. "I don't wish to dissuade you. Quite frankly, I don't think I could. You suffer what I now call 'the Beaumont syndrome.'"

"I beg your pardon?" Rupert wasn't sure if it was an insult or not. "What do you mean by that?"

"Don't get on your high horse. It means when we want something we go after it and damn all else to hell. I did it with Serena. Even your mother did it with your father when she was young."

Robert had compromised Serena. If it had not been for their grandmother and Serena's family whisking her off to France, he might never have admitted he loved her. Rupert could hardly blame only his mother for engaging in relations with his father when they were young. There had been no way for them to know the part her father would play.

"You found partners." Rupert shrugged, not understanding what his cousin was saying. "Someone with whom you could have an *affaire de cœur*. Which is what I desire above all else."

"You must look at how we went about pursuing our loves." Robert's brows drew together. "I almost lost Serena, and your mother did lose Edward for years." He paused again. "Ever since my wedding, you've been intent on marriage. What I think you should consider is whether or not you are giving yourself the time to find the right lady. For the better part of a year you pursued Miss Manning, even after she'd made it clear that she wanted a different sort of life from what you offered. One cannot have a successful marriage when one's goals are not the same."

"I hadn't thought of it in quite that way." Rupert had to give the devil his due. He *had* been so focused on gaining Miss Manning's hand in marriage, he'd failed to even notice her interest in Lord Peter and that gentleman's interest in her. They both wanted nothing more than the life of a diplomat. She would have been miserable living in England all the time.

As for being too young, Rupert felt much older than his years. He had come into his title at an early age, and even when he'd been on his Grand Tour he had missed his estate and his seat in the Lords. Now that he had returned, and despite his age, he was becoming influential in political circles. "What do you suggest?"

"Stand back a bit." They had been strolling in the general direction of Berkeley Square when Robert stopped walking and faced Rupert. "At some point, there will be a lady whom you cannot ignore. She will dominate every waking thought and haunt your dreams. You'll want to fight every man who asks her to dance or accompanies her during the Grand Strut."

"You make it sound like an obsession." Rupert had used a light tone, trying to lessen his cousin's seriousness.

"In a way, it is." Robert nodded slowly, and glanced away. "Yet it's vastly more confounding. When you meet the lady you truly love, you would gladly lay down your life for her."

"Is that what you felt for Serena?"

His cousin gave a harsh laugh. "All that and more. Nothing could compare. Later, after I'd almost lost her, I realized that what I'd thought was love, before her, was a weak imitation." He glanced over at Rupert. "Did you feel that way about Miss Manning?"

He shook his head. "No." After what his cousin had just said, it was clear he had never experienced that type of strong emotion. "She was beautiful, and I thought I was in love, but when she told me she had formed an attachment to Lord Peter, I felt nothing but sadness that it hadn't worked out."

They turned off Piccadilly onto Berkeley Street, which would lead them to Robert's residence in Berkeley Square.

"Then I'd say you have not yet met the woman you were meant to be with."

"How did you know Serena was the right one?"

"From the first time I saw her on that huge roan of hers, I couldn't get her out of my mind." His cousin grinned. "It was a damn good thing too."

From what Rupert had heard, Serena had put his cousin through his paces before she'd agreed to marry him. Even Grandmamma had supported Serena's flight to France to avoid being forced to wed Robert before he admitted he loved her. Robert had been right about Rupert's mother and father. His parents had been separated for years before they could finally wed, only a little over a year ago. Grandfather Beaumont had married Mama off to old Lord Stanstead's only son when she was pregnant with Rupert. Papa's uncle had arranged a marriage for him, and the fact that Mama was increasing was kept from him. Not that Rupert, even now, was able to acknowledge his father as anything more than a step-father, but at least now he knew and was grateful that he'd not been the get of his mother's first husband. He was also glad the title had come directly from the gentleman he had loved as his grandfather, bypassing the man who was legally his father. Although there had been a time last year, after the truth came out, when he would gladly have planted both his grandfathers facers if they'd been alive.

Now that he gave it some thought, perhaps love wasn't something one could dictate or maneuver to occur when one wished it. Still, what was he supposed to do? Wait around until Cupid shot him with an arrow? Arrange for fairy dust? Surely, there was some way to hurry the process along.

When they arrived at Berkeley Square, the door to his cousin's house opened, and the butler bowed. "Welcome home, my lord. Her ladyship and Miss Elizabeth are in the morning room." The man took Rupert's hat and cane. "It's good to see you again, my lord. Lady Malfrey and her son are also in the morning room."

Rupert wondered how much the butler, an old family retainer, knew about his birth—most likely the whole thing. Fortunately, Robert's servants never gossiped outside of the house.

Rupert quickened his step. All his life he'd wanted a real family, including a brother or sister, and now he had one.

Robert opened the door, and Serena glanced up from the floor where baby Elizabeth, Rupert's mother, and his brother, Daniel, were playing. The children had been born less than a month apart. Rupert held out his arms.

Daniel pushed to his knees and rocked, then latched on to the low round table, and pulled himself up.

Rupert sat on the floor next to his brother and the baby made one step before falling into his arms. "You're growing much too quickly. The next thing I know, you'll be walking."

"Rup, Rupie," Daniel chortled.

"When did he start that?" The last time Rupert had seen his brother he'd only just said "mama."

His mother beamed. "You were starting to talk as well as holding on to tables and walking around them when you were his age. I expect he'll be the same."

Activity was not the only way in which they'd be alike. Daniel had the same pale blond curls Rupert, his mother, and Robert had. The mark of a Beaumont. But each also had their father's gray eyes.

Tea was brought in, and a half hour later, Edward, Baron Malfrey—Daniel and Rupert's father—entered the room. Papa's gaze went straight to Mama. "I'm sorry I'm late, my sweet. I was held up in a meeting."

She smiled softly, love shining in her eyes. "It's no matter. You are here now."

Daniel quickly switched his allegiance to Papa. "Papa, Papa."

Edward swung the baby into his arms and laughed. "I've returned. Were you worried I wouldn't?"

That was exactly what Rupert wanted. The only question was, how long would he have to wait until the right lady entered his life? He hoped it wouldn't be past this Season.

After an early breakfast the following morning, Vivian and Silvia were handed up into Clara's huge, opulent traveling coach. The vehicle was painted cherry red, piped in gold, with her crest on both sides of the body. Inside it had deep blue velvet seats and squabs. Extra cushions were tossed around as well. Neatly folded blankets were strapped to overhead racks, as well as a picnic basket. Silvia's and Vivian's trunks had been added to the baggage carriage. Gisila lay quietly in her traveling box, and Perdita lay on a cushion at Clara's feet.

Vivian gave a prayer of thanks that she hadn't heard from Lord Beresford again before they left. Although considering she'd given him no notice of her departure, and, against all odds, Clara had managed to shove them out the door before ten o'clock, that was scarcely surprising. He had not said anything about coming to Town, and Vivian hoped he would not. Or at least not for her. Still, the more she considered it, the greater her conviction that Silvia would make a good match for him. If he showed up in Town, Vivian would have a word with her cousin. Unlike Vivian, who had always felt like an outsider at Beresford, Silvia would be perfect. She already commanded a great deal of respect in the area.

Their first night on the trip, Vivian noticed a couple at the inn her cousin had chosen. The two were obviously in love. Although there was nothing untoward in their behavior, it was clear they could not wait to be alone. That was what she had thought she would have in her marriage. She longed for a lover's touch, yet she'd be devastated if another man looked at her with the same revulsion her husband had. The only way such tenderness would ever come her way was if the man never saw her body. Yet how would she ever arrange such a thing?

She stifled a sigh. If wishes were horses, then beggars would ride. There would be no lover and most definitely no husband.

She would take advantage of this visit to Town. The important part was it took her away from Beresford Abbey and gave her time to find other living arrangements. Thanks to her father's insistence on a generous settlement, she was far from destitute.

"Is something wrong, my dear?" Clara had apparently stopped talking to Silvia.

"Not at all." Vivian smiled brightly. "I'm just so very happy to be visiting London again. My late husband"—she did like saying the *late* part—"insisted I remain on the estate to run it in his absence. As a result, I have not been there since I married."

There was no point in mentioning that instead of allowing her to accompany him to London and actually attending the Lords as he said he did, he'd given his proxy to another peer and taken his mistress to Town. Posing as husband and wife, they had lived in Marylebone, an area catering to middling merchants. Not that Vivian had known about the deception until just before he died.

What she should do was swear off all gentlemen, forever. Other than her father, when he wasn't out looking at dogs, and her brothers, they were not to be trusted. Maybe not even them. She could recall some rousing rows between her parents and a time when her eldest brother walked on egg shells around his wife for several weeks. Her husband hadn't cared at all when she'd discovered his perfidy. In fact, he had been relieved he need no longer hide his behavior.

Vivian removed her gloves, folded them tidily, and placed them in her reticule. Clara was telling Silvia about the entertainments she could expect to attend during the Little Season, and Vivian listened. The plans terrified her. Surely she could find some society of ladies doing good works, or something to become involved in that could be her excuse for not attending the parties.

Two days later, they drew up in front of a large town house on Mount Street. Even though they had stopped along the way, and found their lodgings well before sunset so that Vivian and Silvia could walk, they were all tired of being cooped up in the coach.

Perdita and Gisila had formed a friendship of sorts, sometimes sleeping next to one another in the coach or in a private parlor. Each animal was still happier to remain with her own mistress than anything else.

"Here we are," Clara said as the coach came to a halt. "I shall send a note to my modiste immediately." She continued talking as they climbed down from the carriage and entered the house. "Silvia, I'll show you to your chambers. We shall meet in the drawing room at six o'clock. I know you are used to country hours, and I wish to be up early and out to-morrow morning. We have a busy day ahead of us."

Clara had always reminded Vivian of a whirling dervish. She and Silvia exchanged glances and smiled. They followed Clara up to the landing where she turned. "Silvia, you will be near me. Vivian, dear, I thought you might be more comfortable in the other wing. Ah, here you are, Mrs. Murchison."

A woman who appeared to be in her late thirties, with a pleasant but competent expression, bobbed a curtsey. "Welcome home, my lady."

"Thank you, I'm glad to be back. Please take my cousin to the rose room. Vivian, feel free to treat my house as your home and order things as you wish." Clara linked arms with Silvia. "Come, my dear, I think you'll be exceeding pleased with your apartment. I just had most of the rooms redecorated."

Vivian followed the housekeeper down a corridor to the back of the house as the woman chattered away. "I hope you like it, my lady. As her ladyship said, the rooms have all been refurbished. You'll have a nice view of our garden as well as Mount Street Garden. The area is a lovely place to stroll if you don't want the crowds in Hyde Park."

"Thank you. I'm sure I'll adore the room as well as the view." She glanced around at the chamber. The walls were covered in a pale pink silk, and cream-colored panels. The curtains were deeper cream, almost yellow, and embroidered with a profusion of roses. "It's lovely."

Mrs. Murchison indicated a door. "Right through here is your dressing room and the door on the other side is a parlor. It has views of the park as well."

Vivian strolled into the parlor. It was well appointed with walls and curtains matching the ones in the bedroom. On one wall, long windows flanked a French window which led to a small balcony where one had the promised views of the park. A chaise rested along the inside wall, two comfortable-looking chairs stood before the fireplace, and a writing desk was situated between two windows on the other outside wall.

"I've got the fire going in your bedchamber," the housekeeper said. "If you want I'll have the one here lit as well. Your bath will be up in just a bit."

"Thank you." Vivian smiled. "I don't believe I will want a fire here until later. Do you know if my maid arrived?"

"Yes, my lady. I believe she's pressing some of your clothes, and your cat's around here somewhere. I saw a footman bring her up. Shall I send your dresser to you?"

"Not at the moment." Vivian glanced at the balcony, wanting to get a better look at it. "I will not require her until my bath is ready. Could you please bring me some tea? I find I'm quite parched."

"As you wish, my lady." Mrs. Murchison bobbed a curtsey, then left the room.

Vivian opened the windows, stepping out onto the balcony. A small table and two chairs were situated off to the side. Gisila paced up to her and chirped. Vivian scratched the cat's head, then placed her hands on the wrought iron rail and stretched, sniffing the air.

"What do you think, Gisila? It is not as clean as in the country but not as bad as the other parts of London we passed through."

Gisila sat and stared up at Vivian with large yellow eyes.

"I'm sure Hal will have found a place for your toilet." She sniffed. Actually what she smelled was roses. Sweet with spicy facets. Looking down, she spied a trellis of pink roses. If nothing else, she would enjoy these rooms.

Glancing over at the Mount Street Gardens, a tall man striding as if he would be late captured her attention. He stopped and removed his hat for a moment, giving her a glimpse of his curly, pale blond hair. Even at this distance, something about him was compelling. His dark jacket appeared molded to his torso, and a well-made torso it was. Tight pantaloons encased his muscular legs. She couldn't drag her eyes away from him.

Then he looked up, almost right at her. Oh Lord, she'd been caught! Vivian ducked back into the parlor, hiding behind the curtains. Had he seen her? Inching forward, she peered out again, but he was gone.

Vivian gave herself a shake. *Now you're being silly. You'll probably never know who he is.*

Besides, you need to remember what you went through with a man before. Only fools allow themselves to be used twice.

CHAPTER THREE

The side of Rupert's neck prickled as if someone was staring at him. He glanced up but could see no one. Unsurprising at this time of day, when the outside was much brighter than the insides of the houses. Still, he'd grown used to trusting his senses. It had been a useful trait over the years, particularly when he'd been on his Grand Tour.

He searched the houses on Mount Street. A door to one of the balconies closed. It was probably nothing. Merely someone gazing at the park. He rubbed his neck and continued on in the direction of South Audley Street, where his parents lived during the Season. A few paces later, something made him glance at the houses again. That was when he saw it. Light blue skirts hovering just inside one of the French windows. A woman. Not that it mattered. He couldn't possibly know who she was. Rupert shrugged, attempting to rid himself of the feeling of being watched. For once, he'd let Fate take over rather than attempting to control every aspect of his life. Still . . .

Not many minutes later, he rapped on the door of Malfrey House, the door opened, and Whitsun, the Malfrey butler, bowed.

Rupert handed the servant his hat, gloves, and cane. "I hope I'm not late."

"No, my lord. Her ladyship has not come down yet."

"No need to announce me," he said as he strolled into the hall, continuing on to the drawing room. His father smiled as he entered the room. Closing the door firmly behind him, he turned. "Papa, I have some questions to ask you."

"Very well," he replied, raising a brow. "Will this call for brandy?"

"Probably not, but I would like a glass." A few moments later they were seated in front of one of two fireplaces. Rupert stared into the flames as he enjoyed the burn of the fine French cognac. "You and Mama were very young when you first met."

"Yes." His father nodded. "She was barely sixteen and I was not much younger than you. Why?"

"What would have happened if my grandfathers had not torn you apart?"

Papa took a sip and his brow furrowed. "We would have wed as we'd planned to do. I thought you understood that."

"I'm putting this badly." Setting down his glass, Rupert stood and ran his fingers through his hair. "What I really want to know is, did you miss marrying her, or were you glad you could be out on the Town?"

His father's face became serious. "Even after your mother left, I was never one to be enticed by gambling and brothels." Papa rolled the goblet between his hands. "For one thing, I was studying law and didn't have the funds. For another, no other lady could compare to your mother."

That was very like what Robert had said about his wife, although he had spent years acquiring a well-deserved reputation as a rake, and had known an array of women. "But you married another."

"Yes," Papa said with a grimace. "It was arranged. I—I did my duty by her, but was never able to love her as she should have been loved. Fortunately, she was content. She had affection for me, but nothing more. She believed strong emotions were for people of lower status." He stood, placing his hand on Rupert's shoulder. "I never for a moment stopped loving your mother. Have you met someone? Or are you being told you are too young to marry?"

"No on the first account, yes on the second. Twice since the Season began I've been asked not to fix my attentions on someone's daughter." And he was getting damned sick and tired of it.

"I was advised I was too young as well. If it helps, I think they were wrong." His father's lips formed a line. "When you find the woman you'll love, keep fighting for her."

The way Papa had wanted to fight for Mama. If only he'd known what her father had done, but he'd been at Oxford and hadn't found out until she was already married.

"Thank you for your help. I shall do as you say." Now all Rupert had to do was discover who *she* was.

His father slapped him lightly on the back. "I am glad I can assist you. I missed seeing you grow up."

Rupert's throat tightened as it always did when the subject came up. "If only I had known you were mine, I would have ensured I could see you."

"What has the two of you looking so solemn?" Mama asked as she strolled into the drawing room. Her gaze sharpened. "Has anything happened that I should know about?"

"Nothing at all." Rupert strode to her, picked her up, and swung her around.

"Put me down, you silly boy!" She laughed. "I forbid you to teach Daniel any of your nonsense."

"But you're my favorite mother." Grinning, he set her on her feet and bussed her cheek. "We're just having a father-son talk. You are lovely as always."

She gave him a dubious look, but said nothing else about it. He had no doubt she'd get it out of his father later.

"Have you decided," he asked, "which entertainments you'll attend this week?"

Mama took a glass of wine from Papa. "You do remember Serena is having her first London ball? Naturally, we shall be there. The Eveshams and Rutherfords have balls planned as well."

"Of course. I wouldn't miss them." In fact, Rupert intended to attend a great many balls and other events this Season. "Now that Featherton has married, I shall offer my services to partner any lady my hostess wishes." How better to meet females than by dancing with them.

"That is extremely kind of you," his mother said dryly. "Now do you wish to enlighten me as to what's going on?"

So much for not being questioned. Wasn't it past time for dinner to be served?

His father glanced at him. "We may as well tell her. She'll have it from one of us in any event."

"Indeed I will," Mama said, sinking gracefully onto a chair. "You have all my attention."

By the time Rupert had got to the second request from a father to stay away from the man's daughter, her eyes were shooting fire. "How dare they!" Not a question. "One would think your being a respected peer—an earl, nonetheless—would count for something."

"I actually did consider that to be to my benefit," he mumbled. "But apparently that won't be until a few years have passed."

"Devil a bit." She took a large swallow of wine. "How dare they insult my son in such a fashion? I'll guarantee you"—she narrowed her eyes—"that their wives don't know about this. It appears I have some visits to make."

Rupert debated saying she needn't bother, yet it occurred to him he required all the help he could get. After all, he didn't want to fall in love, have his feelings returned, and have to run off to Gretna Green. That wouldn't do at all.

Whitsun announced dinner, saving Rupert from having to respond. Not that anything he said would have made any difference. His mother was well on her way to preparing for all-out war.

Vivian sat at the small table drinking her morning tea and scanning the park. She had not seen the gentleman with the blond hair in the two days since she had arrived. Of course, she hadn't spent *every* moment watching for him. Even if she'd been inclined to haunt the balcony, Clara had kept Silvia and Vivian very busy purchasing gowns, bonnets, stockings, and other items required for a proper Season.

She did not understand why she was so intrigued by a man she'd only seen walking through the park. Although he hadn't been merely walking. He'd been striding as if he needed to be somewhere quickly, commanding her senses in a way that had never happened to her before.

Vivian dipped the corner of her toast into the baked egg. What would she do if she saw him? Even if they were standing next to each other, she couldn't very well introduce herself. That wouldn't be at all the thing. There was also the possibility that he did not travel in her, or rather Cousin Clara's, circles. Also, she was stupid even to think of a man. Vivian sighed, and glanced once more at the park.

A light patting on her skirt let her know Gisila wished to taste the egg. "Just a moment and I'll give you some."

"Did you say something, my lady?" her maid, Punt, called from the bedchamber.

"Nothing at all." Vivian ate more of her meal before sharing with her cat. "Do you happen to know what is planned for today?"

"The first of your gowns has arrived." Punt stood at the door. "The soft gray becomes you, but just the same, I'll be glad to see you in colors again. I was told you'll have morning visits to-morrow."

"I remember now. We are to be introduced to some of her ladyship's other relatives. I suppose they are also connections of mine in one way or the other." Vivian sat up straighter and smiled. "It will be nice to meet people already well disposed toward me." Or rather, she hoped they would be.

An hour later, she, her former companion, and her cousin were in a bright red town coach headed to Grosvenor Square. The conveyance drew to a halt in front of a large, freestanding building. Two liveried footmen jumped to attend to them. Within a few moments, they were ushered into a cozy morning room done in light yellows and greens with views to the garden beyond.

A petite lady with red-gold hair and dressed in the latest fashion glided toward them. "Aunt Clara." The woman smiled as she held out her hands. "I'm so very happy to see you."

"Phoebe, my dear." Clara bussed the lady's cheek. "Allow me to introduce you to my cousin Vivian, Countess of Beresford, who is also connected to you by marriage, and Miss Corbet, the granddaughter of a dear friend of mine. Miss Corbet is the rector's eldest daughter. Her mother was the Duke of Granville's youngest child. Vivian has just ended her year of mourning, and it is time she embraced life again. Vivian, Silvia, meet Phoebe, Countess of Evesham, my great-niece."

Vivian and Silvia were embraced by the countess and shown to seats on the sofa across from where her ladyship sat with Clara. "I'm so glad to meet you. Vivian, may I call you by your first name? Since we are related, I'd like it so much more if you called me Phoebe." Slightly stunned by the informality, Vivian could only nod. Phoebe continued, "And Miss Corbet, I know we are not related, but it would be very awkward for everyone to be referring to the other by their first names, or, heaven forfend, constantly calling each other *my lady*." Vivian had never seen a smile so bright. "May I call you Silvia?"

Silvia nodded mutely. She was probably as astonished as Vivian was.

"Well then." Phoebe directed the tea tray that had just arrived to be set on the table between them. Once the door closed, she went on as if they'd not been interrupted. "I imagine you'll wish to know which entertainments shall best suit you."

Clara took a cup of tea. "I knew you'd be able to advise us."

Once Silvia and Vivian had their tea, Phoebe passed biscuits and small iced cakes. "My cousin Serena, Viscountess Beaumont, is having her first ball to-morrow evening. I know she would love for you to attend. I'll make sure to have cards sent to you." Phoebe paused, as she nibbled on a ginger biscuit. "If, that is, you are ready for a ball?"

"We are indeed," Clara replied in a bracing tone. "It is time and more for my charges to make their curtseys to Polite Society. Not that Vivian hasn't already made hers, though it has been a while. Silvia was taking care of her widowed father, then offered to keep Vivian company during mourning. This will be her first Season."

Silvia's eyes had gone wide, in the fashion of a scared rabbit. She might have a case of nerves now, but she'd be fine once she settled down. Vivian's palms grew damp. It had been a long while, and she really did not know what she was doing here, other than escaping Beresford, the place and the man. All the rushing around purchasing clothing and other items seemed rather pointless. She was not going to re-marry, and couldn't take a lover. The image of a tall blond man passed quickly in front of her eyes. Preposterous. She didn't even know who he was. Perhaps she could find another purpose for being in Town, such as searching for a small estate to buy. There, that was a good idea. She'd ask her cousin for a recommendation to a land agent.

"Silvia, there is no reason to be concerned. Serena did not make her come out until she was six and twenty. I can tell you are much younger than that."

"T-twenty. Almost twenty-one."

"You see, there is nothing for you to worry about."

They had finished tea and Clara rose. "Phoebe, we shall see you to-morrow evening. Lady Beaumont's ball appears to be the perfect place to acquaint my young ladies with the *ton*."

They bid Phoebe adieu, and as they left the room, Silvia leaned close to Vivian. "I thought that was what all the morning visits were for."

"Be thankful it is the Little Season," she whispered. "Otherwise you'd have to be approved by the patronesses of Almack's for a voucher. You'll like the ball. It sounds as if it will not be much different from the ones I held at Beresford Abbey, albeit the company will be a good deal grander." And she would not have to act as if she enjoyed having her husband's mistress around.

Silvia's lips tightened. "I'll take your word for it." She sighed. "I truly thought I'd be like my sisters and not have to go anywhere or do anything to find a husband. Then I expected I would just remain with Papa. Ah well, there are times Fate intervenes."

"Very true." And not always in the way one wants it to.

Nicholas, Eighth Earl of Beresford, glanced at the gilded-cased clock on the mantel. It was eleven in the morning. Time to visit the dower house again. He'd made a muddle of his proposal. Not that he'd wanted to do it in the first place. He had also managed to anger Silvia. He hadn't thought so before, but it might be for the best that she had not given him the time of day since he'd returned. This was something he could never explain to her. Damn Edgar for going and getting himself run over by a horse.

Nick had given Lady Beresford three days to calm down. In truth, he'd been licking his wounds getting his courage up again. His cousin had always said she had a mild disposition and was not prone to out-bursts. Perhaps he, Nick, had approached her in the wrong way. He'd try once more to keep his promise to his cousin . . . and ensure that this time Silvia wasn't around to interfere. Stubborn, out-spoken fe-male that she was. Though at first glance, or even second glance, no one would expect her to be so difficult. Her glossy sable curls danced around a perfectly heart-shaped face. She was petite but had lush curves, and she moved so gracefully one could swear the air merely parted for her. On the other hand, she never could take advice or even a direct command. She always thought she knew what was best, stat-ing her opinions in a forthright and almost regal manner, her dark brown eyes flashing with indignation that anyone would think she was wrong. He pinched the bridge of his nose. The problem had al-ways been she was frequently right. And there was a time when he'd thought they would make a life together.

Well, he was not a green young'un any longer. He'd served on Wellington's staff and had commanded a battalion of soldiers. Per-haps he'd mention the fact to her. Then again, he'd probably be better served avoiding the shrew. Unfortunately for his peace of mind, that was something he'd never been able to do. If only he knew why she was so angry with him. His uncle, the old earl, and her father said they would explain why he could not take his leave of her. She should have got over any disgruntlement she'd felt about that.

Then again, his duty now was to attempt to wed his cousin's widow. Having Silvia gaze at him with love, as she had a few years ago, would not help either of them.

He strode through the hall. As his butler opened the door and bowed, Nick said, "I'm on my way to the dower house."

The butler opened his mouth, shut it. "Very well, my lord."

Fifteen minutes later, he raised his hand to knock on the door when he noticed the knocker was not there. *What the hell?* He pounded on the black lacquered wood.

After what seemed like an inordinately long time, it was opened by the housekeeper. "What can I do for ye, my lord?"

He unclenched his jaw. "Do you happen to know where her ladyship went?"

"London."

Just what he had not needed to hear. "When do you expect her ladyship to return?"

"She didn't say." The woman stood there with her arms folded across her large frame.

It would be easier getting a recalcitrant jackass to do his bidding than getting information from her. "Very well."

Blast it all to bloody hell! And not a word to him. Now what was he supposed to do? He'd never liked London, filthy place. Give him clean country air any day. And socializing with the *ton* reminded him more of going into a battle. It had never mattered what his father or cousin or even some of his fellow officers had to say, war was simpler.

He was half-way back to the abbey when he detoured to the family graveyard and his cousin's place in it. The edifice that housed Edgar's body was impressive. Constructed of marble, it had taken almost six months to build. Flowers had been planted around the stone and placed in a vase on top of it. Most likely Mrs. Raeford's doing. The woman was still in black, while Edgar's wife was in London. Well, good for Vivian! She deserved to have some fun; her marriage hadn't given her any. Nick wondered if Mr. Raeford had minded. Probably not, the old earl had paid him a fair amount in coin and land to marry his son's mistress.

"I made a damned mess of trying to keep my promise to you, Edgar. I told you I didn't want to do this, but I'll try again. The problem is that I must now travel to Town. I'll see you when I return."

Nick turned and started back to the house. With any luck at all, he'd convince Vivian Beresford to wed him and be back before word got around that he was looking for a wife. After all, he'd never lost a campaign yet. Still, a niggling feeling that he wasn't doing what he ought to hung on his back like a Barbary ape, digging its claws into him. By doing this was he worsening an already bad situation? And what about Silvia? Despite the way she treated him, he still loved her. If only she would talk to him, tell him what he'd done wrong. Bloody hell, this was a fine pickle, and he couldn't for the life of him see his way out of it and retain his honor.

CHAPTER FOUR

Rupert tried not to grin as Wigman, his valet, plucked an invisible piece of lint from Rupert's jacket. It was a ritual they had gone through every day since he was sixteen, when his grandfather Stanstead had insisted Rupert have a valet. Some gentlemen would probably become annoyed with such fussiness, but he believed in encouraging everyone to perform their duties to the best of their abilities. If that meant a few moments' delay in dressing, so be it. "Am I presentable, Wigman?"

"None more so, my lord." Wigman gave a small sigh. "I do regret that Mr. Brummell was allowed to hold sway over gentlemen's clothing. There was nothing like a nice lace cuff or velvet jacket to show a gentleman to perfection."

"I have no doubt you are correct." Truth be told, Rupert thought the previous styles had some merit. "Though, I do have an aversion to wigs and hair powder."

"I must agree with you regarding that particular affectation, my lord." He handed Rupert his watch fob and quizzing glass. "You are fortunate that you do not require padding. One could more easily disguise additions to a gentleman's physique before the styles changed so drastically."

"Fortunate indeed." Rupert clamped his lips together. If he didn't depart immediately, he'd be subject to the litany of faults in Wigman's previous employers. "I have no idea when I'll return."

"Yes, my lord."

Rupert strode out of his Grosvenor Square town house to the waiting town coach. He'd considered walking to Robert's home on Berkeley Square, but dark clouds had hung low all afternoon, and the scent of rain was in the air. Not to mention arriving at his cousin's house for their first ball, soaked, was not a wonderful idea. Rupert settled on the soft brown leather seat, a footman closed the door, and his coachman started forward.

He attempted to tamp down the feeling that something momentous was about to happen. His parents and Robert were most likely correct that he wouldn't meet anyone he didn't already know. Still, he couldn't help a surge of excitement when the carriage came to a stop. Somewhere the perfect lady was out there waiting for him. All he had to do was find her.

The coach door opened, and he caught a glimpse of pale blue skirts moving up the steps before they disappeared into the house. The urge to chase after her, whoever she was, was almost too strong to resist. Rupert could feel his pulse beating a tattoo against his cravat; still, he forced himself to calmly take his place in the line. What were the chances it was the same woman who had watched him as he traversed the Mount Street Gardens? Surely she wouldn't wear the same gown to a ball, yet he had noticed that when a lady favored a certain color, she wore it more often than she did others.

He was being absurd. Even a bit mad. Rupert knew absolutely nothing about the woman, not how old she was, or if she was married, or what she looked like, or if it was indeed the same female. In addition, there were a great many people between him and the lady in blue. Yet there was some force pushing him forward, necessitating that he follow her.

Perhaps this would be an eventful night after all.

"Lord Stanstead." A soft giggle accompanied his name.

Who the devil . . . ah, he saw her now. The young lady who'd spoken was with Lord and Lady Banks. His lordship frowned, and her ladyship smiled.

Mama had apparently begun her campaign.

"Lovely evening, isn't it?" Rupert asked as he bowed over Lady Banks's outstretched hand.

Her smile deepened. "It is indeed, my lord. I think you have already met my daughter, Miss Banks."

"I have. In the Park." She curtseyed prettily as he bowed and took her hand in his. "A pleasure to see you again, Miss Banks."

Rupert straightened and nodded to her father. Lord Banks still appeared none too happy, but his wife had apparently won the argument, at least for now. Miss Banks fiddled with the dance card hanging from her wrist and glanced up at him hopefully.

Taking the hint, Rupert asked, "Would you do me the honor of the first country dance, if it is not already taken, of course."

"It would be my pleasure, my lord." She blushed and extended her arm so that he could write his name next to a reel, the third set.

He was happy to note that she had only a few dances free. The fact remained, even if her mother approved of him, her father did not, and Rupert did not wish to alienate such a powerful ally. On the other hand, he could not be rude to the young lady. One dance with her would be sufficient to attain both goals.

As they reached the head of the receiving line, the Banks's attention was claimed by another couple with a daughter.

Rupert greeted Serena and Robert. "This looks to be quite a crush."

"I know." She grinned. "I'm so pleased it will be a success. Phoebe and Marcus are already here with one of her aunts and two other ladies."

"I'll look for them." Rupert moved on, allowing the next group to greet his cousins. Although he had been in the house several times since Robert and Serena's marriage, Rupert had not been to the formal areas before. The change was remarkable. It was fresher and had the look of a female hand. Stanstead, Rupert's estate, and his town house could use updating as well. His mother was the last lady to have resided in either place. Unfortunately, she'd hated both houses so much the only rooms she'd touched were the nursery and, later, the schoolroom.

When he found a wife, he would make sure she loved him and wanted to make their house a home. He'd also give her free rein to do as she wished.

Rupert entered the ballroom and was announced. The roar of voices barely lowered. Across the way, Marcus leaned casually against a pillar, fondly grinning at something or someone Rupert couldn't see, most likely Phoebe. He made his way through the already crowded room. Snagging a glass of champagne, he wove around clusters of ladies in brightly colored silks, which made a stark contrast with the darker colors the gentlemen wore. He knew most of those present and exchanged greetings as he came upon a circle of acquaintances.

It took several minutes before Rupert was finally close enough to Marcus and Phoebe that he could see the other ladies.

He sucked in a breath. One of the women wore a pale, almost ice-blue gown. Her curls were silvery, much like he'd imagined the color of the snow maiden's hair in a fairy tale his mother had read to him. When the lady glanced at him he could see her eyes were of the same deep blue as the trim on her gown, and the color of the deeper waters he'd seen in the Mediterranean Sea. Not in her first blush of youth, her cheeks were no longer plump. But not that old, perhaps close to his age. She had turned her head toward her neighbor, and her determined chin firmed. God, she was even more beautiful than he'd imagined. Who was she? Rupert was quite sure he'd never seen her before.

He gave himself a shake. Standing there like an idiot wouldn't do him any good at all. He'd never been shy about meeting a lady, yet he couldn't stop himself from staring at her. What would happen when they were introduced? Would she be as fascinated by him as he was by her?

He prayed she wasn't married.

Vivian had the strangest sensation she was being watched. She glanced up and fought to control her countenance. It was him! The gentleman from the park. She was sure of it, and he was staring at her. Their gazes met, and he held hers as he strode forward, apparently not seeing either the footmen who darted out of his way or the other guests attempting to draw his attention.

He was taller than she'd thought, had a strong face with lean cheeks and strong bones. His aristocratic nose was blade straight, reminding her of an ancient Greek or Roman. He carried himself with ease, as if he was the master of his life and the world around him. At first he appeared to be in his early thirties, but when he came closer, she could see no lines bracketing his well-defined lips or marring his smooth brow. The gentleman appeared good-natured, as if a grin hovered permanently around his mouth. In time, she imagined his eyes would have smile lines.

When he reached her small coterie he bowed to Phoebe. "My lady, always a pleasure to see you again."

Phoebe smiled at him. "You will soon rival Kit and Robert in your address, my lord."

Vivian did not know who Kit was, but the only Robert she had been introduced to was Lord Beaumont. The grin Vivian had known was not far away graced the gentleman's lips. "Ah, Featherton is the standard to which all gentlemen aspire. I am a mere pretender to his throne." The man's gray eyes twinkled. "As for my cousin, I trust I have surpassed his address already."

He did resemble Lord Beaumont to a large degree. Both gentlemen had classic good looks, but this man appeared—Vivian searched her mind for the word . . . *vital*. He had an energy about him she did not see in most gentlemen of the *ton*. Even young men, such as he must be, contrived to appear fashionably bored.

"Please introduce me to your friends, my lady," he said to Phoebe as he glanced at Vivian.

Phoebe's eyes seemed to dance, but there was no indication of laughter in her voice. "Certainly. Ladies, may I introduce you to the Earl of Stanstead. My lord, the Dowager Marchioness of Telford, the Countess of Beresford, and Miss Corbet. Lady Telford is my great-aunt, Lady Beresford is her cousin, also a connection of mine, and Miss Corbet the granddaughter of my aunt's friend."

Lord Stanstead bowed over each of their hands. "My pleasure, ladies. We shall all be richer for your presence."

Vivian tried not to let her heart flutter, but it was no good. She drew in a small breath. His voice was as deep and clear as his eyes.

"Does your husband not attend you, my lady?"

"My husband is dead," she responded evenly.

The earl seemed to study her for a moment. "I'm sorry for your loss."

It was all Vivian could do not to tell him she was happy for it, yet that might lower his opinion of her, and for some reason, she did not want him to think badly of her. "Thank you."

Next to her, Silvia muttered something in an under voice.

Vivian looked in the direction her friend was staring. Beresford descended the steps with another gentleman. He paused and scanned the crowded ballroom. If only she could sink back behind the pillar. Perhaps Lord Stanstead's large form would keep the man from seeing her.

A country reel began and Silvia went off with a young gentleman who'd come to fetch her.

Clara was speaking with Phoebe and an older woman who'd joined them. Vivian shrank back, trying to make herself invisible. Just as she had done for six years.

"What is it?" Lord Stanstead's calm tone acted like a balm to her jumbled nerves.

She bit her lip and swallowed. "Nothing." Lord Stanstead raised a brow. "My late husband's cousin. I did not expect to see him here."

He began to turn, and she laid her hand on his arm. "Please, don't. I do not wish him to see me."

Lord Stanstead gazed down at her, his eyes taking on a hard metal sheen. "Has he injured you?"

Oh dear, she had to get herself under control. "No. It is only that I do not wish to—"

"Lady Beresford."

Drat it all. She raised her chin. "My lord. I'm surprised to see you here. I had assumed you did not find London to your taste."

"I normally don't, but I believe we have some unfinished business." Nick Beresford glanced at Lord Stanstead. "Will you dance the next set with me?"

Before she could think of a response, her companion replied in a bored drawl, "Her ladyship has agreed to stand up with me during the next set."

She let out the breath she'd been holding. "Indeed I did, and I am quite sure whatever we have to discuss will wait until a more opportune time." Beresford's friend took his arm, and tugged him away. Once they were out of hearing, she smiled at Lord Stanstead. "Thank you. I won't hold you to the dance. It is a waltz, and I imagine you have already promised it to another lady."

"There is no one in this room I'd rather stand up with." His eyes searched her face. "Besides, you can't very well sit it out when his lordship is still present."

That was true enough. "Thank you, again."

What would it be like to be held by him? Not that it would matter. Nothing could come of it.

"On the contrary, I was about to ask you in any event." He grinned again. "I am honored to be the first."

Heat rose into her cheeks. "I am a bit out of practice, I'm afraid."

"You have only to follow my lead. I'm sure you'll be fine."

Vivian glanced at him, looking for any sign of false flattery, and could find none. "It will be nice to dance again."

"Do you not have assemblies where you live?"

"Yes indeed, but there was never a waltz." Nor had she ever remained past the first hour. Edgar would not publicly shame her by dancing with his mistress, if Vivian made an excuse to leave early.

"Then you shall have a treat denied you at home." Lord Stanstead's countenance had not changed, but she had a feeling he was watching her carefully.

"It is not my home, at least not any longer." Her tone was sharper than she'd wished. "I must apologize. You cannot be interested."

"You are not the only woman to wish to move away from . . . her deceased husband's home. My mother decamped as soon as she was able and has been happier for it."

Vivian was stunned. She had rarely known such sympathetic feeling from a gentleman. "Thank you." It was more than time to change the subject. "Do you make your home in Town?"

His warm gaze told her he knew exactly what she was doing. "Only during the Seasons and for legislative sessions. My main estate is in Kent. I spend a good deal of time there, and I also travel to my other properties."

"I thought most peers allowed their stewards to manage their holdings." Her father and husband had.

A smile pulled at his lips. "I'm sure you have heard the expression, when the cat is away, the mice will play. My grandfather was a great believer that a man must manage his own property. Even the most honest fellow can be tempted to laziness if he thinks no one is looking over his shoulder."

"Stanstead." Phoebe's husband, Marcus, Earl of Evesham, came to stand with Vivian and Lord Stanstead. "I thought you would be making the rounds."

In other words, why was he still conversing with her instead of meeting other ladies?

"Your years out of Polite Society are showing, Marcus." Lord Stanstead's eyes narrowed slightly. "If you must know, I am engaged to stand up in the next set with Lady Beresford and do not wish to be tardy in claiming her hand."

"I understand." Lord Evesham seemed to take a closer look at her. "I must ask your forgiveness, my lady. It was not my intent to be rude. Normally, Stanstead here is the social butterfly."

Lord Stanstead gave an exasperated huff. "Give over, Evesham."

Phoebe appeared and took her husband's arm. "Pay no attention to Marcus at all. He can be just like a mama bear."

Clara strolled over to them with her friend. "Vivian, I'd like to make you known to Lady Bellamny. Almeria, my cousin, Lady Beresford."

Vivian had heard of the lady—who had not? Lady Bellamny had been a leader of the *ton* when Vivian had come out. Nor was she averse to managing situations to her liking. What she hadn't known was that her cousin was friends with Lady Bellamny. Vivian inclined her head. "It is a pleasure to meet you, my lady."

"Likewise." The woman's obsidian gaze focused on Vivian. "Clara has been telling me this is your first time in Town for several years."

Next to her, Vivian could almost feel both Lord Evesham and Lord Stanstead become more alert. Goodness, why all this bother? "I have not been here since I married."

Lady Bellamny nodded slowly. "I'm sure you will discover much to entertain you, even if it is the Little Season."

A volatile under-current seemed to infuse the air around Vivian. Something was afoot. If only she knew what it was. The last set had ended several minutes ago, and now the violins began to play again.

Lord Stanstead held his arm out to her. "Shall we, my lady?"

"Thank you, my lord."

He took her in his arms, and all the stress she'd been feeling fled. It had been so very long since a gentleman had even touched her. Even through his gloves, and her clothing, his hands were warm and sure. Used to being in command. Vivian had to remind herself this was merely one waltz and, likely, the only one.

CHAPTER FIVE

"What the devil do you think you are doing?" Nick growled at his longtime friend and fellow former officer, Damon, Marquis of Hawksworth.

"Saving you from yourself," came the self-assured reply. "Couldn't you see the lady didn't want anything to do with you?"

"I made a promise." Nick clung stubbornly to his desire to have all of this finished, one way or the other.

"Well, if you really do wish to wed her"—Hawksworth's tone was more of a question—"I suggest you leave the lady alone for a bit." He pressed a glass of wine into Nick's hand. "I thought all of you fellows on Wellington's staff had a good deal of address, or did his standards fall after I sold out?"

Nick opened his mouth and closed it again. He actually did want Lady Beresford to refuse him, but he didn't want Silvia any more incensed with him than she already was. Which meant he had to corner Vivian when Silvia wasn't around. "You are generally correct. I merely see no reason to postpone this. If she rejects me again, I shall have to look for another woman to be my wife." Such as Silvia, if he could get her to tell him what he had done to deserve her ire. Conversely, he didn't wish to see another man hurt Vivian again. His cousin had done quite enough of that. "By the way, who was that pup with her?"

"Oho, I'd be careful of who you are calling a pup." Hawksworth gave Nick one of his irritating, superior, *I know more than you do* looks. "That was the Earl of Stanstead, and although he may be young in years, he is not a man to be taken lightly. He boxes with Jackson, fences with Angelo, and the times I've seen him shoot he never missed. If you were to fight him, even with your experience, I don't know that I would wager on you."

Just then, a woman in a cream gown caught the corner of Nick's eye and he turned. *Silvia.* She was enchanting. Even if she could flay a man's skin with the sharp edge of her tongue. Though she didn't look to be doing that now. She smiled up at the gentlemen dancing around her. She'd never smiled at *him* that way, except the once. Nick let out a low moan.

"If you're ill, we should leave," Hawksworth said. Then he apparently got a look at what, or rather who, Nick was staring at. "She is an Incomparable."

"Don't even think about it." Nick surprised himself by snarling. Hawksworth lifted one dark brow. "She may look like a sweet young lady, but she's a shrew. I have reason to know."

His friend's other brow joined the first. "To you or to everyone? Her partner appears to be enjoying himself." Hawksworth's lips formed a sardonic smile. "I never knew you had such a difficult time with ladies. It must have been caused by Waterloo, or are you still upset that you had to sell out? Without the uniform, you now must actually work at being acceptable."

Nick scowled. "At least I'm not aping the Dandy set."

His friend laughed. "My dear Beresford. I never copy. I am leading the Dandy set. Let's depart before you do something that will reflect badly on both of us."

Maybe Hawksworth was right. It was time to retreat and attack at a later time.

The strains of the violins heralded the coming waltz. Rupert escorted Lady Beresford to the floor—after her husband's cousin had left, and he had taken the opportunity to further his acquaintance with the lady, until Marcus poked his nose in their conversation and others of their friends and relatives had joined their little circle.

Rupert learned her given name was Vivian, derived from the Latin *vivus*, meaning *alive*, yet she was not. Something held her back. She had smiled and joked easily with her cousin and Phoebe, yet when forced to converse with the men, she was hesitant and shadows appeared in her dark blue eyes. Although she had stood up to her husband's relative, her hands had trembled slightly, as if she was afraid of the man. Rupert was sure her husband had abused her in some fashion. All his protective instincts came to the fore. He would find a way to help her overcome her fear.

Once Vivian was in his arms she felt as light as a snowflake. For the first several minutes, she was tense, as if waiting for something, then she opened up and became more animated. He asked, "How long have you been in Town?"

"Only a couple of weeks. I cannot say it has changed much in the intervening years."

Rupert knew he shouldn't pry, but she had already let slip some information, and he couldn't help himself. He needed to know more about her. "Did your husband not like London?"

"My"—she pressed her lips together in disapproval—"*late* husband came quite frequently."

It was the way she emphasized *late* that made him understand even more what her feelings were. "You didn't get along."

In his arms, Vivian stiffened. "Let us merely say that there were too many people in our marriage and leave it at that, shall we?"

Feeling easier than he had since he'd discovered she'd been married, he led her through the turn, holding her tighter. "We shall. Have you been anyplace interesting since you've been here?"

"Not really. We've spent a great deal of time shopping and making morning visits."

"If you'll allow me, it would be my pleasure to show you around."

Finally she smiled, and her face lit up. Rupert made a mental note not to discuss her *late* husband again. "I'd enjoy that very much, my lord. Thank you."

"Tell me what you remember about London from before, and I'll fill in the gaps."

They spent the rest of the dance planning outings for the next couple of weeks. Then her brows drew together. "Would you not rather be squiring one of the young ladies around?"

"No. I'm perfectly happy to dance attendance on you."

Her shoulders dropped as she relaxed. "Thank you again, my lord."

"It is entirely my pleasure, my lady."

Rupert fought the urge to tug her against him. Perhaps it was fortunate most of the fathers in Town believed he was too young for their daughters. It gave him the perfect excuse to spend more time with Lady Beresford, Vivian. To him she would be Vivian, until she gave him permission to use her name. Something, Fate maybe, had drawn him to her. Now he wanted to see how it played out.

"May I have the supper dance? It is also a waltz."

He almost lost himself in the blue of her eyes before she replied, "I'd like that exceedingly."

Vivian could hardly believe how divine a waltz was when dancing with a gentleman who wanted to stand up with her and not someone else. She did not stop herself from tightening her grip on his shoulders. Where did Lord Stanstead come by his muscles? The rest of him must be as solid. Which meant he would not be at all interested in what her body had to offer. She was so repulsive to look at no man would be tempted to bed her. She was too fair, and dark hair was in fashion. In short, there was nothing right about her. No matter, she would enjoy his attentions while she could. She wasn't going to remarry in any event.

He'd drawn her closer during the turn and his shoes brushed the hem of her gown, coming perilously close to her leg. Sensations she had never experienced before almost overwhelmed her, and she could feel the heat rise in her chest and face.

"I'm sorry." He loosened his arms. "I should not have held you so closely."

Oh, how she'd love to say he could hold her how he pleased, but . . . "Thank you." Their gazes met as she looked up. "As I said, I am not used to dancing."

His eyes seemed to warm. "It won't take long before you're standing up for every set and dancing until dawn."

"I shall leave that to Miss Corbet. I have more sedate plans." Such as finding a house she could call a home, and dancing with Lord Stanstead once more.

A few moments later the music ended, and he dropped his arms, releasing her. Suddenly she was slightly chilled. "Thank you, my lord. I have rarely enjoyed a waltz so much."

"The pleasure was entirely mine, my lady." He returned her to her cousin just as if she were a young lady. "I shall see you for the supper dance."

The warmth she had experienced before returned. "I look forward to it."

He strolled off, but was quickly waylaid by Lady Beaumont and introduced to a young lady. Vivian tried not to feel disappointed. Naturally he would stand up with ladies who required partners, and although he would honor his appointment to dance with her again, she refused to allow herself to want more. That was not the reason she was in Town.

She glanced around the ballroom. At least Lord Beresford appeared to have left, and she would not be subject to him again this evening. She might be better served by writing to him and informing him that she would not entertain another offer of marriage. If he wished to fill his nursery, he had better look elsewhere.

"Vivian?" Clara's voice brought Vivian back from her thoughts. "What were you scowling about? If anyone were to see you they'd think you were not enjoying yourself."

"I'm sorry. I"—she pasted a smile on her lips—"I'm having a wonderful time, or would be if I knew Lord Beresford was actually gone and not merely hidden by this crowd."

"You may rest assured he is no longer here. I saw Lord Hawksworth take him away."

Some of the tension in her shoulders receded. The less she had to do with any Lord Beresford, the better she'd feel.

Silvia laughed lightly at a quip her dance partner, Lord Oliver Loveridge, made about having to be careful of bumping into others. From the corner of her eye, she saw Nick Beresford glare at her, and she made a point of smiling brightly at Lord Oliver. Nick stalked out of the ballroom with another gentleman. Well, good. The cur wouldn't be bothering either her or Vivian anymore this evening.

Silvia had never known him to press his attentions where they were not wanted. Then again, to her detriment she'd discovered she hadn't known him well at all. And one never knew what his cousin, the previous Lord Beresford, had told Nick—probably nothing about Mrs. Raeford. Normally, Silvia would have thought he'd have known about her. He and his cousin had been close. But since Nick had left Oxford, he had been gone. Except for the month he had spent at Beresford a few years ago. A time she wished she could forget. He was still as difficult as he'd been before. Apparently the army hadn't taught him anything except how to break the hearts of unsuspecting and trusting young ladies.

Suddenly she was jerked out of her reveries by Lord Oliver's bored drawl. "My apologies, Miss Corbet. That oaf should not be allowed on the dance floor. He is ruining the line." His lips formed a sneer. "One wonders how he even obtained an invitation."

She followed Lord Oliver's gaze to a young, slightly overweight man who'd turned a bright shade of red. The lady with him was slightly flushed, but apparently exerting a calming influence on him. How dare Lord Oliver denigrate the other gentleman in such a fashion! Handsome is as handsome does, and Lord Oliver had just lost much of his charm.

Well, she would not allow his behavior to stand in her presence. Silvia pressed her lips together. "Accidents happen, my lord. I'm quite sure he did not mean to cause a problem."

"You are too kind." He cut a glance at the unfortunate man.

"Not at all." She would have pierced Lord Oliver with a look that had made men tougher than he tremble, had he been looking at her, that was. "Let he who is without sin throw the first stone."

Lord Oliver jerked his head back to her. His eyes widened in something akin to shock. "I beg your pardon?"

This was it. What she was about to do would sink her Season before it began. Well, let his lordship do his worst. She would not lower her standards for a shallow, arrogant young man or indeed, anyone at all. "My father is a rector. It is for all of us to be kind to others, and even kinder to those who do not have the same advantages or talents."

"Indeed." Although how he got the word out since he had not opened his mouth, she didn't know.

Fortunately, before she could respond the set ended, and she was soon returned to Cousin Clara and Vivian.

"I never wish to stand up with him again," Silvia roundly informed her group.

Clara glanced around the room as if searching for someone. "I'm surprised not to see his mother about. She'd take him in hand. What did he do?"

"He mocks those less fortunate than he is."

"In that case"—she sighed—"we must find another more suitable gentleman. Unless you wished to spend your life reforming him, that will never do."

"My only concern is that he is just the type to make trouble." Silvia chewed her bottom lip. "I'm afraid I was not reticent in expressing my disapproval."

"I should not worry about it, my dear," Cousin Clara said soothingly. "If he attempts to make fun of you, he'll only look a fool."

"Thank you. I'm sorry to be such a trial." Silvia had known this was not a good idea. She was not malleable enough to please most young men. Unfortunately, her father truly wished her to find a gentleman to love and marry. There was nothing for it. She would do her best, and be grateful that Cousin Clara was more than capable of guiding and helping her.

"Nonsense. There will be a gentleman for you." Clara's tone softened. "I was much like you when I was young. My father couldn't stand missish young ladies, and I had four older brothers. I was never a Diamond, but was considered an Original. I scared off my share of young men, older ones as well, then I met Telford." A misty look entered her eyes. "I told him I couldn't abide fops and weaklings, nor would I take orders from anyone. It was fortunate for him that my father didn't care for my other suitor. Three weeks later we married."

"Was it always wonderful? My parents almost never fought."

"Oh no, not us. We'd go at it like cats and dogs." Cousin Clara smiled. "But the making up was worth it." She cleared her throat. "Now, where is your next partner? Ah, I see him coming. Nice young man, good family. He's not up to your weight, but he'll do for a dance or two."

A tall, slender young man bowed. "Miss Corbet," he said with a toothy smile, "my set, I believe."

He knew the steps to the cotillion and was graceful, but Silvia felt like his older sister. Somewhere there was the right man for her. All she had to do was find him. It would help if Nick went back to Beresford so she could put him out of her mind.

Clara turned back to her conversation with her friend, Almeria Bellamny. "Did you see how young Stanstead and my cousin looked at one another?"

"I did." Almeria shifted her girth on the sofa. "The doctor is right. I must lose some of this weight I've gained. He does have me on a reducing diet."

Clara bit her tongue from commenting. Even as a young matron, her friend's fondness for sweets was well-known. "What do you think about Lord Stanstead and Vivian?"

"It is hard to know." Almeria drew her brows together in a frown. "He is a conundrum. Despite his age, I would normally say it would be a good match, but he made a cake of himself over a young lady last year. Still, when she married another gentleman, he didn't indulge in a fit of dismals or engage in the forms of low entertainment as many of his peers would have done. Which means to me that his heart was not truly engaged. He has been set on making his mark in the Lords. One hears good reports of him there."

Clara was not overly pleased with this report. "I wonder if he is too young to know what he wants in a wife."

"Does any man—or woman for that matter—know what they really desire until they find the right lover?"

"He seems to be a good-tempered man." Vivian would need someone like that if even half of the little Clara had been able to coax out of Silvia was accurate, which Clara had no doubt it was.

"He is that," her friend agreed. "I've never seen him come close to losing his temper. Patient as well."

"Both points in his favor, I should think." She took a glass of champagne from a footman.

Almeria glanced around the crowded room. "I will say, that I can tell you where your cousin is by watching Stanstead."

Raising her quizzing glass, Clara followed her friend's gaze. The gentleman stood with a circle of other men; however, his attention was focused on the dance floor. "Indeed."

Almeria's lips tipped up slightly. "If he takes after the males in his mother's family in temperament as well as appearance, when he falls, he'll fall hard."

"One can only hope." And help ease the path of true love. She had purposely assigned Vivian a room in the other wing where she could come and go as she wished without anyone being the wiser. Perhaps, when they arrived home, Clara would have a small talk with Vivian in order to ascertain her interest in Stanstead. It might be a good match.

CHAPTER SIX

Taking Kit Featherton's place as the gentleman hostesses most wanted was not at all bad. Rupert put down his wineglass and joined Serena Beaumont, who had beckoned him to dance with another lady. For years Featherton had avoided the popular young ladies by only standing up with those who found themselves without dance partners. No hostess worth her name would allow a young female to remain on the sides if a partner could be found.

A half hour later, he had just returned a young woman to her mother when Robert said, "Thank you for helping Serena."

"Of course I'd be of service to her. She is my cousin. Although I find I like dancing with ladies who are not sought after."

Robert grimaced. "If you say so."

"No, truly." Rupert grinned. Before falling for his wife, Robert had avoided *ton* events for years. "They are either extremely shy, in which case I can put them at ease, or so intelligent they overwhelm most men. In either case, it is much better than standing up with females who simper, bat their eyes at one, and have nothing of note to say."

"Such as Miss Banks?"

Robert might be joking, but Rupert noticed the way her gaze had followed him and, with the exception of the one set he had danced with her, he would take care to steer clear of the lady. Not only was he not interested in her, he wanted her father's support on a bill concerning former soldiers. "Precisely."

"Watch yourself around her." His cousin sipped his champagne. "I've seen her like before. One slip and you'll have a quick trip to the altar."

"Your warning is taken." He searched the room until he saw Lady

Beresford sitting with Phoebe and Lady Telford. Vivian was a puzzle he'd happily attempt to put together. Why, for example, did she dislike her husband's cousin so much? That her marriage was not all it could have been, she'd said, but how had that affected her? "I am engaged for this dance. I'll speak to you later."

"One of the young ladies?" Robert asked.

"No, one of the older ladies." Rupert didn't even have to glance back to know his cousin was watching him. No matter how debauched Robert had been in the past, he'd always looked after his family. That was what had drawn Serena to him.

"My lady." Rupert took Vivian's hand, pressing his lips to it. "I believe this is my dance."

She smiled up at him, her sapphire blue eyes shining with joy. "Yes, my lord."

In a matter of minutes she was back in his arms again. For a few moments they said nothing. He spent the time enjoying the feel of her supple form and appreciating her grace as she followed his lead. Although she couldn't be more than five years older than the young ladies making their come outs, she had an elegance about her none of them yet possessed.

He wanted Vivian, but more importantly, he wanted to know her. Her likes and dislikes, what she dreamed of, how she preferred to spend her days and her nights. His interest in her was different than anything he'd felt previously. Yet before he encouraged her affections, he must know that she wanted what he did. How would she feel about living much of the year on an estate and being a political hostess when in London? If their goals were not similar, then marriage to him would make her miserable, and he couldn't bear that.

"You're quiet, my lord."

When he gazed down at her, no anxiety or trepidation showed in her countenance, merely curiosity. "I was enjoying how well you move through the steps."

"It is easy when my partner is so skilled."

"Oh no." She was much more humble and reticent than the ladies he'd met before. Rupert wanted to draw her out, show her how special she was. "I refuse to allow you to throw my compliment back at me. You are by far the most graceful lady I've had the pleasure of standing up with this evening."

He'd wanted to say forever, but something told him she would take that as mere flummery. The last thing he wanted was for her to think him capable of false flattery.

Unlike the other women he'd danced with this evening, Vivian did not blush, stammer, or simper. Her eyes glowed with a quiet pleasure. "In that case, I shall gratefully accept your accolade."

"Why do some females find it so hard to allow praise?"

Her finely arched brows drew together as she paused for a moment. "I believe some of us are taught not to put ourselves forward. After all, a lady is supposed to be modest in thoughts, words, and deeds."

Yet when Lord Stanstead closed the distance between them during the turn, as he always did, Vivian's thoughts were not as modest as they should be. She wondered what he would look like without formal clothing, or any clothing at all. Her heart sped and she glanced away from his chest. She had to think of something else before she started blushing.

A young lady with dark hair and eyes glared at Vivian. How strange. She could not remember even meeting the girl. "Who is the lady in the white gown two couples away?"

Lord Stanstead slid a quick look in the direction she had indicated. "Miss Banks. Why?"

"She was staring at us."

He shrugged. "I wouldn't let it bother you. She's probably admiring the way we dance together."

Vivian didn't think that was it at all. The girl was more than likely interested in his lordship and wishing her in perdition. Not that it mattered. She'd decided not to attend many of the entertainments. Not only did she have a home to find, she should not let anyone think she was ready to marry again. The image of Lord Stanstead in shirt sleeves passed through her mind, and she swallowed a sigh. It would be lovely if she could bring herself to have an affair. If only there were a guide book or something equally helpful to tell her how to go about it.

"Tell me about your home."

He smiled as if thinking of a particularly wonderful memory. "I have always loved Stanstead Court. It is beautiful, with extensive gardens, a natural stream and lake, which are always full of fish."

"I take it Capability Brown did not design it?"

Lord Stanstead gave a dramatic shudder. "Gad no. Although my grandfather did have a few follies built in order to please my grandmother. She was too fond of her gardens to allow Mr. Brown to remove them. Some of my grandest memories are listening to her tell me about her plants. She had a story for each one."

Vivian hadn't known her grandmothers, and she had always missed what she never had. "She sounds like a wonderful lady."

"She was." He came out of his reverie and smiled. "I'm fortunate to still have my grandmother Beaumont. She is a pistol."

Lord Stanstead's good humor was infectious, making Vivian laugh. "I would love to meet her."

He looked at her thoughtfully for a moment. "I think you and she would get along well."

As they danced, Vivian could almost imagine herself in a fairy world. Yet she must remember she was no longer a young girl, and she was definitely not desirable. Was it fair to take up his lordship's attentions when some other lady would be his wife? Or could she simply enjoy this, the dance, their conversation, even though it would not last? She knew enough of the world to understand that in order to make a political career Lord Stanstead must marry, but if he was not ready to make the commitment, what was the harm in her spending time with him? After all, it had only been two sets. He was all that was charming, but it probably meant nothing to him.

Miss Cressida Banks stood with her closest friend from childhood, Miss Emily Woolerton, the daughter of Sir Bertin Woolerton, Member of Parliament. Having grown up on neighboring estates, as girls they had attended the same schools. Having a mutual interest in hunting and politics, their fathers were thick as thieves, and Emily was already betrothed to Cressida's brother, Hector. Fortunately, they got on well and would wed when he returned from the Levant, which should be in the next few weeks.

"Doesn't Lord Stanstead dance divinely?" Emily commented. "Not as well as Hector, of course."

As far as Cressida was concerned, his lordship was a much better dancer, but Emily was besotted and loyal. No one was as good as Hector. "Did I tell you he asked me to dance with him?"

"He did?" Emily's eyes widened only for a moment. "I mean, of course he would. You are beautiful. Any gentleman would be lucky to stand up with you."

Not if Cressida hadn't pushed him. "I practically had to force him into it." She gave a frustrated huff. "Why didn't Lord Stanstead ask me to dance again? I did my best to be encouraging. Instead he's dancing with that older lady."

"Perhaps because of your father?" Emily ventured.

"But Mama *told* him what she'd heard about him being more mature than his age, and made him *promise* not to interfere if Lord Stanstead took an interest in me."

"It would not surprise me if your father has another match in mind."

"Well, if he does, he hasn't said anything to either Mama or me. I just think he's being difficult." A horrific thought came to Cressida's mind. "I will not agree to wed an old man."

"I doubt he would expect you to marry someone elderly. Give it some time," Emily advised sagely. "If not Lord Stanstead, I'm sure another gentleman will come along. Besides, your dance card is almost full."

"I've already had one Season with no offers at all! And he is so handsome." She swung her fan around by the ribbon and stared at Lord Stanstead. He really was the best-looking gentleman at the ball.

"It could be he is wary of your father and does not wish to antagonize him. I've heard he is trying to make a name for himself in the Lords."

Politics! Is that the only thing gentlemen are interested in? "If that is the case, then I must somehow make it easy for him to approach me." After all, he was single and Cressida was single. With her dark hair and his blond looks they would make a stunning pair. "I am positive that if I could contrive to spend a little time with him, he would like me."

Emily lowered her voice. "I know that tone, Cressida Banks. What are you planning?"

"Me?" Cressida rounded her eyes, doing her best to appear innocent. "Nothing bad, I assure you." Though if she happened to find herself alone with Lord Stanstead . . .

"I don't believe you, and you had better be careful." Her friend hid her frown behind her fan as she scolded. "We are not in the country where you can talk yourself out of mischief. Pull the same stunts here, and you will never receive another card for Almack's again."

The more Cressida thought about Lord Stanstead, the more of a challenge he became. If she could manage to be caught with him, she wouldn't want to talk herself out of it, or care about Almack's. It would be the best match she could make. No longer would she be treated like a child. As the Countess of Stanstead, everyone would have to take her seriously. All she had to do now was pay close attention to where he went, and put herself in his way as often as possible.

When the music stopped, Vivian had not been ready for the set to end. Lord Stanstead placed her hand on his arm, and they rejoined their little circle, as she now thought of it. The last time she was in Town, she had been forced to attend event after event, like a horse being shown at Tattersalls. This time, she was allowed to select her own friends and not be at the whim of others. Except when it came to supper with those selfsame companions. Although she discovered she did not mind at all. Perhaps because her new friends were interested in more than clothing and marriageable gentlemen.

It turned out Phoebe and Lady Beaumont were close relatives, and had decided they should all have supper together. Silvia was instructed to bring along the gentleman escorting her. He was a solid man of middling height who spent a great deal of time talking about his home county and appeared slightly in awe of the illustrious company he was now keeping.

It wasn't long before Lady Beaumont was discussing various methods of farming with him, while the rest of them talked of the sights Silvia and Vivian ought not to miss. High on the list were the Elgin Marbles, which she'd heard of but had never seen.

Lord Stanstead leaned toward her, placing his lips close enough to her ear that his warm breath caused a shiver to skate down her neck. "If you're not already engaged, I'd love to escort you to the museum to-morrow."

"I thought you were taking part in the debate on the Corn Laws?" Lord Beaumont said.

Lord Stanstead pressed his lips together. "I'd forgot."

"We can do it another day if you wish," Vivian offered. That there was a debate she did not doubt, yet something, a hardness in Lord Beaumont's tone, told her his cousin was not completely pleased Lord Stanstead wished to spend more time with her.

"Thank you." For some reason he seemed to be sitting closer to her. "May I send a note to you suggesting a day and time?"

"Don't be silly, Stanstead," Clara interjected. "Of course you may. Though, after her success this evening, you might have to wait until next week or so."

What was going on? First Lord Beaumont and now Clara seemed to be against it. Was merely having Lord Stanstead escort her to the museum such a bad idea?

He stared at his cousin for a moment, then turned to Vivian. "The day after to-morrow, if you are free, my lady. I'm sure my cousin is able to vote my proxy if need be."

"I have nothing planned. Thank you. I very much wish to see them."

A fleeting self-satisfied smile graced Clara's face. So that's what she'd been up to, attempting to goad Lord Stanstead into setting a date, not the other way around.

Not long after supper ended, Clara announced that it was time for her and her charges to retire for the evening. Vivian had had a wonderful time but was becoming rather tired, and poor Silvia, who had danced every set, was bravely stifling a yawn.

Lord Stanstead escorted them to the hall. "I look forward to our outing."

"As do I."

He looked as if he wanted to say more, but held back. That was for the best. Spending time together was one thing; expectations were something else entirely.

"Good night, Stanstead." Clara inclined her head. "I must take these two home while they can still stand. It will take a few days for them to become used to the pace of life in Town."

Either not understanding Clara's dismissal, or ignoring it, Lord Stanstead escorted Vivian to their coach. "Have a good evening."

"You as well."

After Clara, Silvia, and Vivian were all in the coach and the pair had started forward, Clara said, "A good first event. I predict the house will be flooded with flowers and other mementos by to-morrow afternoon."

In no time at all—Mayfair was quite small compared to traveling around the countryside—they were back at Clara's house.

Barnes opened the door. "My lady, would you like tea delivered to your parlor?"

"Thank you, Barnes. You always know exactly what I need."

Vivian, her cousin, and her friend made their way up the stairs to the landing and then into the wing in which Clara and Silvia had their apartments. Silvia seemed as if she could barely keep her eyes open.

Clara must have noticed, as she bussed Silvia's cheek. "My dear, you did wonderfully well this evening. It's a shame to-morrow isn't my at home. Nevertheless, I expect to see an assortment of posies, poems, and other nonsense all dedicated to you. Take yourself off now and feel free to break your fast in your chambers."

"Thank you, I am tired." Silvia hugged Clara, then Vivian. "I had a wonderful time. Thank you so much for wanting me to join you."

"Silly miss." Clara smiled fondly. "Your mother and grandmother would have been pleased. Off to bed now."

Vivian felt her eyes closing as well. It had been much too long since she'd even stayed up so late. "I shall seek my couch as well."

Her cousin linked arms with her, guiding her into Clara's parlor. Perdita ran out from under a table, and danced around her skirts. "Yes, my sweet." She picked up the dog and gave her a kiss before setting her back on the floor. "Sit with me for a few minutes. There are some small details I'd like to discuss." The tea arrived, and Clara served. "Did you have a good time?"

"I did. Much more than I thought I would."

"I wasn't sure how you would like being out among the *ton* again."

"It hasn't changed much." Truth be told, Vivian would have been just as happy to have remained home with a good book . . . except for Lord Stanstead, of course. She had enjoyed meeting him.

"Stanstead is a good young man, and I know you will not fall in love with him."

The tea was half-way down her throat and she choked. "I beg your pardon?"

"You may not have noticed the attention all the younger ladies were paying to him, but I did. He'll be wed before the Season is finished."

"I have no intention of . . ."

"Yes, yes, I know, and who could blame you?" Clara smiled. "Enjoy him while you are able."

How was it that she could say the most outrageous things in a completely conversational tone? "He danced with me and is only accompanying me to the museum. I hardly think it shows interest on his part. He is only being kind to a newcomer to Town."

"Of course, my dear. I'm sure you are correct." Clara nibbled on a biscuit. "In any event, he will probably marry for political reasons. His star is on the ascendant." Clara paused, staring at something on the wall. "Most likely that Banks girl. Her father is a powerful political figure."

That ill-behaved child who had been glaring at Vivian and his lordship? Was it possible Lord Stanstead was trying to ensure the lady noticed him by dancing with her? "Indeed." She carefully placed her cup on the table, resisting the urge to slam it down. "If you do not mind, I'm extremely fatigued. I shall see you in the morning."

"I only ask that you not fall in love with him," Clara called after Vivian. "He is exceedingly handsome."

Half-way through the door she stopped. "You exaggerate, and I am not going to fall in love with anyone." *Ever again.* "Good night."

Vivian closed the door behind her. She had fallen in love with Edgar when he'd courted her. On their honeymoon he had been charming and attentive until the night he had finally decided to consummate the marriage. Bile rose in her throat as she remembered her humiliation when he had stripped off her nightgown. Even if he had not said the words then, his revulsion had been writ on his face. His attentions during the act had been so painful she had not been able to stop her tears. She had begged him to stop but he had not. When he'd left shortly afterward, she had felt more alone than ever.

Even if Stanstead was exceedingly handsome, and attentive, and kind, and had a wonderful sense of humor, she had it on good authority she was not what men wanted.

CHAPTER SEVEN

The clock struck three in the morning before the last of Robert and Serena's guests had left. Rupert, holding a glass of brandy, slouched back on a comfortable leather chair in their study while his cousins occupied the love seat opposite him.

"I think it went well." Serena worriedly gnawed on her bottom lip. "Don't you?"

"It was perfect, but I knew it would be." Robert leaned over, kissing her cheek. "Though I expected nothing less from you."

She smiled softly at him, but there was still a slight crease marring her brow. Robert's wife was a wonder when it came to estate management, having run a castle estate in Scotland for many years before she married. The *ton* was still new to her.

"I agree." Rupert took a sip of brandy. "It was a complete crush, which is all you need to make it a success."

Her forehead cleared. "There *were* a great many people. I don't think anyone sent their regrets."

"They would not have dared miss your first ball, my love." Robert's arm slid around her waist.

It was time to leave them alone. Rupert drained his glass, and rose. "I'm off. I'll see you in a day or so."

"I'll walk out with you." Robert stood. "There is a small matter I wish to discuss."

"I shall leave you gentlemen to talk. Rupert, please join us for dinner later this week." Rising, she gave her husband a hug. "Don't be long, my love. We're not going to have much sleep as it is before Elizabeth wakes."

Rupert waited until he heard her climb the stairs before he turned to Robert. "What is it?"

"Lady Beresford. You appear quite taken with her."

There was no point attempting to lie to his cousin, a man who had known him since childhood. "I am, but I shall not make the same mistake I made before."

Robert raised one brow. "Which is the reason you were ready to take her to the museum to-morrow?"

Drat. Was he rushing his fences again? "I'll go slowly." Rupert grinned. "And if I forget, I know my older cousin will remind me."

"I hope you take advice better than I did." Robert grimaced.

"You can be sure I shall." Rupert began walking to the hall with his cousin beside him. "I have no desire to be in either my mother's or grandmother's black book. All I plan to do is to squire her around and see what occurs."

"Harrumph."

"I promise." He was hard-pressed not to laugh. "I won't do anything I should not." After all, he had never had a rakish disposition. Why should he acquire one now?

"Do remember she is some sort of connection of Phoebe's," Robert responded in a dry-as-the-desert tone.

"As Serena is?"

Robert shuddered. "Exactly. Marcus may now think of you as a younger brother, but Phoebe will not be as generous should you break the lady's heart."

Yet another reason to go slowly. Rupert gave Robert an innocent smile as the butler handed him his hat and cane. "No doubt we will meet to-morrow."

As he walked down the steps, he glanced at the sky. The clouds had cleared, and the moon was bright enough to guide his way. A footman held his carriage door open. "Thank you, but I'll walk home."

"Very good, my lord."

Although going down Carlos Place was a more direct route, Rupert soon found himself on Mount Street at the entrance to the garden.

I wonder where exactly she is staying.

He would have to find out soon if they were to visit the museum. His mother should know, or he could ask Phoebe. But he really didn't want all of his friends following his progress with Vivian.

He scanned the windows of the houses bordering the park. She had probably retired at least an hour ago. There was no reason for her to still be up at this time of the morning. Whether she was as interested in him as he was in her might be the better subject to dwell upon. She had the same fair loveliness as Miss Manning, but Vivian's beauty was more ethereal and her demeanor was more mature, yet at the same time she reminded him of the crystal he'd seen blown in Venice, delicate and fragile. For both their sakes, Rupert would need to proceed carefully with her.

A flickering light shining from a window caught his eye at the same time as a man said, "Don't mean you no harm, guv'nor. But a body's got to make a living."

Strolling through the park at this time of night had not been one of his better ideas. He took out his quizzing glass, turned it on the man, and studied him from the top of his greasy hat to his worn-out shoes. Rupert enjoyed helping those less fortunate than he, but that did not mean he would allow himself to be robbed. A compromise that would allow the other man to save face and buy some victuals was called for.

Tucking his quizzer back in his waistcoat, he used his grandfather's you-are-the-dirt-beneath-my-feet tone. "A crown. You'll get no more from me. If you try, you'll receive nothing."

The thief spit and eyed Rupert's tiepin. "Ain't like you can't afford it."

"Ah, but you see"—he pulled out his stick sword, and the man swallowed—"that particular item has sentimental value to me. What's it to be? The crown or nothing?"

"Ain't it my bleeding luck to come across a knowing one?" the thief said in a thoroughly disgusted tone. "I'll take the crown."

Less than a second after Rupert flipped the coin to the would-be robber, the man caught it and melted into the shadows. In the morning he'd have his secretary contact the local magistrate. Something should be done to better protect innocent citizens.

Rupert searched for the light only to find it had disappeared. Tomorrow he'd discover where Vivian was.

Gisila lay on Vivian's chest, making it necessary for her to hold her book off to the side. After a few minutes she gave up the pretense of reading and stroked the cat, who showed her pleasure by purring deeply. "Not that you care, but I neglected to tell Lord Stanstead where I am residing at the moment."

Perhaps it was for the best. Clara was right, he was more than likely amusing himself until he married a younger lady. Vivian just hoped he wouldn't wed that rude girl.

She settled the cat next to her, then blew out the candles. "I will enjoy the Season and find a house to call home. That is all I really want, in any event."

If she continued to repeat it over and over and over again, she was bound to start believing it.

The cat chirped.

"Yes, there will be a garden and terrace. Perhaps in Kent. That is sufficiently far away from Beresford." Yet instead of falling asleep, Vivian gazed at the window overlooking the park. If she rose, would she see Lord Stanstead? She glanced at the clock. It was after three in the morning. Not likely. She turned her pillow, careful not to disturb her cat.

Six hours later, her eyes popped open and she groaned. Lord Stanstead had taken root in her mind. She'd dreamed of dancing with him and walking through gardens. Her nocturnal meanderings had stopped short of kissing, though. That was something to be grateful for. Or was it?

This foolishness had to cease. Simply because he was the first gentleman in a very long time to show her any consideration, did not mean he was interested in her.

Vivian tugged the bell-pull. It was time to get on with her life, which did not include Lord Stanstead.

An hour later, after dressing and breaking her fast, Vivian found her cousin's secretary, Mr. Septimius Trevor, at his desk in his small office. She knocked on the open door, entering a bit nervously. After all, it wasn't every day a lady of her age, even a widow, sought to set up her own household. "Good morning, Mr. Trevor."

He pushed his spectacles up and blinked as if surprised to see her, then rose hastily. "Good morning, my lady. How may I help you?"

She slipped into a chair in front of his desk. "I wish to begin my search for a property on which to live."

She'd expected questions, or at least a modicum of shock, but the young man merely returned to his seat and picked up a pen. "If you will give me an idea of what you are looking for, I shall contact a land agent I have dealt with before when Lady Telford wished to visit Bath or Brighton. He once found a house for her in Scotland. When do you desire to take possession?"

"Sometime in late October would be ideal." Her cousin would allow her to remain until a suitable house was found, and an older companion arranged.

"Plenty of time then." He pulled out a piece of paper. "Shall we begin?"

Vivian began with the bare bones, after which Mr. Trevor questioned and prodded until a much more detailed picture of what her house should look like began to appear. In her mind a fair-sized manor house emerged, situated on a large enough property to support the maintenance, and a home farm as well as a garden. Any doubts she had experienced earlier dissolved as the scheme grew and became more of a reality. "This is wonderful, but do you think I'll be able to find such a place?"

"Indeed I do." He set down his pen. "The question is what condition will it be in, and what will you accept?"

She'd known this was going too well. "I must view the property first. I am not prepared to make extensive renovations." Sitting a little straighter, she smiled. "There is not much for me to do in any event. I shall be able to travel out to any houses that are close to Town fairly easily. Any others may take some doing." Such as convincing her friend and cousin she was perfectly capable of traveling with only her maid and footman. She could not allow Clara or Silvia to leave Town and miss their entertainments.

Rising, Vivian held out her hand. "Thank you, Mr. Trevor. You've been quite competent and very kind."

"Competence is what I do best." He shook her hand. "It was my pleasure to assist you. I'll send this to the land agent immediately."

Vivian made her way back to her apartment and found Punt in the dressing room. "I've done it. Mr. Trevor is going to assist me in my search for a small estate."

The maid turned slowly. "I know you say that's what you want. Just remember, things will always turn out like they should, my lady."

"I do wish you would be happy for me." Vivian wondered if anyone else had these types of problems with old retainers.

"Forgive me for saying so, my lady, but I'm happy you're out of a marriage with a man who didn't deserve you." Punt shook out a gown with a snap. "I think you need to give yourself a chance at more happiness before you bury yourself in the country. After all, that's where you've been for several years now and it hasn't done you much good that I can see."

"I do not intend to secrete myself. I have it in my mind to be active in any community in the area." Vivian resisted the urge to fiddle with the curls framing her face. "And I am unlikely to meet a gentleman who will change my mind about having my own household."

"Harrumph."

The only gentleman who had caught her attention at all was Lord Stanstead. Still, it was impossible. She could not place herself in that position again. If only things . . . if only she were different. Maybe then Lord Stanstead would be interested, and she could trust a man with her heart. Then again, he had only asked to take her to the museum. There was really nothing in that.

Outside of one of the committee rooms in Whitehall, which was being used for meetings to discuss legislation, Rupert saw Lord Banks hail him. "My lord, good morning."

"That remains to be seen. Stanstead"—the older man's voice was low and slightly gruff—"I am to invite you to dine at my house on Wednesday." He drew his brows down so low they almost touched his nose. "If you are not otherwise engaged, that is."

Lord Banks's fierce expression was obviously meant to intimidate. It did not accomplish that, but it was a damned good thing Rupert had no interest in the man's daughter. The question was whether to tell him or not. Although Banks clearly didn't want him for a son-in-law, he most likely didn't want his child rejected either. "I'm very sorry, but I have a previous engagement that evening."

Banks gave a curt nod and said in an under voice, "Thank you."

It was then that a thought occurred to Rupert. "I gather you have another gentleman in mind?"

"Yes. I am happy you understand. Nothing against you, my lord, but he will know how to take a firm hand with my daughter. He is due to arrive in Town later next week." Banks fiddled with his watch, opening and closing it. "The problem, Stanstead, is that you're too dashing."

Rupert's lips tugged up, and he fought the urge to grin. "I'm afraid I have no control over that. I will, however, promise that I will not attempt to court your daughter."

"This must remain between the two of us." Banks had lowered his voice. "If my wife discovered I've spoken to you . . . The thing is, I haven't told her about my choice yet."

Rupert assumed a suitably grave demeanor. It wouldn't do for his lordship to think he found the situation humorous, and he knew exactly how demanding wives could be, even the best of them. "I understand, my lord. From what I have seen, daughters can be the very devil."

"Indeed, indeed, they are. On the other hand, except for bringing them out, they aren't as expensive as sons. I've got enough of them as well. I never have to worry about the girls getting picked up by the watch, or getting into dun territory. Now then"—Banks flipped open his pocket watch—"I believe I can help you muster enough support for your bill providing aid for the war veterans."

Which was the only thing Rupert wanted from the man. "Excellent." He linked arms with Lord Banks. Being seen in close conversation with him and on good terms could only help Rupert gain support. "Shall we go in? It looks as if the meeting is about to start."

Several hours later, Robert and Rupert accompanied Edward Malfrey, Marcus Evesham, and their friends Rutherford, and Harry Marsh, a member of parliament, to Brooks's.

As they strolled down the street, Rupert turned to his father. "I thought we were going to your house for luncheon."

"We were until I realized it is your mother's at home day."

He certainly didn't wish to face a bevy of ladies, especially after the promise he'd made Banks. "I see. The club is a much better option."

If Rupert had known he would meet Vivian, he never would have complained to his mother. It was too late to do anything about that now. He'd just have to stay as far away from Miss Banks as possible. Most families with daughters to fire off would likely arrive on time to the entertainments. He would make it a point to arrive a bit later, but not so late he would not be able to stand up with Vivian. Better yet, he would reserve his dances with her before he arrived.

Marcus led them to their regular table in the back of the large dining room. Taking the chair next to him, Rupert asked, "I offered to escort Lady Beresford to the museum, but failed to ascertain her address. Do you think Phoebe would know?"

"You *are* desperate if you're willing to involve my wife." Marcus grinned. "But you don't have to go that far; I know where she is.

Lady Beresford is residing with Lady Telford at Ninety-Six Mount Street. She and my mother had a long discussion regarding the benefits of living next to a green area."

That made perfect sense. The houses in the middle of the street were the closest to the walking path. Perhaps it was Vivian that Rupert had seen when he'd strolled through the gardens. A waiter came with a bottle of wine and took their orders.

"Thank you." He took a sip of the club's excellent claret. "I felt more than a little foolish for not having asked for the address."

"I had a devil of a time discovering where to find Phoebe when I was attempting to court her. What is your interest in Lady Beresford?"

He set his wine-glass down. "I would very much enjoy getting to know her better. More than that, I cannot say."

Not precisely the truth, but until he knew how strong his feelings were for her and if she returned his regard, that was all he was prepared to say.

Marcus nodded. "Keeping your plans to yourself will stand you in good stead."

Rupert hoped so. He couldn't afford to make a fool of himself yet again.

"We're having an informal gathering on Wednesday evening with Lady Telford and her charges. Would you like to join us? All our friends are getting married so quickly, Phoebe is having to search for unmarried men to round out her numbers."

That would kill two birds with one stone, spending time with Vivian and avoiding Miss Banks. "There is nothing I would like better."

Cressida pretended to apply herself to her embroidery while she waited for her father to return home. Tea came and went, and he still had not returned.

When the clock chimed seven, her mother laid aside her correspondence. "It's time to dress for dinner."

She tucked the fabric and thread into her bag, and did her best not to show her frustration. "When will Papa be home?"

"Soon, my sweet. He is to join us for dinner." Her mother smiled. "I am sure he'll have good news. He can be very persuasive when he wishes to be."

But did he wish to be? He wasn't at all happy that she was interested in Lord Stanstead. Cressida could not bear being unwed for another Season. Most of her friends from school had married in the spring; now even Emily would soon be married. One would think Papa would have arranged a match, yet apparently he couldn't be bothered.

"Be on time and no matter what the answer is, don't pout or argue with him. You must show him you are mature enough to know your own mind."

Cressida sighed. "Yes, Mama."

"Remember, where there is a will, there is a way. I already sent a card to Lord Stanstead for our ball."

That was what Cressida was counting on. She kissed her mother on the cheek. "Thank you. I'll show Papa he can trust me to know what I want."

Three-quarters of an hour later, as she watched her maid dressing her hair, a light knock came on the door and Emily entered the chamber wreathed in smiles. "I wanted to be the first to tell you! Hector has landed in England. He has some business to attend to, but he hopes to be in Town by the end of the week."

Cressida started to jump up, but her maid placed a restraining hand on her shoulder. "That is wonderful! You'll be able to wed soon!"

"Yes." Her friend clasped her hands together. "Oh, he also said he's bringing something for you!"

"Probably some of that pretty silk." She frowned. "I wonder that Papa hadn't heard from him."

"If he's anything like my father"—Emily cast her gaze to the ceiling—"the letter is lying on his desk unopened."

"He has been gone all day." Cressida's maid finished fixing the ribbon to her hair and she rose. "Did you come over just to tell me you heard from Hector?"

"Not at all." Emily looked bemused. "Your father invited us to dine with you. Did he not tell you?"

"As I said, he's not been here." Cressida pulled a face, funning. "I only wonder if he told Mama."

"Well!" Her friend placed her hands on her hips. "How awkward. Gentlemen can be truly absent-minded. I do hope your brother is not similarly afflicted."

Cressida took her shawl from her maid. "I dare say if he is, he won't be for long once he is married to you."

"Indeed." Emily's voice softened and a gentle light came into her eyes. "I shall be so glad to see him."

"As will we all." Cressida stifled a sigh. If only she loved someone as much as Emily loved Hector, and was loved in return. Even if Cressida didn't love Lord Stanstead, he would be very easy to fall in love with.

CHAPTER EIGHT

At eleven the following morning, Vivian closed the book she had been attempting, not very successfully, to read. Against all her desires, her mind strayed from the romantic hero to Lord Stanstead. If only romances came true.

Laying the book aside, she glanced down at her cat. "Surely someone must be up by now."

Gisila slowly blinked her eyes once.

"I do wish you were a bit more communicative." That is what she got for having a silent cat. Bending down, Vivian stroked the soft, gray feline. "If nothing else, I'll enjoy the change of scenery." She stuck her feet into her slippers, left her chambers, and headed for the morning room. Maybe it was the lack of industry that had her feeling blue deviled. By this time of day, she would normally have completed a full schedule of meetings, and who knew what else. Being in the dower house had given her back the sense of competence she had lost while married to Edgar. She gave herself a little shake. That must be it, and when she had her own estate, she would be back to her usual good spirits.

Voices and laughter drifted down the corridor from the back of the house. Aha, her cousin and friend must finally be about.

When she ambled through the open door, Silvia was in the process of giggling over a note. "Have you ever heard of anything so absurd?"

Clara shook her head and had a self-satisfied expression. "I told you you would be a success."

The room was filled with bouquets, posies, notes, and what looked like paper fans with verse written on them. "I'd say Clara was right. You certainly made an impression."

"Oh, Vivian, listen to this. Lord Oliver sent it. After what I said to him, I thought he would hate me.

"'Rose that you are, stab me no more with your thorns. I was but a fool who thinks himself wise. Please dance with me again and save me from my demise.'"

"Very droll." Vivian grinned. "Shall you stand up with him?"

"Yes. I believe I will give him another chance." Her friend jumped up. "We were going to send for you. I've never known you to sleep so late."

"I didn't. I was waiting for the two of you."

Silvia plucked a card from an exquisite arrangement of pale pink roses. "This is for you."

She handed the card to Vivian. The writing was strong, masculine, yet neat, unlike the scribbling of her father and brothers. Imbedded in the wax seal was a crest. Who would have sent her such lovely flowers?

"Open it." Silvia practically bounced with excitement.

If only Vivian could take them upstairs to her rooms and read the note in private, but her cousin looked on expectantly as well. She carefully separated the wax from the paper.

> *Even the beauty of these roses cannot match yours.*
> *Yr obedient servant,*
> *Stanstead*

He had found her. Warmth wound its way through her body as she bent to smell the flowers. "They are lovely."

"I've never seen anything like them before," Clara said.

The blooms were cup shaped with multiple layers, and although the first impression was indeed a pale pink, the petals ranged from almost white on the outside to a deeper pink in the middle. Vivian fluffed them and the scent became more prominent. "Neither have I. Where in the world could he have found them?"

"Who sent them?" Silvia asked as she sniffed the flowers.

"Lord Stanstead." He must have gone to a great deal of trouble. These were not the usual hot-house blooms.

Vivian ruthlessly shoved down a sense of joy. He was not for her. She must remember that.

Her friend pointed to an arrangement of autumn flowers. "This bouquet is for you as well."

On the card, Vivian's name was scrawled in cramped handwriting. She opened it and cast her eyes to the ceiling. "Lord Bumfield."

A fresh pot of tea and toast arrived. Clara poured a cup, handing it to Vivian. "Practical, but hardly romantic, although he probably thinks it is."

She was definitely not interested in Lord Bumfield. The man was nice, but a widower with several children, prone to flatulence, and stout. No, she'd do much better on her own than tied to a husband like his lordship. If she *were* to be interested in a gentleman, it would be Lord Stanstead, and there was no point in even thinking of him. Even if Vivian was in the market for a husband, he would choose a younger, better connected wife.

She glanced at her cousin. "What are our plans for the day and this evening?"

"We have morning calls and three entertainments this evening." Clara placed her cup on the low oval table between the sofas. "Which means we must be dressing."

Two hours later, after visiting several houses, Vivian was ready to return to Mount Street. Surely there must be houses where the rest of the company didn't consist of young ladies who could speak of nothing but fashion, and giggled over who was to dance with them. Then again, neither did she have much in common with the women discussing children or people she didn't know. She wondered if there was any way she could politely excuse herself from accompanying her cousin and friend without having to plead a headache.

The Dunwood House butler bowed them into Phoebe's home.

"My ladies, please follow me."

They were led to a large drawing room where, thankfully, all the women appeared older than eighteen.

Phoebe greeted them. "Welcome. I think you know everyone. We were just discussing the Worthingtons' soirée. Will you be there?"

"Unfortunately, I was forced to decline," Clara said. "I must do my duty by Miss Corbet and my cousin."

"I understand." Phoebe bussed Vivian's cheek. "We will be discussing politics most of the evening."

This might be exactly the escape she wanted. "Although I must confess to being a complete novice, I am extremely interested in politics."

"I'd be happy to send a carriage to fetch Vivian." Her hostess slid a glance at Clara. "She may dine with us as well."

"Naturally, if she would enjoy that more . . ." Clara's voice faded as she studied Vivian.

Goodness, it was past time to start standing up for herself. "I do believe I would prefer the Worthington event." Vivian gave a rueful grin, more to apologize to her cousin than anything else. "My feet still ache from last night."

"Very well," Clara said. "That is settled. Vivian, you will be introduced to the leaders of our country's liberals."

"Wonderful." Phoebe smiled. "I shall send the carriage for you at seven o'clock."

"I look forward to it." Vivian returned the smile. She had never been encouraged by her father to discuss politics, and her husband had let her know in no uncertain terms that he had no interest in her views.

Despite all that, she did keep up with the current issues and had some definite opinions of her own. Perhaps she might have something to contribute to the discussion this evening and, hopefully, issues in common with the ladies here. Yet as this was a morning visit, after the prescribed fifteen minutes, she, her cousin, and her friend said their good-byes.

As they were leaving, a lady even more flamboyantly dressed than Clara entered the house.

"Lady Evesham, how lovely to see you again!" The woman was wearing an elaborately embroidered silk robe, the like Vivian had never seen before. Atop her head was a turban made of different colored silk strips.

"Lady Thornhill, how wonderful that you've returned." Phoebe took the woman's outstretched hands, kissed her cheek, then turned to Vivian. "Her ladyship has been traveling in the Far East for the past two years."

That probably explained the fantastical garments. "I envy you, my lady."

"We have missed her drawing rooms greatly. No one was able to replicate them." Phoebe quickly made the introductions and the talk turned to Lady Thornhill's travels. Unfortunately, Clara ushered them out, but not before they received an invitation to attend any of the lady's drawing rooms they wished.

Finally, Vivian was finding entertainments and people she would enjoy being around, and she had not thought of Lord Stanstead for at least ten minutes. That had to be progress.

Rupert's secretary, John Milford, handed him a letter with the Evesham seal on it. He opened it, quickly perusing the contents. "I am dining with Lord and Lady Evesham this evening if I have nothing else scheduled."

"You are not otherwise engaged, my lord." Milford reached into the top part of a stack of cards, extracting one. "You have an invitation to Lord and Lady Thornhill's drawing room on Thursday."

"I saw him at my club. He has brought several interesting artifacts back with him. Accept it."

"Yes, my lord."

"You had the roses sent?"

"Indeed, my lord. They should have arrived sometime this morning. Your gardener brought them from the estate and had words about taking so many from the plants. He almost insisted on taking them to the lady herself. However, Cook was able to convince him he should eat."

"I'll bet he did." Rupert smiled. "I don't suppose you reminded him that I found the things and braved the hazards of bringing them back from Persia, and therefore should be allowed to do as I wish?"

"I am not so bold." One side of John's mouth turned up in a crooked grin. "He still hasn't forgiven me for stealing daisies when I was eight."

John was the third son of Rupert's rector. They were of an age and had been together almost constantly until Rupert went off on his Grand Tour. He wouldn't have gone at all if John hadn't been at Stanstead to oversee the estate while he was away. "If I recall correctly, you did not steal them, I told you to pick them for your mother."

"Unfortunately, you didn't get your gardener's permission first," his secretary responded in a dry tone. "The back of my legs still hurt."

"I couldn't sit down for days." And he'd discovered just how much weight his courtesy title held. None at all.

"My hand was cramped from writing out over and over again that I would receive permission from a responsible party before accepting an invitation to take anything."

"Someday," he grumbled, "I'll be in charge of my own gardens."

"I wish you luck."

"If you need me, I'll be in my study until it's time to dress for dinner."

"And if you require me, I shall be right here."

Rupert gave a short laugh. "Where you always are, unless I've sent you haring off somewhere."

He took the stack of invitations from the desk and opened the door to his study. There were times that he still thought he could see his grandfather, or the man he'd thought of as his grandfather, from the corner of his eye as he entered the paneled room.

He separated the invitations into two piles, one for acceptances and the other rejections. A richly engraved card caught his eye. The Marquis of Sudbury was having a masquerade. Rupert didn't know the man well. Sudbury never married and carefully cultivated his reputation as a rake, but they had more than a passing acquaintance, his lordship being a friend of Rupert's grandfather Stanstead.

In England, masked parties still had a rather risqué reputation, but in Venice they had been all the crack. Even if it turned out to be "not quite the thing," as his mother would say, the party might be fun. Rupert put the invitation on the acceptance pile.

A few hours later, he strolled into the drawing room of Dunwood House in Grosvenor Square, and stopped. Vivian was here, looking even lovelier than he remembered. His heart-beat grew more rapid. As if she could sense him, she glanced at the door and smiled. His ears rang as if they'd been boxed. He had definitely never had that kind of reaction to any female before.

"Rupert, come in." Marcus shook his hand, tugging him into the room. "We have sherry if you'd like some."

"Yes, please." Rupert dragged his eyes from hers. "Sherry would be perfect."

After she'd gone back to her conversation with Phoebe, Anna, Lady Rutherford, and Serena, his head began to clear.

"I think you know everyone present?" Marcus poured the excellent sherry he and Phoebe were famous for keeping. It was rumored that her uncle had laid in a store of it before the war.

Rupert gratefully accepted the drink. He sipped carefully, resisting the urge to drain the glass and ask for more. He would really worry his friends and cousins if he did that. "Yes. I believe I do."

"You know how things are when you take your pot-luck with us. Nothing formal, just mill around until dinner is announced."

Rupert did know. Having lived in the West Indies for years, Marcus was never as ceremonial as many of their peers. He snoodled over to Vivian and bowed. "My lady, it is a pleasure to see you again."

Her cheeks turned a pretty shade of pink, almost the color of the roses he'd sent. "Thank you, my lord, for the compliment and for the flowers. I've never seen such beautiful blooms."

"I found them during my travels. That you enjoy them made it worth the trouble."

She gave him her hand, and he lightly kissed her fingers. Straightening, he greeted the other ladies and gentlemen, which included his cousin and Serena.

Robert raised a brow, and Rupert shrugged in answer. As soon as he knew in which direction the wind blew, he would tell his cousin. "What are you discussing?"

"Anything and everything," Vivian responded. "We are solving the country's woes."

"Or attempting to," Serena added. "We ladies have some ideas that Vivian might be interested in."

It pleased him that his cousins were now on a Christian-name basis with Vivian. That Serena felt comfortable enough with Vivian to be informal said much of the lady he was interested in.

Rupert made a point of remaining next to Vivian as they resumed their discussion. "I'm still bothered over the Seditious Meetings Act. It is much too broad."

"Will you attempt to bring a bill to modify it?" Rutherford asked.

"If I thought I could get enough support." Rupert took a sip of sherry. "At the present, I'm more concerned about the one I am sponsoring concerning our returning soldiers."

The air stirred next to him as Vivian shifted. "I agree. Some areas of the country have had too many problems with roving bands of former soldiers who are unable to find work."

He wanted to touch her. Put his arm around her waist, or place his hand on the small of her back. With the exception of the two of them, everyone else present was married, and small touches, sidelong glances, and fleeting smiles abounded.

He forced himself to switch his glass to the hand nearer her in order to inhibit any unconscious gestures. "I agree. In my county, we have made a point of finding work or apprenticeships for them. Some of the soldiers are no more than children."

"Indeed." Vivian rubbed one finger absently over her bottom lip, and Rupert wished it were his lips touching it, tasting her, learning her sounds of pleasure as he made love to her. "There are the widows and children as well. Even widows of officers can have a difficult time making ends meet if they have no family to help them."

He listened as she and the others discussed measures they'd taken. The longer she spoke, the more impressed he became with her intelligence and grasp of the political realities. This was a lady who could help make a political career.

Dinner was announced and he escorted her into the dining room. Fortunately, Phoebe and Marcus had invited only close friends, and they sat informally at the table, giving Rupert an opportunity to take a place next to Vivian. If only he knew if she had any feelings for him or if the emotions were all on his part, or how long he'd have to continue this dance before she responded to him. Rupert refused to consider the possibility that he would not win her. This urge he had to protect her, to care for her, was too strong to be ignored.

A footman held out the tray to him. "Pheasant, my lord?"

He speared a piece of the breast. "Lady Beresford, this slice looks particularly good. Will you sample it?"

Rupert wanted to be the one to attend her, selecting the most delicious foods, accompanying her to the most interesting places, and showing her what she had not yet experienced. Slowly learning her likes and dislikes.

He would take this one step at a time, being careful not to scare her. All evening she had claimed his attention in a way no other woman had done before. And the better he came to know Vivian, the more convinced he was that she was for him. Just as he had thought the first time he saw her.

CHAPTER NINE

"Thank you, my lord." Vivian took a bite of the pheasant he had put on her plate.

If Lord Stanstead had not said her name, she would still be daydreaming. She had never been around a circle of people with whom she had so much in common.

Her only problem was keeping her reactions to Lord Stanstead under control. From the moment he had entered the drawing room and caught her eye, her heart had throbbed painfully in her chest, and she'd had to remember to breathe. If only she would not have such a dramatic response to his mere presence, she could be perfectly at ease.

She held her knife and fork more tightly than necessary to keep her hands from trembling as he served her a piece of game pie from the tray. What she was feeling was ridiculous. She was no longer a giddy girl and would do well to remember how being attracted to a gentleman had turned out the last time. And *this* was much worse.

He grinned at her and his eyes lit up. The only time her husband had appeared that happy was when his mistress was present, never around Vivian.

"I take it you will attend the soirée this evening?" His deep, gentle voice washed over her, once more taking her breath away.

"Yes, with Phoebe."

"It's a shame there is no dancing." Lord Stanstead angled himself closer to her. "However, the Framingham ball is on Wednesday. I'm sure Lady Telford received invitations."

"I believe she did." Head bowed, Vivian applied herself to her food.

"I would be honored if you would dance the first waltz with me."

Her mouth dried and she reached for her glass of wine. She would never be able to eat a thing at this rate. "It would be my pleasure."

The memory of being in his arms flooded her senses, and she yearned for him to hold her again.

"And the supper dance. I dare say our friends will once again take supper together."

"Yes, of course."

What was she doing? This way would only lead to heartache. Once he saw her body, he wouldn't want anything to do with her. A pain started in the center of her heart and exploded. She must cease thinking of him and wanting him.

Vivian raised her gaze to his, and was shocked to see the warmth in them. She had to say something to distract him. "What of Miss Banks?"

He raised his brows in surprise. "Miss Banks? Why would you think of her?"

Vivian twisted her serviette. "She is young and seems quite interested in you."

"Too young, and I have no interest in her." His stare bored into Vivian, as if he could will her to understand what he was not saying. "She is here to catch a husband, and her conversation is full of inane chatter."

If only she could trust her instincts, maybe then she'd know what he wanted. Perhaps he merely wanted an older woman with whom to dally. If only she could bring herself to have an affair, on her terms, but she couldn't even do that. She would not take the chance of being seen leaving a gentleman's house, she could not bring him to Clara's home, and she must never forget that her body was anathema to the male sex.

Still, he did not turn away. "When I wed, the lady must be capable of helping me run several estates and be interested in being a political hostess as all the ladies here are."

She allowed his voice to caress and tempt her again. That was the life she thought she was getting before, and it had all turned out to be a lie. A footman appeared with sole in butter sauce and almonds. "I would love some fish."

Lord Stanstead studied her for a moment before serving her the sole. "Anything you wish, my lady."

The problem was, he sounded as if he meant it.

On her other side, Lord Rutherford claimed her attention, giving Vivian a chance to stop herself from falling into Lord Stanstead's gaze. "My wife tells me you are interested in orphans."

"Indeed I am." After her husband's death, she had finally been able to set up a home for them. "As is Lady Rutherford."

"Although we like to keep our children close to home, Anna and I have been discussing setting up more programs in London. I do not know if the subject was raised, but she, Phoebe, Lady Marsh, whose husband is my brother-in-law and a Member of Parliament, and Serena have already begun an orphan asylum. Those children are apprenticed out, and we have now turned to other children who live at home but whose families are desperately poor. Is that a project you would be interested in supporting?"

For a moment Vivian was startled; a gentleman had never before asked for either her opinion or her help. "Of course, I would love to be involved."

"Mention it to my wife or any of the others, and I am sure they would be grateful for your support."

She was more than thrilled with the way this evening was going. It had far surpassed her wildest dreams. "Thank you, I will."

He glanced over her head for a moment, then grinned. "You're welcome. I'm always happy to see another lady who is interested in the plight of the less fortunate."

When the ladies retired to the drawing room, Vivian brought up the subject with Anna.

"How good of Rutherford to bring it up." Her brow creased for the merest moment. "I think we should hold a meeting soon. One must never allow forward momentum to slow down."

"I agree. Ideas such as this must go forward quickly, so that others do not have the time to back out."

Anna gave Vivian a strange look she could not decipher. "Absolutely."

Not many minutes later, in fact, a great deal sooner than she had expected, the gentlemen joined them. Each man found his wife, and Lord Stanstead came over to her. That made sense as they were the only unmarried ones present.

"What did you and Rutherford discuss?"

She told Lord Stanstead about the program. "I think it is a wonderful idea."

"As do I." He took two glasses of wine from Lord Evesham, handing her one.

Vivian could still not bring herself to call Phoebe's husband by his first name. There was something about his demeanor that made her think he didn't quite trust her. "Thank you."

For what was left of the evening, Lord Stanstead managed to remain with her most of the time. He'd placed her hand on his arm, cupped her elbow, and in small, seemingly insignificant ways, driven her to distraction. His large body seeming to hover, ever ready to refill her glass of wine, or bring tea to her when it was served. His fresh but masculine scent wended its way around her, and his presence made her feel protected.

By the time Phoebe's carriage delivered Vivian home, her senses were raw. She was exhausted and more confused than she had ever been in her life. She knew she should arrange to stay as far away from Lord Stanstead as possible, but her heart and body longed to spend more time with him. If only she knew how to fulfill her wishes and protect her heart at the same time.

Rutherford came up to stand beside Rupert as Phoebe's coach pulled away from the townhouse, carrying its precious passenger. "Thank you for the hint."

"I thought you might need some help. Staring meaningfully at a lady is all well and good; engaging her interests and mind is, at times, more productive."

"Is that what you did with Anna?"

"That was my mistake with Anna." His friend's lips tightened. "I almost lost her because I failed to understand that she required more than my love." Rutherford paused for a moment. "Allow me to restate that: She required to be her own person as well as my love. At the time, I took it as a rejection of me instead of her need to be herself."

Robert had also had to learn something of the sort, and that was exactly what Rupert had ignored about Miss Manning. By the same token, he loved how Vivian came alive when discussing social issues and politics, and he would not want to take that away from her. Rather, he wished to encourage her interests. "Thank you for telling me."

His friend gave a sardonic grin. "I am merely attempting to keep a friend from groveling the way I had to."

Surely, that wouldn't happen to him. What did he have to grovel about? Thus far, he had done all that he could to attach Vivian's feelings, and this time he was right: Her emotions were as engaged as his were. Each time he'd touched her, she had responded. Sometimes there was a quickening of her pulse, or an intake of breath. At other times, she leaned into him slightly. She blushed so easily when he caught her looking at him.

Now that he was certain of her, there was no time to waste in fixing her affections in a more permanent fashion.

To-morrow when he escorted her to the museum would be the perfect time to begin. More flowers were in order, but not roses this time. Something in light blue, as that appeared to be her favorite color. Hmm, the lupines would be almost gone, but his delphiniums should still be in bloom. Old Gregson wouldn't throw a fit about them.

His town carriage pulled up and a footman asked, "My lord, do you plan to walk home?"

That was what he had intended, but riding would enable him to send to his estate for the flowers more quickly. "No"—before his footman could jump off the coach, he pulled open the door and climbed in—"drive on."

In only a few minutes, the door to his residence opened and his butler bowed. "Good evening, my lord."

"Evening, Harlock. Send to the stables and have one of the grooms awoken. I have a missive to send to Gregson."

"As you wish, my lord." The butler closed the door, took Rupert's hat and cane, then spoke softly to one of the footmen still on duty.

Rupert strode to his study, pulled out a piece of foolscap, sat behind his desk, and wrote out his order for as large a bouquet as could be managed to be delivered to Lady Beresford in Mount Street no later than ten o'clock the next morning. He was about to ring for Harlock when a sleepy-looking groom was ushered into the room.

"Take this to Miss Gregson and have her give it to her father." Gregson was an old fussbudget, but he wouldn't go off on his daughter, who was the second housekeeper. She would have to read the letter to him in any event. Rupert handed his groom the missive. "Remain there for the rest of the night, and return with the flowers."

"Aye, my lord."

He poured a glass of brandy as Harlock closed the door, leaving Rupert alone. Although not as busy as the regular Season, the Little Season still had plenty of entertainments. Getting up a party for the theater or the opera shouldn't be difficult. Unless he had to invite Lady Telford and Miss Corbet along with Vivian. That gave him pause. The number of single gentlemen he knew was rapidly shrinking. There was, of course, Hawksworth, but he needed someone older as well. What Rupert really wanted to do was find a way to have Vivian attend the masquerade. Yet how to arrange it escaped him at present.

He leaned back against the soft leather of his chair and swirled his brandy, watching as the colors changed from lighter to darker amber. The real question was who did he know who was closer to Sudbury than Rupert was, and old enough to be in a party with Lady Telford? He'd have to give that some thought. In the meantime, he would invite Vivian for a carriage ride during the fashionable hour in the Park and discover which entertainments she planned to attend.

He drained his glass, placing it on the desk. To-morrow couldn't come soon enough. He could barely wait to see Vivian again.

A knock came on the door and Harlock entered. "This came for you along with a message that it was urgent."

Rupert opened the sealed letter. "Is someone waiting for my answer?"

"Yes, my lord."

> *My dear Lord Stanstead,*
> *I have the support you require to bring the bill to the*
> *Lords, and I have arranged for a committee vote to be*
> *held at ten in the morning.*
> *Yr. Servant,*
> *Banks*

"Is it bad news, my lord?"

"No, quite the opposite." Rupert glanced at the clock. By the time he got John Milford down here it would be too late. The missives must go out immediately. "I'll need three or four footmen immediately."

"Yes, my lord."

"They will have to wait for answers, or, in a few cases, hunt the gentlemen down."

"I understand, my lord."

Rupert sat down at his desk and began writing letters to all his fellow peers who had already promised support for his bill. Once the notes had been sent, he wrote a message to Vivian explaining to her the situation and that he might be slightly late picking her up for their outing. Not exactly how he wished to begin courting her, but he prayed she would understand.

Vivian lay in bed listening to Punt hum as she went about her work. When the tune grew louder, Vivian knew it was time to get up, even though she would rather pull the covers over her head and hide. Some way or another she would have to survive the museum visit with Lord Stanstead without letting him know how much she was coming to like him.

She should have known how it would be after her first meeting with him. She had expected him to be a bit callow, like other young men his age. Yet he was not. Rather, men much older than he, listened when he spoke. His ideas were well thought out, and he knew to a nicety how far he could push a point without making himself appear foolish or too eager. At the same time, he had managed to keep her attention. He would make whichever lady he married a wonderful husband.

"My lady"—Punt stood next to the bed—"a letter was delivered for you, and I have your tea."

Vivian pushed herself up against the pillows, took the missive, and opened it.

> *My dear Lady Beresford,*
> *Please forgive me, but I have an important meeting to attend this morning at Westminster if I wish my bill regarding the war veterans to be heard in the Lords.*
> *I shall try not to be late for our appointment, but count on your generous nature if I should be.*
> *Yr grateful servant,*
> *R. Stanstead*

Laying the note down, she took a sip of tea. "When was this delivered?"

"I'm not sure. Sometime last night, I think. It was on the tray when I went down to the laundry at six."

"Thank you." Vivian wouldn't be at all surprised if he had to cancel their trip. And she could not blame him; the bill was extremely important to him and to the poor returning soldiers.

She glanced at Punt and a tall vase with blue delphiniums caught her eye. "Where did the flowers come from?"

Punt picked up the card that had been set amongst the blooms. "Since I haven't started reading your mail, you'd better see for yourself."

Vivian opened it. *Stanstead.* They were beautiful and in her favorite color.

Oh dear, how was she to stop herself from caring about him when he was so . . . so wonderful? If only her body was not so horrible to look at. If it was as pretty as she'd been told her face was, everything would be fine, but it wasn't, and she would not be rejected again. Spending her life alone was a preferable option.

She must get on with finding her own place to live, and resettle as soon as possible. "Please send a message to Mr. Trevor that I wish to meet with him after I break my fast."

"Yes, my lady."

Hopefully, the land agent had found some possibilities. If she was quick, she could find out what was available and be free when Lord Stanstead came to fetch her.

An hour later, after rushing through her toilet and having breakfast brought to her room, Vivian sat with her cousin's secretary.

"I wrote Mr. Jones as soon as I received word you wanted news as to the progress." Mr. Trevor tapped his pen on the desk, in a thoughtful manner. "I trust it will not be too soon to expect results."

"I hope you are correct. The more I think of it, the more I wish to be settled in a house of my own. It will give me something useful to do."

As well as get her out of London and away from Lord Stanstead.

"Indeed, you cannot be comfortable situated the way you are. Lady Telford is extremely kind, but every lady should have an abode of her own."

Vivian twisted her handkerchief in her hands. She detested waiting. "Precisely. I'm so glad you see my point."

A footman entered with a good-sized packet. "For you, Mr. Trevor."

"Thank you, Corey."

As Vivian sat as still as she could, Mr. Trevor cut the strings and smoothed out the sheets of paper. "We have some possibilities." He frowned. "What is this? Obviously not for you." He set aside two pieces of paper from the stack. "Now then. They are arranged by county. Shall we go through them together, or would you rather look at them by yourself?"

"By myself. I shall bring back the ones that appear most promising, so that you can arrange a viewing." She rose and bent over the desk. From her angle she could read the information on the house he had rejected and saw the land agent's name. Jones and Son. Not difficult to remember. "Thank you."

Mr. Trevor had risen as well. "Not at all, my lady. It is always a pleasure to be able to assist you."

For reasons she would consider later, Vivian took the information about the house Mr. Trevor had rejected and pushed it under her stack of papers, picked up the pile, and left the room.

Twenty minutes later as she perused the estate offerings in her parlor, a light knock came on the door. "Enter."

"Vivian?"

"Silvia." Vivian placed the documents upside down on the elegant cherry desk. Once her plans were firm, she would tell her friend. "I didn't expect to see you up so early. Would you like some tea?"

Silvia sank onto the small sofa next to the desk. "No, thank you, I've had hot chocolate." For a few moments she fiddled with the silk belt of her robe. "I have a question for you."

Vivian raised a brow. "Go on."

"I know you were . . . unhappy in your marriage," Silvia said haltingly, "but was there ever a time when you thought all would be wonderful?"

It was hard to remember, but . . . "Yes, before we wed and for a few weeks at the beginning." If Vivian had known before she had married her husband what she'd learned later, she would have attempted to stop the match. Yet she had been so young and naïve, so full of hope. She'd known she wasn't really pretty, even her father had told her that, but she had tried so hard for so many years to be a good wife. Until she walked in on her husband and his mistress during a fête at the estate.

Vivian had been looking for him to hand out some prizes when she'd heard noises coming from a parlor. She had opened the door. Her husband and Mrs. Raeford were half-dressed on the sofa. The woman's chemise was tucked around her waist, and Vivian's husband was on top, plunging into her. She should have left but her feet refused to move, as if they were stuck in deep mud. Finally they finished, but not before they had declared their love over and over again. And suddenly so many things she not understood made sense. Bile rose in her throat, and she thought she would be sick right there in front of them.

"My love," Mrs. Raeford had said as she smiled smugly at Vivian. "We have an audience."

Her husband had glanced over his shoulder. "So you finally know. It's about time. I dropped enough hints, but you were too stupid to figure it out."

She wished she had been able to make a retort. Instead she fled to her chamber and wept until she had no more tears left. She had wanted to leave, but her parents would not have taken her back. She had wanted to die, and if her husband had not had the accident, she might have taken her life. It might make her a horrible person, but she was glad he was dead.

"Before you married, did you have any feelings that you should not join with his lordship?"

"That is an interesting question. I'm not sure that I did. I think I was too young and excited to be betrothed, and my parents were so in favor of the match my wishes were likely to have been overridden. What I remember most was the shopping and wedding arrangements. Why?"

"I have a feeling Lord Oliver will propose, and I do not think I should marry him. He is all that is witty and engaging, but something is not quite right."

Vivian reached over, taking her friend's hands in hers. "Then my advice is to follow your instincts. You are wise beyond your years and have much more knowledge of mankind than I did when I wed."

"Thank you." A small smile trembled on Silvia's lips. "I needed to hear someone else confirm my beliefs."

Punt entered Vivian's parlor. "Lord Beresford is downstairs waiting to see you, my lady."

"Just who I do not need to see right now. I wish he would give up this mad idea. I've already rejected him once." Vivian rubbed her hands over her face. "I'll be down in a few minutes."

"No." Silvia's lips had firmed into a straight line, and she stood.

"I shall tell his lordship that he is not welcome." She glanced at Punt. "I won't be more than a few minutes."

Vivian waited until the door closed behind her friend. "If I did not think I would be caught out, I'd be tempted to listen in on that conversation. There is much more there than meets the eye."

Silvia's maid was waiting when she strode into her chamber. "I need to dress immediately."

How dare Nick Beresford come around to bother Vivian? He never could take no for an answer. Well, he would now. Silvia splashed water on her face and brushed her teeth. She would send him away with a flea in his ear.

Less than fifteen minutes later, she entered the front parlor where he'd been put. "Lady Beresford is not available to see you. If you give me a message, I promise to see it is delivered. How did you find out where we are residing?"

He gave her such a smug smile she itched to slap his handsome face.

"It was not exactly a secret, especially after the way you've been gallivanting all over Town with Lady Telford."

"Gallivanting indeed. How dare you! We are doing nothing that is not normally done during a Season."

"Silvia—"

"Miss Corbet to you, my lord." Rage at what he'd done years ago, and how he'd left her, burbled up inside, threatening to explode. "*You* no longer have any right to use my name."

A lock of thick, dark brown hair fell over his forehead and he shoved it back. "Very well, *Miss Corbet*, I am not here to argue with you. I merely wish to put forth my proposal to her—"

"The same proposal as before?" She glared at him. Really, some men could be so thick, and he was the epitome of blockheadedness. "The one she already declined, and told you she would not entertain?"

"Yes, now would you please—"

"No. I will not."

He let out a huff—actually it sounded more like a growl, but she chose to ignore it—and prepared to continue arguing.

His face flushed. "I would like to be able to finish at least one sentence."

"Very well." She crossed her arms over her chest. "Go on."

"I shall leave my direction." She opened her mouth, but he held up one finger and she closed it again. "If she would like to contact me."

"She won't."

"At least I tried," he muttered more to himself than to her. Silvia Corbet was going to drive him to distraction.

Nick had to get out of there before he took her over his knee and spanked her, or did something infinitely worse, such as kiss her. God, she was beautiful when she had her ire up. The only problem was that she was standing between him and the door. "I'm leaving now."

She swept aside, her hands now on her nicely rounded hips. Where the devil did they come from? She reminded him of a Portuguese fishwife with her chin jutting out, ready to do battle. He needed to keep that in mind and off her more pleasant attributes.

"I thought you said you were leaving."

Fishwife. "I am."

He grabbed his hat from the butler stationed in the hall. "Thank you."

He strode down the street and was several houses away before he realized he was going in the wrong direction. That woman was a menace, and the sooner she married some poor unsuspecting man and moved away, the better off he'd be. Why the hell did he let her get to him? He wasn't even sane when she was around. He slapped his hat against his thighs. Christ. He should be used to it by now.

Ten minutes later, as he was nearing his town house, he heard his name called.

"Beresford." Hawksworth was standing less than two feet away. "I realize you haven't spent much time around the *ton*, but even *you* should know giving your friends the cut direct is not at all acceptable."

"I'm sorry. I didn't see you."

"That was obvious. What has you so upset?"

"Not what—who." He took off his hat again, this time raking his fingers through his hair, then set it back on his head. "I went to see Lady Beresford to renew my proposal, but Miss Corbet greeted me in her stead."

"Ah, the lady at whom you were staring the other night."

"Yes, and I was not staring at her. She merely happened to pass in front of my line of vision."

Hawksworth linked arms with Nick. "You sound as if you could use a drink."

"I'm not sure that would help." Which was a sad state of affairs when one thought of it.

"Then perhaps this will. The betting at White's has it Lord Oliver will be wed to the lady before the Season's out."

"White's? I thought you belonged to Brooks's."

"I have membership in both clubs. Which is how I happen to be so knowledgeable."

"Who the hell is Lord Oliver?"

"The gentleman you saw her dancing with."

Nick wanted nothing more than to plant someone a facer. "That popinjay? She'll run rings around him."

"Don't be so sure about that. The man has been known to have a nasty temper."

Blast! "Then he'd damn well better keep it to himself. If he lays a hand on her . . ."

"Why do you care?" Hawksworth asked in an amused drawl.

"I don't bloody care." Nick glanced around hoping someone would do something deserving of being beaten. "I don't hold with abusing women, any woman. Not even Silvia."

"Silvia, is it?"

"I mean Miss Corbet. God blast it, I've known her all my life. Besides, it would upset her father."

"Hmm, we can't have that."

Nick stopped and glared at his friend. "Would you stop sounding as if nothing matters?"

An amused gleam entered Hawksworth's eyes. "My dear boy, one of us must maintain a fashionably bored demeanor, and you're doing a miserable job of it. I would take you to my club, but I'm afraid you'd pick a fight. Come along to Jackson's with me instead. At least if you hit someone there, they'll be expecting it."

"Good idea." Pummeling someone was just what he needed. Nick allowed his friend to guide him to Bond Street. "I don't understand why I allow her to needle me. You'd think I'd know better by now."

"Just a thought, mind you, but is it possible that you wish to be in the lady's good graces and never quite manage it?"

"Ridiculous. I couldn't care less what she thinks of me." That was a bald-faced lie. "I'd just like to be able to best her in an argument. Is that so much to ask?"

"Beresford, at some point someone must have told you never to argue with a lady. It is absolutely pointless. They will invariably talk rings around one and never make any sense while they are doing it. They end up getting exactly what they want, and the gentleman ends up at his club, wondering how it happened. No wonder you act as if you're ready for Bedlam."

The only problem with that line of thinking was that Silvia could not only talk rings around him but she could out-maneuver him as well. She needed a man who would stand up to her. But if Lord Oliver meant her harm, he'd have to go through Nick first. Someone must watch out for her. Not every man had his tolerance for her foolishness, or deserved her. If only he knew what the bloody devil was going on in her pretty head.

CHAPTER TEN

Rupert glanced at his pocket watch as he hurried down the steps of Whitehall. It was the middle of the afternoon. His first stop would be Lady Telford's house. He hoped there was a chance Vivian had not given up on him. Hailing a hackney, he climbed in.

Realistically, he couldn't be too upset about the time the negotiations had taken. After hours of haggling, he'd won the vote to push forward his bill to the full House of Lords. Rupert hoped Vivian would be as happy as he was.

Several minutes later, he jumped down to the pavement, threw some coins to the driver, and took the steps two at a time. A footman answered his knock, and Rupert presented the man his card. "Is Lady Beresford at home?"

"Sorry, my lord. She left not a half hour ago."

Drat. He had missed her. Well, it was no more than he deserved. "Please tell her I called."

Well, blast it all. At least he had tried, and she would know he came, even if it was several hours later.

In no hurry now, he strolled to his house, letting himself in. On the round onyx hall table lay a letter placed on the silver salver. His title was written in a strong yet feminine hand. Rupert picked it up and carried it to his study, where he popped open the seal.

> *Dear Lord Stanstead,*
> *I wish you luck to-day. However, I had some urgent*
> *errands to perform and could wait no longer.*
> *Your friend,*
> *Vivian, Countess of Beresford*

Rupert held the paper to his nose. It had her scent. He could almost feel the warmth of her fingers as she penned the note. He may have missed her, but Robert had said she was once again accompanying Phoebe to this evening's entertainment. Rupert would apologize and tell her everything that had occurred.

Glancing at the mound of paper on his desk, he debated attempting to find her or going to his club. Discretion won. About twenty minutes later, he was passing White's when Lord Sudbury came down the steps.

"Stanstead." The older man waved. "I heard about your success. Congratulations, my boy. Your grandfather would have been proud of you." The older gentleman paused. "He wouldn't have agreed, but he would have been proud."

How could Rupert have forgotten? Sudbury had been friends with old Lord Stanstead. The grandfather who was no blood relative to Rupert, but his mother's husband's father. In truth, blood relatives or not, none of his grandfathers were anything to brag about. They all colluded to keep his parents apart, and for years had succeeded. "Thank you, sir. I believe the world is changing and we must change with it."

"All you young people say the same thing. Never mind that. You received my invitation?" A hopeful look appeared on Sudbury's countenance. "My sister is visiting for several weeks and wanted to entertain. She normally resides in the country. Not my usual thing; it will be rather tame," he said, as if to excuse the nature of the masquerade. "Still, one must maintain good relations with one's family."

Rupert grinned. "I not only received it, but accepted."

"Good, good. It was hard to know who to invite. M'sister's got definite opinions on what should and should not go on at a party."

He didn't say anything for a few moments. Sudbury was not only an old roué but an inveterate gossip as well. Nevertheless, Rupert wanted him to issue an invitation to Vivian. "If you are searching for other guests, I can recommend Lady Telford. She is in Town with her two charges, a widow and a young lady she's bringing out."

The man's eyes brightened. "Lady Telford, you say? I had no idea. I haven't seen her in an eternity. Thank you, Stanstead." Sudbury turned to go, then stopped. "What is her direction?"

"Mount Street."

"Good of you to tell me. M'sister, you know, will be pleased."

As Sudbury strolled off down the street, Rupert wondered if the man had carried a torch for her ladyship all these years. At least now he knew Vivian would be invited.

Vivian's hands grew damp and her stomach clenched as she entered the land agent's office. Even though she had her maid with her, it was not the *done* thing for a lady to visit a business office. She should have had him come to her. Yet if she had, then everyone would know what she was doing, and she didn't want to answer the questions that were sure to be asked.

Of course, her cousin and Silvia knew she did not intend to remain at Beresford, but Vivian had not been specific about her plans. Clara probably assumed Vivian would marry, and that was not going to occur.

A clerk quickly jumped to his feet. "May I help you, ma'am?"

She straightened her shoulders. "Yes, you may. I am here to see Mr. Jones regarding several property descriptions he sent to Mr. Trevor for my review."

"My father is not in at the moment, but I'm sure I can assist you." The younger Mr. Jones opened the door to a room filled by a large rectangular table and several chairs. "If you will make yourself comfortable, I'll fetch some tea and biscuits for you and your companion."

She entered the room with Punt following closely behind her.

"Speaking of companions," Punt said, "I don't suppose you've given any thought to who is going to be yours?"

"Not yet. I thought I'd purchase the property then speak to my cousin about indigent relatives who might require a position."

Punt snorted. "And when do you plan to tell your mother?"

Leave it to Punt to ask that question. Mama would not approve of Vivian setting up her own household. "When it's too late to change anything. The first person she will tell is Papa, and I do not want his interference." Which would be forceful and loud. She almost winced at the thought of confronting him. "As it is, I'm surprised I haven't heard from my father."

"I did think he'd have another match in mind." Her maid waited until Vivian had selected a chair, then sat next to her.

"At the moment, he is too concerned with a match for his prize bitch." Which turned out to be a very good thing indeed.

Mr. Jones returned, balancing a tray in one hand and a sheaf of folders in the other. Once she and Punt had consumed their cups of tea and a few biscuits, he arranged the files on the table.

"I have them sorted by location with relation to London, my lady."

"Thank you." Punt handed Vivian her notes on each of the properties in which she was interested. "You might wish to look at my thoughts on which ones I think will suit me best. At some point in the next few weeks, I will travel to the estates closest to Town."

"Very good, my lady." He scanned the papers she'd given him. "Excellent. I shall have the answers to your questions in the next few days."

Vivian rose. "Thank you. Please send them directly to me."

The young man jumped up, almost turning over his chair. "I shall, my lady."

That had gone well and was not nearly as fraught with difficulties as she had imagined it would be. On the other hand, the elder Mr. Jones had not been present. Perhaps Vivian would be better off dealing with the son on a permanent basis. He appeared anxious to acquire his own clients.

Vivian arrived back to her cousin's house in time for tea. When she entered the morning room, Clara held a large gilt-edged card and what looked to be a letter.

She glanced up. "Well, this was a surprise."

"What is it?"

"We've been invited to Lord Sudbury's masquerade. Normally, I would not entertain taking either you or Silvia, but his sister, Lady Mansfield, wrote me a lovely letter assuring me it would not be one of his lordship's usual parties."

"What on earth does that mean?" Vivian sat next to her cousin, who handed her the letter. "Goodness, how bad is his lordship?"

"He was always a bit of a rake. Since he never wed, he had taken to enjoying a different circle of people."

"I understand." Or she thought she did. Nevertheless, she did not wish to inquire further.

"It's a shame he has not had the benefit of the restraining hand of a lady to guide him," she mused.

Vivian bit back a bitter laugh. She'd had no luck at all in *restraining* her husband. "Indeed?"

"Oh yes. Gentlemen have no notion how to go on without a female showing them the way. He'd asked for my hand, you know."

Vivian had not, but was certain she was about to be told. "I
thought your husband was your one true love."

"In many ways he was, and we had an excellent marriage." An
odd look that Vivian could not decipher came into Clara's eyes. "It
was a difficult decision. I was enamored of both of them, you see. For
different reasons, naturally, but my papa picked George over Sudbury, and there you have it. I always thought he would find another
lady and wed, yet he never did." She folded her serviette. "I blame
myself."

That was interesting. Could Clara still be interested in his lordship? "When is the masquerade?"

"In a few days. We will have to decide on costumes immediately.
I might have some things in the attic if the moths haven't got to
them."

Tea arrived with the small sandwiches Clara preferred over biscuits. Perdita showed herself, sitting hopefully at Clara's feet.

Vivian poured. "Where is Silvia?"

"Gone to an outing to Richmond with a group of other young
people. I don't expect to see her for another hour or so. Lord Oliver
arranged the party."

"It looks as if his lordship is growing fond of her."

"Yes." Clara took a sip and frowned.

"Is something wrong with the tea?"

"Of course not. I am not sure I like Lord Oliver. He is not at all
like his parents and the older brother. Very unsteady. I trust Silvia
will keep her head about her. She is not normally a fanciful girl."

Vivian thought back to the conversation she'd had with her friend.
"I think she will be able to separate the wheat from the chaff, as it
were."

Clara tugged on the bell-pull and Barnes immediately stepped
into the parlor. "My lady?"

"I want the trunks of old clothes in the attic brought down here."

He bowed. "Yes, my lady."

"There now, we'll see what we have."

An hour later, Clara had pieced together her costume, and held up what looked to be a long, sheer piece of cloth. "This is perfect for you."

"I beg your pardon?" Vivian's throat was so tight she had trouble croaking the words out. "There is nothing to it."

Her cousin glanced at the fabric. "I suppose you could wear a shift underneath."

"I—I could not. Truly, Clara, I would be almost naked."

"Come now." Her cousin advanced upon her. "Don't be so dramatic. I'm sure it is not as bad as all that." She held up the cloth, which was much thicker than Vivian had first thought. "There is a black wig as well. No one will know who you are."

Clara called for their maids, and before Vivian knew it she was gowned as the Egyptian queen Cleopatra.

"I found some of that kohl as well, my lady." Punt stood back, nodding her head approvingly. "Add a few bangles and a gold necklace, and it will be perfect."

If only there were a mirror in the room, Vivian could object to the details of the costume, which she was sure was too scant. On the other hand it might not be as bad as she thought. Her maid would not allow her to go out in anything scandalous. "If you think it will be all right?"

"As rain, my lady."

Vivian had never been to a masquerade before. Would Lord Stanstead be there? If he was, could she be with him and pretend she was someone else? Another lady entirely?

Later that evening, Phoebe Evesham's town coach arrived for Vivian to carry her to the Worthington's party precisely as Silvia and Clara started toward their carriage.

Clara shooed Silvia into the town coach, then turned to Vivian before entering the carriage herself. "I am so pleased you and Phoebe have hit it off."

"I am as well." Vivian fastened the top button on her cloak. The days were still warm, but the nights were becoming cooler. She counted herself fortunate indeed. It had been such a long time since she'd been around people she could trust. "It is pleasant to have made friends."

She waved as her cousin's coach drove off before giving the Evesham's driver the order to start. Lord Stanstead had not responded to her message this morning. Although he might not have received it before he had left his card at the house.

Despite telling herself she could not form an attachment, she wished she knew if he was attending the same entertainment she and Phoebe were. Still, if he was searching for a wife, he would most likely attend one of the balls Clara and Silvia would visit.

Vivian was tempted to give herself a good scold. It was silly to want him to spend more time with her. She would be leaving Town soon, and he should be going about the job of marrying and producing an heir.

Yet when she entered the first room in a series of large rectangular connecting parlors, the first thing that caught her eye was him, leaning elegantly against the wall, speaking with Lord Rutherford.

A smile lit his lovely gray eyes as he captured her gaze and sauntered forward. "My lady. I had hoped you would attend Lady Worthington's drum." Without her leave and before she could object, Lord Stanstead appropriated her hand, tucking it into the crook of his arm. "I am deeply sorry I missed our trip to the museum. You must allow me to make it up to you." His voice was soft and made her feel as if she were the only person in the crowded rooms. "Please say yes."

Vivian's skin warmed with his touch. She'd never had a gentleman pay her such attention. "Yes, of course." And she enjoyed it far too much. "Tell me how your bill went this morning."

"First, I want to know if I may escort you to the museum to-morrow."

Most gentlemen would have immediately begun speaking about themselves. It pleased her that he did not. "I would be delighted." Vivian glanced up to smile at him and sucked in a breath. There was nothing of the boy in him now as he focused all his considerable attention on her.

Lord, he was a handsome man, as well as strong and kind. Everything any lady could wish for.

If he knew how deformed she was, he would not be here now. She should find a way to tell him. Instead, wanting to enjoy his company for a while longer, her lips wobbled into a slight smile. "Now about your bill."

As they strolled the rooms, he told her about the battles he faced. From the bickering about where the money would come from, to those who believed the government owed the former soldiers nothing. There was apparently more sympathy for the widows of officers than anyone else. Most likely because they were ladies, not part of the masses. Several times they stopped and he introduced her to other friends and allies of his as well as those she now knew as well. How easy it would be to live in this world of politics, power, and forward thinkers. With these people her intellect might be valued and she could make herself useful.

As the house had no ballroom, the carpets were rolled back for dancing, the music was supplied by a string quartet, and she found herself in Lord Stanstead's arms again. If only she could encourage him, if only her body wasn't somehow disfigured.

"Have I told you how well you dance?" His breath caressed her ear.

Her heart went flying straight to him and she was not sure she would be able to recover it. "Not this evening, but thank you."

"I would not want you to forget. A lady as talented as you should know you are appreciated."

Vivian's chest contracted painfully, afraid of being hurt again. If only, if only, if only.

CHAPTER ELEVEN

Vivian paled and her eyes widened almost in trepidation, as if Rupert had said something to frighten her. No matter what she had been through before, he vowed she would know that he cared for her above any other woman.

From the moment Vivian entered the drawing room, he'd fought to remain as close to her as possible, showing her how his affections were growing, edging out other gentlemen who attempted to stand next to her. He'd make damn sure the other men knew she was his, as well.

The entire time he escorted her around the rooms, his fingers itched to touch her, from her small bottom to her firm breasts. His arms wanted nothing more than to hold her. But mostly, he wanted to taste her, her mouth, and every inch of her body. It was hell not being able to carry her off. Damn if Robert hadn't been right. She was turning into his obsession, and more. Rupert could barely let her go at the end of the set.

Before the end of the Season she would be his. He would make sure of it.

When a waltz started, he gave thanks to the Deity.

Bending his head, he whispered into Vivian's ear, "Dance with me."

She nodded shyly, and he took her in his arms. They moved gracefully together. As if they were meant to be one.

"What made you so interested in politics?" Vivian asked.

"From the time I was born I was taught it was my responsibility to care for my dependents; taking my seat in the Lords was part of that duty. Seeing the damage the war did to the people and lands on the Continent made me decide to help anyone I could who was in need.

I'm fortunate that I already had a group of friends who thought like me."

"You mean the Eveshams, Marshs, and Rutherfords?"

"Yes. There are other friends as well. The Earl of Huntley and Viscount Wively are not here this Season. They both married several months ago and have new babies." He wanted to add that she would meet them later; perhaps at their wedding. But it might be too soon. "You would like them as well."

"I'm sure I would." She smiled, yet her voice was sad.

Rupert took advantage of the turn and drew her in closer, tightening his hold on her. "I believe the ladies are planning a campaign to garner support for some of the legislation proposed. I'm sure they would appreciate your help."

The corners of her lovely pink lips tipped up. "That would be enjoyable."

"You should mention it to Phoebe."

"Yes, I shall."

Her tone was fainter than usual, and although it could be that the noise level of the parlor had risen, Rupert didn't think so. Something was wrong with Vivian. She was not enjoying the evening as she should.

The music stopped. Tucking her hand in his arm, he snoodled with her to where his friends were gathering, moving as slowly as possible, enjoying having her next to him and not wanting to share her with anyone else.

By the time they arrived, the next set, a country dance, was starting. He glanced at Marcus, raising a brow.

"My lady"—Marcus bowed to Vivian—"may I have the honor of this dance?"

As before, her lips tilted up, however, the smile did not reach her eyes. "You may, my lord."

Rupert bowed to Phoebe, and she shook her head. "Keep me company, if you would. I'm feeling a little tired."

"Of course." He hailed a footman and procured a glass of lemonade for her. "Unless you'd like champagne."

"No, lemonade is just what I need."

"I can remain here with you," Vivian offered, concern shadowing her eyes.

"No, please. You dance and enjoy yourself." Phoebe smiled, playfully shooing Vivian away. "I expected this. I was tired for the first three months the last time as well."

He looked at Marcus, who grinned broadly. "We are hoping for a girl this time."

"Congratulations." Rupert stole a quick glance at Vivian. Perhaps by next year they would have a child to celebrate as well.

The music began again, and soon he was left alone with Phoebe. He settled on one of the chairs next to the sofa, and she turned to him. "You seem quite taken with Lady Beresford."

"Does it show so much?"

She raised one quizzical brow. "Have you been trying to hide it?"

"Not really." Not at all, truth be told. "I want to ensure she is . . . taken with me as well. I can only do that by spending time with her."

"I wish you well, Rupert. You know that. And, despite what others have said, I do not think you are too young to marry. I will say that I have been given to believe something was very wrong with Lady Beresford's marriage, and that may make her shy of a second one."

"She said something that gave me the same impression." He scrubbed his face with a hand. Did the path to love never run smoothly? "I do not wish to frighten her, but I don't know how much slower I can go."

A peal of laughter rang out. "My dear, if this is your idea of moving slowly, I do not know that I wish to see you moving quickly. You have only known her for about a week."

"Do you not believe in love at first sight?" He took out his quizzing glass and turned it upon her. "I thought you were more of a romantic."

"Only now." Her gaze was drawn to the dance floor and her husband. "Marcus swears he fell immediately in love with me. It took me much longer."

Rupert had heard something of the idiot Marcus had made of himself before he'd been banished to the West Indies. Phoebe had not taken what she'd seen as his betrayal at all well, and for years she had held a grudge against him. Given that Vivian had been married before, her experience could have been much worse than Phoebe's. Rupert might have a harder time than he had expected bringing Vivian up to scratch. "Thank you. I needed that reminder."

Phoebe reached out, tapping his knuckles with her fan. "If you truly love her, don't give up. She needs a gentleman who will care for her."

"I won't. I only wish I knew what I was up against." He slid a hopeful look at Phoebe.

She was quiet for a few moments, then apparently caught sight of something across the room, before saying, "I would not betray a trust, but if I can help you, I shall. I think she cares for you more than she will allow herself to acknowledge."

"You will have my heartfelt thanks." Rupert knew that his friends had helped one another secure their ladies, or gentlemen, as the case may be.

"Yes, I know"—Phoebe grinned—"and you shall name your first-born child after me."

"Not if it's a boy!" He drew back in mock horror.

Phoebe giggled. "You will make an excellent husband."

The look on his friend's countenance was the type of happiness he rarely saw on Vivian's face. What had happened to her? More importantly, would she allow him to help her?

Vivian and Lord Evesham came together again as they performed the simple steps of the reel. She glanced at Lord Stanstead and found him looking at her as well.

"You seem fond of young Stanstead."

"Young?" She didn't want to talk or even think about her feelings for Lord Stanstead. That would lead to nothing good for her. "He does not give that impression."

"No, he came into his title early." The steps of the dance separated them again. "Because of that and a natural tendency toward conscientiousness, he is older and wiser than his years."

"How old is he?" Not truly wanting to know the answer. That she was falling in love with a child would make it worse.

"Two and twenty."

Good God! Two years younger than I. No wonder Lord Stanstead's friends were protective of him.

"My lady?"

Vivian just stopped herself from shaking her head in an attempt to focus. "I beg your pardon, my lord, but I hardly know how to answer you." She raised her chin and a brow. "He has been kind to me."

"Hmm. It think he is fond of you as well."

"I doubt his attention is more than that of a friend." Thankfully, at that point they changed partners, but she could tell he didn't think she was being truthful, and she hadn't been.

Lord Evesham was being impertinent asking her such a personal question. Especially one she did not wish to answer. He did not press his inquiries further though, and she began to relax. Her next partner was Lord Rutherford, while Lord Stanstead partnered Anna Rutherford.

Sometime later, Lord Stanstead claimed his second dance with Vivian, another waltz. Did it mean anything that all the other ladies were now dancing with their husbands? Come to think of it, no man out of their immediate circle had asked her to stand up with him. Surely, it was a coincidence. She had always been told gentlemen did not live in their wives' pockets. Still, all of her new friends seemed to have special relations with their mates.

Lord Stanstead's large palm rested on her waist, stealing her ability to concentrate on anything or anyone but him. No other gentleman had ever held her so possessively, and she liked it, as if she was to be protected and cared for. Was Lord Evesham correct? Could Lord Stanstead truly have feelings for her?

His low voice cut in on her thoughts. "Are you having a good time?"

"Yes." More fun than she'd had in years. "Do I not appear to be?"

"You do now." He smiled at her as if no one else was present or could see them. "I noticed that you appeared nervous or perhaps distracted earlier."

"I am not used to large gatherings." Or ones at which her husband . . . dead husband . . . had not made a point of saying something cutting to her. "But I am finding the more political events make me feel less on display."

"Maybe it is that intelligence is valued over what one is wearing."

Or how young one was, or how one's body might look. "I believe you are correct." She dreaded having to attend the balls Silvia was finding so delightful. "Did you know that Phoebe and the other ladies have started charities to help widows and their children, as well as schools?"

"Yes, and not only that." He grinned ruefully. "They do not actually trust the politicians will do anything to the purpose. Anna won't be happy until ladies have the vote."

Which was an excellent idea, but unlikely to occur. Even peeresses in their own right could not vote. "I must say I agree with her."

"Not you as well!" Lord Stanstead exclaimed jokingly. "Polite Society will soon be taken over by radical thinkers."

Vivian laughed and he drew her closer.

"You are in good company," he said. She closed her eyes for a moment, allowing his tone to caress her. "My mother demands a full accounting of what is going on at the Lords and assists my step-father in drafting speeches and legislation."

"How horrible," she teased, "for you to be surrounded by so many forceful ladies." Was that what he looked for in a wife?

"Did you know they all have one feature in common?"

"Do they really?" She caught glimpses of Anna and Phoebe. "None of them look at all alike."

"No, but they have one feature in common." He nodded. "Each of them has a determined chin."

Lord Stanstead made Vivian wish she had a determined chin as well. Then again, not much was right about her, so one more thing hardly mattered. After the masquerade she would make an excuse to spend several days away from London. She could view properties and, without his presence, bar his lordship from her mind. And her heart.

"Where is Lady Beresford?" The angry voice of Nick Beresford growled from behind Silvia.

She clamped her lips together. If she were not so well bred, she would have rolled her eyes. Though she could swear her knuckles still stung from the last time she'd made that mistake, which had been at least ten years ago.

She turned to face her tormentor, clipping her words. "Not. Here."

"That, I can see," he snapped. "Is she hiding from me?"

The man was going to drive her mad. Silvia breathed deeply through her nose, letting out the breath. She could not raise her voice in Lady Framingham's ballroom. "I doubt she has given you the slightest thought since you visited Lady Telford's home. She has developed her own set of friends. Something you would be wise to do as well, my lord."

He narrowed his eyes at Silvia. "What makes you think I don't have friends?"

"If you did"—she poked her finger at his chest, closer than ever to losing her temper—"you would not be here badgering me."

"I asked a civil question."

"I haven't heard you ask anything in a civil tone since you were ten years old."

"That is not—"

"Miss Corbet?" Lord Oliver's *ton*ish drawl cut through Nick's more belligerent one. "I believe this is my set."

She gave him a blinding smile. "It is indeed, my lord." And just in time. She'd been about ready to kick Nick Beresford, and that would have brought down someone's wrath on her, or broken her toe, maybe both. "Lord Beresford"—she curtseyed—"please excuse me."

Nick didn't say a word, but his sharp brown gaze followed her to the dance floor.

"Who is that fellow?" Lord Oliver bowed before taking her hand.

Was that suspicion in his tone, and for what reason? Silvia's temper hung by a thread, and she wasn't about to put up with another difficult man this evening. She looked straight into Lord Oliver's eyes, challenging him. "Someone I know from my home county. Why?"

"No reason." His tone was softer now, placating. "I thought for a moment he meant something to you."

"Not at all." Less than nothing. A mere thorn in her side. They took their places in the line. "I wish to enjoy the dance and not think about him."

"Your wish is my command." Lord Oliver smiled, but it didn't touch his eyes.

They went through the complicated movements of the cotillion. She really had to get ahold of her temper around Nick. Why did he infuriate her so? Every time he was present, it was as if all her nerves were being rubbed raw. Not only that, he was the only person she had trouble being civil to, and he wasn't even the most irritating person she knew.

She glanced at Lord Oliver. He was handsome, sophisticated, charming, and completely false. It had taken her a while to put her finger on exactly what it was that was off about him. He laughed, flirted, and smiled, all without any emotion. She would prefer Nick to Lord Oliver.

Good God, what was she thinking? Nick was the last gentleman she wanted to be with.

The back of her neck itched. As she made the next turn, Silvia glanced around. She should have known. Nick. Lounging against one of the many columns separating the ballroom from the deep alcoves where the older ladies sat. With him was a man she'd never seen before. Nick stared back at her, and she looked away. It wouldn't do at all for her to allow Nick Beresford to think he had anything other than her disdain.

"You're staring at her again," Hawksworth commented.

"I'm just making sure nothing happens to her." Nick dragged his gaze away from Silvia Corbet. Damned chit. Ever since she had turned sixteen, he had not been able to get her out of his head. They had talked of marriage, yet now he was expected to try to wed Vivian Beresford. Although there probably wasn't much chance of that happening, she was doing an excellent job avoiding him. What the devil was he supposed to do?

"And what, exactly, do you expect to happen to your young lady on Lady Framingham's ballroom floor?"

Blast Hawksworth. Nick growled. "She is not *my* young lady."

"So you say, but whoever she is, what do you think will happen to her?"

His eyes had strayed to Silvia again. "I don't trust Lord Oliver."

"Well, you have a point there." Hawksworth finished off his wine and gave the glass to a footman. "He's said to be playing deep recently."

That didn't bode well for Silvia. "Is he into the money-lenders?"

Hawksworth made a point of inspecting his glove. "I don't know, but I could find out. If it's important to you, that is."

"No one else seems to be watching out for her, so I suppose I'd better do it. Where the hell is her chaperone?" Nick pretended to study the room, but Silvia was the only one who commanded his attention.

"Over in the northeast quadrant of the ballroom speaking with Lady Bellamny." Hawksworth shuddered.

"Isn't she your godmother? I wish you would stop acting like a blasted fop."

"Not a fop, dear one." Hawksworth flicked an imaginary piece of lint from his jacket. "I have decided to be an Original. I'll take part in all the sports, but at the same time dress as well as the Dandies. My valet agrees I shall be able to replace Brummell."

Nick started to scowl, but laughter shot out. "You're as bored as I am."

"Much, much more so." Hawksworth lowered his quizzer. "At least you have your estate to keep you busy, while I'm supposed to pretend to love the Season."

"I'm surprised the duke isn't trying to get you married."

"You really do not have a wonderful grasp of my family." Hawksworth raised a sardonic brow. "Now that I have proved my ability to lead men, I am supposed to dance to my father's tune. An heir is the last thing he is concerned about. Did you know he began naming the boys in Latin numbers because there are so many? Aside from that, I have always had the feeling he does not care for me as much as he does for my brothers and sisters."

"You've never said that before. Why?"

"He and my mother didn't get along well at all. I suppose if I didn't look so much like her it would be different."

Silvia caught Nick's attention again. "Where is he taking her?"

Hawksworth straightened, shoving himself off the pillar. "Outside. It appears as if you were right to be concerned."

Before he had finished his sentence, Nick had started making his way around the edge of the room, his friend following close behind, just as they had in the army.

Silvia and Lord Oliver were not far from the French windows to the terrace, when Nick heard her say, "This is perfect. There is a slight breeze."

"It will be much cooler on the terrace itself."

"I have no doubt, but my shawl is with Lady Telford, and I do not wish to catch a chill."

He hung back. If she could handle the situation, he would let her. God knew she wouldn't thank him for interfering.

"Very well then, perhaps another time." Lord Oliver's voice was calm, but there was a hint of frustration underlying his drawl. "I'll escort you back to her ladyship."

Silvia nodded her head once. "Thank you, my lord."

Nick started to trail her at a reasonable distance when a gloved hand, adorned with rings, stopped him. "I don't believe I've made your acquaintance, sir." An older woman with a purple turban complete with large floppy feathers addressed Hawksworth. "Hawksworth, make the introductions, if you would."

Nick wanted to bark a laugh as his friend paled.

Hawksworth bowed. "My lady, allow me to introduce the Earl of Beresford. My lord, Lady Bellamny, my godmother."

Ah, the dragon of the *ton*. Only Almack's patroness had as much influence. "My lady, a pleasure to meet you."

"Well, you're one of the few young men who think so."

He choked, quickly turning it into a cough.

"I'll leave you now before you have apoplexy." She patted his arm. "Miss Corbet is safely back with Lady Telford. If you wish to court her, here is your chance."

It was apparently Hawksworth's turn to change a laugh into a cough.

"You misunderstand," Nick said firmly. "I have no interest in the lady, nor does she have any in me."

"Indeed." Lady Bellamny leaned toward him a bit. "In that case, the two of you should not spend so much time watching one another."

Before Nick could think of a reply, she left to accost another innocent guest.

"Better you than me," his friend muttered. "Thank you for absolutely nothing."

Hawksworth shrugged. "When it comes to Lady Bellamny, it's each man for himself. The woman scares me to death when she's in Town, and I have known her all my life. However, if you wish to marry she will do all she is able to assist you into the parson's mousetrap."

Nick scanned the ballroom. Silvia was being led out to dance with a man of middling height who looked to be several years older than he. "Who is she with now?"

"Lady Bellamny?"

"No, Miss Corbet."

Hawksworth fixed his quizzing glass on the dance floor. "Bumfield. He is a widower with several children. Perfectly harmless." Nick must have done something, for the next thing out of his friend's mouth was, "Why the devil don't you just ask her to stand up with you?"

"She won't do it," he answered, hoping his tone wasn't as petulant as he felt.

"Oh, I think she will. As long as there is a space left on her card. After all, if she turns you down, she can't dance for the rest of the evening."

Nick had forgotten that small nicety. She would probably annihilate him later, but it might be worth it. "Do you know Lady Telford?"

"Yes, why?"

"You'll have to introduce me. I plan to do a bit of reconnaissance before springing the trap."

Hawksworth shook his head. "You were in the army for far too long."

"Be that as it may." Nick grabbed his friend's arm. "I need an introduction, and you will need to perform it. And I was in only a year longer than you."

A few minutes later, Nick bowed and Hawksworth did his duty.

"It is a pleasure, my lord." Lady Telford glanced from Hawksworth to Nick.

He cleared his throat. "I'd like to ask Miss Corbet to stand up with me."

The older lady languidly waved her fan. "Then ask her."

His cravat tightened. "I wanted to know if she had any sets left this evening. She is quite popular."

Her ladyship's lips curved in a catlike smile. "She is indeed, and your luck is not in this evening, my lord. However, I believe she still has a few dances open to-morrow for the Torrington ball."

As luck would have it, he had accepted an invitation to the event. "Thank you." He moved to the side a bit and watched Silvia gracefully perform her part of the cotillion. It might be a good idea to ask her with her ladyship close at hand.

He waited until Silvia's partner returned her to Lady Telford and bowed. "Miss Corbet."

Her fine dark brows drew together. "My lord?"

"I wish to ask you to dance with me at the Torrington ball."

She opened her mouth and shut it again. "I—I don't know what I have available. My dance card for that entertainment is at home."

"Come, my dear." Lady Telford seemed to purr. "I remember you had a country dance and the supper dance. Though I believe Lord Oliver intends to request the supper dance. It is a waltz."

Lord Oliver be damned. "I'd like the supper dance." Hawksworth poked Nick in his back. "If you would be so kind."

Her ladyship nodded approvingly, while Silvia's glare shot darts at him. But his friend was right. He had trapped her. She couldn't do anything but accept.

With a smile he knew he'd pay for later, she responded, "Thank you, my lord. It would be my pleasure."

At least she hadn't gritted her teeth.

"I look forward to to-morrow." He bowed to both the ladies before making his escape. If he remained too long, she was sure to think of a way out of standing up with him. "That didn't go badly at all."

"I hope she doesn't carry knives," Hawksworth remarked.

"No, not metal ones at any rate." Though her tongue could flay the flesh off a man.

CHAPTER TWELVE

The following morning, Vivian was donning her gloves when Lord Stanstead was announced. She attempted to tamp down the increasing sense of pleasure being in his company gave her. "Tell him I'll be right there."

She took one last look in the mirror. Her cherry-colored carriage gown was dramatically different than the shades of light blue she normally wore. The color brought out the pink of her cheeks, and it was time for a change. No longer would she allow her life to be ruled by men to whom she was nothing but a method to gain what they wanted, without concern for her.

One more day, that was all she would allow herself to have with Lord Stanstead, then she would start finding reasons she should avoid him.

Taking a breath, she blinked back the tears threatening to form. Now she was being silly. After all, one must live with oneself as God made one.

As Vivian made her way down the stairs, Lord Stanstead turned and gazed up at her. "My lady, forgive my being forward, but you look even lovelier than when last I saw you."

A thrill of happiness caused her heart to flutter like the wings of a small bird. "Thank you. A lady always likes to be appreciated."

"Shall we be off?" He held out his arm. "We should be able to avoid most of the crowds."

It *was* much earlier than the fashionable were usually abroad. Even Silvia had not yet come down. Vivian tried not to give in to her disappointment that he did not wish to be seen with her. Dancing was one thing, but this . . . "Yes, let's."

His phaeton was waiting with a small boy in livery holding the horses. Once he had helped her up and taken his place, he gave the order to release the pair. The tiger hopped onto the back of the carriage. She'd heard of tigers, but was dubious about allowing young children to be in charge of blood cattle. "Is it safe to let a young lad take care of your horses?"

"I know there are those who think they should not be allowed to do so, but quite frankly, Stuie will get into trouble if not gainfully employed. I require him to attend classes with the other servants' children. He is extremely bright, but inevitably finishes before the rest and requires occupation. As he loves horses, this seemed to be the best place for him. This pair is as gentle as they come. Now, I would not allow him near my grays."

She felt like an idiot. Lord Stanstead was nothing if not thorough, a fact she should not forget. "Forgive me—"

"There is no need." He waved one hand, keeping ahold of the reins with the other. "It's a valid concern." He flashed another of his smiles that made her catch her breath. "Especially from one who worries so much about the well-being of others."

Her cheeks warmed and she knew she was blushing. "Thank you."

"Were you able to speak with Phoebe?"

"I was. She and Anna have several projects that I am interested in." Endeavors Vivian would have liked to institute at Beresford, had she been allowed to do so.

"Do you enjoy gardening?"

"Very much. My mother has a lovely old garden that she refused to allow to be destroyed for a lawn."

"When I went on my Grand Tour, I brought back dozens of plants . . ." Lord Stanstead regaled her with stories of his old gardener, who appropriated the flowers and vegetables he took to his estate. "Now he acts as if they belong exclusively to him." He slowed his horses. "Here we are."

The drive to the museum was much shorter than she'd thought it would be. "Already?"

"Yes, normally it takes much longer." He set the brake, threw the ribbons to his tiger, then came around to her. Rather than pull down the steps, Lord Stanstead lifted her as if she were as light as a feather. Having both of his hands around her waist sent pleasurable tingles through her torso and did nothing at all for her composure. This was not good. She'd never been breathless with a gentleman before. Perhaps now was the time to begin putting distance between them.

He set her carefully on her feet, placing her hand on his arm. "I think you'll like the Elgin Marbles. They are all everyone has been talking about."

"So I have heard. One is made to appear provincial if one has not visited them at least once." She rested her fingers lightly on his arm, even though she would have preferred to hold on with both hands.

He paid the small fee at the entrance before guiding her unerringly to the famous artifacts. "I never thought there were so many!"

"Yes, it's as if Lord Elgin shipped back most of the artifacts in Europe. The Greeks are already asking that those belonging to their country be returned."

Vivian studied the sculptures and other pieces that clearly came off buildings. "Do you think they will be sent back?"

"Not after the price our government paid for them."

"I have to say, some of my enjoyment in seeing them is lost. It's as if I'm looking at stolen goods."

Lord Stanstead leaned closer to her and now her stomach behaved like butterflies had taken up permanent residence. "I agree, but we mustn't say anything. It would be considered not *the thing*. They are here to be admired, not criticized."

Vivian swallowed as the warmth of his body sank into her. "I understand. Perhaps we could leave now."

"If you wish. Or we may visit other parts of the museum. There are some magnificent paintings."

"Thank you for understanding."

They spent the next hour or so touring the other collections, and discovered their taste in art was the same. Vivian had rarely enjoyed herself more. Gradually, other visitors began to arrive, most of them children with governesses and tutors, and she understood the reason Lord Stanstead had wanted to arrive early. It was much nicer to have the museum to themselves.

Once they regained the pavement, his horses could be seen being led by the tiger. "He is not driving them."

"No. He's only allowed to walk them."

Lord Stanstead lifted her up into the phaeton. Vivian thought she would be able to ignore his touch if she knew it was coming, yet the anticipation made it much worse. A sense of longing she'd never experienced before invaded her senses. They were half-way back to Mount Street before she had control of herself again.

The instant the carriage slowed, one of her cousin's footmen let down the steps, but just as Vivian was about to allow the servant to help her, Lord Stanstead lifted her down again.

She couldn't take much more of that and maintain her composure. All she wanted to do was throw her arms around him. "Thank you for taking me. It was lovely."

"The pleasure, my lady, was all mine." His voice was low, warm, and seductive.

Her body prickled with awareness. She did not dare look up, but she knew Lord Stanstead was gazing at her. If only she could allow herself to want him, but it was no use. Once he saw her unclothed, he would not desire her.

"Thank you once more for the lovely outing." She started to turn, but he took her hand. Oh Lord, what was she going to do if he continued to touch her?

Fighting the urge to peel off Vivian's gloves and kiss each finger one at a time, Rupert brought her hand to his lips, touching it lightly. Until now, he'd never understood why Robert had felt it necessary to attempt to compromise Serena into marriage, yet his actions were increasingly comprehensible.

From Rupert's perspective, the day had been a disaster. Vivian had been amiable but not willing to be charmed. Her smiles had at times appeared forced, and when he had placed her hand on his arm, her touch was different than before, cooler. What exactly had occurred between last night and this morning, he didn't know, but he would damn sure find out.

He drove to his house, giving the horses over to his tiger. "Take them to the stables, and tell Harlock I'll be back before dinner."

No more than thirty minutes later, he was at Jackson's Salon, stripping.

"Is there anyone interesting here?" he asked one of the great Jackson's assistants, hoping to find an opponent he hadn't fought before.

"Lord Hawksworth brought a friend. Looks like he'll show to advantage, if I do say so meself."

"Good. I need a challenge." Surprising how one recalcitrant lady could bring on the need for violent physical activity.

"I'll ask the gentleman if he'd like a sparring partner."

"Thank you." A short while later Rupert strode out of the changing room into the boxing area, inclined his head to Hawksworth, and stopped.

Next to him was the man whom Vivian had been avoiding. Rupert's day had just taken a turn for the better. He could vent his spleen on someone who deserved to be pounded into the ground. His soon-to-be challenger was almost equal to him in weight and reach, although Rupert thought he had a slight advantage in height and age. "Hawksworth."

The other man turned. "Stanstead, here for a round or two?"

"Indeed."

"Allow me to introduce you to the Earl of Beresford. Beresford, the Earl of Stanstead. I recommend each of you to the other." Hawksworth moved aside and murmured, "I shall keep track of the betting."

Rupert and Beresford entered the ring and waited until the attendants had affixed boxing gloves to their hands. Several other gentlemen and some of Jackson's assistants gathered round. Hawksworth said something, and slips of paper were handed to him. The wagering had begun.

Having taken notice, Jackson himself came over and stood between Rupert and Beresford. "You may begin, my lords."

As soon as the great man stepped aside, Beresford lunged, feinting as though he meant to attack from the left, but Rupert was wise to that trick and landed a hard strike to the other man's jaw.

Beresford shook it off and advanced again. "You're good."

"So are you," Rupert replied, refusing to be distracted.

They danced around for a bit, sizing each other up, before he managed a punch to Beresford's gut. A whoosh of air burst out of him, and he charged, catching Rupert on the shoulder as he once more attempted a flush hit to the other man's jaw.

"I hear," Beresford panted, "that you've been spending a lot of time with Lady Beresford."

Rupert leapt out of reach. "What does it matter to you?"

"I asked her to marry me." Beresford closed the distance between them.

"I plan to do the same."

Beresford stopped, and his brows came together in a puzzled expression. "Do you care for her?"

"*That* is really none of your business." Rupert swung, knocking Beresford off balance. "But if you must know, yes, I do, a great deal. Do you?"

"No. I did it for duty."

God damn the cur. Vivian deserved to be loved, not seen as a burden. Anger surged through Rupert, but that wouldn't help him win this fight. Suddenly the bout became all about Vivian, protecting her and making her his. This match was for her. Doubling up on his punches, he aimed for his opponent's head and stomach.

No more than thirty seconds later Beresford collapsed to the floor, gasping for air. "She says she'll never wed again."

The reason for that was what Rupert wanted to know. The attendant took off one of Rupert's gloves and Rupert held out his hand, grasping Beresford's. "I know a pub where the ale is the best you'll find in London."

Beresford climbed to his feet and nodded. "Excellent idea. You're bloody good, by the way. I've never been taken down before."

"It's all in the technique and concentration." Two things Beresford lacked. "I never allow myself to be distracted from the task at hand." Nor would Rupert now. Winning Vivian was his main focus, and if he could convince Beresford he need not wed Vivian, the man might be the key to accomplishing Rupert's nuptials to the lady.

Less than a quarter hour later, they strode out of the boxing saloon, down Bond Street, through the labyrinth of small streets making up Soho, to the Dog and Duck. Rupert kept the conversation to a minimum until they entered the pub, found a table in the back, and called the bar-maid over.

A girl who couldn't have been more than fifteen swung her hips provocatively as she greeted them. "What you hav'n, me lord?"

"Two pints, if you would, Meg."

She speared a young man behind the bar with a look. "I just loves the guv'nor. He's a real gent."

"Ah, Meggie, give a chap a break." The young man screwed his face up. "We can't all be like his lordship here."

"Harrumph." Tossing her head, she flounced off.

Rupert glanced over to her father, who rolled his eyes as the man watched Meg drive her betrothed mad.

Once the ale was served, Rupert took a long drink, wanting to carefully form his questions. What he learned about Vivian's prior life might be crucial to convincing her to marry him.

As before, Beresford jumped in. "Look, call me Nick, if you like, or Beresford if you don't want to be so informal. I can see you don't like that I proposed to Vivian, er, Lady Beresford. If you think you can give her a better life, I'll stand aside."

That was unexpected, but fitted into Rupert's plan. "You said she would never wed again. Why is that?"

"She was married to my cousin Edgar. The union was less than desirable for both of them. Although Vivian tried to be a good wife. My cousin had been and was until he died, in love with another woman. She was the exact opposite of Vivian in every way, from birth to appearance."

Rupert leaned back against his seat and listened.

Beresford took a long draw of his ale. "Edgar and Vivian's marriage was arranged by their fathers. I honestly think Edgar did his best for the week or so after the ceremony. I do know that Vivian fancied herself in love with him, but that didn't last long. Their honeymoon was cut short by my uncle's death, and Edgar was furious that he was stuck with Vivian. He became involved with his mistress, Mrs. Raeford, again, and convinced himself that if he'd waited, he would have been able to find a way to marry her. Which was rubbish. The earl had her married off to an older gentleman farmer as soon as he saw which way the wind was blowing. The old man didn't mind Edgar keeping her on the side, and paid her husband to turn his head, but he'd be damned if he let his son wed the chit."

No matter the reason, Rupert couldn't countenance any man purposely hurting a woman, particularly one he was duty-bound to protect, but he wasn't an innocent and knew it happened. "Was he cruel to her?"

"He didn't beat her." Nick drained the rest of his glass, and Rupert signaled for another. "But he became so angry that he couldn't be with the woman he wanted, I expect he said things he should not have, and he always compared her to his mistress. I don't have to tell you that Vivian did not fare well."

No, she would not have, yet this type of abuse was not what Rupert had expected. Still, it made sense. When he'd complimented her today, she had pulled back. She might be afraid of the same pattern occurring again. "Did he flaunt his mistress?"

"I was gone much of the time"—Nick shook his head thoughtfully—"but I don't think she knew until close to the end."

That meant she had been denigrated and had no clue of the reason. Not that knowing would have made it better. "You said you asked her to marry you out of duty. What did you mean?"

"My cousin asked me to. I arrived on the heels of his fall. Edgar knew he'd treated Vivian badly and wanted to make amends." Nick's lips formed a grim line. "I told myself I'd ask her twice. The problem is that I'm in love with someone else, as well." He stared into his empty glass. "For reasons I don't know, she hates me, but there you have it."

Rupert stared out the grimy window, watching the passersby. "When did Lady Beresford tell you she would not marry again?"

"When I proposed." Nick raked his hand through his hair. "I'm a military man. Plain speaking is what I do best. I was always in line after Edgar, but never expected to inherit. If he had done his duty by Vivian, they would have had children. God knows he had several by the other woman. I didn't know what else to promise her, so I told her I'd give her children."

Rupert had never heard of a worse proposal in his life. Even Robert's to Serena had been better than that. Thank God Vivian had had enough pride left to refuse.

For the first time, Rupert wanted to laugh and did, long and hard enough that Beresford started to flush with anger.

"I don't think it's that funny," he groused. His lips began to twitch. "It wasn't at the time. Although, it probably saved me from a wife I didn't want."

"No wonder she turned you down." Rupert chuckled again. "Not to mention how awkward she would have felt remaining Lady Beresford."

"There is that." Nick grimaced. "Looking at it from your point of view, it almost seems as if Edgar used me to insult her from the grave."

It was time to stop the man from offering for Vivian again. "I think you can leave her ladyship to me." Rupert drained the rest of his ale. "Now that I know what I'm up against, I'll figure out a way to deal with it."

Nick stared as if he couldn't believe what he had heard. "You really do care deeply about her?"

"More than I ever thought possible." And Rupert was sure she was beginning to feel affection for him as well.

His heart ached for her and what she must have suffered. His mother had been ignored by her husband, but that was exactly the way she had wanted it. He could not imagine the pain Vivian must have suffered being compared to a woman her husband considered the love of his life.

Rupert knew, not from experience but from watching other married men, that once they fell in love, their wives were beautiful to them, no matter what others thought.

His grandmother had told him everyone had their match. He just had to prove to Vivian he was hers.

CHAPTER THIRTEEN

Silvia sipped her cup of chocolate. A tray with toast, a pot of jam, and two poached eggs lay across her lap.

Her lady's maid, Hattie, rummaged around the dressing room gathering Silvia's clothing for the next few hours. It was ridiculous how many times a day the fashionable in London changed their garments. Although it did provide much needed employment. Come to think of it, the entire way the *ton* lived appeared to support a great many people.

She tried to focus on the greater issue of the poor, to no avail. Unfortunately, ever since Nick had asked her to dance, she could think of little else. Try as she might, Silvia could find no way to get out of it. If only she didn't know him so well, the cur. If she pretended to be ill this evening, he would only ask until he caught her without a dance partner.

She didn't know what devious scheme he was plotting, but there was no way she would allow him to make a dupe of her again. Once was quite enough for a lifetime. Thank you very much.

She picked up a piece of toast and took a bite, chewing slowly. *Drat, drat, drat.* Why couldn't she find a workable solution?

What she needed was a long walk to clear her head. Eying the white muslin day gown hanging on the wardrobe, she swallowed the toast. "I shall need a walking gown."

"Yes, miss. Don't forget you have an appointment with her ladyship to go shopping."

"I won't." So much for a *long* walk. "I shall also require a footman." At home she tramped all over the country without an escort, or with Hattie. Here in London, she was required by Lady Telford to have a footman for walks, and a groom to ride out.

What would happen if Silvia took her ladyship into her confidence and told the lady why she didn't wish to stand up with Nick? No, that was too risky. Silvia had vowed to herself never to tell anyone what had once been between her and Nick. Before he had returned to Beresford, she was sure she'd got over him. Yet being around him made the pain he had caused her come rushing back.

Her hands curled into fists. If she were a man she would have challenged him to a duel or hit him in the eye or something gruesome. Of course, if she were a man, none of it would have happened.

"If you want to have any time to walk, miss, you'll need to finish eating and get out of bed." Hattie poured water into the porcelain washing bowl. "I'll send a message to have a footman waiting."

"I'm coming." Silvia finished her breakfast in short order. There was no point starving herself because of the blasted man. By the time she had washed, her maid was back, ready to help her dress. "How much time do I have?"

"About an hour."

"I'll be quick." She adjusted her bonnet, tying the bow off to the side. An hour was enough time to make it to the Serpentine, the river that snaked through Hyde Park, and back.

Several minutes later she entered the Park from the east end and lengthened her stride. Silvia was almost to the water when she heard Lord Oliver call her name. What the deuce was he doing up at this hour?

Biting the inside of her lip, she stopped. "Good morning, my lord."

His eyes were rimmed with red, and there was evidence of a cut on his jaw. Surely he didn't shave himself, yet his garments appeared thrown together as well. He gave her a polite smile. "Good morning to you."

"I'm surprised to see you strolling so early."

"Allow me to escort you." Without waiting for her answer or responding to her question, he took her by the elbow, and the unpleasant scent of gin almost made her ill. "Where are you going?"

Not where she was before. "Back to Mount Street. I would not wish to take you out of your way."

"No problem at all." He began ambling back the way Silvia had just come, at a much slower pace than she preferred. "I am glad to have seen you. Will you reserve the supper dance for me this evening? I believe there is only one ball scheduled."

The image of a scale popped into her mind. On one side was Lord Oliver and the other Nick. To her dismay, Nick had the advantage.

"Miss Corbet has already given me the pleasure of that set."

Oh, good heavens! Just what she needed, the both of them at one time. "Good morning, my lord."

In contrast to Lord Oliver, Nick appeared well rested, shaved, and neatly dressed. "Good morning. Up to your walks again, I see."

"I have a footman with me."

"For all the good it's doing you," he said in an under voice.

Next to her Lord Oliver puffed up like a bantam rooster. "What, exactly, do you mean by that?"

Nick eyed the other man for a moment and seemed to make a decision. "Nothing at all. I'll come along. I enjoy a pleasant stroll in the morning."

This was too much. All Silvia had wanted was time alone to think. "I thank you both, but I simply wish to walk at my own pace." Sweeping a curtsey, she started off. Let them make of that what they would. She had reached the gate leading to Mount Street when she glanced back. Of course it would be him. "Lord Beresford, don't you have anything better to do?"

"Than protect you from that rascal? No."

"He is not a . . . Oh, why bother." If it wasn't so undignified, she would have stamped her feet. "The only one I require protection from is you."

She turned to step out into the street.

"I'm still dancing with you this evening," he said, using his I-won-the-round voice and almost pushing her temper over the edge.

Pressing her lips firmly together, she continued on. There was absolutely no point in getting into an argument with him. It would be like lying down with pigs. They'd both get dirty, but he would enjoy it. Unfortunately, she was afraid she might as well.

The evening of the masquerade, Vivian held her arms up as her maid placed the gown over her head. A belt of gold cloth went around her waist. This was it, her last London entertainment for a while. She must get away from Lord Stanstead before she either did something stupid or lost her heart.

Between to-morrow and when she left, she would make up excuses to remain at home. Sick headaches always worked well. They covered myriad minor conditions.

Punt applied the kohl around Vivian's eyes, then fitted the long black wig. She truly did look different. Not at all like herself. The starched linen garment from the last century made her hips and bust appear fuller. That was an unlooked-for improvement.

"There you go, my lady." Punt stepped back.

"Thank you. I do not believe anyone will recognize me."

"Are you sure you wouldn't like some scent?"

Vivian glanced at the bottles lined up on her dressing table, all of them intended to entice her dead husband into her bed. Why had she even brought them? She glanced at the fireplace, wanting to hurl the expensive fragrances into the flames. "No. You may give them away or toss them in the rubbish. I do not wish to keep them any longer."

A knock sounded on the door, and Clara strolled in and struck a pose reminiscent of one of Queen Elizabeth's portraits.

Vivian grinned. "You look splendid and very regal."

"I've always been fond of our virgin queen." She patted her curls. "It must be the red hair."

With a credibly straight face, Vivian said, "Or your forceful personalities."

Her cousin nodded. "Very possibly. She was a lady we can all learn from. It was a pity she never married, though. I cannot imagine any descendent of hers being booted off the throne by Cromwell."

"Indeed." She wasn't going to get Clara started on the English Civil War. It would take more than a century and a half for her to forget what Cromwell had done to her family. "Shall we go?"

"Yes. Please do not say anything to Silvia; she is a lovely girl, but I will not miss playing gooseberry for a change. I had no idea how tiring it is to chaperone a young lady, as well as"—Clara's voice became as dry as dust—"listening to the mamas try to shove their daughters forward." She graced Vivian with a brilliant smile. "I know I do not have to worry about you."

Perhaps that was part of the problem. She had been a dutiful daughter, a dutiful wife, and now, it appeared, a dutiful widow. Not that she'd had much choice in the matter.

She gave herself a shake as Edgar's voice rang in her head. *"Put your nightgown on. How do you expect a man to think about getting an heir looking at that?"*

No. Vivian would never be put in that position again. Much better to remain alone.

Rupert stared at his image in the mirror. "I can't believe my grandfather wore such a thing."

"If you had wanted to select your own costume, my lord, you should have begun earlier."

Normally, he appreciated the plain speaking of his older retainers. This was not one of those times. He damn well knew he should have begun earlier. "I always thought he'd go as Henry the Eighth or some other powerful historical figure."

"I see your point." Wigman fixed a short sword to a belt circling Rupert's waist. "Be thankful your legs have the muscle to carry the costume off. I saw a gentleman once who had stuffing in his stockings in order to make his calves more shapely. It all slipped down around his ankles."

"Indeed." He probably wouldn't be the only gentleman to have bare legs this evening.

A long red cape and gold chain came next. Mark Antony. Of course. With Grandfather's love of Shakespeare and his classical education and travels, who else? Now, if only Rupert knew how Vivian would be gowned.

"There you are, my lord."

"Thank you." Rupert donned a gold half-mask. "I don't know how late I'll be."

"It's no matter, my lord."

His town coach was waiting when he walked down the steps. A footman opened the door, and as soon as Rupert was seated they started forward.

Even though this entertainment wasn't to be risqué, he prayed Miss Banks or others of the younger ladies were not in attendance. He wanted to concentrate only on Vivian, once he found her.

The short line on the steps into Lord Sudbury's house moved quickly, and there was much oohing and aahing over the various costumes, but no sharing of names. The unmasking, as usual, would come at midnight.

In only a few moments Rupert reached his host, who *was* dressed as Henry the Eighth. "Welcome, my lord. So far all my guests have wonderful disguises. I don't think I recognized more than a quarter of them. Midnight will bring some interesting revelations, eh?"

"As it always does." Rupert greeted his hostess, then followed a footman to the ballroom, wondering if Vivian had arrived yet.

Crystal-and-gold chandeliers hung suspended from the ornately plastered and painted ceiling upon which cherubs, maidens, and men cavorted. He searched the ballroom and thought he recognized Vivian, yet when he came close, a cloyingly sweet perfume assailed his nose.

Definitely not her.

Taking a glass of champagne from a fountain set up off to the side of the room, he wove his way through the crowd, searching, not with his eyes, but with his senses.

Finally, the fragrance of a fresh meadow—lemon verbena, lavender, and bergamot—had him turning toward a very modest Cleopatra. He would swear she was wearing stays and a chemise under her costume.

The sound of violins readying for a waltz floated through the air. He finished his wine, but his mouth remained dry. "My queen, may I have this dance?"

She licked her lips and stared at him. "Yes, you may."

Leading her to the dance floor, he bent down and whispered, "It appears as if we are the only Antony and Cleopatra here."

"Yes, it does, my lord."

"Then you were obviously meant for me."

Vivian appeared confused as Rupert held her closer than proper as they made the turn. His knee pushed briefly between her legs, and a light gasp escaped her lips. He grinned; she was responding to him physically, as she had intellectually, just as he wanted. She had to have recognized him as well. He was positive she would not allow another gentleman to take such liberties.

She trembled slightly as he slid his hand from her small waist to the top of her buttocks. Their small talk was forced, as if they truly were strangers, and when the set ended, instead of trying to find her cousin, he grabbed one glass of champagne for the two of them and gave it to her. "Drink."

She took two small sips before Rupert plucked the glass from Vivian's fingers, drained it, then tucked her hand in the crook of his arm and headed for the balcony. "Come with me. I want to stand up with you again, feel you in my arms."

Vivian hesitated. "The dance floor is the other way."

"I know." The last few days of being in her presence, and always with others, had decided him. She was his, and this evening he would not share her. It was past time she was made to realize how he felt, how much he wanted and desired her.

Rupert placed his lips close to her ear. "I wish to be alone with you."

Her eyes widened in surprise. "You do?"

She was so beautiful, his heart ached with wanting. The pulse at the base of her throat throbbed, as his must be doing as well. "More than anything."

He guided her around the edges of the rapidly filling ballroom, onto the balcony. It was blessedly empty. The music began, and he took her in his arms. For a moment she was stiff, then she relaxed and allowed him to pull her close. "You are intoxicatingly beautiful."

Behind her mask, her lashes lowered. "I have to say, I've never seen a more handsome Mark Antony."

"Nor I a more lovely Cleopatra. Stay with me."

"But I can only dance with you twice."

"Not to-night. That is one purpose of a masquerade. Who is to know who we are?"

"Oh, I see." She pulled her full lower lip between her teeth. "I—I . . ."

Twirling her into the shadows, he brought them to a halt. With one finger, he raised her chin. "Be with me."

He lowered his lips to hers. Touching softly, tasting, allowing her to grow used to his attentions. After a moment she responded, pressing her breasts against his thinly clad chest. He trailed his tongue along the seam of her mouth, but didn't receive the reaction he expected. How much of a lout had her husband been? "Open for me, my Cleo."

Her lips parted slightly, and he entered. Slowly at first, gradually possessing her mouth as he planned to possess the rest of her.

Vivian moaned as he tilted his head. God, she'd be the death of him. He had never wanted, no, needed a woman as much as he did her. He didn't know how he could take the courting of her slowly when his body demanded he take her now, and she wanted him as well. He slid his hands down her back to her nicely rounded derrière, easing her closer. She'd been married. Surely she would know what his hard shaft meant. How much he desired her.

Voices filtered from the ballroom's French windows. Coming closer than Rupert would have liked. No matter what, he would not compromise her. He broke the kiss and, under the guise of waltzing, guided Vivian around the corner of the terrace, keeping her hidden from anyone standing near the ballroom.

"Now we're safe for a few moments."

The lanterns in the garden flickered, reflecting in her eyes. "Are we?"

"Yes." Taking her in his arms again, he lowered his head. This time she met him. Their mouths and tongues tangled in an intimate dance, and he groaned. "Cleo." Rupert didn't dare call her by name. "You taste so sweet."

"And you, sir, taste of danger."

"Never. I would never harm you." He palmed her firm, small breasts. One day soon, he would give them the attention they deserved.

Vivian's hands roamed over his chest and back, her fingers sinking in greedily. If he allowed this to continue, they'd be making love on the terrace.

"We must stop." It almost killed him to say the words.

"Just a little while longer." Her voice was breathy and filled with longing.

"Oh God. How can I resist you?" Especially when it was the last thing he wanted. He should propose soon.

CHAPTER FOURTEEN

"No more than I can resist you." Vivian pressed against Lord Stanstead's hard, muscled chest. He kneaded her breasts, and when his finger brushed over her nipple, something sharp and thrilling shot straight to her mons. She had never felt anything like it before. Between her legs she grew wet and willed him to touch her there as well.

"I want you." His tone was gruff and filled with emotion.

So this was what it was like to want a man, to desire to bed him, have him desire her. And his kisses. Vivian had not known one could use one's tongue to such wonderful effect. Nothing would come of it, but she had to give herself the opportunity to be with a man who wanted her, even in disguise. "Yes."

The voices grew louder, and he broke their kiss again, taking her hand and leading her through a door into the house. A clock chimed.

"What time is it?"

"Almost midnight."

A cold chill swept over her. They couldn't go back in now. How had so much time passed so quickly? "Someone will notice."

Lord Stanstead wrapped his arm around her waist. "Come, I'll take you home."

"No." He couldn't be allowed to know who she was. Lord Stanstead was too much of a gentleman not to marry her, and she would never again wed a man who had been forced to marry her. "I have my own way."

Vivian tore away from him and darted into the corridor. In a few moments, she was in the hall. A footman opened the door and she fled around the corner and into the mews. It was only two blocks to Mount Street.

Despite Lord Stanstead's kisses and the way he had touched her, she had been correct that he didn't truly want her as his wife. If he had, he wouldn't have kissed a strange woman.

Most likely it was her black wig that enticed him. Her husband had detested her fair hair. The problem was that she wanted what Lord Stanstead had offered. If only she was brave enough to have an affair.

She had been moving rapidly down the street, but she slowed her pace. What was stopping her? Her husband had demanded she be naked, until he saw her, that was. There could not be a rule that she must show herself. She could continue to wear the wig and would refuse to allow him to see her body. No harm would be done, and she could finally experience lovemaking. After all, Lord Stanstead would have no idea it was Vivian he was bedding, and, if she were clever, he would never know.

Covering her mouth with her fingers, she gave a nervous giggle. She had never had such wicked thoughts before. Nor had she ever considered she would actually look forward to being with a man and enjoying it. The decision seemed to lift a weight from her shoulders.

That is exactly what she'd do. Cleopatra would send him a letter, and Vivian knew just the place she would conduct her illicit meetings with him. At the town house described on the paper that Mr. Trevor had attempted to hide from her.

Her skin tingled. Every nerve in her body was alive as it had never been before. It wasn't until she was in her apartment at Clara's house did Vivian think of what her cousin would say to her leaving the party early. She must send a message saying she hadn't been feeling well.

As she sat down at the desk, her door opened. "I didn't expect you until much later. My lady, are you all right?" Punt crossed the parlor to Vivian. "You're flushed. I hope you're not coming down with a fever. I'll make up a tisane and send a message to her ladyship that you're home."

Tucking her feet under her gown, Vivian nodded, and thanked God for her maid. "I am feeling a little warm." Just not for the reason Punt thought. "I'll go to bed immediately. A good night's sleep is what I need."

Vivian didn't want to have more than one argument with her maid. She needed help to make all the arrangements, and if her maid thought she was ill, she would never agree to assist her. It would be difficult enough talking the poor woman into her scheme at all.

Punt stepped into the corridor, and Vivian slipped into her bed-chamber behind the screen, where her nightgown was ready for her to don. It was the work of a minute to remove the costume. She hadn't worn stays, and her breasts were still full and tender from Lord Stanstead's ministrations. If nothing else, she would know how a woman should feel with a man.

Morning couldn't come soon enough.

Vivian washed her face, brushed her teeth, blew out the candle, and climbed into bed. Her door opened and closed again. Good, Punt probably thought Vivian was already asleep. Though try as she might, each time she began to drift off, the thought of Lord Stanstead's hands and mouth played havoc with her senses.

How long she'd remained awake, Vivian didn't know, but when she opened her eyes, gray light filtered through the window.

Could she really go through with her idea? Her body began to tingle again reminding her of the reason for her decision. She could, she would, and on her terms.

Vivian closed her eyes and listened. It must be early. There was no indication her maid was in the room. Reaching out, she tugged on the bell-pull, and a few moments later one of the lower housemaids entered her chamber. "Your maid says she'll be up in a minute or two and for me to ask if I can get your tea or anything."

Vivian sat up against the pillows. "Please. I would like tea, toast, and a poached egg."

"Yes, my lady."

Once the door closed behind the girl, Vivian threw her legs over the side of the bed. After convincing Punt she was not going to hell for a wanton, Vivian would take a hackney straight to the land agent's office. She prayed the town house was still available. She'd finished washing and had just donned her robe when her maid entered, carrying a stack of clean linen, followed by the same young housemaid.

"Here you are, my lady."

"I need to speak with you."

Punt nodded, and supervised setting out Vivian's breakfast. She'd been hungry before, but now her stomach twisted itself into knots.

"You're up before times. Are you feeling better?"

"I am wonderful and well rested." There was no point in not being forthright. After all, she was a grown woman and a widow. "I need you to accompany me to the land agent."

"About a house?" Punt's lips pressed together in disapproval, and Vivian ignored it.

"About a town house." She sat at the square table near the windows overlooking the garden, and poured her tea, adding two sugars and milk. She wasn't able to meet her maid's eyes, but said in an even tone, as if every day she told Punt that she was going to try to have an affair, "I have decided to have a liaison with Lord Stanstead, and I shall need your help." The room was so still, so silent, it was deafening. Vivian took a sip and swallowed. "If you won't help me, I'll be forced to find someone who will." It was blackmail.

After several more uncomfortable moments, Punt finally said, "You've thought about this, have you?"

Vivian's heart pounded in her chest. "A great deal."

"I don't suppose you'd ... no, never mind." Punt shrugged. "If that's what you want, I can't have you trusting yourself to strangers, and someone's got to look out for you."

Vivian let out the breath she'd been holding. This was really going to happen. "My indigo carriage gown, I think."

"I'll get one of your bonnets with a veil as well. No point advertising."

She turned in her chair. "Thank you."

"Don't know if I agree with you, but there it is." With that cryptic response, Punt disappeared into the dressing room. "Finish eating."

Less than an hour later, Vivian entered the office of Jones and Son Land Agents.

Young Mr. Jones jumped to his feet. "My lady, I would have attended you."

"I was in the area," she lied. "Circumstances have changed a bit. I still require an estate, but I also need a town house for the rest of the Season." She handed him the listing. "That one will suit nicely, if it is not already taken."

His face flushed red. "Are you sure, my lady? I mean it's—it's . . ."

"Furnished?" Vivian smiled. "That is precisely what I need."

"Perhaps my father should speak to you," he squeaked.

"Nonsense. I understand Hill Street is a perfectly respectable neighborhood."

"It is." He gave dissuading her another attempt. "But the house is not decorated for a"—he ran his finger under his cravat—"as it should be for a lady."

"If that is all that's worrying you"—she smiled again—"I am sure it will be fine until I can have it refurbished. I would like to view it now."

Mr. Jones swallowed. "Yes, my lady, but I can't leave now."

"Very well, I'm capable of entering the house by myself."

"But—but—"

Vivian wiggled her fingers for him to produce the keys. "You cannot possibly think I would damage anything?"

"No, my lady." He rose, dragging his feet to a cabinet, and took out a set of keys. "Here you are."

"Wonderful. Now if you will prepare the lease and have it sent to me at Mount Street, I'll sign it today and arrange for the funds to be transferred."

That apparently cheered him for he finally lost his panicked look. "Thank you, my lady."

Punt shook her head as she and Vivian left the office. "First time I've ever seen you bowl someone over."

"I have a feeling there will soon be a great many firsts in my life." At least she hoped so. Until now, her presence on this earth had been a disaster.

Another hackney took her to the house situated toward the corner of Hill Street and Waverton Street. Not too far from her cousin's house, which was helpful as Vivian must return every night if no one was to discover what she was about. "It doesn't look as if a mistress lived here."

Punt choked. "Is that why Mr. Jones was trying to talk you out of the house?"

"Yes." Vivian gave her maid a wicked grin. "I wonder what the inside looks like."

"Open the door and we'll find out." Punt waited as Vivian took the key from her reticule.

"If I didn't know better"—Vivian cut her maid a funning look—"I'd think you were happy for me."

"The only thing I ever wanted for you, my lady, was your happiness," Punt replied, as stoic as ever. "You've had very little of that. If I was worried you'd turn into a trollop, things would be different."

With Lord Stanstead, Vivian could almost imagine giving herself over to him. Yet that was too dangerous. She had done that once, and she would not repeat the mistake. "Thank you for your support. I shall be circumspect."

The lock and hinges were well oiled as the key turned and the door swung silently open. Vivian stepped into the hall and came to a halt. "Oh my."

Marble, gilt, expensive vases, and statuary were tastefully displayed, or so one would think when first entering. Upon a second glance, she noticed that the vases had men and women in interesting positions, and each of the three pieces of statuary placed in alcoves around the half-moon hall was the slightest bit erotic. The center one depicted a woman leaning back against a man's chest, but instead of having his arm around her waist, one hand covered her breast; in the second his other hand was on her mons; and in the third, she had her hand on his member. But the shaft on the statue did not resemble her husband's. It was much more erect.

"Well, I understand now why Mr. Jones tried to keep me from this house." She glanced over her shoulder at Punt. "Let's see the rest of the place."

The subtle erotica was in all but two of the first floor parlors, one in the back facing the garden, which must have been the morning room, and a front parlor.

On the next level, only the master's bedchamber was out of the ordinary. The walls were hung with carmine-red silk, and the bed curtains were blossom pink, but the cover was red. Gilt trim decorated the white plaster ceiling, the bed, and curtain ties as well as the other furniture.

"Well, I've never seen anything like this in my entire life." Punt's eyes practically popped out of her head.

"Neither have I." Vivian laughed. "But it is perfect. Staid on the outside and decadent on the inside."

"I'll manage to get some bedding over here," Punt said pointedly. "And visit the employment agency. You'll need two or three day maids, and a cook."

Vivian widened her eyes. "A cook? Whatever for?"

"Men like to eat."

"Oh yes, of course. You'd better try to find a Frenchman. It's really too bad we don't have a list of the servants who were here before." She rubbed her hand over her brow. "Tell them I'll pay a year's wages. In return, I want discretion and a good job done." She took out a small purse from her reticule. "We can walk back to Mount Street, then have Barnes call you a hackney." Making their way back down the stairs—she had no reason to inspect the attic—she locked the door after them. "If at all possible, I would like everything in place by to-morrow evening."

Punt heaved a sigh of long suffering. "In for a penny, in for a pound. I'll get it done."

Vivian was so happy she could have danced back to Mount Street. She couldn't believe how easy this had been, or how daring she was being. Wicked, as well. The only thing left to do was write Lord Stanstead and invite him to have an affair with her.

Rupert rolled out of bed with more energy than he'd had in months. Last night, his dreams had been full of Vivian in his arms, living in his home, and bearing his children. She would also be a perfect political hostess, and a good mistress.

Considering how much sleep he hadn't had, he should have been tired, but he couldn't wait to see her again. Unfortunately, it was too early to pay a call, and the sky was a dull gray.

He sniffed the air. Rain. No taking her out in the carriage to-day. If only he had thought to have flowers sent from Stanstead, he could take them over to her. The only other option was a bouquet from the Covent Garden market. They were sure to be open.

He rang for his valet, who arrived with warm water.

"Send a message to Cook that I'll want breakfast in a half hour." He'd never seen the point of waiting until ten to break his fast. No matter what time he got to bed, he was always up early, and hungry.

Wigman stepped into the corridor. "It will be ready, my lord."

Thirty minutes later, he went downstairs. "Harlock, have my carriage brought around. I want to leave as soon as I've eaten."

Under an hour later, he hopped into his phaeton. "Let 'em go."

"Aye, my lord." Stuie jumped on the back. "Where we off to?"

"Covent Garden. I won't be long, but I have an errand to run." Once they arrived, he set the brake. "Keep a sharp eye out."

"I will, sir."

Rupert quickly found the flower ladies and began looking over their blooms. "Isn't that a sea aster?"

"Dunno, I just sell 'em." The woman yawned.

He cupped the flower with his fingers. Definitely a *Tripolium pannonicum*. "I'll take all of them." A yellow flower adorned with a purple pistol caught his eye. *Clematis tangutica* cultivars. That would go nicely with the white and yellow asters. "I'll take the vine with the yellow flowers as well."

A few moments later he paid for his purchase and headed back to his carriage. Two older men flanked Stuie. The boy's chin jutted out in a belligerent manner, his stance was wide, and his hands curled into fists.

Rupert slowed, keeping his horses between himself and the ruffians, effectively shielding him from their sight as he approached. After carefully placing his flowers on the carriage seat, he cleared the team's heads, putting himself on the same side as the others, but out of reach of the larger man. "Can I help you?"

The fellow jumped. "No, guv'nor. Nothin' going on here. Jus' askin' if the young'un needed some help."

Stuie spit on the ground. "Not likely, my lord."

Rupert eyed the other man, who'd turned his head. "You're a long way from Mount Street."

"Bloody hell," the would-be thief mumbled. "I would have to run into you ag'in."

In the daylight, he was able to see the tattered remains of a uniform. "What unit?"

"Fifty-second foot." The former soldier made a gesture with his hand. "Both of us. Ain't been able to find work since we got back from Waterloo."

"What did you do before you enlisted?" Rupert watched the men carefully. One never knew when someone might stupidly attempt to attack him. "Something tells me you weren't thieves."

"Nah, raised on farms, we were," the other man said. "No place for us there now."

"Don't know where ta go but here."

Rupert took out his card case and a pencil. He wrote an address on the back. "Go see this man. If anyone can find you work, he can. As long as you don't mind leaving London, that is."

The former soldier took the card. "Thank ye."

"Where'd you send them?" Stuie asked as the men walked off.

"Fenniman."

"Ain't he the one that found you your last tenant after old Jerry died?"

"He is." And if need be, Rupert would find a place for them. He needed to have his secretary scout around for more land for sale.

"You think they'll go?"

"They headed in the right direction." Rupert climbed into the phaeton. "All I can do is try."

"Got your flowers?"

"Yes. I only hope the lady likes them."

"She the same one you been sendin' flowers to?"

Rupert raised a brow. "You're full of questions today."

His tiger shrugged and scrambled on to the back. "People are wondering if we're going to see changes."

By the time he got back to Mayfair, the morning had advanced sufficiently to allow him to stop in Mount Street. When he pulled up in front of the house, Stuie got down, taking charge of the horses.

The door opened as Rupert reached the top step.

"Welcome, my lord. The ladies are in the drawing room. It is Lady Telford's at home day."

Giggling came from behind a door, and he paused in the act of taking off his hat. "How many ladies are here?"

"It's early yet; only about seven."

There was no way in hell he'd enter that room. He'd made the mistake once at his mother's at home. Clearing his throat, he indicated the flowers. "I'd like to leave these for Lady Beresford. Do you have a piece of paper I could write a note on?"

Rupert could swear he saw the slightest twitch of the butler's lips. "Indeed, my lord."

A few minutes later, he strode out of the house, but not before another carriage drove up. *Damn and blast it.* Lady Banks and her daughter. Before they could hail him, he drove off.

The last thing he wanted was to jeopardize the support Lord Banks was giving Rupert in the Lords.

After having joined his friends for luncheon, he finally arrived home in the late afternoon. Once again a letter from Vivian lay on the hall table. He picked it up, popping off the seal as he strode to his study. Half-way down the corridor he came to an abrupt halt. *She wants to do what?*

* * *

My dear Lord Stanstead,
I had such an enjoyable time last evening that I wish to
continue our acquaintance. I shall be waiting for you at
Number Forty Hill Street at eleven o'clock to-morrow
night.
Cleopatra

What the devil was she about and how the hell had she found that house? He raked his fingers through his hair. The only thing she could be planning was an affair, although she hadn't struck him as the type of woman who would have relations outside of marriage. Or had he seen only what he wanted to, yet again?

No, he was right about her. This latest start must have something to do with her husband.

He glanced once more at the missive. Eleven was a deuced odd time. Why not earlier or later? Well, he'd find out soon enough, to-day if he could manage it. Who was this woman who intrigued him so much?

CHAPTER FIFTEEN

"Well," Mama said, "he must not have seen me wave."

Oh, Lord Stanstead had seen them and run, but what had he been doing at Lady Telford's house? Cressida pasted a polite smile on her lips. "Probably not. In fact, we haven't seen him at any of the entertainments for a week or more."

"Your father said the Lords have been extremely busy."

The door opened and the butler bowed. Mama handed him her card. "Come this way, my lady."

When they entered the drawing room, the other ladies were exclaiming over a bunch of beautiful yellow and purple flowers Lady Beresford held.

"They are perfectly lovely! Who sent them?" one of the women asked.

Lady Beresford shook her head, smiling. "Barnes, please have these placed in water. I shall arrange them later."

"Oh, pooh!" Another lady pouted. "I cannot believe you are so cruel as to keep us guessing."

"Everyone must have their secrets." Lady Telford did nothing more than add an inflection of scolding in her tone for the subject to change to a bonnet seen on Bruton Street, but Cressida knew.

Lord Stanstead must have brought them over himself. Yet for the life of her, she didn't know what he saw in Lady Beresford. Her face was pretty in an older sort of way, but she was much too thin to be fashionable.

Fortunately, Mama must have made the same connection as Cressida had. As soon as they could politely excuse themselves, they did.

Once they were back in the carriage, Mama gave her sympathetic look. "I'm sorry, my dear. It appears Lord Stanstead's interests lie elsewhere."

"Yes, Mama." Clearly, there was no point in discussing the matter. Her mother was ready to give up, but Cressida knew that Lord Stanstead was meant to be with her. She would simply have to find a way to show him that. "Where has Papa been in the evenings?"

"There have been political entertainments he was required to attend. However, he will be accompanying us to Lady Jersey's ball. Everyone will be there."

Including Lord Stanstead, Cressida hoped. If she could be found alone with him there, he'd have to marry her.

Silvia stood still as her maid laced her gown. Despite racking her brain all day, she had found no way to thwart Nick's plan to dance with her. She might as well give in gracefully. She'd had to stand up with other men she hadn't cared for; all the young ladies did. At least he danced well, and she would not end the set with sore toes.

"There you go, miss. Do you want the pearls?"

"Yes. They will do nicely." Because she was the eldest, most of her mother's jewelry had come to her. Much of it was not suitable for an unmarried young lady.

Though it did not matter, she had no desire to show off any wealth. She and Cousin Clara had agreed that there was no need to mention the amount of Silvia's portion. It would only attract fortune hunters, and she was determined to ensure whoever she married wanted her, not her money. Mama and Papa had wed for love, as had her sisters. She would as well.

When Silvia reached the drawing room, Lady Telford and Vivian were enjoying glasses of wine. Silvia poured one for herself. Normally she didn't drink much, but to-night she required a bit of help to face what was coming.

She took a seat on the sofa next to her ladyship, and only then noticed that Vivian had not dressed for the evening. "Are you not feeling well?"

"I have a little bit of a headache and thought to remain in. I'm sure it is nothing to be alarmed about."

"I agree, my dear, taking a few days to yourself is an excellent idea," Lady Telford said. "You've been up late and out early."

Vivian appeared flushed. "Do you have a fever?" Silvia asked. Not that Silvia wanted her friend to be ill, but then perhaps she could remain home to nurse Vivian, and put off the inevitable for a while longer.

"No, I might be a bit warm, but that happens sometimes." She set her glass on the small square end table. "You two run along and have a good time. I'll be fine with a night's rest."

They chatted a few minutes longer before her ladyship rose. "It is time we leave. You should know, Vivian, Lord Beresford has asked Silvia to stand up with him."

Vivian's brows knit together for a brief moment, then her brow cleared and the corners of her lips tugged up. "I knew it."

"Knew what?" Silvia wanted to sink right through the floor, run back home, or in some other way disappear.

"He never really wished to marry me. I have no doubt my husband put him up to it. Edgar had a great many regrets as he was dying."

"Harrumph." Lady Telford snorted. "A pity he didn't have them sooner."

There was that. Maybe Silvia standing up with Nick would stop him from distressing her friend. "If my dancing with him means he'll stop bothering you, then it will be worth it." Neither of her friends needed to know that Nick Beresford's only objective was to irritate Silvia to death.

She placed the back of her arm across her forehead, assuming a suitably tragic pose. "I will suffer in your place."

Vivian chuckled. "You do not believe me, but you will."

If they knew the truth about her history with Nick Beresford, neither Vivian nor Cousin Clara would be so light-hearted about the situation.

"Let us be off." Her ladyship moved toward the door. "We'd better get there if you're going to sacrifice yourself on the altar of duty."

The ballroom was already crowded when they arrived.

"Miss Corbet, you are finally here." Lord Bumfield rushed up to her. "I was so afraid you would miss our dance."

"I'm sorry, Lady Beresford is not entirely well, and I did not wish to rush off and leave her."

"No, of course you would not." He bowed. "It is nice to see a young lady who cares about the travails of others. What a true friend you are."

She watched her toes carefully as they went through the steps of the country dance, but she needn't have worried. Lord Bumfield had vastly improved since the first time she had stood up with him. She merely wished he had not transferred his affections from Vivian to her.

"After I trod all over your feet at the last ball, I hired a dancing master."

"You are doing extremely well, my lord."

He grinned. "Yes, I believe I am."

Her card was full, and Silvia did not sit out one set, yet all too soon, Nick was bowing to her. "Miss Corbet, my dance, I believe."

Although it was what almost every gentleman said, from him it sounded smug, as if he was claiming more than a dance. "It is, my lord."

Silvia vowed she would have no reaction to him. She would go through the motions as if he were no one special and never had been. Yet the second his gloved palm rested on her waist and his hand engulfed hers, shivers of sensation raced through her, the same as the last time he'd touched her.

This was not good. Silvia couldn't breathe and the sparrows in her stomach were making her ill. She couldn't do this. "Nick."

Silvia's voice was so low Nick could barely hear her. He searched her face. She had paled. "Silvia, what's wrong?"

As the music began, he wrestled with what he should do. Then she took a large gulp of air, and her color improved. Quickly he started twirling her around the floor. "What was it?"

She shook her head. "Nothing. I don't know why you're doing this to me."

After leaving her the way he had a few years ago, he deserved that. He should have said adieu himself instead of leaving it to another. Despite his hopes, Silvia had apparently never forgiven him. Nick supposed his first hint should have been when she failed to answer the letters he'd received permission to send her. How was he to respond to her now, though? Tell her in the middle of a ball that he still loved her?

"Is this part of a wager?"

What the devil was she talking about? "A wager? Is that what you think of me? That I'd wager on you?" Wonderful, now he was growling at her in the middle of the bloody ballroom. "No, it is not part of any stupid wager."

"Then what?" She gazed at him warily.

"I—I want to make it up to you."

"Well, you cannot." Silvia practically spat the words. "And I refuse to have this discussion here."

"No, not here." He glanced around. "On the terrace."

"You must be mad. We haven't even finished the dance yet. You would create a scene."

Damnation. She was right. "After supper."

"I have another dance partner."

Why the devil had he thought standing up with her was a good idea? Carrying her off would have been much more efficient. "Then you name a time."

"Never." Silvia's voice was hushed but fierce. "Don't you understand? I do not ever wish to see you again."

He lowered his voice, making sure no one but Silvia could hear him. "I'm not sure what you heard, but it didn't happen the way you must think it did. Just hear me out." Her eyes flashed, but her countenance was frozen in a polite smile. Christ, he was going to have to beg. "Please, Silvia."

"Very well. Day after to-morrow in the morning. Come to Mount Street. I'll give you ten minutes."

"I'll be there."

And Nick would make her listen to him. It could not merely be that her father had said good-bye on his behalf. There must be something more. For better or worse, he'd discover what the hell had happened to make her so angry with him.

The next day, after returning from morning visits, Vivian had gone to find the bouquet Lord Stanstead had sent. She looked first in the rooms the other bouquets had been placed, searching in the family drawing room and the morning room. She finally found them in her parlor. What did it mean that someone had placed them here?

The vase was large, and she set about arranging the blooms to take full advantage of the color contrast. How he had found sea asters in Town, she didn't know, but they were beautiful and one of her favorites.

Half-way through last evening, she had almost regretted remaining at home. Although, it was not as if he would have told her if he had received the letter she'd sent him. Her stomach clenched. Would he come? Part of her hoped that he had been a little mad when he was kissing her in her disguise and now regretted his behavior. That it was the dark hair he could not resist. Yet the other part wanted desperately to be with him and wished he would have kissed her when she was not disguised.

As for tricking Clara and Silvia, guilt had pricked at Vivian's conscience when she'd lied about feeling poorly. Still, if she had seen Lord Stanstead last night, she could not have trusted her reaction to him. Better to wait until to-night.

She stroked the soft petals of the clematis, and its light, sweet fragrance wafted into the air. He certainly knew how to please a lady.

Shortly after she completed the arrangement, Punt entered the parlor. "It's all ready. The cook won't be able to start until to-morrow."

One worry fell from Vivian's shoulders, only to be replaced by another. What would she do when Lord Stanstead arrived this evening? "I couldn't have done it without you."

"There is still time to back out." Her maid's tone was hopeful, as she busied herself packing items into a bag.

"No, I have to go through with it." Otherwise she would never know what it was like to be with a man who seemed to want her.

"As you will, then." Punt straightened. "I'm going to take these things over to the house."

"Perhaps you could arrange a bottle or two of wine and something to eat as well."

"Already done, my lady." She turned, her hands on her hips. "The other servants will be gone when we arrive. I won't pretend to know why you've taken this start. It seems to me there was another way, but I promised your mama to protect you as best I could, and that I'll do."

Vivian's throat closed as tears blurred her sight. "Thank you. I do not expect this to last for long."

Her maid gave a curt nod and left the room, bag in hand.

The plan was for Vivian and Punt to depart the house shortly after Clara and Silvia did. Vivian had told her cousin she had an engagement, but did not fully answer the question of which one it was. If Lord Stanstead arrived at the appointed time, she could be home by midnight at the latest.

Although the day had been filled with shopping, morning visits, and a walk in the Park, the clock seemed to move at a snail's pace. Finally it was time for dinner. She dressed in a silk evening gown, which she would change once she arrived at the house on Hill Street.

"Vivian, dear, are you still ill?" She lifted her head to find Clara and Silvia staring at her with worry.

"I am well." Vivian's stomach cramped, but she had better eat or her cousin would insist she remain home. She dipped the spoon into her soup. "I am a little preoccupied with what I will do after the Season ends. I've been thinking of setting up my own household."

"You may reside with me if you wish," Clara said without expressing censure. "I have invited Silvia as well."

"Thank you." Vivian tried to smile but had the feeling she wasn't quite successful. "I wish to have my own home."

"I do understand. You are aware you will incur censure due to your age. Still, my offer is always open. The best advice to give you now is to enjoy the Season." One corner of her mouth tipped up. "I certainly intend to. Which reminds me, Lord Sudbury has invited all of us to the theater next week."

"Oh, how lovely of him." Silvia clapped her hands. "I have never attended a play in a real theater before."

"I'm sure we shall have a wonderful time." Vivian drank a sip of wine. That went down better than the soup had. She'd have to be careful not to over imbibe. Going to Lord Stanstead on the go would *not* be a good idea. "It has been a long time since I've had the opportunity to enjoy the theater as well."

She stole a surreptitious glance at the clock. God, would the hands never move? After an eternity, her cousin rose. "Come Silvia, we must leave." Addressing Vivian, Clara asked, "What time will you depart?"

"Shortly after you." Vivian took another drink of wine, careful to sip a small amount. She was so nervous, she could easily continue to imbibe.

She followed the others up the stairs, before fleeing to her apartment. She had to calm herself, or she would never make it through the evening.

She entered her room, where her maid was waiting. "How much longer?"

"As soon as the coachman sees her ladyship drive off, he'll come around."

"I hope Barnes will not mention to my cousin that I've left in a hackney."

"If her ladyship asks him, he will." Punt smoothed her skirts. "Which was the reason I hired a town coach for the rest of the Season."

Another worry abated. "You think of everything."

"If I can't talk you out of this," Punt said caustically, "I can keep you from ruining your reputation."

"Thank you." Perhaps she was correct, and Vivian should not have an affair with Lord Stanstead. What if he did discover it was her? She couldn't bear for him to think badly of her.

A knock sounded on the door. "My lady, a coach is here for you."

"I'll be right down."

Punt stood. "I'll meet you at the corner. It won't do for me to be going out with you."

Another point Vivian had not thought of. She really was not very good at this type of thing. "Maybe I am making a mistake."

"You'll make me a happy woman if you stay, but you do owe his lordship an explanation, and you'll have to give it to him in person. I can stay in the room if you like."

She pulled her gloves on. Was it nerves, or should she call the affair off before it began? She'd have to make a decision, and soon. Lord Stanstead would be at the house in less than an hour, and she still had to don her disguise.

CHAPTER SIXTEEN

Rupert had excused himself from dinner and a small card party with his mother and father. As he normally tended to linger, they would think it strange if he left too early.

He tied his cravat in a simple style, one easily undone. Would Vivian come as herself or as Cleopatra? Earlier, he had been tempted to seek her out, but as he had strolled to the house on Mount Street, he'd seen Lady Telford's carriage, with Vivian and Miss Corbet inside, leaving the house.

Musing about this evening was useless. He would have to wait for his answers.

The clock struck the half hour. Not long now. "Wigman, I want my plain black town coach."

There was no point in advertising his presence at the house.

"Yes, my lord."

A quarter hour later, he climbed in his carriage. "Take me to the corner of Hill Street and Waverton Street. I'll make my own way back home."

"As you wish, my lord."

After he'd done everything he could think of to protect Vivian's reputation, Rupert leaned back against the soft black leather squabs, but he couldn't relax. It was almost as if he'd never had a liaison before. He wondered if Vivian was equally nervous.

The coach rolled to a stop. "We're here, my lord."

He stepped out, took his bearings, and turned right. The small town house was two buildings down. The door opened as he approached. A stern-looking woman, likely in her forties, eyed him appraisingly.

Trying to shrug off the feeling that he was not wanted, Rupert smiled. "Good evening."

"Sir. If you will follow me." She led him up one flight of stairs, down a corridor to a largish chamber in the back of the house. "In there."

Rupert opened the door and stopped.

Whatever he'd been expecting, it was not this. Standing in the center of the room, Vivian was once again gowned in the costume, and trembling like a virgin sacrifice might. Any remaining thought that she could be an experienced seductress fled.

He ambled forward until he stood in front of her. "Your Majesty." Taking her hand, he kissed each finger. "Thank you for seeing me."

She gave a tight little nod. Wide eyes searched his face. "You came."

Her tone held surprise and something else. If he didn't know better he would think it was a hint of sadness. Yet why would she be unhappy that he was here? She blinked rapidly. Was she going to weep? Good God, anything but that. "I could not have stayed away."

She jerked her hand from his. That was obviously not the right thing to say. A tray with two glasses and a carafe of red wine stood on a small rectangular table. "Shall we have something to drink?"

Once more she nodded.

"I believe we are both a bit nervous." He snoodled to the table, poured two glasses, returned to her, and pressed the goblet into her hand. "Take a sip."

He set his glass on the table as she gulped down most of her glass. Much more and she'd be in her altitudes. "Here." He took the goblet from her, placed it next to his, then bent his head, touching his lips lightly to hers. "We will take this slowly. If you wish to stop, you have only to say the words."

Gradually, her lips opened to his, and the heat that had been between them the first time rose. Careful not to alarm her, he placed his hands on her slender waist.

Her palms slid up his chest to his shoulders, and soon wrapped around his neck, as her firm breasts pressed into his chest. Rupert groaned, and deepened their kiss.

His shaft was already hard, and he wanted her with a fierceness he had never felt before, yet rushing her wouldn't help either of them.

First he needed to know how experienced she actually was. He trailed his fingers down her back, closing them over her bottom. She moaned, pressing into him more fervently and rubbing against him. Did Vivian even know the effect she was having on him?

He palmed one breast, flicking his thumb over her nipple, causing her to squirm. Toeing off his evening pumps, he walked Vivian backward to the large bed filled with so many pillows it wouldn't matter where they landed. "I want you."

"I want you too." Her voice was breathy and full of desire.

He found the clasp to her costume, but the second he began to release it, Vivian froze. "No, I don't wish to undress."

Rupert slowly moved his hand down her back. "Very well. Whatever you wish." What the devil had her husband done to her? He pressed kisses to her neck as he eased her onto the bed. "Tell me what you like."

A tiny sob escaped her. "I don't know."

Christ, she was going to break his heart. It was a damn good thing her cur of a husband was dead, or he'd see to it himself. "There is no need to worry. When I touch you, let me know if you enjoy it."

"My lord—"

"Under the circumstances, I would rather you call me Rupert."

"Rupert." Vivian's heart pounded out of control. "I am sorry."

"Don't be. Let me pleasure you."

What else he could possibly do to give her more delight, she didn't know, yet he seemed to want to be with her. "All right."

Then he twirled Vivian's nipples between his fingers, and flames shot through her. She couldn't get close enough to him. Her breasts swelled, and she was lost in a bliss so intense she could never have imagined it. Rupert kissed her again, deeply, as if he would possess all of her. Her hips lifted, and he made a low, groaning chuckle.

The next thing she knew, cooler air moved up her legs, and she stiffened. Every time her husband had touched her there it had hurt. "No."

Rupert ceased, then placed one of his legs between hers. He moved his firm lips down over her jaw. "Let's try it this way."

Fear threatened to overwhelm her. "You'll stop if I want you to?"

"Always." His mouth closed over her breast as his knee moved bit by bit to the apex of her thighs.

Her hips lifted, rubbing against him as he rubbed her. Lovely frissons flooded her, and her body tensed. She needed more, there must be something more. She pressed her hip against his leg and his knee rubbed her. Suddenly the tension broke, and her body pulsed, and she'd never known such completion. "Don't stop. Don't let me go."

Rupert's lips curved against her breast. "I won't." He kissed her again, this time lightly on her lips. "Sweetheart. My beautiful darling, I'll be here for you as long as you want me."

If only what he said was the truth. Still, now she knew she'd go through with the affair. "Will you come back?"

Rising onto one elbow, he gazed into her eyes. "Yes." He arranged her so that she was tucked against him. "For now, rest a while."

Vivian had never felt safer than she did cuddled next to Rupert. She closed her eyes, sure she would be unable to sleep, but when she opened them again, the candles had burned down so low she jerked up.

He stroked her hair and pressed his lips to hers. "It is time I left. We wouldn't want the neighbors to see me."

She almost forgot he had no idea she didn't live here. "You're right." She couldn't see the clock over his shoulder. "What time is it?"

"Almost three." Rupert rolled to a sitting position. "I'll call your maid to you as I leave."

"Thank you." Vivian watched as he tied his shoes. His jacket and cravat were crushed. If anyone saw him they'd know he'd been doing something. Lifting her hand, she cupped his cheek. "Until to-morrow."

He leaned down, grinned, and possessed her mouth as if he couldn't get enough. "Until later this evening."

A few moments after Rupert left, her maid entered the bedchamber. "You must change and go home. I sent for the coach."

In much less time than it had taken to don her disguise, it was off, the kohl cleaned from her eyes, and everything put away. Hugging her cloak around her, Vivian strode through the garden to the gate in the back. Punt opened the door, making a come-quickly motion with her hand, and they climbed up the steps to the carriage.

"I told him to drop you off in the front, my lady. I'll go around to the side gate."

"I have decided to go forward with this."

Punt nodded. "I thought you might."

A sleepy footman answered the door at Clara's house, which meant her cousin and friend had already returned. He bowed Vivian in. "You may go to bed now," she informed him.

Later, as she lay in the much smaller bed than she had shared with

Rupert, Vivian smiled. Except for the fact that he didn't know he was making love with Vivian rather than Cleo, this evening had been perfect. She punched the pillow. She could not have everything, so she would have to be content with what she'd been given. At least he was much nicer than her husband had ever been.

Nick strolled into the Pigeon Hole, an exclusive gaming hell in Mayfair, accompanied by Hawksworth. There was no point in attending any more of the *ton*'s entertainments until he'd spoken with Silvia, yet this was not his preferred form of entertainment. "I don't know why you brought me here. You know I don't like to gamble."

"That is because you are so very good at it, and you hate fleecing fools," Hawksworth drawled as he raised his quizzer and surveyed the room. "Speaking of fools, Lord Oliver appears to be in his cups and with little to show for it."

The number of counters and coins on the table in front of his lordship was pitifully small. Nick snorted. "Idiot. This is what comes of giving a man too much money and no responsibility."

Hawksworth handed Nick a glass of wine. "Apparently, the good duke has threatened to cut him off unless he marries. Upon which time, he will increase Lord Oliver's allowance."

"He should be making his own way." Nick couldn't stand the excess he'd seen in London. More than one family had been left destitute because of gambling and other vices.

"But, my dear friend, that is what he intends to do." Hawksworth raised a black brow. "He plans to marry his way into solvency."

Nick grabbed his friend's arm. "Miss Corbet?"

"Mind the jacket." Hawksworth scowled. "My valet is notoriously fussy, and I don't wish to lose him."

Nick dropped his hand, but had to stop himself from growling. "I asked you if he wants to improve his finances through Miss Corbet."

"Who else has he been dangling after?" his friend asked in an exasperated tone. "Not that I think he likes her over-much, but needs must."

"How does he know anything about her portion?"

"It seems to be common knowledge amongst the dowagers and older ladies that her sisters had large dowries. Naturally, it makes sense that she would as well."

Silvia would loathe anyone who wanted her for her money. He'd bet his fortune that she had no idea Lord Oliver was aware of her worth. "Bloody worm."

Hawksworth heaved a sigh. "Could you please speak in full sentences? One could easily forget you are well educated."

"As you wish." Nick narrowed his eyes at Lord Oliver. "I said he is a bloody worm that should find somewhere other than in England to reside."

"There, now you have a purpose, and you will be doing the lady a service." Hawksworth pulled out a chair, kicking one out for Nick. "Probably his father as well."

"I don't give a farthing for his father."

"No," his friend murmured, "you wouldn't. How do you propose to remove Lord Oliver from Miss Corbet's surroundings?"

"I know a sea captain who wouldn't mind taking him to India. He could probably get a good price for—"

"No." Hawksworth interrupted. "Marrying for wealth is a perfectly acceptable way of repairing one's fortune. You simply do not like him or that he has selected your Miss Corbet." He waved his hand, and two chairs appeared at Lord Oliver's table. "Let's join him. I'm sure you are bound to come up with a better idea."

"One that causes more suffering," Nick said in an under-tone, but as they took their places, Lord Oliver rose.

"Give me a few moments, gentlemen. I shall return directly."

Lord Oliver strolled toward a corridor leading off the main room. A few moments later, a scruffier-appearing man glanced around before following.

"I don't like the looks of that." Nick motioned with his head. "I'll be back straight away."

Hawksworth laid a restraining hand on Nick's arm. "Do you want me to come as well?"

"No, it might look odd. I won't engage them."

He sauntered from the room as if he didn't have a care in the world. The corridor was lit by candles in wall sconces. Neither gentleman was visible. Nick opened the first door he came to, which turned out to be a privy. Making his way to the end of the corridor, he finally spied a heavy wooden door that probably led outside. Pushing it open, he heard Lord Oliver's well-bred voice.

"I'll have the money as soon as I convince the lady to marry me. It won't be long now. M'father doesn't expect a large wedding."

"I'm sure your lordship can think of a way to hurry her along." The English was proper enough, but the man sounded as if he was from the Rookery. "Get her alone for a while, and make sure you roger her good."

Nick clenched his hands, fighting the urge to beat the speaker into the ground and anyone else who happened to try to stop him.

"I won't rape her," Lord Oliver insisted urgently. "If my father ever found out, I'd be banished for good."

"May I make a suggestion?"

Ah, that must be the scruffy gentleman.

"A simple abduction would work well. All you'd have to do is take her out of London for a night. I'm sure she and her family would see the sense of an immediate wedding."

"Very well," Lord Oliver said. "If she refuses me, I'll do it."

"If she refuses you, you'll never get the girl in a coach," Rookery said. "You have a week, or I'll take care of it for you."

Nick was half-way tempted to just kill Lord Oliver now, but Hawksworth was right. There must be a better way of dealing with the man, and murder was too quick. His lordship deserved to suffer for a long enough time to learn the error of his ways.

The next morning Rupert woke at his usual hour, surprised to find he wasn't at all tired. That could only be due to Vivian. He was convinced he loved her, now all he had to do was show her she could trust him. Their nightly meetings would go on, and he would court her during the day as well. Eventually, he would help her be comfortable enough that she no longer required her Cleopatra costume. He hoped her troubles did not run deeper than he knew. That would present a problem.

After breakfast he went for a ride. The easy motion of the horse helped him think. Normally, Rupert would go to his father or mother for assistance, but he didn't feel right approaching either them or his cousin. What was between Vivian and him was private. She would feel betrayed if he told anyone, and rightly so. Yet what to do? He might be able to get some measure of aid from her maid, if that's what the older woman was.

"Stanstead!" the familiar voice hailed him.

"Beresford, well met." Rupert waited as Vivian's cousin by marriage rode up.

"I have a bit of a problem and was told you have a wide circle of acquaintances."

"How can I help you?"

He listened as Beresford told him about the conversation he'd heard the night before. "Do you know how you want to handle it?"

"I initially wanted to run him through." Beresford grinned merrily. "But I decided a longer period of suffering was called for."

"Interesting, the fashion in which you take pleasure in another man's pain." On the other hand, if it was Vivian they were discussing . . . Rupert could not find it in his heart to object further. "However, I must admit, he deserves to be brought to heel." In addition, anything that harmed Miss Corbet would distress Vivian, and he would not have that. "I have known Lord Oliver for a number of years. I can't say that I like him. He is a gossip, doesn't think twice about hurting the feelings of others, and, in general, has a weak personality." Rupert urged his horse forward. "I did not know the duke was pressing him to marry. That may present an opportunity for someone who has done me a good turn or two. If you like, we may call on him now."

"What!" Beresford uttered in amazement. "Visit a member of the *ton* before noon and on horseback? Are you sure he won't faint or refuse to see us?"

Rupert grinned. Now that Nick wasn't pressing Vivian to marry, he liked the man enough to count him as a friend. "Ah, there is the rub." Rupert lowered his voice to a loud whisper. "He is *not* a member of the *ton*."

"It won't do," Nick replied glumly. "I've already promised that I wouldn't load the cur up on a boat to India."

If nothing else, having a conversation with Beresford was entertaining. "Not to worry. I have something much different in mind."

They exited the Park, riding along with the early morning traffic until Rupert turned off the busier street and into Russell Square, stopping before a large white house that always reminded him of an elaborate white wedding cake. "Here we are."

"But where are we?" Nick stared up at the edifice, his jaw dropping.

Rupert laughed. "We are in Russell Square at the home of Mr. Chawner, wool merchant, and exceedingly proud of it."

"Let me guess. We're going to sell Lord Oliver as slave labor? As long as he remains in England it will work. I don't think I promised not to do that."

"Not quite, but something close. Mr. Chawner has a daughter, who he dearly wants to marry into the *ton*. He had her fired off a few years ago, but she didn't take, mostly due to her lamentable habit of refusing to be ashamed of her antecedents."

"Indeed? Sounds like a formidable young lady. Naturally, that raises the question, would she marry Lord Oliver?"

As they dismounted, a footman took their horses.

"Wait until you meet her." Rupert pulled the bell next to the door. He too wondered what Miss Chawner would make of Lord Oliver.

CHAPTER SEVENTEEN

The door opened and Mr. Chawner, a man of around fifty years, still fit, with steel-gray hair, stepped out. "My lord, how many times have I told you I'd be happy to wait on you in Grosvenor Square? Ain't proper you comin' to me." He bowed, then took the hand Rupert offered. "Don't know what the peerage is coming to."

Nick had managed to close his mouth, but he continued to stare around him, much like one is tempted to when visiting Prinny's Pavilion at Brighton.

Rupert called him to order. "Lord Beresford, may I introduce you to Mr. Chawner?"

Beresford stuck his hand out and shook Chawner's before the older man could protest. "My pleasure, sir."

"Pleasure's all mine." A speculative glimmer entered his eyes. "What kind of lord are you?"

Although the corners of Beresford's mouth twitched, he didn't smile. "An earl, sir."

"Come in, come in, we're breaking our fast. I'll introduce you to my daughter, Maggie."

"Thank you, we would be pleased to join you." Rupert followed Chawner up curved marble and gilt stairs, leaving Beresford to bring up the rear. "It is Miss Chawner we have come to talk with you about. Not on Lord Beresford's account, his affections are already engaged and we hope to have an announcement soon."

"Who do you have in mind, my lord?"

Miss Chawner, a tall young lady with shiny brown hair and a sprinkling of freckles across her upturned nose, came forward. "Welcome, my lord. From upstairs I could hear Papa tell our butler to open the door, but I see he beat poor Bagley to it." Even though her tone was a slightly severe, the loving look she gave her father more than made up for her chastisement. "Please join us. Papa is having coffee, but I know you prefer tea." She glanced at Beresford. "And you, sir."

"He's not a sir, poppet, he's an earl. This here is Lord Beresford."

She sank into a graceful curtsey. "Welcome, my lord."

Her father showed them into a breakfast room painted a bright yellow. Gas lamps were affixed to the walls, and gilt edged the white trim. Curtains with a cream background and a riot of brightly-colored flowers framed the long windows.

"She seems too nice for Lord Oliver," Nick whispered.

"She is extremely nice, with a will of steel. I don't like seeing people go to waste, and that is exactly what is happening with Lord Oliver." Rupert took the seat Miss Chawner indicated. Beresford sat next to him.

They feasted on rare beef, ham, eggs, toast, tea, and coffee as they discussed commerce, tariffs, and the state of England's economy. After several minutes, Miss Chawner set her cup down. "What brings you here, my lord?"

"There is a gentleman who must marry well. His name is Lord Oliver Loveridge, the third son of the Duke of Stafford. He is not himself a peer, but his family is influential, if not abundantly wealthy. The duke will settle a small estate on Lord Oliver when he weds, as well as raise his allowance to support a family."

Creasing her forehead slightly, she glanced at her father. "I have heard of him. He is not perfect husband material, but I believe I can make something of him."

"He has gambling debts," Nick added.

She shrugged lightly. "What man in search of a wealthy wife does not? His gambling will have to cease, as will his late nights." Once again she looked over at her father. "What do you think, Papa? I'm not growing any younger."

"If you decide you want him, poppet, you shall have him. I'll wrap him up all right and tight, Bristol fashion."

"Very well." She turned to Rupert. "Please make whatever arrangements you must for me to meet with him."

Nick, who'd been watching her with something akin to fascination, set his coffee cup down. "You don't have to accept him."

Miss Chawner's eyes widened. "What an idea. Of course I do not. I shall meet with him and make my decision." A wicked grin appeared on her lips. "If we agree to wed, he will dance to my tune, or he will not dance at all."

Beresford swallowed. "I understand."

Deeming it time to take their leave, Rupert stood. "Thank you. I'll be in contact soon."

She and her father rose, and Mr. Chawner accompanied Nick and Rupert to the door. "Thank you, my lord. I'm glad you came by."

Once on their horses and headed back to Mayfair, Nick said, "I don't understand why she wants to marry into the *ton*. Wouldn't she have a more pleasant life with a man of her own status?"

"It was her mother's dream, and she intends to honor her memory." They rode on in silence for a few moments. "Make no mistake, Miss Chawner is the type who makes her own happiness. Like a cat, she'll land on her feet."

Apparently accepting how the matter with Miss Chawner stood, Nick turned to the business at hand. "How do we approach Lord Oliver?"

"We don't. I know his father and will make the suggestion. In the meantime, it's your job to keep Miss Corbet safe."

"Bloody hell!" He urged his horse to a trot. "I'm supposed to meet with her this morning. She'll have my head if I'm late."

"Do you know your way back?"

"I'll find it." Nick saluted as he cantered off.

For a man who swore with such fluency and had led troops into battle, he was interestingly afraid of Miss Corbet.

Rupert considered changing, then going to Mount Street, but he decided against it. He would send the flowers he'd ordered from his estate instead. He must also apply his mind to finding a way to get Vivian out of that Cleopatra costume. Obviously, she was afraid to be naked; therefore, it behove him to find something more comfortable for her to wear. Preferably with less starch.

An hour later, he dashed off a missive to Madame Lisette, a well-known and extremely expensive modiste his mother and most of his female friends patronized. How soon she could do what he wanted, Rupert had no idea. Still, even if it took a day or two, at least he'd have achieved his goal.

He'd just finished changing when Harlock notified him Madame had arrived. "Bring tea. I'll be down directly."

Madame Lisette was perched upon one of his large, comfortable leather chairs, sipping a cup of tea, when he entered the room. Fashionably but simply gowned, she gave an impression of competence.

She rose when he entered the room, and he greeted her with a grin. "Madame, thank you for attending me here."

Rupert motioned for Madame to be seated, and he took the chair opposite her.

She inclined her head. "I am well acquainted with your lady mother and your cousin, Lady Beaumont, milord. I think I must tell you that I do not dress ladybirds." She gave a one-shoulder-Gallic shrug. "My *clientèle* is exclusive and would not approve. However, with anything else I am happy to aid you."

That put him in his place. "There is a lady, but not of the demimonde. She is the woman I hope to wed." Hmm, how should he put this without giving too much away? "She had an unfortunate experience with her late husband." Rupert felt his neck growing warm. He hadn't expected to embarrass himself. This might not have been such a good idea after all. "Perhaps I should not have asked you to come."

"I think I understand, milord. *Moi*, I was in France at the time of the Revolution. Many women were treated badly. You wish to help your lady in an unusual way. Am I correct?"

Rupert had the strange urge to tug at his cravat. "Yes."

She nodded encouragingly. *"Continuez."*

This conversation called for brandy rather than tea. "I'd like to have you design a nightgown, a modest nightgown that shows nothing."

Madame Lisette's lips formed a moue. *"Oui?"*

"Yes." This may not be so bad after all. "That is the first one. The next one should be a little less modest."

"How long do you plan to continue with these nightgowns?"

"I have no earthly idea." He blew out a frustrated breath. "As long as it takes."

An interested sparkle entered Madame's eyes. "Tell me more about this lady."

Rupert froze. He could not reveal Vivian's identity to this woman. "Come, come. How am I to dress her if I do not know her size?"

"Oh yes, of course." Why hadn't he thought of that? "She is quite slender and very fair. Of moderate height." He stood, placing his hand on his collar bone. "Her head comes to here."

Madame had pulled out a notebook and was writing. *"Eh bien. I understand you. I have something that might work. Another customer* ordered it. An older lady who loved beautiful things." Madame crossed herself. "Unfortunately, she recently passed away. The gown is white, with blue flowers the color of a summer sky embroidered on it."

"Perfect. Her favorite color is light blue." Thank the Deity. His scheme was going to work after all.

She slipped the notebook and pencil back into her reticule. "Where shall I send the garment?"

"Send it here. I'll have it delivered to her."

Rising, she curtseyed. "It will be my pleasure to assist you and the lady to a happy occasion. I am always pleased to see a woman wed to the right gentleman."

Rupert would be as well. Pleased to have Vivian married to him, and in fairly short order if he could manage it.

Sooner than he had expected, the package from Madame Lisette arrived. Perfect; now all he had to do was figure out how to get it to Vivian. It would not do to simply arrive and ask her to change. It was clear she took a great deal of effort with her disguise. Somehow he had to get the nightgown to her lady's maid, yet the whole house would know the second he asked for the woman.

Stuie slipped into Rupert's study through the French windows. "I'm to ask if you got anything for me to do, my lord."

Mr. Dermot, the tutor Rupert had hired to teach the staff, had probably sent his tiger to him. "Tell me you weren't disrupting class."

"Nothin' like that." The boy gave a cockapert grin. "Mr. Dermot said I could go as I already knew what he was teachin'."

"Teaching." Rupert couldn't go to Mount Street, but Stuie could. "As a matter of fact, I do have something I need help with."

"I'll get the phaeton."

"No, this time we're walking."

Stuie's shoulders drooped, but he'd been too well trained to object. "Yes, my lord."

Rupert picked up the package. "I'll explain on the way."

Not many minutes later, he stood, waiting impatiently at the entrance to Mount Street Gardens, when he spied his tiger and the maid he had met the night before coming from the park. Lady Telford's house must have a gate leading out to the garden.

"This here is Lord Stanstead," Stuie said by way of an introduction.

"Thank you, Stuie." Rupert had taken one glance at the maid's stern countenance and decided he did not need an audience. "I won't be long, and I'll need the carriage when I return."

The boy all but bounced, but bowed instead. "I'll see right to it, my lord."

In a matter of moments, the lad was a blue streak running home. Rupert inclined his head. "Miss . . ."

"Punt." The woman's tone, if not hostile, left no doubt she wasn't pleased.

"Let me first say that I wish to wed your mistress."

Vivian buried her nose in the bouquet of delphiniums and clematis that had been delivered to her. Without even glancing at the card, she knew they were from Rupert. How lovely to think of him and call him by his Christian name. She tried to imagine what she would say to him if they ran into each other, and couldn't think of a thing.

Last night he'd been so tender. No man had ever held her before. Even her father was more likely to pat her on her head or shoulder as if she were one of his hounds, than hug her. If only it was Vivian he was making love to and not Cleo.

The thought had dogged her mind all day. She had made her disguise too well. The makeup, wig, and lowering her voice had worked to perfection. The truly bad part was she had to stop lying to herself and admit she wanted him to love her. She was tired of never coming first in a gentleman's life.

What a mess she'd made of it all. Yet, if Rupert was going to fall in love with her, he would not now be with Cleo. That was one fact she had learned the hard way: It was impossible to make a man fall in love with you if he loved another. Why did this have to happen to her? Twice!

Her chest constricted, and tears pricked her eyelids. She would not weep over a man again. It never helped. She would find a way to deal with Lord Stanstead during the day and Rupert at night.

A light knock came on the door and Silvia entered. "I have a favor to ask."

Vivian hastily wiped her eyes. "Yes, of course. What do you need?"

"Are you all right?" The concern in Silvia's voice made Vivian determined to show her friend all was well. "Have you been crying?"

"Not at all. I am merely having a reaction to something." Fortunately, her nose didn't become red when she wept. "What can I do for you?"

Her friend blushed. "Nick, Lord Beresford, is here to speak to me. I need someone to play gooseberry, but I don't wish anyone to hear us." She pulled a face. "It's liable to become quite a heated discussion. I thought the back of the garden would be more appropriate."

"And you would like me to remain on the terrace?"

Silvia rushed forward in a swish of muslin and took Vivian's hands. "Yes, if you would. I know it is a great deal to ask . . ."

"Not at all." It would be nice if one of them found love this Season. "Let us go. We should not keep him waiting."

"Oh"—Silvia waved one hand airily—"that doesn't bother me. As far as I'm concerned, he can wait a bit longer. I just want to get it over with."

Then again, that did not sound promising. Vivian grimaced. "Try not to be too loud."

Silvia led the way as if marching into battle, which she might indeed be. From what Vivian had seen in the past few weeks, Nicholas Beresford could be a formidable gentleman. On the other hand, he was the only man she'd seen who was up to her friend's weight.

When they reached the main staircase, he was pacing like a caged lion. He glanced up, and it was clear he had eyes only for Silvia. "Well?" he barked. "Will you talk to me?"

"I told you I would." Silvia's tone was as belligerent as his.

"Barnes," Vivian said. "Please fetch some tea and lemonade to the terrace. You may take your time; I believe his lordship and Miss Corbet would like to take the air."

Vivian took Silvia by the arm. "My lord, this way, if you please."

When they got to the morning room, Vivian released her friend. "Go outside. I can see you from here."

CHAPTER EIGHTEEN

Vivian thought she'd faint when Barnes announced Lord Stanstead was here to see her. She could not sit with him while the drama between Silvia and Nick was playing itself out across the garden. "Is her ladyship in?"

"Yes, my lady."

"Would you please ask her to attend me?"

Barnes, bless him, bowed and went back into the house. Vivian had known that she had to be able to intermingle with Rupert outside the bedchamber and behave in a reasonable manner, yet she thought she would have time to think of how to do it. On the other hand, putting the encounter off would not make it easier.

A few minutes later, Clara sat down at the table, glancing toward the garden. "Are they courting, or can we expect fisticuffs?"

"I'm not quite sure." Vivian pulled a face. "They appear to be doing both at the same time. She has struck him twice, but, as you see, he will not release her hands, and they are still talking."

"Intelligent man."

"I think you are right." Truth be told, Vivian could not think of a better match for Silvia than Lord Beresford. "Lord Stanstead has come to call."

"Off with you then." Clara's gaze seemed to be fixated on the young couple. "If one of them pulls a weapon, I shall intervene. Until then, I'll leave them to sort it out on their own."

Vivian leaned down, bussing her cousin on the cheek. "Good luck."

"Mm-hm." Clara shooed Vivian away with the wave of a hand. "Go tend to your gentleman."

Vivian shook out her skirts and made her way to the hall.

The butler bowed. "He is in the front parlor, my lady."

"Thank you, Barnes." She opened the door and Rupert turned from the window. "You wished to see me?"

Grinning boyishly, he came forward. "I realize I did not make plans with you and for that I'd ask your forgiveness, but I would like to take you for a carriage ride." He held out his hand to her. "Will you come?"

What was he up to? He'd seemed perfectly happy with Cleo's company last night. There was no reason to have Vivian's as well. Still, as she'd told herself only a few minutes ago, she had to learn to be around him during the day, and there was no time like the present. "It would be my pleasure, my lord."

His fingers touched hers, and she sucked in a breath. This would not do at all. She had to get hold of herself. She pasted a polite smile on her face as he led her through the hall, then out to his phaeton. Knowing what would come next, she braced for the flood of sensations as he lifted her into the vehicle.

Oh, good God. This was far worse than before. His simple, innocent touch had her wishing for more. Rupert's energy, his physical intensity, swamped her senses. Vivian wanted his lips on hers, and his hands caressing her.

Her mouth dried. How was she to survive this ride without betraying herself? She fidgeted alternately with her gloves, her skirts, and her bonnet ribbon, before being able to speak again. "What an unexpected pleasure."

"I'm glad you think so. I hope you'll enjoy yourself." He slid a glance at her, then his attention was on his horses.

"I'm sure I shall. Where are we going?"

"Around the Park." His lips curved into a smile. "Where else?"

"Surely it is not time for the Grand Strut?" She gasped for air. If she was not careful she would stop breathing. Never before had she thought that possible.

"We are a bit on the early side." He looked at her again. "Something you said made me think you might like to take a drive when you are not fully on display."

"I'm surprised you noticed. It's true. I am not completely comfortable in situations that are purely social." If he'd perceived that, what else had he discerned?

Keeping his eyes straight ahead as they maneuvered through the busy streets, Rupert responded, "You might be surprised what I pay attention to." She couldn't think of a response. After a few moments, he continued. "My lady, this is merely a carriage ride. I beg you enjoy it." She should, she would. "Yes, of course. I'm sorry. When you arrived I was chaperoning Miss Corbet and Lord Beresford. My mind was still on them."

Rupert laughed so suddenly, Vivian jumped. "I understand now why you are so on edge. If I had to play that role, I believe I'd give them boxing gloves. A more fractious pair I have rarely come across."

Her spine sagged with relief. "They are, indeed. Yet for all that, I do believe they care very much for each other, but are unable for some reason to express their feelings."

"All I can tell you is that he has deep feelings for her." Rupert spared Vivian a sidelong glance.

His horses were fresh and not the mild pair he'd had the other day.

"I thought as much. It is hard to tell with Miss Corbet. At times there is a softness in her eyes when she looks at him, but the minute he approaches her she becomes Boadicea."

"The warrior queen?" He feathered a corner in the neatest fashion. Rupert was an exceptional whip. "I agree with your analogy. Miss Corbet is quite fierce."

"She's had to be, looking after her sisters and father as she did."

"I did not know." The corner of his lip turned up. "I'm sure Beresford has his work cut out for him."

For some reason, even though she had made the comparison, she did not appreciate his humor. "And you find that amusing, my lord?"

Rupert gave her a steady look, his brow raised in a quizzical fashion. "I have had the opportunity to spend a great deal of time with Beresford lately. If I were a less cultured man, I'd say he is the closest thing to a barbarian I've ever seen, but I have met those who are true barbarians."

She had yet to meet a more well-traveled, educated gentleman than Rupert, or one as manly. There was no doubt he would one day be a leader in the House of Lords. Other than his lamentable tendency to prefer Cleo over Vivian, she could find no fault with him at all. Though that was rather a large defect in his character. "In your travels?"

"Indeed. Years before he died, my grandfather Stanstead arranged for my Grand Tour. In addition to the more sedate parts of Europe, I traveled to the Levant and Constantinople. I was fortunate that the war ended when it did."

"He must have cared for you a great deal." She had been thinking lately about her own parents. When Vivian had complained to her mother about her husband, shortly after their marriage, Mama had told her there was nothing to be done but put up with it.

"His goal was to raise a man who could be trusted to care for the earldom." Rupert's tone was unusually severe, and the corners of his mouth, which usually held a smile, turned down.

"I too was molded into a being who would do as she was bid." Such as marry Edgar and live unhappily until his death. No matter what fate threw at her now, Vivian was determined to be happy.

"I was fortunate that my mother had different ideas. She was the one who taught me to love life and those around me. Where my grandfather taught duty toward one's dependents, she showed me that caring for them from my heart was the way to help them." He blinked several times. Was he close to tears? Vivian had never seen a man so moved. "I'm sorry to bore you."

"No." Vivian had responded in the polite tone she'd been taught for years to use, but she wanted to shout it. "You should never feel that I am not interested." *Oh God, now what?* "I am intrigued with your life. I mean to say, you seem to know so much for . . ."

"For my age?" Rupert replied, his tone as dry as the dirt on the path.

"Of course not." He didn't act like any of the young gentlemen she had ever met.

"I must apologize again." This time his tone was even but distant. "It's been a trying couple of days."

As it had for her. "I'm sure whatever your concerns are, they will come out to the good."

A coach ahead of them had stopped as two elderly ladies exchanged greetings.

He looked at her with an expression she could not decipher. "I pray you are right."

Silvia glanced first at Vivian then at Nick. At the ball, he had said it wasn't what she thought. Silvia didn't believe him, but she supposed she should hear him out. Then she could send him on his way with a clear conscience, and they could both get on with their lives.

He placed her hand on his arm. "Where is the best place to go?"

"Near the wall." She firmed her jaw. There was no point in allowing him to think she would forgive him. "That way, if you start yelling, no one will be able to hear you."

Silvia could almost feel his teeth grind, but he didn't say a word. When they reached the end of the path, she stopped and faced him. "What do you want to say?"

Nick took a large breath and blew it out. "Silvia, I made a terrible mistake."

"I shall not disagree. There is nothing new in that." She infused her voice with as much disdain as she could. As far as she was concerned, he'd spent his life making them.

His large form was suddenly hovering over her. "Only when it comes to you."

What the deuce did he mean by that? She didn't want to look at him, but she did. A crease marred his broad forehead, and for the first time since she was sixteen, he appeared unsure of himself. "What did you do now?"

"Not recently, although I suppose I could have behaved better and told Edgar to go to the devil." Nick rubbed his hand down his face. "Four years ago, when I left, I should have told you the reason."

Silvia bit the inside of her lip. She really did not want to hear this. "What reason could there have been but another woman?"

"What?" He jumped back from her. "Why the devil would you think that?"

"Could you please moderate your language?" He hadn't been this bad before. "My father told me."

"Why, that wily old . . ." He reached out to take her hands, and she whipped them behind her, taking a step back for good measure. The last time he'd touched her, she had ended up kissing him. *That* would definitely not occur again. Nick closed the gap between them. "Tell me exactly what he said."

"Why do you want to know? Why do you even care?"

"Because the . . . *he lied.*"

To the best of her knowledge, her father had never told a falsehood, although he had prevaricated about his new wife. Fury shot from Nick's eyes, but it did not seem to be directed at her. She had nothing to hide.

Why not tell him everything? "I saw one of the servants from the abbey, and she said the old earl had sent you away. I—I thought— You had made me believe you were in love with me, so I was going to find out where your unit was and follow you." She blinked back the unwanted tears threatening to fall. "After all, you said you wanted to . . . well, never mind."

"Marry you."

Nick loomed over her, and Silvia tried to step back again but hit the hedge. "I went to the blacksmith's because his son was in the same unit, and asked him. He was in the process of telling me when Papa came in with something that needed to be repaired. When we got back to the rectory, he told me about the woman, your woman." She crossed her arms across her bosom and raised her chin. "What happened to her anyway?"

"Nothing." He stared at the sky for a moment, then met her gaze. "There was never anyone else." Nick's lips formed a thin line. "I'm a blasted fool."

Well, she wasn't going to argue with him, and said with all the haughtiness she could muster, "You are just now making the discovery?"

"I should have known you wouldn't make this easy."

"Truly, I have not the slightest clue what you are talking about." She moved to go around him, back into the house. The next thing she knew his arms were around her and he'd claimed her lips. For a moment she refused to kiss him, but God help her, she had missed him so much.

He growled and held her tighter, as if he would never let her go. She opened her lips, and he possessed her as he had done years ago. This kiss was even better than the last one. She felt herself melting into him, returning his caresses, running her fingers through his hair.

She could not allow this to continue.

Using all her will, she forced her head away. "No."

He still held her, but touched his chin to the top of her head. "You don't understand."

"No," she sobbed, unable to hide her hurt and heartbreak any longer. "You're the one who does not appear to understand. You may not kiss me then walk out of my life. I could have been with child!"

"I don't want to—" The pulse at his throat quickened. What had she said? Pregnant? "Silvia, did anyone else touch you?"

Nick heard the crack of Silvia's palm against his cheek before the stinging set in.

"You are the only one."

This didn't make any sense. Not only that. No wonder she was so bloody angry with him all the time.

God Almighty! Pregnant!

She was turning to walk away, and he had to stop her. "I would never, never have left you if there had been even the slightest chance you could have been carrying my child." She stopped and turned slowly to face him, tears streaming down her cheeks, but her gaze was militant. "Silvia, I loved you and I still do. I could never have abandoned you that way." She stared at him as if he belonged in Bedlam. Maybe he did. "Please, tell me, why did you think you might be with child?"

Her eyes widened and her jaw dropped. "My mother told me if I kissed a man I could become pregnant. Did you think I was so innocent I didn't know that?"

Bloody hell. She really believed it. If this weren't so damn serious, he could have laughed. The problem was, how could he convince her he was telling the truth? His plan to pick off all her objections one by one wasn't going to work. It was time to counterattack, while he tried to think of who he could trust to tell her how one got with child.

At this point, Silvia needed to know the truth. All of it. "Your father saw us kissing and asked me to leave. He even prevailed upon the old earl to help with the promotion I'd been wanting so that I could support you."

"But—but . . ." For a moment she looked as if she'd swoon. Silvia never swooned.

"Here's the bench." He made sure she didn't fall off the thing when she plopped down on it. "Your mother had been gone less than a year. Your sisters were young, and he depended on you to run the house and take care of them. At first I thought he was being selfish, but he convinced me I was the one thinking only of myself. That your sisters needed you more than I did. I was a fool to have left without at least speaking to you. To have trusted him. He told me he would explain everything to you, but was afraid that you would insist on going with me if I told you." He caressed her cheek with his thumb. "I wanted to marry you then, Silvia. I was a fool not to have taken you to the closest place in Scotland I could find. Please marry me now."

Her open palm connected with his face, and he jerked back. Only one other person had ever landed two blows on him; he could barely believe he'd let his guard down with her. For Christ's sake, he should have expected it. "What was that for?"

"For being a dunderheaded, addlebrained, care-for-nobody . . ." Nick tugged her against him, covering her mouth with his, and for several searing moments she leaned against him, trembling.

He lifted his head, grinning down at her, and she scowled. "Twiddle-poop."

"Twiddle-poop?" He grinned more widely, holding her hands captive. Being slapped twice was enough.

She took a breath and swallowed. "Yes, and you are a ramshackle slibber-slabber," she added, warming to her topic again. "If you—"

He placed his fingers against her lips. "I love you and I have for years."

She tried to jerk her hands from his, but he held fast. "Do you think I am a complete fool? All you've been doing since you took the title is chase after Vivian. I will not be your consolation prize."

CHAPTER NINETEEN

This time, Silvia pushed back, but he held her firmly. "I did that to keep a promise I made to my cousin."

"Vivian said something to that effect, but I don't believe you. He didn't care enough about her to attempt to extract promises on her behalf. The only woman who ever mattered to him was Mrs. Raeford."

Beresford winced. "You knew about her?"

"The only one who didn't know was Vivian, until she walked in on them one day."

"He didn't tell me that." The damned self-serving fool. "Yet the fact remains that before he died he asked me to offer for her." He glanced at the sky and swallowed. Somehow he had to make her understand. "After all he'd done for me as a child and as a young man, I couldn't deny him his last wish."

"He was not that much older than you, and he didn't come into the title until a few years ago. How could he have—"

"Edgar convinced his father to pay for my education when my own father would not, and pay for my commission, including all but the last promotion. He made a point of having me invited to Beresford Abbey during school breaks. He gave me a sense of family when I would have had none."

"That's the reason you were there so much." Her tone softened. "I never knew."

"No." Nick barely croaked the word out. He didn't like feeling all these emotions. He damned sure didn't want to talk about them. Getting into a ring to work things out was much easier, and it didn't hurt nearly as much. "It wasn't anything I'd discuss."

"What would you have done if she'd accepted?"

"I don't know, but I think part of me was sure she wouldn't have me. I did not know you were with her. If I had . . ."

"Harrumph." Silvia started tugging her hands away again.

He couldn't let her go. If she didn't listen to him now, she might never agree to see him again, and he'd lose her for good.

Finally she ceased. "That still doesn't explain why you continued to visit Vivian after she refused you."

"Once." He gave her the look that had sent experienced lieutenants scrambling. "I visited once more. Before I left the abbey, I made a promise at my cousin's grave that I would only ask twice. But I couldn't do it again." Nick nuzzled her temple. "The only thing I've wanted for years was for you to marry me. Silvia, please don't refuse me." She shook her head. "If you do, I will not give up until you say you'll be mine."

Silvia frowned, a sure sign she was thinking about it. "I am not sure it would work. We bicker constantly."

But she'd never been so angry with him before. At least now he knew the reason. He gazed down at her and smiled. "You are amazingly stubborn."

"Me! Why, you once claimed the sky was green and—"

Nick kissed her again. She tasted like the sweetest honey. If he could manage it, he'd stay there all day. "I would have done anything to gain your attention and keep you with me. As long as we did not come to an accord, you'd stay until your mother called you in." He dropped to one knee. "My beloved Miss Corbet, please make me the happiest of men and agree to argue with me for the rest of our lives."

A burble of laughter escaped her lips, and, finally, she smiled. "My lord, you must ask my father first."

"I already have, and he has given me permission to address you." He couldn't keep the grimace from his face. "He also told me he would be pleased with the marriage, now that we are older and your sisters have married." What the old man hadn't told Nick was that he'd poisoned the well.

Nick's heart tightened as she stared down at him until he couldn't stand it any longer. He pulled her down to the ground.

"Nick! My gown!"

How could she think about her gown at a time like this? Didn't she know how hard this was for him? "I'll buy you another. I'll buy you a hundred; just please say yes."

"Thank you very much, but I'll purchase my own clothing." Rising, she shook out her skirts. "I'll tell you my decision in the morning." She left, sweeping grandly back into the house.

Damnation! That had not gone as he'd wanted it to. Then again, when had anything with Miss Silvia Stubborn Corbet gone the way he'd wished the first time? Standing, he brushed off his pantaloons. He'd have to think of something between now and the morning to convince her to wed him.

Silvia's head spun as she made her way unseeing back to the terrace. Memories of their first kiss melded with the ones they'd just shared. Frissons of pleasure still coursed through her body. As a girl she had thought he was wonderful until they argued with each other, yet even then she'd wanted to spend more time with him.

Still, she had to think about this. Was Nick lying when he told her about her father, or had Papa lied? That would have to be worked out first. And what about her mother? Nick hadn't said that what Mama had told her about kissing was false, but he had seemed terribly surprised. She must ask someone how one became pregnant. She must also sort through her thoughts and emotions. If everything he'd said to her was the truth, then she had been wrong to detest him for so long and wrong to treat him as she had been doing.

"Silvia." Lady Telford joined her at the table on the terrace.

She blinked. "Where is Vivian?"

"She had to go out." Her ladyship's gaze traveled from Silvia's head to her hem. "How are things going with Lord Beresford? I almost stepped in a time or two, but you seemed to have the situation well in hand."

Oh no! She must have seen Nick kiss her. "I'm not sure. He said some things, and I don't know if they are true or not."

Clara gave Silvia a shrewd look. "Is there anything I can help you with?"

"Perhaps." She had to ask someone, and her ladyship had given birth to several children. "Can a lady become pregnant by kissing a gentleman?"

Brows snapping together, Clara asked, "Is that what you were told?"

Silvia sat in one of the chairs and fiddled, pleating and unpleating her skirt. "Um, yes."

"Well, that is certainly an interesting tale to tell girls, but it is not the truth. Getting with child is rather more involved than that." She paused for a moment. "Though not much more, and I suppose when one gets down to it, kissing eases the way."

"But it takes more than kissing?"

"Yes. Vastly more."

That answered one question. "How long do you think it would take for a letter to get to my father and for me to receive his response?"

"The question you really need an answer to is how long will it take him to respond." Clara's lips firmed. "Something tells me you've been fed a quantity of Banbury tales. If you will tell me what exactly is going on, I may be able to give you the truth you deserve, not what others wished to tell you."

Silvia was so tired of all of this. Of fighting her feelings for Nick, of not knowing what her future held, of her father clinging to her until he found a replacement for her mother. "Before Mama died . . ."

In the end, Clara had the whole story, including the part about Vivian's dead husband.

"All of this makes much more sense now." Clara ordered wine and poured them both a glass. "I do not know Lord Beresford well, but"—Silvia opened her mouth, and Clara held up one finger—"I do not believe he is capable of calculated cruelty, especially toward someone he cares for. Look at what he did for his cousin after the man's death. Even if he thought Vivian wouldn't accept him, he was taking a risk." She took a sip of the chilled wine while Silvia let Cousin Clara's words sink in. "I also now understand why you were so angry with him." Silvia nodded so hard a curl fell down, then her friend continued. "But would you have eloped with him?"

"Before Mama died, I was to have come out that next spring. I was almost seventeen."

"Yes, my dear," Clara said kindly. "Yet would your father have allowed you to marry and leave with Beresford? If he thought you would have remained at home, he might have countenanced the match, but"—Silvia hated buts—"would you have been content to remain in Beresford while your new husband went off to Spain or wherever he was going?"

Silvia took a large drink of wine. "No. I would have insisted upon going with him."

"Precisely my point."

"Was Nick—were we—being selfish, wanting me to leave?"

"No, child. You were being in love." Clara reached over and covered Silvia's hands. "Your father was most likely afraid to lose you as he had your mother, and there were the younger girls he had to think about."

"What you are saying is that I can believe Nick when he claims to love me and that he would not have left me if he thought I was breeding?"

Clara's brows raised, and although she pressed her lips together, they twitched. "If that young man thought you were *enceinte*, you would have been on your way to Scotland, and no one would have been able to stop him from marrying you."

She was right. Nick would have carried Silvia off on horseback if necessary. All the anger that had been building toward her father burbled up. "What Papa and old Lord Beresford did wasn't right."

"No, it was not. Your father should have sat down with you and Beresford and discussed the problems as he saw them. From Beresford's and your father's devil's bargain, Beresford came out with a promotion, but you, my dear, had nothing but your anger."

And the knowledge, false though it was, that Nick had betrayed her.

Suddenly Silvia was tired. She'd spent so many years being angry with him, and the moment he came back into her life she'd attacked him. Not to mention hitting him twice to-day. She wanted to run to her chamber and cry, and at the same time she wanted to travel straight to her father and tell him what he'd done was wrong. Now she had to make it up to Nick and beg his forgiveness. She'd probably choke doing it, and he'd laugh at her. "I don't know what to do."

"I think Lord Beresford understands a good deal more now than he did when he got here. All you have to do is decide if you want him."

"Yes." Silvia nodded more to herself than her friend, and she did want him, more than ever before.

Rupert had tried to keep the tone of their conversation light, but had failed. There were times he thought he did not have the experience to convince her to confide in him. And at other times, Vivian appeared so much younger and more inexperienced than he was.

"Perhaps I could help." She was searching his face, and her own countenance appeared troubled. "I'm told I am a good confidant."

How the deuce was he to answer her? "Thank you for your offer. However, this is a problem I must work out for myself." If only he could ask what her husband had done.

Earlier today when he'd managed to arrange a meeting with Vivian's lady's maid, the woman had not been at all surprised to discover Rupert knew Cleo was Vivian. Once the maid had understood he wanted to marry her mistress, her hostility had dissipated. During their short discussion, Rupert had come to understand that Vivian did not have a clue he knew her identity. She apparently thought he wanted the imaginary Cleo instead of her. It bewildered him that she could not realize her essence was hers alone. He would recognize her anywhere and in any disguise. Yet now what was he to do? If he simply told her, she might be so embarrassed she would run away from him.

They had finished the circuit, and Rupert searched for innocuous conversation. If he thought relations between him and Vivian were complicated now, how much more so would they become unless he could figure a way out of this tangle? He must find a way to reveal his knowledge so as not to humiliate her in the process. "Would you like to return home, or shall we make one more turn?"

"I'm ready to leave." Her features appeared as strained as he felt. "I think my cousin has plans for us, and I am concerned about Miss Corbet."

"I shall take you back to Mount Street."

"That would be for the best." Vivian had glanced at him for a moment from beneath her long pale lashes, before fixing her gaze straight ahead.

Damn and blast it! Perhaps this had not been such a brilliant idea, yet Rupert couldn't stay away from her. Was he any further ahead now than when he had gone to fetch her? He spared a brief look at the lady who was fast becoming the center of his life. Yes. He now knew that she would not be able to handle her deception well or for long. The question was, would she bolt before he could convince her to marry him?

Another meeting with her maid was in order, but first he'd have to make certain she would see him. "I don't know if you've heard of Lady Thornhill, but she is famous for her drawing rooms. Her first one in a very long time is to-morrow afternoon. I would consider it an honor if you allow me to escort you."

The number of people in the Park had been increasing dramatically, and Rupert had to watch his pair. Even with his attention on them, Vivian seemed to be taking an extraordinarily long time in answering.

He was trying to think of something else to say when she finally replied, "Thank you. I would be delighted. Lady Evesham told me about Lady Thornhill, and I am glad to have the opportunity to meet her."

One hurdle over. Now if he could cover the rest of the ground that easily. "I shall fetch you at two."

Except for a few comments about the weather, the remainder of the ride back to Lady Telford's house was mostly silent. Both he and Vivian seemed to have lost the ability to make small talk. How had he got himself into this position and what the devil was going on in her beautiful head?

When they arrived at Mount Street, Rupert motioned the footman away and lifted Vivian down from the phaeton, carefully lowering her feet to the pavement. He took her hand and smiled. "I shall see you later."

Vivian's heart was thudding in her chest, and she couldn't breathe. If only he knew how soon they would meet. "Yes, to-morrow." She had to get away, now, before she ruined everything and told him she was Cleo. "I look forward to it."

Despite the footman's presence, Rupert escorted her to the door. "As do I."

His voice was low and gravelly, as if it pained him to speak. Did he feel any guilt at all about making love to one woman at night and spending time with another one during the day? Probably not. Men were different from women in that respect. Even the best of them.

Vivian's mother had told her she must overlook her husband's infidelities. Yet she had thought Rupert was different, and her heart wrenched at the deceit. She should tell him, but then he'd leave her, and she desperately wanted more of what he'd given her last evening.

"There you are." Pulling her gloves on, Clara came down the stairs. "I thought you'd forgot we have been invited to drink tea with

Lady Worthington." She gave Vivian a critical run-over. "You'll do, and here is the coach." Her cousin blinked as if just realizing they weren't alone. "Stanstead, you may assist Lady Beresford into my carriage."

Vivian was going to swoon if he picked her up again. Every nerve in her body was attuned to his touch. "I'm sure his lordship does not wish to leave his horses standing."

"Nonsense, it will only take a moment." Clara called over her shoulder, "Silvia, are you ready yet?"

"Coming, Cousin Clara."

"I'm happy you are feeling better, my dear."

Silvia's cheeks bloomed as the footman assisted her into the coach.

Rupert, although he'd not said a word, had kept hold of Vivian's arm and appeared reluctant to let her go.

"Thank you, my lord."

"Think nothing of it." He gave a slight bow. "I am yours to command, my lady."

Her stomach tightened painfully. "Thank you. Until to-morrow."

At first she thought his lips had tightened, but one corner tilted up. "Indeed."

She slid onto the bench next to her cousin, while Silvia sat on the rear-facing seat. Clara gave Vivian a calculating look, and she decided to deflect attention from herself. "Silvia, did you straighten things out with Lord Beresford?"

The younger woman chewed on her bottom lip. "I'm not sure. Although, I can say I have a different perspective of him than I did before." She placed her reticule on her lap. "Time will tell."

"I do believe," Clara said as she turned from the window, "Lord Oliver is on his way to my house. Pity we won't be there to greet him."

From the tone of her voice she was anything but disappointed.

Silvia frowned. "I thought you favored him."

"Oh no, my dear." Clara settled back with a smug mien. "I favored the effect he was having on others. Now that the situation is close to being resolved, I have no further use for him."

Stratagems. Vivian was simply happy they were not directed at her. Why did life have to be made so complicated? Not that she had any right to talk. Allowing Rupert to think she was another woman wasn't exactly simplifying her life. Maybe being dutiful should have been enough for her. Still, Rupert had a way of making her feel like a precious jewel, and Vivian could not yet give him up.

Sir Walter Scott had it right when he'd written in his great work *Marmion*, "Oh what a tangled web we weave, when first we practice to deceive!"

"Did you say something, my dear?" Clara asked.

"Nothing of import." Vivian knew herself too well to think she could keep up her pretense for more than a few weeks. First Cleo would have to disappear, then, a week or so later, Vivian would take a journey out of Town to view properties. That would give Rupert time to find a wife, something he should be attending to rather than dallying with her.

If only he did not dally so well.

CHAPTER TWENTY

A block away from Lady Telford's house, Rupert brought his phaeton to a halt. "Lord Oliver. A word if you please."

The man inclined his head. "I'd be happy to, but another time would be better. I have a matter I must attend to first."

"On Mount Street?"

"Yes, as a matter of fact." Lord Oliver made to start his horses again.

"I just came from there. The ladies have gone visiting." Rupert watched the other man carefully. Despite what Beresford had said, Rupert wanted to assure himself that Lord Oliver's feelings were not engaged. That would make marrying him off to Miss Chawner more difficult than it would probably already be.

"Devil a bit." A look reminiscent of a panicked horse entered the man's eyes. "I don't have time to waste chasing her all over Town. Do you know when they'll return?"

"I was not privy to that information. However, if you're considering asking for Miss Corbet's hand, I think you've missed your mark."

"What do you mean?" Lord Oliver's already fair complexion paled even further. "I've been dancing attendance on her for weeks now. You must be mistaken."

"Hardly that long. I believe Lord Beresford and Miss Corbet have an understanding. You should know I am rarely wrong." Rupert glanced around. "We should not speak of this here. Give your carriage to your groom, and we'll go to a tavern I know of not far from here. I believe I can help you."

"How can you possibly—"

"The world of the *ton* is quite small."

He waited, watching while myriad thoughts and emotions crossed

174 · *Ella Quinn*

Lord Oliver's countenance. Mostly anger, but there was fear as well. Fear won out.

"Very well." Tossing his reins to his groom, he jumped down from his curricle and climbed into Rupert's. "Although I do not know how you think you can do anything."

Rupert drove them to the Museum Tavern across from the British Museum and only a short distance from Russell Square. He had visited the inn a few times with Mr. Chawner. Lord Oliver kept up a steady stream of conversation about absolutely nothing as Rupert considered how to approach marriage with Miss Chawner. Once tucked into a back corner table, with pints of ale in front of them, he surreptitiously studied the other man. His complexion was a bit pasty and his clothing not as neat as usual. Lord Oliver was clearly worried about his fate, and the news that Miss Corbet and Beresford were making a match, which Rupert hoped they did sooner rather than later, had scared Lord Oliver. Fortunately, he didn't appear to be planning anything nefarious, though Rupert would wager his last groat that Nick Beresford would cut short the life of anyone who attempted to harm his beloved.

After several moments, Rupert set his mug down. "I've heard you are in need of making a good match."

"You seem to know a great deal." Lord Oliver took a long pull of the ale. "Then you always did seem to be a downy one."

"I've found it to be to my benefit."

"The thing is, I'm at *point non plus*. I got taken in by a Captain Sharp and made the mistake of going to the bloodsuckers. I'm in deep. I have no way to raise the wind, and I can't go to m'father. He told me the last time my dibs weren't in tune that if it happened again I could leave Town for good." Lord Oliver gave a fatalistic shrug. "The only way to come about is to marry an heiress. I thought Miss Corbet might do, but she seems to have cooled toward me lately."

If the lady had ever really been interested, which Rupert doubted. "I know an heiress. Her father is a wealthy merchant, and she is his only child."

Lord Oliver gulped down the rest of his ale and signaled for another. "It's not as if I'd be the first one to marry down for money. If she behaves anything like a lady at all, I don't suppose the parents will mind. She would have to give up her connection to her father, of course."

"She is every inch a lady, but she will not give up her father or pretend she comes from somewhere else." Rupert watched the other man's countenance turn a shade close to green and took pity on him. "Don't worry that her father will try to insinuate himself into your circle. He will not."

Lord Oliver pushed his glass away. "What is her name and when can I meet her?"

"Her name is Miss Chawner. They live not far from here." Rupert kept his smile to himself. He'd not been entirely sure the man would act reasonably. "We can go over now and at least leave our cards."

He called for his carriage to be brought around and checked his pocket watch. Mr. Chawner might not be home yet, but his daughter was sure to be. It might be better for her to inspect Lord Oliver before her father saw him.

Several minutes later, they were shown into an opulent gold and red drawing room that must have been decorated by the same man Prinny used. As Rupert had never been in the parlor before, he could only assume it was meant to impress and awe visitors.

A low, pleasant, feminine voice drifted in from the hall. "There was no need to put Lord Stanstead in the gold room." The door opened and Miss Chawner appeared dressed neatly and expensively in an emerald-green day gown. She gave Lord Oliver a curious glance, then understanding dawned, and she smiled at Rupert. "My lord, Papa has not yet returned. How may I help you?"

"Miss Chawner, may I make you known to Lord Oliver Loveridge, a younger son of the Duke of Stafford."

She sank into a graceful and appropriately deep curtsey. "My lord, it is a pleasure to meet you."

Satisfied Lord Oliver was suitably impressed, Rupert continued. "Lord Oliver, Miss Chawner."

The other man bowed and took the hand she offered, bringing it to his lips. "The pleasure is entirely mine."

"There is no need to beat about the bush," Rupert said before any uneasiness could set in. "The other day I mentioned you to Miss Chawner, and she expressed an interest in a meeting. I think you will deal well together."

"Indeed, my lord." Her tone was calm and well modulated. If she had any trepidation, it did not show. "I am no green girl who wishes to be swept off my feet. A marriage of mutual interest would please me."

For a moment Rupert couldn't read Lord Oliver's intent at all, then he laughed. "I'm not sure I have ever met such a forthright young woman. It is refreshing."

Her eyes twinkled. "We may repair to the morning room where we can discuss our mutual interests. Naturally, my companion will be present. However, she will not interfere with us." She glanced around, her lips in a moue. "Lord Stanstead, I feel badly leaving you in this monstrosity of a parlor. Papa loves it, but I think he and our regent both have dreadful taste."

"It's quite all right." Rupert grinned. "I've been to Brighton. I think I can manage this for a while."

Once the couple had left, Rupert sat and took out his notebook and pencil. He had enough business to keep him occupied until they returned. Yet rather than focusing on his affairs, he found himself sketching Vivian.

Several minutes had passed when Lord Oliver returned alone. "I have been invited to stay for tea. Miss Chawner assures me she can arrange for my transport home."

"And?" Rupert asked, wondering if his matchmaking scheme had worked.

Lord Oliver nodded. "Thank you. She is even more strong-minded than Miss Corbet, but I believe you were correct. We will deal well together. After spending this past half hour in her company, my opinion is that she is getting the worst end of the deal." He grinned. "I have sent a note to my mother asking that she receive Miss Chawner and me in the morning." He held out his hand and Rupert shook it. "All's well that ends well."

"A favorite saying of my mother's. I shall see you later." At least he was able to resolve someone's problems, even if it hadn't been his own.

Rupert recovered his hat from the footman at the door. He was going to his parents' house to dine, after which he'd have to make an excuse to be excused from the theater in order to meet Vivian. Now that all the tertiary issues were resolved, he could concentrate on his own courtship.

Vivian could easily have screamed with frustration. It wasn't that all the conversation revolved around the most eligible gentlemen in the *ton*, but with several young ladies who were just out and accompanied by their mamas, too much of it did. Not to mention that every time she'd spoken with Lady Banks, her daughter's eyes were shooting arrows at Vivian. What on earth did the girl have against her?

A Miss Emily Woolerton had accompanied them, and her talk was of nothing but her impending marriage. Unfortunately, although her betrothed was back in England, he was delayed in arriving in London. After just a few minutes of listening to the wedding plans, Vivian was praying the gentleman would soon arrive and the couple would be married.

Why Vivian had even come was beyond her understanding. She should have known what it would be like, considering the Dowager Lady Worthington had a daughter who was out as well. Nevertheless, she was a friend of Clara's, and Vivian would have not embarrassed her cousin by refusing to attend when they had been especially invited, which meant they were there for much of the afternoon.

At least Miss Vivers. The Dowager Lady Worthington's daughter, had conversation about other issues than the gentlemen.

The only saving grace was that the Banks ladies must depart soon. Their fifteen minutes were almost finished.

Truth be told, Vivian should not be nearly as bothered by the conversations as she was. After all, she was no longer on the Marriage Mart, and she should be glad about it. Yet with Silvia and Miss Woolerton brimming with happiness and the speculation about other potential matches this Season, Vivian's mood sank further into a gray morass.

To make matters worse, as they had the other day, no matter how many times she looked, the arms of the clock refused to move at more than a snail's pace. She still had hours to go before meeting with Rupert. And there was dinner to get through.

"Lady Beresford, have you decided when you will re-marry?" Lady Banks's lips curved into a small, polite smile.

"I have decided I shall not." There, Vivian had announced her intentions to the whole world. Or, unless she missed her guess about Lady Banks, they would shortly be apprised of her choice. "I am searching for a small estate and hope to visit some properties in the next few weeks."

Miss Banks's eyes widened. "That is a splendid idea. I cannot wait to have a home of my own. With a husband, of course, but you have already done that."

The little shrew. Unable to stop herself, Vivian mimicked the girl's wide-eyed look. "Indeed I have, and I can assure you that your husband's house is not your own."

"But—" Flustered, the young lady turned to her mother. "Mama, won't you always live at Meadowfield?"

"Cressida, what a question." Lady Banks gave her daughter an exasperated look. "Naturally I hope to die there, but if your father should pass away first, and your brother marries, I shall move to the dower house. This is the reason settlement agreements are so important. A lady should always know what will become of her if her husband dies." She patted her daughter's knee. "Naturally, Papa will take good care of you. Now let us speak of more pleasant topics. Lady Beresford will not wish to be reminded of her loss."

Vivian made her best effort to appear suitably relieved at the change of subject. If she'd thought no one would see her, she would have danced on her husband's grave. Fortunately, this time when she glanced at the clock, it had made progress.

Lady Banks and her unpleasant daughter left, only to be replaced by more guests.

"I thought morning visits took place earlier," Vivian mumbled more to herself than anyone else.

"Normally they do, but with all the children, Lady Worthington has her at home later in the day, when they are out taking their exercise."

Twenty minutes later, Clara finally rose. "I've had a delightful time, but we must rest before this evening."

"Yes indeed." Vivian had never been happier to leave an event.

The Dowager Lady Worthington stood. "I shall see you out." Once in the hall she said, "Thank you for coming. Your conversation has helped keep me sane."

"It was the least we could do for a friend." Clara bussed the lady's cheek. "We had a lovely time." By the time the farewells were said, their coach had arrived. Unfortunately, not much escaped Clara. "Vivian, dear, are you quite well?"

"Of course." She settled onto the coach bench. "Why do you ask?"

Her cousin frowned. "You snapped twice at Miss Banks. That is very unlike you."

"But don't forget," Silvia interjected, saving Vivian the need to answer, "Miss Banks did bring up a painful subject for Vivian. I thought Miss Banks was amazingly rude. Did you not see her glare at Vivian as well?"

"Hmm, I didn't notice the looks, but she did seem terribly relieved when Vivian said she was looking for an estate and intended to leave Town for a while." Clara turned her attention to Vivian. "Have you found anyplace suitable to view?"

"Yes, a few houses." Naturally, Clara would know Vivian had spoken to Mr. Trevor. Nothing happened in that house about which Clara was not aware. Except perhaps when Vivian and her maid had slipped back in last night. Yet if her cousin didn't mention it, neither would she. "I'll take Punt with me and a couple of your footmen, if you have no objection."

"With all that on your mind, no wonder you have been looking strained."

Thank God they had arrived in Mount Street and Vivian could escape. Though to what she didn't know. She truly did not wish to be by herself, nor did she want to be with others. It was as if her skin didn't fit properly anymore. If only what her head told her to do was the same as what her heart demanded she do.

When they gained the hall, she took off her bonnet. "I think I shall rest until dinner."

Silvia's forehead creased, but she didn't say anything.

Clara merely waved Vivian away. "That is a wonderful idea. I believe I shall do the same. Will you be attending the rout with us?"

"I don't think I'll be up to it." She made her way quickly to her apartment. She could not be around all those young ladies wishing to wed.

"You look as if a nice cup of tea wouldn't be amiss." Punt stepped out of the dressing room with an almost spritely gait.

Vivian removed her fine-grain kid gloves. "If I have any more tea, I shall drown in it."

"Then a sherry."

A few moments later, she was in a comfortable chair, her feet up, with a glass of wine. "Thank you."

"Will you be going out with her ladyship this evening?" Punt asked almost cheerfully.

Either Vivian was more exhausted than she'd thought, or there was something different about her maid. Had Punt met a man she was interested in? It seemed to be going around this Season. "No. I don't want to try to think of an excuse to leave early."

"Probably for the best. You've been racking about a lot, and you don't want to start burning the candle at both ends, as they say."

Definitely different than her usual staid self. "You seem happier."

"Me?" Punt glanced back at Vivian. "I've finally decided that this visit to London will be good for you."

"Indeed." She raised her brows. "And what brought that about?"

"The fact that you haven't fretted once over your dead husband." Her maid went back to the dressing room.

Until today, when Miss Banks had brought up her husband, Vivian had not given him as much thought as she had at Beresford.

No matter what Vivian had to do, she would be free of him, and when she had a house of her own, no one would be able to tell her she was doing something the wrong way and countermand her orders. Anger and embarrassment surged through her at the memories, feelings she'd hidden for years behind a polite and dutiful façade.

Did she even know who she was anymore? She had been so young when she'd wed; had she ever known herself? The only times she'd ever felt as if she had any power were when she'd moved to the dower house and now, with Rupert. He was the only gentleman who had ever done as she asked.

Vivian closed her eyes, willing the memory of his caresses back. Tonight she would experience even more, if she allowed herself to do so. Yet could she?

CHAPTER TWENTY-ONE

Shortly after leaving his parents' home, Rupert arrived at the house on Hill Street. Vivian's maid, Miss Punt, opened the door. This time she smiled. "Good evening, my lord."

He handed her his hat, cane, and gloves. "Good evening, Miss Punt. How is her ladyship?"

"Nervous as a cat." She didn't lose her grin. "You'd better work fast."

He had already heard from his mother that Vivian planned to go on a house-buying search. Although he'd like nothing more than to let her depart and follow, it might cause a great deal of speculation. Politically and socially, Rupert had put himself in a position where he could no longer move in the shadows. "Would it be possible for us to have a slightly longer conversation in the next day or so?"

"That would be best. During the middle of the day I can come and go without anyone taking notice."

"To-morrow afternoon, around two o'clock. We may meet at the circle at the end of the gardens, where we cannot be seen from the house."

The maid nodded sharply. "I'll be there."

"Thank you." He took the stairs two at a time. By the time he and Punt met, he'd also have the next nightgown for Vivian.

Knocking once, he opened the door. She sat in front of the fire-place, which had been lit against the night chill. The glass of wine in her hand was full, as if she had just poured it. The white of the gown almost glowed in the dim light.

"Thank you for wearing my present. Do you like it?"

Vivian turned swiftly, one hand going to her throat as droplets of wine splashed over her other hand, to the rug. "Forgive me. I didn't hear you enter."

"No, it is for you to forgive me." He snoodled over to her, approaching her as he would a frightened animal. Rupert drew out his handkerchief, wiping her hand and setting the glass on a small round table next to her. "I should have knocked more loudly. Will you?"

"Of course I will." She smiled softly. "Thank you for the use of your handkerchief. If you leave it—"

Reaching out his hand, he stroked Vivian's cheek with his finger, interrupting her flow of words. "The gown is beautiful on you."

Her breath hitched. "And much softer."

He trailed his finger over her jaw and down her neck to the top where the tiny button started. "Yes, much softer."

Finally, she leaned into his caress. "I've missed you dreadfully."

"As I have you." Rupert covered Vivian's mouth with his own. Gently, he pulled her up, bringing her fully into his arms. "I've thought of nothing else but you since I left this morning." He ran his palm down her back, pressing the tips of his fingers into her spine. "Shall we have a glass of wine and a bite to eat, or will you let me make love to you first?"

She melted into him, sighing when he palmed her breast. "Love me. All I want is for you to love me."

Good Christ, he did, but now was not the time to tell her. Earlier to-day he had finally understood how fragile she truly was, and he only hoped he could help her to heal from the scars her husband had inflicted on her psyche. Rupert swept her into his arms and carried her to the bed.

Laying her down as he kissed her, he quickly removed his jacket, cravat, waistcoat, and shirt as he toed off his shoes. When he took his place next to her, she touched his chest, as if she'd never felt a male body before, and perhaps she hadn't. Rupert attempted to think how he would act if forced to be with one woman when he loved another, and could not. The one thing he knew was that he would not hurt her. Now, he must show her how much he loved her, mind, soul, and body.

"You look better than the Marbles." Her tone was breathy and full of wonder.

He could have chuckled, but her countenance was too serious as she studied him.

She touched his nipple. "May I kiss you there?"

"You may kiss me anywhere you like. My body is yours to command."

Vivian grinned. "I feel as if I am exploring a new continent."

She nuzzled his chest, placing feather-light kisses on him. By the time she touched her tongue tentatively to his nipple, he was harder than he'd ever been in his life. Should he wait until she agreed to be his wife before they consummated their union, or should he show her what their love would be like?

Vivian continued her innocent explorations, and Rupert began cataloging his plants. It was a damned good thing he'd left his pantaloons on, or she would probably run away in fear.

He sucked in a sharp breath as her teeth raked his nipple.

"Did I hurt you?"

There was so much concern in her eyes, he could have wept. How seriously had she been wounded? Was that the reason she hadn't wanted him to touch her mons? "Not at all. It feels good."

"Then I'll do it again." Against his chest, she smiled.

As she moved against him, the embroidery of her gown teased his stomach, increasing his need. He switched from plants to multiplication, all the time reminding himself that his forbearance was for Vivian. They could not have a full life if she was still afraid of what he might do to her.

Rupert stroked every part of her he could reach. Soon they were both panting and moaning, creating a symphony of their own. He reached down, gradually raising the edge of her nightgown higher, waiting for her to say no. Instead, she latched on to his lips with her own. Soon their tongues tangled in an intimate dance. Her fingers moved down his back and over his bottom.

God, this was torture. Sweet torture, but torture nonetheless. Finally, he covered her labia and stroked. Within seconds Vivian came apart in his hands.

"Oh God, oh God," she screamed. He held her until her breathing evened. "Rupert, I never knew anything could feel that good. Even better than last night."

Rupert wanted to place her hand over his hard shaft, to bury himself in her slick heat. He bit his inner cheek hard. "May I assume you like when I touch you there?"

"It never felt good before."

"I'll always make you feel good."

"You will, won't you?" Awe filled her voice.

For the rest of our lives, if you allow me. "I promise you I shall."

He held her as she fell asleep, trying to think of ways he could murder a dead man.

Vivian woke with a start. The candles had burned down in their holders. Rupert still had his arms wrapped around her, and once more the sense of safety she always experienced with him seeped through her skin into her bones. Even if she had wanted to, at this moment, she could not have left him. And he would keep his promise, until he discovered she was Vivian or saw her deformity. Even then, he would do nothing to harm her, but would gently set her aside. That is what would break her heart, and she must leave before that happened.

Smoothing her hand down the nightgown, she smiled. It was truly beautiful. The white work was a wonder in itself.

When she had donned the garment earlier, she'd been concerned it would be too revealing, but the way it was constructed, the gown covered everything. It was simply lovely and soft. Much better than the starched linen of her costume.

Next to her Rupert stirred. If only time could stop and she could remain here with him forever. Not wishing to wake him, yet unable to keep her hands off his glorious body, she lightly wended the light blond hairs covering his muscular chest. If only they could remain here forever.

His stomach rumbled before she heard his words. "Are you hungry?"

Ravenous. Which was a surprise. Normally, she didn't eat much, and when Edgar had visited her she'd lost her appetite for days afterward. "I am."

"Let's see what we have."

Holding her hand, he led her to the table, which had been set with not only the fruit and cheese from earlier, but with small, tart-like pies. "I wonder what these are."

"They appear to be a type of filled pastry."

Rupert held a chair for Vivian before taking his own place, then put a little of everything on her plate. As she hovered her fork over the tart, Rupert bit into it and sighed.

"Is it that good?"

"Heaven. You didn't tell me you had a cook here, or that he was French."

"How do you know he's French?"

"These, my dear, are made with a type of dough only the French and Italians make."

Naturally, he would know. She ate a piece. Pork, but so tender it melted in her mouth, and perfectly spiced as well. "This is wonderful." Then she remembered that Vivian knew about his travels, but Cleo did not. "But you must have traveled widely to recognize the crust."

He gave her a quizzical look, and for a moment she thought he knew. "Before the war ended I traveled to the Levant as part of my Grand Tour. The entire journey was shorter than those of my contemporaries. I don't like leaving my estate for extended periods, yet I visited places they did not. I simply did not stay as long."

This time she could answer truthfully. "I wish I could have traveled. London is the farthest I've been from home."

"I'll take you to France one day." He wolfed down another pie.

If only she could live her life as Cleo instead of Vivian. Cleo was as adventurous as Vivian was not, and Rupert desired Cleo, not Vivian. She choked down the rest of her pie. "I'd love to go to France with you."

"Then we shall." He covered her hand with his and smiled with his eyes as well as his lips. "As long as you are with me, you can do what you wish."

Lord help her. She fell into his warm gaze and deeper in love with Rupert. She dragged her eyes away from his. "We shall see." Somewhere in the house a clock chimed half three. "We should be going."

"Soon." He stood. "Have you had enough to eat?"

As if she could eat anything else with her stomach once again tied in knots. This time of her own making. "Yes."

"Then let me love you once more."

Rupert kissed her and it occurred to Vivian that she had a better chance of throwing herself off a cliff than resisting him. "Yes."

This time, she came more quickly and harder than she'd done before, but still he caressed her and kissed her as if, like her, he couldn't get enough. Under her nightgown, his nimble fingers touched and toyed with her bare skin. Setting her on fire. He gave a gravelly chuckle when she reached completion a third time.

Was he falling in love with Cleo? That was the only reason Vivian could think of. Why else would a man continue to pleasure a lady when he received so little? Not that she would complain. Every time her husband had exercised his marital rights, it had been excruciatingly painful. Tonight, she began to believe that with Rupert, it would not be.

Yet if they did mate, and if he was falling in love, he would surely hate her when she told him the truth. Perhaps she should simply leave without saying good-bye.

When he lifted his head, he was breathing heavily. "Will you keep until to-morrow?"

Regardless of her worries, she laughed. "Are you concerned I'll not come?"

He gave her a wicked grin, and it took her a moment to realize what she'd said. Vivian could feel her cheeks heating in a blush.

"I might be." He cradled her face. "But know this. I would hunt you down and bring you back."

The strong, stern lines of his face and intensity in his eyes told her he would do everything he said. She placed her hands over his. Tears pricked her eyes. Never again would she find a man like Rupert, and it scared her to death. She had lost herself, her heart to him. She should leave Town in the morning and never return. She should allow him to find a lady to marry. "I'll be here."

He took her in one last searing kiss, scattering her wits to the wind, before gathering his garments and striding out of the bedchamber.

A few minutes later, while Vivian was still wondering at the way Rupert made her feel, Punt entered the room. "It's time for you to change, my lady."

Vivian went through the motions she had gone through thousands of times before, yet she couldn't remember a thing, other than Rupert's last kiss. It was as if he had branded her as his own. How could she leave him, but how could she not?

CHAPTER TWENTY-TWO

Miss Punt had showed Rupert into a lighted room with a mirror. He pulled his shirt over his head, the fine linen grazing the exact places Vivian had kissed. Wasting no time, he donned the remainder of his clothing.

As long as she was with him, in his arms, he knew she was his. What would happen when she had time to think, he did not know, and that worried him. One thing was true, she was ready to bolt, and if she did, Vivian would discover just how swiftly he'd follow. It would rain in hell before he would let her go.

What Rupert experienced with Vivian was nothing he'd ever come close to feeling before. He knew now why his cousin and friends never allowed another gentleman to waltz with their wives. He didn't even know if he could be civil if he had to watch another gentleman stand up with her for a country dance.

What he did know was that he would lay down his life and all his possessions if that was what it took for her to stay with him. He gave a mirthless laugh. It was a good thing Beresford had decided not to bother Vivian any longer. Rupert would have had to ensure the man left for the Season. No one and nothing would ever be allowed to injure her again. He couldn't change her past, but he would guarantee her safety and happiness in the future.

A knock came on the door, and Miss Punt poked her head in. "We're about ready to leave, but we'll be walking."

"I'll be close behind. What happened to her carriage?"

"The coachman didn't come."

Damn the rascal. "I'll take care of it from now on. If he shows up to-morrow, tell him he is no longer needed."

188 · *Ella Quinn*

She gave him a satisfied nod. "Yes, my lord. It will be a pleasure."

He went to a room overlooking the garden and waited until Vivian and her maid were almost to the back gate. Moving silently, he opened the back door, then closed and locked it, slipping the house key Punt had given him into his waistcoat. She had given him a key to the gate onto the mews as well, making his ingress and egress to the house less noticeable.

Once in the garden he lengthened his stride. There would still be a good deal of traffic, foot and carriage, this time of night, and he would not allow Vivian to travel the streets with only her maid as guard. Staying far enough away that she wouldn't notice him, he trailed them through the maze of narrow mews housing horses and carriages for Mayfair's town houses.

However, behind the Mount Street houses bordering the gardens, there was no mews. He closed the distance between Vivian and him as they entered the Mount Street Gardens. She and her maid quickened their pace, then made their way to a high brick wall and through the gate.

He'd almost breathed a sigh of relief when movement caught the corner of his eye. Ah, his old friend. "What are you doing here?"

The man held up his hands. "Nothin', guv'nor. Nothin' bad, leastwise. We're patrolling. I picked this park 'cause not much goes on."

Rupert flipped him a yellow bob. "Did you see those women?"

The man deftly caught the coin. "Couldn't miss 'em."

"Anytime you see a female come out of that gate, watch out for them and there'll be more where that came from."

The old soldier saluted. "Yes, sir, and thank you for pointing us to your friend."

"Do the same for anyone who needs help and watch out for the ladies, and you'll have repaid me."

Rupert lingered until candle-light lit the windows of Lady Telford's house before continuing on his way home. Since he'd met Vivian, she had taken over his sleeping and waking thoughts. Tonight his dreams would include a future as well.

Silvia had attended the evening's entertainment with trepidation. She'd had the horrible feeling Lord Oliver was going to ask for her hand, and she did not want to even stand up with him. Yet, surprisingly, he was not present. Nick, though, was. God had never answered her prayers so quickly and with such accuracy.

After another long conversation with Cousin Clara and being completely honest with herself, Silvia had decided how to answer his proposal. There was only one waltz on her dance card, and after Nick was done complaining about stodgy old people, and making sure his name was on her dance card for the waltz, he had finally decided to ask for her remaining country dance.

Once they began the cotillion, Silvia decided she must not have been paying attention any of the other times she had performed the steps. Each time she came back to him, he grinned as if they were sharing a secret. Every time she twirled and caught his eye, Silvia wanted to shout with joy. How had she not known he danced so well? Surely other gentlemen not so practiced and athletic must be at a disadvantage. Even through their gloves, her hands tingled with his touch. She ended the dance breathless and happier than she had been in a very long time. "Take me outside. It's stuffy in here."

"Are you sure?" He gave her a quizzical look. "People might see us."

"Let them talk. What can they say when they discover we are betrothed?"

He took her arm and almost dragged her out onto the terrace. In short order, her back was against an ivy-clad wall, his hand braced next to her head as he leaned in. "Don't play with me, Silvia. If this is an attempt to get back at me—"

She grabbed his face with both hands and kissed him. "Do not be an idiot. I love you and I have for more years than I wanted to. Yes, I'll marry you, but I will not have my father perform the ceremony."

"Thank God." He gathered her in his arms, and she threw her arms around his neck. "No one will ever take me from you again."

"I know." She laid her cheek against his chest. "It took a while for me to understand, but I know that now."

Nick kissed her, long and deep, exploring her mouth in a way he hadn't before. Someone cleared their throat, and he shielded her with his massive body, placing one finger over her lips.

"I shall keep my back to you," Cousin Clara said. "But you must realize that when Beresford left the room with you in such a precipitous manner, tongues started to wag. May I assume that an announcement of marriage is imminent?"

Nick grinned at Silvia. "You may, ma'am. I am happy to be able to tell you that Miss Corbet has done me the great honor of agreeing to be my wife."

"Oh, wonderful. That makes my job so much easier." She gave an airy wave of her fingers. "Carry on. You have a few moments before the curious start to appear."

He lowered his lips to Silvia's with a ferocity he never had before. As if he had been starving and she was his manna. "I love you."

"I love you, and I've never been happier." Tears started in her eyes, and she blinked them away. "Although, I don't know if I'll ever forgive my father."

Nick grunted. "Is that the reason you don't want him to marry us?"

"Yes. If you do not mind, I'd like a small wedding by special license."

"Silvia, in order to marry by special license, one of two things must occur. Either I have your father's permission—"

"No. I forbid you to ask him."

"Or," he continued in that patient tone she used to hate, "you must have attained your majority."

"But I—"

He placed a finger over her mouth. "Will have to wait three days and about one hour to become my wife and the Countess of Beresford."

"It's almost midnight," Clara interjected dryly.

Silvia shook her head and giggled. "Three days and not a moment longer."

"Agreed." He held out his arm. "We should go back in before everyone comes looking for us and we are the Season's latest scandal."

They found Clara waiting near the door. When the three of them went in together, shoulders shrugged and eyes were no longer fixed on the entrance to the terrace. Nick winked at Silvia. How Cousin Clara had done it, Silvia did not understand. Although later, she had every intention of thanking Clara for her help.

The strains of a waltz caused a surge of movement toward the dance floor. Nick escorted Clara to a chair, and Silvia to where the other couples were taking their places. She felt lighter than she had in years, as if she was in one of those hot air balloons sailing through the clouds. If only she did not have to act as if she wasn't dancing on the moon. "I'm happy."

His larger hand engulfed hers, and he placed his palm on her waist. "That makes two of us. I'll write your father informing him of our marriage upon our wedding day."

"That would be best. I do not know if he would attempt to interfere again; after all, he did say you could ask me, but I no longer feel such loyalty after what he did. Even if it was for my sisters."

"I don't blame you at all, my love."

Silvia wanted to cry for all the waltzes they had missed, and the years they had spent apart.

Once the set ended, Cousin Clara decided to sit with friends, no doubt to tell them about their pending nuptials, leaving Nick and Silvia to sup alone, or as alone as one could be with two hundred other guests.

Potted palms and other large plants separated the tables against the walls and punctuated the room, giving a feeling of privacy that was as false as it was welcome.

A high, peevish voice on the other side of the plants next to their table interrupted Silvia and Nick's murmured conversation. "But why isn't Lord Stanstead here? Even Papa is present, so there cannot be a political event this evening."

"Cressida, keep your voice down," a hushed but equally young voice answered. "I'm sure you will see him soon."

Apparently unable or unwilling to lower her voice, Cressida continued, "I can't marry him if I cannot get him alone."

Nick raised a brow, tilting his head toward the plant. Silvia did the same. She'd had no trouble recognizing Miss Banks's voice and, despite teachings to the contrary, Silvia did not feel the tiniest bit guilty for eavesdropping.

"Maybe he's decided not to look for a wife this year after all." The speaker must be Miss Woolerton. The two were almost inseparable.

"Nooo! I want to be his wife. Next Season might be too late."

Silvia motioned to Nick for them to leave. As they passed by the table, the two young ladies were still in close conversation. "We must find a way to warn Lord Stanstead."

"I'll take care of it," Nick said in a grim tone. "First one, now another."

She didn't understand him. "What does that mean?"

"It means," he grumbled, "that I am going to be your shadow until you have signed the register making you my wife."

A lovely shiver danced through her. "I cannot think of anything I'd like more."

Finally, she had Nick's complete attention when she wanted it, and they were going to be married. Her thoughts turned to Beresford and the abbey. "Nick?"

"Yes, my love." He tugged her a bit closer.

"As you know, I am not an extravagant person."

"Silvia." He sighed. "Just tell me."

"The abbey must be entirely refurbished."

"What the dev . . . deuce made you think of that now?"

A slow heat rose up her neck. "Mrs. Raeford has horrible taste."

"Ah." He was silent for a few moments as they climbed the stairs back to the ballroom. "We shall make a brief visit, whereupon you may make notes, and give instructions for the changes to be accomplished on our honeymoon."

Leave someone else to supervise the work? Was he mad? "But Nick—"

"No, we *will* have a wedding trip, and if the changes are not to your liking when we return, you'll have to do it all over again."

"Oh, I suppose that will work."

He gave her a wicked grin. How her life had turned out so well, Silvia did not know. She supposed much of it was due to Nick, who had refused to give up on her. Unlike her father, with whom she would have a discussion when she returned home.

The following morning, Vivian stared down at the letter on the tray. It lay beside the stack of invitations, isolated and most definitely unwelcome. The writing was neat, almost feminine, and it belonged to her father's secretary. She was half tempted to consign the missive, unread, to the fire. Father never wrote her about anything pleasant, at least not pleasant for her. Normally she received at least one piece of correspondence a week from her mother, but, now that she thought of it, she'd not received anything since being in Town. What could have prevented her mother from writing?

Praying Mama wasn't ill or worse, Vivian tore open the note. Her eyes narrowed as she read down the sheet. *"Damn him to hell!"*

"My lady, what on earth?" Punt rushed into the room. "In all the years I've served you, I've never heard you swear before."

Vivian crumpled the letter, pitching it into the fire. Her hands clenched as the wadded ball blackened and shriveled. "I should have known he couldn't let well enough alone."

"Maybe I should ring for her ladyship?" Her maid tugged the bell-pull.

A chirruping sound caused her to glance down. Gisila stared up with unblinking yellow eyes. Vivian swept the cat into her arms. "Give me a moment to compose myself, and I'll go to her."

Punt nodded and left the room. Vivian sank onto a large French chair next to the fireplace, stroking the large furry beast as she forced her thoughts to focus on the problem at hand. With all her other troubles, she did not need to deal with her father's interference in her life as well. Unfortunately, his meddling in her affairs was not unexpected. Although she had fooled herself into believing that since so much time had passed, he would leave her alone. Perhaps it was her fault Papa thought he could simply take it upon himself to arrange another match for her. Unlike Silvia, Vivian had never asserted herself with her father.

Nevertheless, legally, he could not force her to re-marry. Even if she hadn't been of age, as a widow she was considered to have attained her majority. Yet while there was no legal force Papa could bring to bear, familial pressure was another matter. He might also be able to ruin her. If he and the other gentleman decided to tell their cronies or, heaven forbid, send a notice to the newssheet, she would, at the very least, appear ungrateful. At worst she would be labeled a jilt, and that would cause a scandal. The only positive aspect of this whole quandary was that she had full possession of her property. Thank God she had not yielded to her mother's offer to go home.

Even now and at this distance, Vivian cringed at the prospect of writing to inform her father she would not agree to the marriage. A better idea would be to leave Town as she had intended. In fact, this might be the perfect time to travel to the Continent. Surely he wouldn't follow her over there. If he could even find her. She would disguise herself. Lord knew she now had plenty of experience.

Vivian drew in a shaky breath. Father and her prospective husband were not due to arrive for another week. That would give her time to think and coordinate her travel. Clara could pretend Vivian had not received the letter. On the other hand . . .

The door opened and Clara glided in. "Your maid said you were in a taking. What has happened?"

Vivian waved her to the chair opposite hers. "I received a note from Father telling me he has arranged a match. All that is needed is my signature on the settlement documents. He and the other gentleman shall arrive in London next week. He plans to open Brackford House and expects me to remove there until my wedding."

"Is *that* all?" Clara's tone was light, but her chin firmed, ready to do battle. She rose, went to the sideboard, poured two glasses of wine, handed one to Vivian, and resumed her seat. "If I were not a lady, there are a great many appropriate oaths I can think of to utter at the moment."

"I believe I already did." Vivian grimaced. "I do not understand how he thought I would simply go along with his scheme. That was the reason I chose not to go home to my parents after my husband died."

"Who knows how gentlemen think." Clara cast her eyes to the ceiling. "It is a mystery to me and always has been. Although, it is most likely your history of doing as you are told that got him this far. Not that it is at all your fault. Any reasonable man would have at least approached you with the idea before making all the arrangements."

"Well, I shall not agree to his proposal." Vivian twirled her glass of wine, took one sip, then another. She must keep her wits about her, and she couldn't do that if she tried to drown her problem. Not only that, she had a drawing room to attend with Rupert in a few hours. "I shall put forward my plan to visit properties."

"When asked, I would, of course, say it was not my business to inquire of you exactly where you had gone." Her cousin sipped her wine. "But unless you intend to hide forever, he will keep pushing you to do as he wishes."

"You're right." Vivian dropped her head into her hands, wishing there was another way. She dreaded the contretemps her decision would cause. "I shall have to confront him. I'll inform him that I will not re-marry."

Clara studied Vivian for a few moments. "Wait a few days. It might not hurt for you to write him as you're leaving Town."

"That is exactly what I will do." She gave her cousin what was probably a wan smile. "Thank you."

"We shall muddle through." Clara grinned like a sly cat. "Some resolution is bound to reveal itself. It always does."

"I shall trust you to be right." As they rose, Vivian hugged Clara tightly. "I'm glad you have had more luck than I."

"It's time your life took a turn for the better." And on that bracing thought, Clara strode out of the room.

CHAPTER TWENTY-THREE

Three hours later, Vivian descended the stairs dressed in a Mexican-blue Gros de Naples silk walking gown. Rupert was already waiting for her. When he smiled, a look came into his eyes very much like the one he used with Cleo. Could it be he was attracted to both of them, or was he a rake in sheep's clothing?

When Vivian glanced at him again, the look had disappeared. It must have been her imagination, and her wish that a gentleman could want her that way.

She placed her hand on the arm he held out. "Good afternoon, my lord."

Rupert inclined his head. "Good day, my lady. Shall we go?"

"I wouldn't miss it." She gave him a warm smile. "Thank you for this treat."

"One of many I have planned for you," he responded in a soft tone that sent pleasurable shivers down her spine.

She was going mad if she thought he actually meant anything by it. Hadn't her husband courted her on their honeymoon and the minute they returned to Beresford gone back to his mistress? Well, this time she knew the game. Rupert would be with Cleo at night, and escort Vivian during the day. Perhaps he had decided it was not time to marry. What better way to avoid marriage-minded misses than by escorting a widow about Town?

If only she could cease her growing feelings for him. Still, the few times her husband had been in bed with her, he had never been kind, and Rupert was much more than that. He was loving and everything any woman could want from a man. Every time she tried to make sense of it, her head swam. She would certainly go mad if she kept this up.

"Oh, this isn't your phaeton." Vivian gazed at the light blue landau trimmed in gold with Rupert's crest on the door. The darker blue convertible top had been put down. "It's beautiful."

"I'm glad you like it." He waited as a footman opened the door, then assisted her up the steps. "The phaeton would have been impractical. This will be taken home and will return in a few hours to collect us." He settled himself next to her on the seat. "Although, I'll wager you will be having so much fun you won't want to leave."

Her heart lightened. He was fun to be with and she always had a wonderful time with him. The only thing to do was stop worrying and overthinking what was happening between them. In less than a week, they would go their own ways. She would be a pleasant memory for him, and she would find a way to recover from her broken heart. For now, she was determined to enjoy his company. "As long as the conversation is not about young ladies finding matches, I am positive I will have a perfectly lovely time."

Rupert barked a laugh. "I see you've been attending too many morning visits and teas." He took her fingers in his hand and held them. "To-day you will be subjected to discussions on art, poetry, and radical political thinking." He glanced down at her and his eyes danced with mirth. "And those are merely her usual guests. Only God knows who her ladyship has invited now that they are back from the Orient."

A few minutes later they rolled to a stop in front of a perfectly normal-looking town house. However, once inside, Lord and Lady Thornhill's love of travel could be seen everywhere. The couple greeted them dressed in long, brightly colored and embroidered robes over petticoats.

"Stanstead." Lord Thornhill shook Rupert's hand. "I'm glad you could come."

Rupert's other hand was securely on the small of Vivian's back. "Thank you for asking me. My lady, please allow me to introduce you to our host, Lord Thornhill. My lord, Lady Beresford."

The older man, still trim, with salt-and-pepper hair, bowed. "A pleasure. This"—he chuckled—"as you might guess, is my beautiful wife, Lady Thornhill."

Her ladyship held out her hand, and Vivian shook it. "My pleasure to see you again. Lady Evesham told me about your drawing rooms, and I've looked forward to them."

A smile creased the corners of Lady Thornhill's eyes. There appeared to be little artifice about the woman or her husband. The couple were clearly masters of their universe, a state of being Vivian admired and envied, particularly in her current circumstances. "You will see the Eveshams in a little while, I'm sure. In the meantime, feel free to introduce yourself to anyone you don't know, or join any conversation."

"Before we join your other guests," Rupert said, "please tell me where your garb comes from."

"Japan," Lord Thornhill answered. "We were inspired by the bright colors and ease of movememt."

As they strolled toward the voices drifting down the corridor, Vivian almost froze. Just walk up to someone and start talking? Introduce herself? How on earth was she to get along here?

Rupert must have sensed her unease for he whispered, "You won't flounder. You are as intelligent, if not more so, than anyone present. Besides, I'll be here for you."

"Thank you." She breathed in and out again. "I'll be fine."

"You shall." His ever ready grin was present. "I have faith in you even if you don't have it for yourself. Come, let's see if I recognize anyone."

They were shortly involved in a conversation about whether the government should send the Elgin Marbles back to Greece. A short while later they left that debate only to be embroiled in a conversation on how best to bring about universal suffrage. The lady espousing the viewpoint was firm in her opinions that women as well as all men should have the right to vote. Vivian had read about the idea, but the thought that ladies were actively promoting it was something she had never considered.

"Universal suffrage will not happen in our lifetime," Rupert said. "But I have hopes for my children or grandchildren."

"If we continue on the path to social reform that we have begun, I think it may occur more quickly," the lady responded.

"Ah, but you are forgetting," a gentleman chimed in, "the fear instilled in the more conservative segments of our government by the French Revolution and the uprisings in the countryside."

A small hand touched her elbow. "I agree it should be sooner rather than later," Anna Rutherford, opined. She gathered Rupert and Vivian with her glance. "Phoebe and Marcus are here as well. This is a good place to have a comfortable coze." She linked arms with Vivian. "Are you enjoying yourself, or is it a bit overwhelming?"

"It is certainly not what I am used to." Vivian struggled to describe what she was feeling. "I find it exhilarating."

"I think that is the reason I enjoy these drawing rooms as well. One is introduced to different ways of thinking."

Phoebe and Anna, who had claimed the long window seat overlooking a side garden, moved over to make a place for Vivian. She had never felt so included in a circle before. These women had become friends so quickly. They had instantly accepted her for who she was, not who they wanted her to be.

Their husbands were friendly as well, but she knew they were concerned about her intentions toward Rupert. She stifled a laugh. If only they knew about Cleo, they would not be apprehensive.

Footmen walked through the room with drinks and small tidbits of food. Rupert snatched a glass of what Vivian had thought was tea in a small cup. She took a sip and almost sputtered it out. "What is this?"

"Sake," Marcus answered. "Wine made from rice." He held up a small roll that had been fried. "This is a spring roll. Keep your mind open, and you'll find a number of new dishes."

"How do you know about them?"

"All sorts of races live and pass through the West Indies," he said. "I enjoy new experiences and different foods."

"Give me an English meat pie anytime," Lord Rutherford said.

Anna cuffed him on his shoulder. "Don't be stodgy."

His eyes warmed. "You love coffyns."

"I do." She raised her chin and took a bite of one of the spring rolls. "I also like these."

Phoebe laughed. "She doesn't allow him to get away with anything."

Marcus laid his hand possessively on her shoulder. "And you do?"

"Never." Phoebe's eyes softened as she gazed upon her husband. "It is a woman's job to keep her husband moving forward."

What it would be like to have that sort of love and respect in a marriage, Vivian could not imagine. Her mother and father certainly did not have a marriage like her friends did.

Salts and spices she had never tasted teased her lips as Rupert held a small amount of a spring roll to them. She opened as she had done for him last night. Vivian wanted to moan remembering how he had possessed her.

"Try it."

She bit down. Unlike English pasties, the roll crunched and splintered. Holding her serviette under her chin, she chewed. Even the vegetables were unusual. "Umm, this is delicious."

"It is." Heat lurked in his eyes, making them silver. The color they were when she was Cleo.

He was so close that for a brief moment she thought he would kiss her. Here. In front of everyone. Then he blinked and increased the distance between them. Her heart sank. She should not have got her hopes up. Still, she wanted to be in his arms again, even if he thought she was another woman. And despite enjoying the drawing room, Vivian wanted nothing more than for the hours until this evening to fly, so she could be with Rupert again. In his arms and in bed.

"Taste this as well."

"What is it?" Vivian asked as she opened her lips.

"A type of seafood called crab meat." Rupert waited until the morsel was in Vivian's mouth before he ate another piece. "Do you like it?"

"I do, and I sincerely hope this type of entertainment becomes all the crack."

Vivian smiled at him, making him wish they were alone on Hill Street. He wanted nothing more than pull her into his arms and make love to her. Feed her these delicacies in bed. If he lived to be one hundred, he could not conceive of a lovelier lady, a more interesting woman, a more perfect person to spend the rest of his life with. If only he knew how long it would take before she would agree to be his.

Several hours passed before he looked at his watch. "We are all going to be late for dinner or anything else."

"I can't eat another bite," Vivian said just after swallowing another glass of rice wine.

"I am satisfied as well." Anna leaned against the window embrasure.

Touching her now rounded stomach, Phoebe gave a comical frown. "I'll be hungry in an hour."

"Shall we make our way home?" Marcus glanced around the room. "The company is thinning."

"I think we must." Rupert held out his hand to Vivian as she dislodged herself from the comfortable window seat. "Let's find Lord and Lady Thornhill."

Several rooms on the main floor were open for their guests. Vivian exclaimed over the art and fabrics bought in faraway places that were displayed in the long gallery.

Vivian had said she'd never traveled, and he would enjoy taking her to see other countries and seeing her pleasure in them, allowing her to experience the differences in culture. The steamships he had seen being developed would make travel faster than the sailing ships, and allow them to make trips that did not require long periods of time away from his estates.

They found their host and hostess in another room holding forth on some of their artifacts, and bid them adieu.

As they strolled to the hall, Vivian glanced at Rupert. "Do you think they obtained all their art and whatnot legally?"

"Oh yes. Lord Thornhill made a comment about how dear some of the items were and the thoroughness of the inspections the authorities conducted when they left the countries. The Thornhills insisted upon ensuring they took no national treasures." He paused for effect. "Except for the cook. I think they may have smuggled him out."

Vivian's laugh was everything Rupert wanted. "I would have smuggled him out as well," he said.

"I'm going to have to rest before this evening."

He kept his voice even as he asked, "Which party are you attending?"

"I may not." Vivian's tone was airy, but there was an undercurrent of uneasiness. "Cousin Clara and Silvia are going out, of course, but I may retire early."

Blast it all. When would she work it out that he knew she was posing as Cleo? He'd been dropping subtle hints by looking at her as he had last night. If she didn't do it on her own, he would be forced to enlighten her. That, he was not looking forward to.

When they arrived in Mount Street, he escorted her to the door. "To-morrow, shall we drive out to Richmond? It's lovely this time of year."

She swayed a bit. The rice wine must have affected her more than he'd thought.

"That sounds wonderful."

Rupert kissed Vivian's hand. "Until we meet again."

Thirty minutes later, Miss Punt scurried out the gate to the gardens. "What did you do to her ladyship?"

He held up his hands in surrender. "Not me. There was a different type of wine at the gathering, and I think she might have imbibed too much."

"She did at that." The maid shook her head. "I hope she doesn't have a headache."

"As do I." He handed her the parcel that had arrived from Madame Lisette while he was out. "This is for your mistress."

Miss Punt nodded. "How long do you think your plan will take? Her father wrote her this morning and said he'd made a new match for her."

Rupert bit off an oath. "When?"

"He'll be here in a week."

"Before then." Of all the bad luck. Vivian deserved to be courted and wooed, not badgered into another bad marriage. "What can you tell me about her husband?"

"Dead is a good place for him to be." Miss Punt's lips firmed into a straight line. "I don't know what exactly happened, but my poor mistress cried herself to sleep while that whore he kept acted like she hadn't a care in the world. Everyone, except her ladyship, knew how things were. None of the servants took her orders unless they verified them with his lordship. Like as not, he'd change them, and do something his mistress wanted."

By the time she'd finished, the maid's bosom was heaving with indignation, and Rupert didn't blame her at all. No lady, no wife, should be treated the way Vivian had been, but he still didn't know if the late Lord Beresford had physically hurt her. "Did she ever have bruises?"

"Never on the outside, but there are plenty on the inside. Not that she would ever say anything to me, she keeps her own counsel, but whatever he did left her thinking no man would ever want her."

Bloody hell. "Did she confide in anyone?"

"Maybe Miss Silvia. When we were at Beresford, I'd find her in her ladyship's room late at night."

Past tense. At Beresford, but not here? "Why do they no longer converse?"

"Lady Telford put Miss Silvia next to her and my lady is in the other wing, and she met you."

Interesting. Rupert made a mental note to find out more about Lady Telford. "If you cannot bring her to Hill Street this evening, I'll understand."

"Thank you, my lord." Punt turned to leave and stopped. "I'm that glad you came into her life."

Rupert nodded. "Thank you for your help. She's fortunate to have such loyalty."

When he arrived home, Nick Beresford was pacing Rupert's study. "This looks serious. What can I do for you?"

His friend scowled. "You've got more problems than you think."

He poured two glasses of brandy, handing one to Nick. "Have a seat and tell me about it."

Nick took a long pull on his brandy. "For one thing, Miss Banks is after you. Miss Corbet and I heard her talking with a friend last night. She plans to get you alone and compromise you into marrying her."

That news was nothing more than Rupert had expected. In order to remain on Lord Banks's good side, Rupert had asked to be warned of which parties to stay away from. "One of the reasons I've been avoiding events where young ladies are present. Go on."

"This next piece isn't much better. Lady Telford told Miss Corbet that Lady Beresford's father wrote about a match he's already arranged. The old man even had the settlement agreements drawn up."

That was far worse than Rupert had thought. He moved his jaw that had clenched painfully. Punt had said Vivian was leaving. Running away was more like it. Had any of the men in her life treated her well? He was almost afraid to ask, but . . . "Anything else?"

Nick suddenly had a cat-who's-eaten-a-canary grin. "You may wish me happy. I'm to be married in two days."

"That *is* good news. Congratulations." Rupert poured Beresford another glass of brandy. "Am I invited?"

"If you're not on your wedding trip, you are."

Rupert rubbed his chin thoughtfully. If he and Vivian were to wed in a few days, he must obtain a special license. "I will not run away. It never helps, and always creates a false impression. I do need to secure my lady's hand immediately. I see a trip to Doctors' Commons in my secretary's future."

"By the by"—Nick set his glass down—"have you seen or heard of Lord Oliver?"

"As a matter of fact, yes. I introduced him to Miss Chawner yesterday. After several minutes of discussion he actually appeared happy, which, I can tell you, surprised me to no end." Rupert lifted his goblet in a salute. "My last loose end is Lady Beresford. If I can convince her to marry me quickly, I believe all of our problems will have been sorted."

"I'm happy you and Vivian found one another. It never occurred to me . . ."

"What?" Rupert would not allow anyone to slight Vivian. She had apparently gone through a life time of that, and it would cease now.

Nick took another drink. "I just didn't imagine an out-and-outer like you falling for Vivian. She was always so quiet. I don't think I'd heard her say more than a dozen words aside from greetings or other pleasantries in all the time I've known her."

Perhaps because your reared-in-a-cow-byre brute of a cousin treated her so badly. "I do not know what she was like before, but the lady I know and love is quick, intelligent, and cares deeply for the plight of others."

"You blame Edgar."

"Why would you come to that conclusion?" Rupert kept himself from tossing back his brandy, but still drank deeply.

"I don't think I've ever heard anyone give such a speech with his teeth clenched. You're angry at how she's been treated, and it stands to reason you think my cousin is at fault."

"He was not the only one. I don't think I'll get along at all well with my future father-in-law."

"Hawksworth was right. You are not to be underestimated." Nick rose. "I'll thank you for helping me and leave you to your plans. I don't envy Vivian's father or the proposed husband, but I shall do everything possible to be there when they discover their scheme has been circumvented."

After Nick left, Rupert went to his room to dress for dinner. He must move his plans for Vivian forward, and he might not be able to wait to consummate their *affaire de cœur*. She obviously had no idea how desirable she was, and it was up to him to show her.

CHAPTER TWENTY-FOUR

Vivian woke to a darkened chamber. A moonbeam played hide-and-seek with the curtain as it fluttered with the breeze. She hadn't thought she'd had that much to drink, but it was enough to make her want to sleep. Something she never did during the day. Lying still, she took stock of her head and body. No headache. Her mouth didn't taste like a barn floor. Yet, that did not tell her what would happen when she arose. There was no time like the present to find out.

Carefully, she propped herself up on her elbows. So far, so good. Then swung her legs off the bed and sat up. Amazingly, she didn't feel bad at all.

Lighting a candle, she padded over to the clock. It was nine thirty. If she hurried, she would have enough time to prepare for Rupert's arrival at the Hill Street house. Where was her maid? "Punt, we must leave now."

Silence answered Vivian's call. "Well, drat. She must have thought I would be out all night."

She went back to the bed and yanked on the bell-pull.

Vivian had finished brushing her teeth and washing her face when Punt rushed into the chamber. "I didn't expect you to be up until morning."

"I have no lasting effects of overindulging. We must hurry."

Forty minutes later, they were in Vivian's dressing room on Hill Street. Her maid adjusted her wig.

"Bring me the nightgown."

"He sent a new one." Punt shook out a lovely white gown embroidered with blue and yellow flowers.

"It's beautiful." Vivian rubbed the fabric between two fingers. "Not as substantial as the last one, but it will still cover everything."

"I don't suppose," her maid said as she dropped the gown over Vivian's head, "that you would consider telling his lordship who you are."

If only she could, but then he wouldn't want her any longer. "I cannot. What would he think of me?"

"He seems pretty taken with you already."

"With Cleo, not me." Since she had decided to be honest with herself, she could admit she wished it were different. That he truly did want her, but the fact remained she was not the type of woman men desired. If she could keep her persona as Cleo and not be discovered, Vivian thought she might try continuing the masquerade. Perhaps it was just as well her father had given her a chance to leave.

"He keeps escorting you places."

"Yes, but only to avoid the younger ladies." Vivian's throat closed, but she refused to allow the tears to come. "I've been over this time and again. There is no point to this discussion. It is what it is, and he'll be here soon." She rose and glanced around the opulent red and gold chamber. "Bring the wine and some food."

"As you wish, my lady."

Punt left and Vivian set about arranging the candelabras away from the bed. She should leave instructions for them to be left where she put them each night. Still, it gave her something to do while she waited to be in Rupert's arms again. A tear rolled down her cheek. She wiped it away and blew her nose. At least she had him tonight and for the next few days. She would depart as soon as Silvia was married.

Rupert slipped through the garden door in the back of Vivian's Hill Street house, then into the corridor. Punt waited with a candle. "How is she feeling?"

"She says she is well. I tried to convince her to tell you who she is, but she won't."

That was not surprising. "Leave it with me."

In silence they mounted the stairs.

This time he knocked, and waited.

A moment later the door swung open, and Vivian was in his arms. "I'm so glad you're here."

Rupert gathered her to him. "There is no place I'd rather be." He lowered his lips to hers. "Or anyone I'd rather be with." Brushing his thumbs over her cheeks, a drop fell on his finger. *Good Lord.* "You've been weeping."

"It is of no consequence." Her voice was rough and thready.

Meaning that she was of no consequence. "It is to me. You matter to me." He gently moved them to the table. "Let's share a glass of wine." He filled one goblet, holding it to her lips. "Drink a little."

Vivian chuckled wetly. "Yes, my lord."

Rupert set the glass down, sat on a chair, and pulled Vivian onto his lap. "Tell me what is troubling you."

She toyed with his cravat, appearing to focus all her attention on his pin. "I must soon leave Town. I have some issues to resolve."

Such as her father's latest proposed marriage. "I see. When shall we depart?"

Her head jerked up and her eyes flew to his. "We? But . . . but you cannot. You have business here."

"You are my only concern." He nuzzled her gently curved jaw, and his chest tightened. There was no way on earth he'd allow her to leave without him. "Now that I've found you, did you actually believe I would simply allow you to disappear?"

"You cannot mean that." She shook her head as if her denial could make it true.

Taking her chin between his thumb and forefinger, he kissed her again. "Yet I do. Have you no idea how much I care for you?"

Vivian's tears flowed freely now. "No."

Holding her firmly to his chest, he stood. "Then it's time I proved it to you."

Laying her down on the bed, Rupert undressed faster than he ever had before. In the mood she was in now, she might flee before he could kiss her again. The mattress dipped as he lowered himself beside her. "I want you to be mine forever."

He claimed her lips, stifling her protests. Soon her body hummed with his caresses, and she held on to him as if she were drowning.

But when he tried to remove the nightgown, she froze. "No, please."

What she was afraid of, he didn't know, but, for now, he would honor her wishes. Instead he tasted her breasts through the fine muslin covering them. Soon she was moaning again. Her palms stroked his back to the top of his buttocks, and stopped. This was the first time he'd been naked with her. Not giving her time to think, he possessed her mouth again, exploring with his tongue as his fingers stoked her need higher.

Finally, she caressed his bottom. "It's so firm."

"I'm glad you think so." Rupert moved over Vivian. "I want all of you."

She bit her lush, swollen bottom lip and nodded.

Slowly, he trailed his tongue lower until he reached the silvery-blond curls of her mons. The only part of her she would allow to be uncovered. She tasted of musk and spice. His heart swelled with joy as she bucked against him, grabbing his hair, urging him on. She flung her head from side to side, as she cried out for relief before she shattered at his hands.

Rupert had never enjoyed pleasuring a woman so much, and he knew pleasuring Vivian would only get better with time.

She was flushed and beautiful, and ready for him. "Rupert, I'm afraid. It has never felt good before."

"Do you trust me?"

"Yes."

"I won't hurt you. If you need me to stop, I shall."

Vivian couldn't bring herself to stop Rupert. He'd been so kind to her, he deserved some joy for himself. She braced for the pain, but the only feeling was a stretching, and fullness. He sank into her as if he had done it a thousand times before. Nothing had ever felt so good, or so right. She blinked rapidly, determined to stop her tears of delight mixed with sorrow from falling. She could never give him nearly as much as he had given her. Leaving him would be unbearable, but she should not think of that now.

Rupert drew back as if he'd withdraw, and she tightened her grip on his derrière. "No."

In answer, he plunged deeper into her. "I'm not going anywhere, my love. Wrap your legs around me."

Vivian did as she was told, and the luscious tension returned. "Good, so good. I want more."

"Your wish shall be granted." His voice was harsh and low, but his touch was gentle.

She didn't know what she'd done to deserve a man like him. Frissons of sensual pleasure speared through her, until finally, she was trembling beneath him.

Rupert kissed her as if the world would end, until he shuddered and collapsed off to Vivian's side, drawing her to him. No matter how long she lived, she would never forget this moment. The first time she felt beautiful and loved, when their hearts beat together and she knew she cared for him more than her life.

His lips pressed against her temple. "I love you. Never believe otherwise."

Vivian was too happy to argue that the woman he cared for was nothing more than a wig and kohl. "As I love you."

Later, they ate her cook's small meat pies, perfect for a chilly night after making love yet again. Rupert fed her grapes, and she fed them to him. His eyes were the color of molten silver, and he looked at her as if he could see her soul.

As she brought the wine-glass to her lips, she lowered her lashes. If only someone had told her how dangerous to her heart falling in love would be. If only she had heeded her own warnings. To-morrow she would leave him a letter telling him the truth. She owed Rupert that much at the very least.

Rupert flashed a wicked grin, picked her up, strode to the bed, and dropped her. Before she could move, he was kissing her again. "Are you up for another round?"

Her heart, *she*, was lighter, more joyful than she'd ever been. "I am. Are you?"

She loved his teasing. Her husband could barely bring himself to touch her, but Rupert couldn't seem to get enough.

"Oh, my lady, you have no idea." His fingers worked their magic, and he laughed as she moaned. "I'll never have enough of you."

A few hours later, Rupert listened as the clock struck three. Next to him, Vivian was curled up, her hand and head on his chest.

He had never loved anyone the way he loved her. She was his sun, moon, and stars, and it was up to him to convince her that she deserved to be loved and cared for. Still, no matter how he'd attempted to reassure her, she had slipped away at times. If he wasn't certain her maid would contact him, he would be terrified Vivian would attempt to leave Town without him and he would lose her.

"Come, my love. It's time to go home."

"I'm too comfortable." Her tone was warm as honey, and sleepy.

So was he, but one of them had to keep propriety in mind. If any-one caught them, she would believe he had been forced to marry her, and that was the last thing she needed. "Give me a kiss, and I'll see you to-morrow."

Still mostly asleep, she puckered her lips, and he touched them lightly with his own before leaving her.

Rupert dressed quickly, then called Punt to attend Vivian. He met the maid outside the bedchamber door. "I'll tell the coachman to have the carriage ready. Do not allow her to do anything rash until I see her to-morrow."

"I'll do my best, my lord."

"I know you are acting in her best interest and would not normally betray her confidence, but please promise me that if she makes plans to depart Town, you will send me a message."

Punt swallowed and nodded. "With as much as I've done so far, I might as well continue. Only, mind, because you make her ladyship happier than I've ever seen her."

"Thank you." He breathed a sigh of relief as the maid went to at-tend Vivian.

Once again, he waited until he saw the women were safe before making his own way home. Later that morning, he would ask for her hand. What he wasn't looking forward to was explaining that he had known her secret from the first.

He gained his study, penned a missive to Nick Beresford asking him to come to Stanstead House as soon as he received the note, and left it to be sent first thing in the morning. Rupert and Vivian didn't have a great deal of time before her father and prospective husband arrived. Before then, he must be apprised of the extent of her prop-erty for the marriage settlements.

Several hours later, he had just sat down to break his fast when Harlock tapped on the side of the door. "My lord, Lord Beresford to see you."

"Show him in and bring more tea."

Rupert's butler bowed, only to reappear a few moments later with Beresford.

"Help yourself to the sideboard. Tea should arrive shortly." Rupert waited until his friend had one cup of tea, before broaching the reason for his summons. "I intend to ask Lady Beresford to marry me to-day. If she accepts, I will need to know the extent of her estate in order to draw up the settlement agreements. I plan to transfer all her property into trust for her benefit, and later that of our girl children."

Nick leaned back in his chair. "Generous of you. A damned sight better than her father would do. If it comes to that, other than me"— he gave a devil-may-care grin—"I can't think of any other gentleman who'd do so."

"You would be surprised at the numbers." Rupert kept his tone dry, though he couldn't stop his lips from twitching. "I'll make a point of introducing you to the ones I know. You have been in an excellent mood since Miss Corbet accepted you."

Nick went to the sideboard and returned with a large piece of rare beefsteak. "Nothing like knowing you're going to be wed to the love of your life." He sobered. "There was a time I didn't think it would happen. Especially after Edgar made me promise to ask Vivian to be my wife."

"He appears to have been a master at making those around him happy." Rupert hid his scowl behind his tea-cup.

"For most of my life, he was good to me, if only he could have stood up to his father about marriage." His friend seemed to sink into bittersweet reminiscence.

He had to end this conversation before he said something to alienate Beresford. "Vivian's property?"

"Yes, of course." Nick stabbed distractedly at his meat. "I'll have the document sent straight over."

"How go the wedding plans?"

Beresford's brow cleared. "Exceedingly well. Lady Telford will host the wedding breakfast and has arranged for a clergyman to perform the ceremony at her house. My residence isn't up for it yet, but I'm sure Silvia will take it in hand. Hawksworth will stand up with me. I'm not sure who Silvia is asking. My only duties are to procure the special license and the ring."

"If you give me your details, my secretary can pick up your license when he does mine. As for the ring, I had planned a visit to Rundell and Bridge's. You are welcome to accompany me."

"I'll do that. I had thought of sending for something from Beresford, but decided I would prefer something made especially for Silvia."

"I'm sure that can be arranged." Rupert grinned as he placed his serviette on the table. "Shall we go?"

"If you'll give me the loan of paper and pen first I'll write a note to my solicitor about Vivian's portion."

Rupert led Nick back to the study, and a short time later, they strode out of the house toward a group of hackneys.

"Why not take your phaeton?" Nick asked.

"The shop is located on Ludgate Hill in the City. We may be a while, and I don't want to keep the horses waiting."

Early that afternoon, they finally left the jewelry store. Nick had ordered a ring to be made for Miss Corbet, while Rupert had found exactly what he wanted in a selection of older rings. All he had to do now was convince Vivian they belonged together for the rest of their lives.

He arrived home to find a letter on the hall table.

"It was delivered by messenger," Harlock said, "with instructions for you to read it immediately."

The seal had no crest or any other indication of its author. He opened it, squinting at the cramped writing.

> *My lord,*
> *You must come quickly. Her ladyship has taken it in*
> *her head to leave in the morning.*
> *Yr. friend,*
> *A. P.*

Short and straight to the point, just like the woman herself. "I don't know when I'll return," he said to Harlock.

Heart pounding, Rupert rushed out of the house, found a hackney at the entrance to the square, and a few minutes later, he was knocking on Lady Telford's door.

"Come in, my lord." The butler raised a brow of inquiry.

"I'm here to see Lady Beresford."

"I shall see if her ladyship is at home."

In other words, if she would agree to see Rupert. He clenched his teeth. Not that it mattered; he'd find her if he had to search every room in the house.

Lady Telford appeared from a corridor on the right side of the hall. "Lord Stanstead, I will take you to Lady Beresford."

"Thank you." He'd barely croaked the words. Damn it all, he must compose himself. Vivian would be high enough in the boughs. He didn't need to be there himself. Someone must keep their head about them.

CHAPTER TWENTY-FIVE

When Vivian had finally managed to force her eyes open, the door had just closed behind Rupert. Rolling over, she breathed in his clean, spicy scent from the pillows and fought back her tears. Every time he left, letting go of him was harder. She lay there memorizing the way his normally perfect curls became tousled when she slid her fingers through them, the way the corners of his lips curved up first before he smiled, and his elegant gait when he entered the room and came to her.

Vivian buried her face in his pillow. This had to be the end of it. If she did not break it off with him now, she might never be able to. An ache started in her chest, making it hard to breathe. Why had she had to fall in love with Rupert? Yet how could she leave him?

Rising, she donned her chemise. Once Punt arrived, it was a matter of minutes before they were ready to depart. As usual, the coach waited for them in the mews, and soon they were at the Mount Street house.

Punt lit a candle that was on a small table next to the garden door, and Vivian followed her, unseeing, up to her rooms.

"Let's get you into bed."

She stood, as she'd done all her life, while her maid unfastened and unlaced her gown and stays. Once in her own nightgown, she crawled into the cold bed, wishing Rupert was still with her. She prayed for a dreamless sleep, but as soon as she closed her eyes, he was there, speaking soft words of love, caressing her, taking her to a place she could not have dreamed existed.

There was only one thing to do, and she would attend to the arrangements in the morning. At least she would have another night with him.

* * *

"My lady?" Punt's hand shook Vivian's shoulder, waking her.

"What time is it?" She yawned, struggling to sit up, expecting her maid to lay the breakfast tray across her lap.

"Not that late, but this came for you by special messenger."

The letter Punt handed her was from Mama and not franked. Vivian sat up straighter. "I hope nothing is wrong."

She tore the seal off as she opened it, smoothing the sheet out over her lap.

> *My darling Vivian,*
>
> *I can only suppose that you received your father's letter. Believe me when I tell you that I did my best to talk him out of this outrageous scheme of his. Unfortunately, he left for Town yesterday. I didn't dare write you until he was out of the house.*
>
> *I have always regretted that I was unable to help you when you confided to me about your marriage. I had wished better for you. Sadly, I cannot think you will like Lord Tewkesbury any better than you did Beresford. The man is a widower with several daughters and two sons. If you choose to wed again, it should be your choice. Drat that hunting bitch.*
>
> *All my love,*
> *Mama*

Vivian looked at the date and froze. Her father could be in Town to-day, to-morrow at the latest. "I must make immediate arrangements to depart. Papa could arrive at any time. Fetch me the estate information. I hope the visits can be set in short order."

Her maid opened her mouth, snapped it shut, then said, "You should tell her ladyship."

Vivian glanced at the clock. It was already past noon. "Why did you let me sleep so late?"

"You needed it. If you don't mind me saying, these late nights are running you a bit ragged."

She couldn't argue with that. "I must eat." She'd never been so hungry. "After which I'll speak to my cousin. I am certain she will be able to keep my father at bay until I can escape."

"That she will, and you never know what other help will show up." On that cryptic remark, Punt disappeared into the dressing room.

After breaking her fast and dressing, Vivian found her cousin on the terrace outside of the morning room at the back of the house. "I received a letter from Mama . . ."

Clara's brows lowered as she narrowed her eyes. "I think it best if you stay close to the house to-day. In the event your father arrives, I shall have him turned away until you can sort out what you wish to do."

That was easy: Vivian would flee. "Whatever happens, I shall not agree to marry Lord Twiddlededum."

"I agree, it does not sound like a good match at all." Her cousin patted her hand. "You will come about. I place great faith in Fate."

Barnes tapped on the open door. "Lady Beresford, Lord Stanstead is here to see you."

Vivian couldn't see him now, not when she was so distraught. She would do or say something that would ruin everything. "Please tell him I am not—"

"Vivian, my dear, he can be very helpful. Stanstead has a good head on his shoulders. I'll fetch him." Clara gave Vivian a stern look. "Do not run away."

She wrung her hands. She wished more than anything that he could help her. If only he could take her away, but he wanted Cleo.

Vivian rose as Clara, followed closely by Rupert, strode onto the terrace. He took Vivian's fingers in his. "Let us speak alone."

"I think that is a wonderful idea." Clara beamed, closing the French window to the terrace. "I shall be right here."

Vivian led Rupert to a rose arbor in the back of the garden. "I will miss our outings."

He gave her a quizzical look. "I gathered from what Lady Telford said there is some sort of problem. However, that does not change my reason for being here."

It was too early for Rupert to have come for the carriage ride he had proposed. So . . . "Oh, did you come to say you could not go this afternoon?"

"I came for this." He dropped to one knee. "Vivian, would you do me the great honor of being my wife?"

She stepped back, covering her lips with her hand.

It is happening all over again! How could Rupert betray her in this way? "I cannot. You don't love me. You love Cleo."

As Rupert rose, he stared at Vivian as if she was mad. Perhaps she was. After all, ladies did not mention *chères amies*, and since he was unaware of her deception, she should not know about Cleo even if they were one and the same. Still, it didn't feel that way. Cleo was loved in a way Vivian never would be. She blinked back the tears threatening to fall. "I went through one marriage with a man who loved another woman. I cannot do it again." She turned her back to him, and stared through blurred eyes out at the garden. "Please go, just go away and leave me alone!"

Yet instead of stomping off in anger, Rupert's warm breath tickled the back of her neck. "Vivian, you are the only woman I love." She took a breath, preparing to argue with him, when he forestalled her. "Did you think I did not know to whom I was making love?" The tip of his finger traced her ear down to her cheek. "That I could not recognize the delicate shape of your ear beneath the wig, or I could forget the gentle line of your jaw? From the first moment we met, your scent filled me. It was as if you were my home. I knew when you sent the letter it was you. The paper and ink could not hide the perfume of fresh meadows and wild flowers; your fragrance."

She couldn't believe what he was telling her. How could he have known? Cleo was everything Vivian was not. Dark, bold, and adventurous. "But with the cosmetics and the wig . . ."

Rupert turned her so she faced him. "They could not hide your eyes when they smiled at me, or your voice when you cried out in pleasure, or the soft tinkling of your laughter, or most of all, your spirit." He nibbled the corner of her lips as his hands held her waist. "Marry me, Vivian. Be my lover and my wife forever." His palms cupped her breasts, and his voice was low and gravelly as it washed over her. "You are the most enticing woman I've ever known, and I want no other."

She was becoming lost in Rupert as he continued to caress her, but could she trust him with her life? Clara's words came back to her. *He will marry someone like Miss Banks.* "You might want another woman, a younger one."

"Vivian, how old are you?" he asked as one hand left her breasts.

"I am four and twenty."

"And I'm twenty-two. Hardly any difference at all. As a matter of fact, just last month a woman from the village near my estate wed a man my age; she was forty." Vivian sucked in a breath, as his clever fingers began to stroke her back. "Think of it as ensuring that you will be pleasured for a long time." His lips curved into a smile against her neck. "Many years more than if you married someone older."

"I wish I could say yes." She pleaded with him to understand. "I want to, but there is something wrong with me." Unable to look at him, she hung her head. "My body is deformed."

"Deformed?" His tone was incredulous, then his form went rigid, and he growled, "Did someone scar you?"

"No, it's nothing like that." She almost wished it was. "I do not know what it is. My husband said . . . he could not even look at me." Rupert put his finger under her chin, raising it so that she had to look up to meet his gaze. "I couldn't bear for you to be repelled as well."

Rupert watched as Vivian's eyes swam with tears. There must be a special place in hell for people like Edgar Beresford, who would take a beautiful woman and make her feel ugly. "We're going to Hill Street."

Her jaw dropped, but Rupert had apparently shocked her enough she was no longer threatening tears.

"Now?" she asked in an offended tone. "But it's daylight. Everyone will see us."

"We will arrive separately and go in the back way. Get your maid while I ask Lady Telford for a carriage."

"Rupert, what are you planning?"

"Do you trust me?"

"Always, but . . ."

Not giving Vivian a chance to argue further, he grabbed her hand and walked as rapidly as he could to the house. When they regained the morning room, he kissed her, hard, on the lips. "I'll wait here."

She nodded as if she was in a daze, but did as he had asked. All he had to do was keep her with him.

Rupert found the lady in her parlor. "I need a carriage for Vivian."

Lady Telford tugged the bell-pull. A footman popped his head in. "Get the plain black town coach readied. Keep it in the mews." Raising one brow, Rupert glanced at her. "Vivian received a letter from her mother. Her father could be here at any time. I do not wish her to leave from the front of the house where she may be seen."

"Very well."

Lady Telford handed him a glass of wine. "Do I need to ask your intentions?"

"I wish to marry her. If she'll have me."

"Splendid." She smiled. "Nothing gives me greater pleasure than to see two people in love take their vows." Rising, she said, "I'll see if I can speed things along, shall I?"

"Excellent." Rupert paced, then after what seemed like an eternity, Vivian and Punt finally walked into the morning room. He held out his arm. "The coach is around the back. I'll meet you there in a few minutes."

He escorted them to the gate, saw them into the carriage, and walked down the mews. He needed to give Vivian enough time to change. It was a pity he had not had time to have the latest gown delivered. Yet perhaps she could wear it for their wedding night. When he reached the back of the Hill Street house, he took out his watch and waited another five minutes before using his key to open the gate.

A few minutes later, he strolled into the bedchamber. Vivian turned, eyes wide, staring at him. Her gorgeous silver-blond hair was loose and reached her hips, her petal-pink lips slightly apart, and she was trembling like a blancmange.

In two strides, she was in his arms. "You said you trusted me. Believe me now when I tell you there is nothing wrong with you."

She swallowed. "The last time a gentleman saw me naked, it did not turn out well."

"That man was a stupid fool." A bloody, selfish, care-for-nobody.

He kissed her, sweetly, teasing her bottom lip with his teeth. A long mirror stood in the corner of the room, and he positioned her in front of it as he stood behind her.

"I don't think I can do this." Vivian hung her head, refusing to look into the mirror.

"You can and you shall. Let me slay your dragons, my lady." Slowly he unfastened the top five ivory buttons, exposing her shoulders and the tops of her breasts. "Do you see anything odd?"

"No, but this can be seen in an evening gown."

"Fair enough." Rupert unbuttoned the next several buttons and the gown fell to the top of her hip, exposing a reddish, heart-shaped birthmark. "What about now?"

Her answer came out on a sob. "The question is can you live with me damaged as I am?"

"I'll tell you what I see." Rupert stroked the birthmark. "A lovely woman with high breasts tipped with nipples that remind me of light pink French roses. Your skin is so silky and perfect, it would make an angel cry in envy, and you carry your heart not only in your breast, but on the outside as well." She relaxed a little against him. "Shall we go on?"

She nodded tensely, clearly still unsure of herself.

Gradually he eased the gown over her slim hips. With a soft swoosh, fabric fell to the carpet. "Vivian, you are the most exquisite woman who has ever existed, and I wish to spend the rest of my life worshipping you and your body's faultless form."

He turned her to face him and just when Rupert expected her to smile and agree, her face crumpled. "Why did he do that to me? Why did he lie?"

He cuddled her closer. "From what Nick told me, your husband was in love with another woman."

She nodded against his chest. "I know."

"I cannot imagine treating a lady the way he treated you. But, after meeting you, I do understand not wanting to make love to anyone else."

Kissing her tears away, Rupert carried Vivian over to the bed. She untied his cravat, then busied herself doing what she had never done before—undress a man. Even though it was still light out, her maid had lit the candles, giving the chamber a softer glow.

She still had trouble believing Rupert thought she was beautiful. On the other hand, she knew *he* was. She ran her palms over his chest, all hard muscle. Soft, springy hairs lightly covered his flesh. She touched the tip of her tongue to his nipples. They were darker than hers, but then again, he appeared to have spent time in the sun without a shirt on. As soon as his pantaloons were off, he wrapped his arms around her and climbed onto the bed.

After they made love, when she was cuddled in his arms, she kissed the palm of his hand. "Will you ask me again to marry you?"

"I will ask until you say yes." He shifted, looming over her, the corners of his eyes crinkling. "My beautiful, darling Vivian, will you be my wife?"

"Yes. I would love to be your wife." A lifetime with Rupert Stanstead was exactly what Vivian wanted and no one would take it away from her. Especially her father and Lord Twiddlededum. "We must do it soon, before my father finds out."

She started to rise, but Rupert pulled her back down. "We shall wed with all due speed, but we will not give the impression we are running away."

His face was strong and his expression firm and unyielding. The only problem was that she had never defied her father. An image of her hiding behind Rupert sprung into her mind. With him she would be safe. He was equal to anything and would take on anyone, including her father. "What do you suggest?"

"I have already sent my secretary to buy a special license. I understand Lady Telford has a clergyman arranged for Beresford and Miss Corbet, or we may wed at St. George's. It is for you to decide. We have friends we will wish to invite to our wedding breakfast, which I propose we have at Stanstead House. The next morning, a notice will appear in the *Morning Post* that we have married. Sometime during the next day or two, we shall inform your father, either in person or by mail."

She was amazed. Not that he could plan it all out, but that he had. "I find nothing to disagree with."

"Good." He gave her one of his boyish grins. "Do you wish to have a new gown made?"

Vivian mentally reviewed her wardrobe. Madame Lisette had delivered several garments yesterday, including one in white with silver netting. "No, I have something suitable."

Rupert rose from the bed, taking his warmth with him. "Give me a moment." He rummaged through his waistcoat pockets, bringing out a small velvet bag.

"What is that?"

"If you will hold out your hand"—he sauntered to the bed— "you'll find out."

CHAPTER TWENTY-SIX

Rupert slowly opened the sack, making a show of it, before sliding a ring on Vivian's right hand. The wide band was made of white gold. In the middle sat a large sapphire and on either side were several smaller diamonds. "The next time I place this ring on your finger, it will be during our wedding ceremony."

"It is exquisite. Where did you find it?" Vivian flung her arms around his neck. "It looks ancient." For some reason she could not explain, the ring made marrying Rupert real to her.

"Only from the fifteenth century." He lay back down beside her. "When I saw it, I knew my search was over. Fortunately, your ring finger is almost the same size as my little finger."

She held up his hand. "I wondered about that."

Rupert touched his lips to hers, and a knock sounded on the door. "My maid."

"Most likely. As much as I would love to remain here, we should probably return to Lady Telford's house."

"Give us a few moments," Vivian called.

"My lady," Punt said from the corridor side of the door, "Lady Telford asks that you return as soon as possible."

Rupert gave Vivian an incredulous look. "Did you—"

"No! I would never tell anyone. The only reason I told my maid was that I didn't know how to go about setting this"—she waved her hand—"up." Vivian began thinking back. "I wonder if she did not mean something of this sort to occur. She gave me apartments in a different wing and has not questioned my not accompanying her or, indeed, going out at all lately. I am getting the sneaking suspicion that she has known about this, and us."

He rolled his eyes. "Never underestimate old ladies. Let's be on our way." He dressed quickly, except for his cravat, waistcoat, and jacket. Those he threw over his shoulder. "I'll send your maid to you and meet you downstairs."

Punt was waiting when Rupert opened the door. She raised a brow and he nodded.

Vivian watched the pair. What was that all about?

He'd just got his jacket on when they came down the stairs. "The coach is ready. If you don't mind, I'll ride back with you."

Vivian tucked her hand in the crook of his arm. "I wouldn't have it any other way."

When they arrived in Mount Street, Silvia, Nick, a young gentleman Vivian didn't know, and Clara were drinking tea.

"Here they are now." She rose to greet Vivian and Rupert. "Our other betrothed couple."

"She must have mice that spy on people," Rupert whispered. Then loud enough for the others to hear, he said, "Indeed we are."

Nick shook Rupert's hand and Silvia hugged Vivian.

Nick and the young man had sprung to their feet.

"Please meet Mr. Octavius Trevor, one of our Mr. Trevor's brothers. He is currently on his way to take up a living outside of Birmingham and has agreed to perform your ceremonies if you have no objection."

"One of his many brothers." The young man laughed easily. "After the first two were born, he ran out of names."

Rupert glanced hopefully down at Vivian, a question in his eyes. No matter what he wished, he was giving her the power to choose. In the short time she had known Rupert, he had shown her more respect and given her more freedom than she had ever had in her life.

She smiled up at him. "I do not mind if you don't. This is your first marriage, where I have had a large wedding."

"The only thing that matters to me is spending my life with you."

"It is settled then." Vivian turned to her cousin. "Lord Stanstead and I would love to have Mr. Trevor officiate."

Clara glanced at Nick and Silvia. "You two are excused for your carriage ride in the Park." After Nick closed the door, Clara continued. "When would you like to marry?"

"The day after to-morrow," Rupert and Vivian said at the same time. She added, "We don't wish to interfere with Nick and Silvia's plans."

"Excellent." Clara beamed. "You'll make it an early evening tonight. To-morrow we shall all attend Lady Jersey's ball. It will be the event of the Season and the perfect time to let the *ton* know of Beresford and Silvia's marriage and your betrothal. Vivian, if you will allow Rupert to return to his home, we may discuss the details."

"My lady," Rupert said. "Excuse me, but I wish to take Vivian with me when I tell my parents and cousin."

For a moment Clara appeared flustered. "Of course, how could I have forgotten they are in Town? Vivian, we shan't have much time to prepare."

Vivian leaned down and bussed her cousin's cheek. "Feel free to make the plans. I'll be happy with whatever you decide to do. The only preference I have is the time. I would like the service to be at ten o'clock."

"As you wish, my dear." Clara kissed Vivian.

"Mr. Trevor," Rupert said as he and Vivian were about to leave, "may we give you a ride anywhere?"

"No, thank you. My eldest brother's carriage will be here to pick up Septimius and me. You may know him. His courtesy title is the Marquis of Hawksworth."

Rupert tilted his head. "I do indeed; not well, but we've met several times. He is a close acquaintance of Lord Beresford's. Is there a reason you do not use your title?"

"They were in the same army unit together." The young man grinned. "In a professional environment, I have found the title to be more of a burden than an asset. As has my brother, I might add."

Rupert's brows drew together. "I know very few heirs who have been allowed a commission. Did you have a brother who was the eldest?"

"No. Our father doesn't believe in heirs in waiting. We are all expected to have an occupation. I, of course, was too young to know, but I have been told that when Hawksworth wasn't interested in learning land management, Papa bought him a pair of colors."

"I was army mad myself. Unfortunately, my grandfather wasn't of the same opinion." Rupert took Vivian's arm. "We shall see you in the morning."

"I sometimes forget," Vivian said, "how small the *ton* truly is."

They were half-way to the gate to the mews, when he stopped, drew her into his arms, and kissed her. "You do realize that less than a century ago they would have burned your cousin as a witch."

She giggled, feeling giddy for the first time in years. "She would have been too smart for them to catch. I would ask how she knew, but I don't think I wish to know the answer."

"I agree."

"Tell me, what type of greeting may I expect from your mother and step-father?"

Rupert waited until he and Vivian were in the carriage before answering her question. "The first thing you should know is that he is my natural father, not merely my step-father."

"Oh my. If you would rather not tell me, I'll understand."

"No, you will shortly be my wife, and it is no secret to the family." The coach started forward, and he took her hand, more for his comfort than hers. Other than Robert's wife, Serena, who'd been there when all the details had come to light, Vivian would be the first outsider to know. "The short story is that my mother and father were in love when they were young. She became pregnant with me. He was at Oxford and had not a clue of her condition. My maternal grandfather, Lord Beaumont, discovered her situation. He and his good friend Lord Stanstead arranged a marriage between the Stansteads' son and my mother."

"But why not simply tell your father?"

"He was second in line to a modest barony. Stanstead's son would never have children." Rupert paused, trying to think of a not-so-shocking way to put it. "He preferred men."

"I've read about that," Vivian said mildly and squeezed his hand.

"It's not as uncommon as some think. That wasn't the worst of it. He had friends who were sick. One of them liked children." Only his mother knew what he was about to tell Vivian next. "We spent most of our time at Stanstead, where my grandfather—" God help him, even after all Lord Stanstead had done, Rupert still thought of him as his grandfather. "When I was six, Mama and I were visiting Town, and her husband came to the town house late one evening accompanied by a friend. I woke up with the man standing over my bed. The falls of his breeches were undone."

Vivian clasped her hand to her mouth and gasped.

"Fortunately, one of my nursemaids slept nearby, and she woke screaming. Nurse—you'll meet her when we go to Stanstead—went after him with a fireplace poker. Mama had decided to sleep on the nursery floor, and she came running in. Her husband and his friend were made to leave, and early the next morning, we returned to Stanstead. Grandpapa sent his son overseas. A few years later we received confirmation of his death. So you see"—he grinned at Vivian— "I'm quite happy that Edward Malfrey is my father."

"I completely understand," Vivian said primly. "I would be as well. It is a shame you cannot acknowledge him as such."

"I'm glad you understand." Rupert raised their still clasped hands and kissed her knuckles. The coach came to a stop. "Don't be frightened. I'll be next to you the entire time." Unfortunately his parents weren't at their home, but visiting Serena and Robert. Rupert returned to the coach. "Berkeley Square."

"Why are we going there?" Vivian's voice held more than a note of panic.

"My cousin's house is on Berkeley Square. Don't tell me your family's house is as well?"

"Yes. I had almost forgot. I knew the Eveshams live on Grosvenor Square, but as that was the first entertainment I'd been to, I didn't catch the address. The last time I was at my family's townhome was six years ago, and then only for a short while."

"If you can remember the location, we shall drive by to see if your father's arrived yet."

She gave a nervous titter. "Only if I can slide down in the seat so no one can see me."

"Just sit back. I'll lean forward."

"I don't know the number, but it was directly across from Gunter's. I remember my father complaining about the traffic."

Using his cane, Rupert pounded on the hatch. "Drive around the square once."

"Who is the gentleman your father picked for you to marry?"

Vivian opened her mouth, made a face, then shook her head. "This is horrible. I was so angry, I started calling him Twiddlededum." Her fine blond brows drew together in thought. "The name began with a T and it was odd—Twiddlebury?"

Rupert slid his arm around her and chuckled. "Does Tewkesbury sound familiar?"

"That was it. Do you know him?"

"More I know of him. He gives his proxy for the Lords to friends. My grandfather knew his father, which means the man is likely in his forties. He has several children."

"That is what my mother wrote to me. She is not at all in favor of the match."

What more did Rupert know about the man? Dogs. "He breeds hunting dogs. My grandfather had a pair, but he only gives them to those he likes or wants something from."

"You now have the reason for the match." Vivian's voice was as hard as Portland stone, and bitter. "My father probably wants one of his dogs."

His mind boggled at the thought that a father would trade his daughter for a dog. Yet, Vivian seemed certain. It was a damned good thing they had found each other and would wed soon. "You'll be much better served by being a political hostess."

She nuzzled Rupert's shoulder. "Indeed I shall."

The carriage slowed.

He kissed the top of her head. "Carefully, look out, and tell me if you recognize the house."

"The one with the green door." She pressed her back into the squabs. "Do you see anything?"

"The knocker is still off the door."

Vivian heaved a sigh. "Thank God."

"Is your father that bad?"

"He is used to having his way, and I have never gone against him. If the past few years hadn't been so difficult, I probably would have simply accepted his choice of husband without argument. I dislike shouting, and that is how he gets his way."

Rupert had no problem confronting the bully, but he didn't want Vivian upset before she was his forever. Tewkesbury was most likely of the same ilk. If they weren't in Town yet, they wouldn't find her until after the wedding.

Once again the coach stopped. Rupert hopped down to the pavement, then lifted Vivian from the carriage. She had that frightened-deer look again. "There is nothing to worry about. They have already met you."

"I know." But not as Rupert's betrothed. As long as no one shouted in anger, Vivian would be fine. She squared her shoulders. She'd lived through hell with a man who didn't love her. No one would keep her apart from the man who did. "I'm ready."

A footman was on duty at the door. "I'll announce myself and my betrothed. You go fetch a bottle of my cousin's best champagne."

The young man bowed and gave an order to a younger footman.

Laughter and other loud noises floated down the corridor. How nice it would be to marry into a family who had fun together.

Rupert opened the door, standing aside to let her enter first. Two babies, one blond, the other a redhead of about the same age, were on the floor with their mothers and fathers, and there appeared to be a race going on. Although she couldn't tell if the fathers, who were on all fours, were racing or the babies were doing it. She and Rupert watched for a few moments, then the blond baby looked at Rupert, bounced on his bottom, and screeched, "Rupie, Rupie."

All eyes turned in Vivian's and Rupert's direction. He lifted the baby. "Vivian, allow me to introduce Mr. Daniel Malfrey. Dan, meet my betrothed, Vivian." Rupert smiled at her. "I don't think he's interested in titles yet."

She reached out and took the drooling baby. "A pleasure to meet you, Daniel."

The adults had scrambled to their feet. A woman she recognized as Rupert's mother strode over to them and embraced Vivian. "Welcome to the family, my dear."

Rupert's father—she could clearly see the resemblance now that she knew—slapped Rupert on the back. "Glad to see you figured it out."

Serena and Robert joined the group, and Serena hugged Vivian. "I thought it would turn out this way."

Robert shook Rupert's hand. "You were right," Rupert said. "It is a madness."

Vivian didn't understand that at all, but it didn't matter. What was important was they were all happy for Rupert and her.

The door opened and a butler followed by three footmen entered carrying champagne and glasses. Once the flutes were full and everyone had a glass, Edward, as she had been instructed to call him, raised his glass. "Congratulations to Rupert and Vivian. May you have a long and happy life together."

"When is the wedding?" Freddy asked.

"In the morning." Rupert slid his arm around Vivian. "There is no point in waiting."

"At Stanstead House or on Mount Street?"

"The wedding will be at Lady Telford's and the wedding breakfast at my house. Her ladyship sent a runner to inform my staff."

"You'll want to inspect the house." Freddy raised her brows at Rupert. "Shall we come with you?"

Vivian almost choked on her wine. "Now?"

"No time like the present." Freddy set her glass down. "Whitsun, have my coach brought round." The butler bowed and left the room. "Even though you are a widow, you'll not wish to be seen going into Rupert's residence without a chaperone. Serena and I shall accompany you for propriety's sake. Our husbands can take care of the children."

"After you see the house," Serena said, "we can go with you to Mount Street where you can change, and we'll all meet back here for dinner."

"Excellent." Robert gave a slow smile. "We can all tell Vivian stories about Rupert's childhood."

"Only the most embarrassing ones, I'm sure," Rupert shot back.

"Naturally. That's what families are good for. Have you told Grandmamma yet?"

Rupert grimaced. "I didn't think she was in Town."

"She arrived back today." Robert bounced his daughter. "Ever since she was introduced to that French modiste, she's been going to Paris for her wardrobe."

Rupert's arm tightened around Vivian's waist. "I suppose that will be our next stop."

"If you give me a moment," Serena said, "I'll send Grandmamma an invitation to dinner."

"My lady." Whitsun bowed from the doorway. "Your coach is waiting."

Once again, it was only a matter of minutes before they arrived at Rupert's house in Grosvenor Square. The door was opened by a white-haired butler who stood as erect as a soldier.

Rupert kept his palm on the small of Vivian's back. "Harlock, meet your new mistress, currently Lady Beresford."

The servant bowed. "We received the information about your marriage, and I speak for the entire staff when I say we have been a long time without a mistress, and it will be our pleasure to serve you."

"What he means," Freddy said dryly, "is that I never liked the place, which had nothing to do with the staff, and the last female to live here was Stanstead's grandmother."

Well, that was plain speaking. Vivian was glad Rupert had told her what had taken place here. She inclined her head to the butler. "I'm sure Lord Stanstead and I will put things to rights soon enough."

"This is your house, my lady," Rupert said firmly. "It is not for me to interfere with your management of it."

If only he knew how much that meant to her. She would thank him later, when they were alone. "In that case, is the housekeeper available? She might wish to accompany us as we tour the house."

"If you will consent to drink tea in the morning room, I shall have Mrs. Honiwell prepare what will be necessary."

"Thank you, Harlock. Rupert, lead the way."

No more than twenty minutes later their little coterie had consumed several delicious biscuits, most of a cake filled with nuts and fruit, and two pots of tea.

A plump woman in her middle years with light brown hair knocked on the door and curtseyed. "My lord?"

"Ah, there you are, Honey." Rupert stood, helping Vivian to rise from the low chaise. "My dear, allow me to present your house-keeper, Honiwell. Honey, my future wife, Lady Beresford."

The housekeeper curtseyed again. "A real pleasure, my lady." She smiled as if Vivian was the answer to all her prayers. "I have my note-book, if you'd like to begin with a short tour. We shall have a full inspection later, if you agree."

"Certainly." There wasn't time to-day to look at everything. "Perhaps in the next week or so."

"More likely after we return from our honeymoon." Rupert took Vivian's hand. "I have a surprise planned for you."

Her cheeks warmed in a blush. "What a time to tell me."

"I could hardly tell you before you agreed to marry me."

Her face was going to be beet red at this rate. Naturally, she would have thought he had meant to take Cleo. "Very true. How bad is the house?"

Rupert gave her a sly look, but Honiwell responded, "We've kept it clean, my lady, and the linens are in good repair, but there has been no one to select new hangings."

"Or furnishings or any of that sort of thing. Am I correct?"

"Yes, my lady."

"Rupert"—Freddy stood—"don't you have something to do in your study? I'm sure we shall go on much more quickly without you."

"As a matter of fact, I do." He bowed. "It has to do with my surprise."

"Devil," Vivian said to his back as he ambled out of the parlor.

Serena raised one brow. "For all that his name is Stanstead, he is truly a Beaumont."

Vivian and her future relations followed the housekeeper out of the room and up the stairs.

As they entered the first bedroom, Freddy pulled a face. "I must apologize to you. I did not raise my son to be interested in domestic matters. I had so little interest myself."

"No matter. I'm perfectly capable of taking them on." *Ecstatic* would be the word. Since Vivian was thirteen, she'd been looking forward to having a home to do with as she would. Beresford was a bitter blow. Yet, with Rupert by her side, she would move forward to a new and much better life.

CHAPTER TWENTY-SEVEN

Sun flooded Silvia's bedchamber. This was her wedding day. She couldn't believe that after having hated Nick for so long, she was finally going to become his wife. Not that it had been Nick's fault. Her father had a lot to answer for. She and Nick would deal with Papa later. This day was to be celebrated.

She had been dressed for the past several minutes, waiting for Vivian and Cousin Clara. Not long ago, Silvia had heard a carriage drive up to the front of the house, and she wondered how soon the visitors would leave.

The door opened and Cousin Clara entered in a froth of brightly colored shawls and skirts. "We are almost ready to go. Lord Beresford sent this over earlier." Clara opened a box. "For you to wear."

Silvia's jaw dropped. She'd never seen anything so striking. Displayed on a Prussian-blue velvet cloth was a necklace with pearls and rubies interspersed on three strands, matching earrings, and a bracelet. On closer inspection, the bracelet appeared to be new, but the other pieces were quite old. "Where did he find them?"

"I have no idea. They are not part of the Beresford jewels," Vivian said prosaically. "I brought you one of my blue handkerchiefs to borrow for today. I think Beresford has taken care of the old and the new."

Although Silvia knew it was customary for a gentleman to give his bride something on their wedding day, she hadn't given it any thought. The sense of a pleasant dream deserted her, leaving in its place an excitement she hadn't experienced since before Nick had left to return to the army. She wanted to jump up and down and skip as she had as a child. "Someone put them on me, please."

Clara chuckled. "Give me a moment." She made Silvia sit at the dressing table before fastening the necklace.

All Silvia could do was gaze in the mirror. "I feel different, as if I'm no longer a single lady."

"If you're going to wear the rest, don them." Clara's voice was slightly hoarse. "Beresford will be waiting."

Silvia quickly inserted the gold wires through her ears and slid the bracelet on her wrist. "I'm ready."

Even though Cousin Clara had offered the use of her house for the wedding, and Mr. Trevor had agreed to officiate, in the end Silvia and Nick had decided to have the service performed at St. George's. She might still be angry at her father, but she had been raised a rector's daughter and church was where she wanted to be for her wedding.

Nick, his friend Lord Hawksworth, and Lord Stanstead were already at St. George's when she, Clara, and Vivian arrived. Nick glanced up as they entered through a side door, and gave her a crooked grin. Dressed in black and snowy white, he'd never looked so handsome.

He held out his hand. "Shall we begin?"

"Yes, I'm more than ready."

Silvia was radiant and exquisite, and Nick was going to have one hell of a time being civil to her father when they returned to Beresford. The old man had made them wait years for this moment. But right now, Nick was simply happy she was going to be his. Everything else could wait.

In typical Silvia fashion, she had wasted no time joining him. Her grip on his hand was sure and firm. She would make an excellent wife and countess. Most importantly, she would be his lover and the mother of his children.

"Who gives this woman to this man?"

Silvia seemed to grow taller as she gave the clergyman a look and said, "I give myself to him."

"Umm, most unusual." The man coughed. "My lord?"

Stanstead raised a brow, ready to step in if needed.

Nick gave an imperceptible shake of his head. "Is there a law against it?"

"No, but—well."

Silvia's lovely chin had turned mulish. He had no doubt she was prepared to argue canon law with the vicar.

"In that case, she will give herself away."

The man coughed. "Very well. Nicholas James . . ."

After they signed the register, he gathered her into his arms. "I'm glad you're my wife."

She rose on her toes and kissed him. "I'm glad you're my husband."

"We have a pathetically small wedding breakfast waiting for us."

"We'll have a larger celebration when we go home to Beresford."

He placed a light kiss on her lips. "You think of everything."

Silvia grinned and Nick saw the sun, moon, and stars at the same time. "I do, don't I?"

"Come along, minx. We need champagne."

"Yes, I rather think we might."

Their wedding breakfast included the same people who were at the church, but Lady Telford had done a splendid job of hosting a small but elegant feast.

An hour later, when Silvia and Nick were departing for his house, he finally got to kiss his new bride. "Do you really want to attend Lady Jersey's ball?"

Silvia's lips formed a pout. "Under other circumstances, no, but Cousin Clara is correct. It is the perfect time for the *ton* to see us married. After all, we cannot leave Town until after Vivian and Lord Stanstead are wed."

Nick stifled a sigh. "At least we have the rest of the day."

As soon as they arrived at his house, he introduced her to his small staff, and escorted her to their bedchamber.

Nick had waited for this moment for years. He, Silvia, and a bed.

He gave her time alone to change when he would rather have undressed her himself. Yet he must be careful not to alarm her; she was a rector's daughter, after all, and had thought kisses could make her pregnant.

He knocked, strode into the room, and stopped. She was the most beautiful woman he'd ever seen. Her blue-black hair tumbled to her waist over the highly embroidered gown. When he'd looked his fill, he closed the distance between them. Removing his cravat, he kissed her. But instead of letting him take the lead, she put her hands on his chest and began pushing off his jacket.

"Silvia, love. Slow down."

"Take it off. I'm already in my nightgown, and you haven't even undressed."

"I didn't wish to scare you," he said in his defense. What in blazes had got into her? Her hands went to the placket of his breeches. One by one the buttons were unfastened. This was truly going to be a shock. "You might wish to wait."

His waistcoat was shoved down over his arms, and she tugged at his shirt. "Take it off."

"Silvia, have you any idea what you're doing?"

"Of course I do. Cousin Clara explained everything."

"Never let it be said I don't give you what you want." He toed off his shoes and pushed down his breeches while bending over to allow her to remove his shirt. Once he was naked as the day he was born, he started unbuttoning her nightgown. "How many blasted buttons does this thing have?"

"I don't know. I made it too long ago to remember." Her voice was breathy as she rubbed her palms over his chest, playing with the hairs covering it.

"Silvia, I can't get the blasted buttons undone."

She pushed his fumbling fingers away but had no better luck than he had, and grabbing both sides of the gown, ripped apart the fine muslin fabric.

For several long moments he could only stare at her as full, dark-tipped breasts greeted him. Finally he found his voice again. "Oh God! You are gorgeous."

A blush rose in Silvia's cheeks. Not as worldly as she thought she was. All the better for him. He stroked her back, over her lush bottom, and smiled as she moaned. He nibbled her full, deep-rose bottom lip, encouraging her to open for him. When she figured out what he wanted, he dived in, exploring the warm cavity. Soon their tongues were dancing and battling. This is how it would always be with them.

Sweeping her into his arms, he threw her onto the bed and jumped in after her. Suddenly, it creaked ominously.

"Nick, I think we should go to another room."

"It will be fine. Kiss me."

The next thing he knew the mattress, with them on top, collapsed to the floor. "Damn, blasted thing."

"Watch your language."

Then the sound of wood popping shot through the air. "Damn!"

Grabbing Silvia, Nick rolled them off the bed just before the heavy wooden canopy came crashing down.

For a moment she was so still he thought she'd been injured. "Silvia, talk to me."

"Truly." Her tone was so calm it almost scared him. "Nicholas Beresford, you do not wish to know what I would say."

"No." He grimaced. "You're probably right."

Sun streamed through the window, and someone started pounding on the door. "My lord, is everything all right?"

Blackford. His butler.

"Give me a minute." Nick rummaged in his wardrobe and found a robe for Silvia, then donned his breeches. "Come."

The door opened a crack at first. Blackford's eyes widened. "What happened?"

"The blasted bed crashed, that's what happened." Nicholas raked his fingers through his hair. "Did you or anyone else bother to inspect this furniture in the past twenty years?"

Looking affronted, his butler replied, "That is the housekeeper's job, my lord."

"Where the devil is she?"

"We haven't had one since Mrs. Murray went to live with her daughter."

"When was that?"

"Before the old lord stopped coming to Town."

Silvia began to laugh. "Nick, how could you not notice you had no housekeeper?"

"I don't know," he muttered. "I've never had to bother with one before. My mother always dealt with them."

Casting her eyes to the ceiling, Silvia shook her head. "Blackford, which of the bedchambers are fit for use?"

"This is the only one left on this floor."

"I'm going to murder someone." Nick was rapidly losing control of his temper. "Why the devil didn't you tell me?"

His butler straightened. "It is not—"

"Your job." He strode over to the window before he said something he shouldn't. Why of all times did the bloody bed have to break on his wedding day? Part of the fallen canopy caught his eye. "Worms. I wonder how much of the furniture is rotten?"

"That will be all, Blackford. Please call my maid and his lordship's valet." Silvia crouched down and inspected the bed. "This has been going on for a while." She rose. "The only thing to do is go to Cousin Clara's. She has more than enough room."

"We can go to the Pulteney."

"I would not feel comfortable at a hotel." Wrapping her arms around him, she leaned her head against his chest. "She'll understand. To-morrow we can look at some warehouses for pieces that are already built, then order the rest." She reached up and pulled his head down. "We shall be fine. Come, husband, I still want you to bed me."

"Vixen." Despite his foul mood, Nick smiled. "You would have made a fine soldier's wife."

"I know. Let's find different quarters, Colonel. We still have a ball to attend."

Shortly before eight that evening, Rupert descended from his town coach and up the steps of Lady Telford's home. He had distressing news for her, and wasn't looking forward to her reaction.

Barnes opened the door. "Good evening, my lord. Her ladyship will be down shortly."

"Is Lady Telford here?"

"She and the new Lady Beresford are in the drawing room. I'll announce you."

What the devil was Silvia Beresford doing here? Had Nick angered her already? "Thank you."

"Stanstead, good to see you." Nick greeted him with a glass of wine. "I know you must be surprised to see me, but the thing is"—the man actually flushed—"we had a mishap and are staying here until the house can be redone."

Rupert moved toward the sofa, only to see Silvia blushing a deep red. "Lady Telford, Lady Beresford, good evening."

"Don't mind them." Lady Telford shook her head at the younger couple. "Never thought I'd see a military man turn missish. Their bed broke, and it turned out most of the furniture was rotten. That's what happens when a house doesn't have a mistress."

"Cousin Clara!" Silvia blushed even harder if that was possible.

Rupert gave brief thanks to the deity that his furniture was still sound, and struggled not to laugh. "I'm sorry to hear that."

"Better check your own, Stanstead," the older woman remarked caustically.

"Yes, ma'am."

"Rupert."

Vivian entered the drawing room. Every day she was lovelier. He kissed her cheek before leading her to the window seat. "Your father has arrived. I drove around Berkeley Square before coming to fetch you. The lights were on and the knocker is back on the door."

She gave a tight nod, and drew a breath. "That is unfortunate. Clara, I believe you will be having a meeting of some Ladies' Benevolent Society here in the morning."

Rupert was all at sea. What the deuce was she talking about? "I'm happy his arrival hasn't thrown you into a panic, but why would you want your cousin to have a houseful of women when we are marrying to-morrow?"

"Not a real one." Vivian giggled. "Father is terrified of groups of women. Particularly of ladies who do good works. He will leave his card and slink away until it is safe to return."

"And by then, we'll be at my house for the wedding breakfast."

"Exactly. I decided there was no reason to be afraid of him." She smiled, and Rupert wanted to take her in his arms and kiss her in front of everyone. "I've made my decision. I signed the settlement agreements, and there is really nothing, other than bluster, he can do about it. He'll simply have to find another dog."

"This is not the first time you have mentioned a dog. What does an animal have to do with all of this?" Clara stared at Vivian as if she'd lost her sense. After a moment, she must have finally understood. She snapped her wineglass down. "Tewkesbury. Of course. I should have made the connection before now. That cur. Your father should breed himself to a dog. I would like to say I cannot believe he would trade his daughter for a bitch, but that is exactly what the muttonheaded idiot did, is it not?"

Vivian nodded, but Rupert was pleased to see that she did not seem nearly as upset as she had earlier.

"Isn't he the fellow who has the prize hunting hounds?" Nick asked.

"The very one," Rupert replied, ready to strangle Vivian's father. "But you'd better be prepared to give up your firstborn daughter for the privilege of owning one."

"Well, of all the corked-brained ideas," Silvia added. "I cannot believe, in this modern time, he'd do such a thing."

"I can." Clara tugged the bell-pull. A moment later, Barnes entered. "Please ask Lady Beresford's maid to pack everything but what she'll need to-morrow. Notify the coachman that I want them removed to Stanstead house this evening." She shifted her gaze to Vivian and Rupert. "Your father may have a louder bark than he does a bite, but Tewkesbury is another matter. He can be a nasty customer."

Vivian paled, but she straightened her shoulders. "I will not be afraid of him."

Lady Telford's lips formed a straight line. "Stanstead, I suggest you take yourself off to White's after dinner this evening before you attend the ball. If Tewkesbury is in Town, he'll be there. You'll want to know what he is saying."

Rupert would take his father and cousin as well. "Yes, ma'am."

She shooed them out the door. "Have a good time and give your grandmother my regards."

Once they were in the carriage, Rupert took Vivian's hand in his. "I'm sorry."

"It's not your fault."

"Trust me to protect you."

She tilted her head and kissed him. "I shall."

Whatever happened to-night, by to-morrow at this time he'd be a married man, and no one would stop him.

After they arrived at his parents' house, Rupert took his father and Robert aside, and explained what Lady Telford had advised him to do.

By the time he'd finished, Mama, Serena, and Silvia had joined them.

"I've sent a message to the kitchen that we'd like to dine as soon as possible." His mother squeezed his father's arm. "You will go with Rupert?"

"I, and Robert as well. We'll return in plenty of time to escort you to Lady Jersey's ball."

"Do any of you actually know Lord Tewkesbury?" Despite what Clara had recommended, it seemed to be a great waste of time to be waiting for the man when none of them could recognize him.

"I do," Edward Malfrey replied. "Enough to point him out."

Rupert took Vivian aside. "We won't be long. I simply wish to see if the man has mentioned the betrothal."

CHAPTER TWENTY-EIGHT

Rupert, his father, and Robert Beaumont sat in the main room at White's, waiting for the large dining room to thin of company. Robert had gone to look at the wagering book when Nick and Hawksworth entered.

"We thought we'd join you."

"Even if the man's here, I don't expect fisticuffs." Rupert was beginning to think all this was for naught. "I'm surprised your bride let you out of the house."

"She practically pushed me through the door. Lady Telford's information about Tewkesbury may not have worried Vivian, but Silvia is determined to protect her."

Robert reclaimed his seat. "Rupert, you're in the book. The wager was running in your favor to marry Lady Beresford. This evening it changed to Tewkesbury."

"Now we know he is making the match known." Nick glanced around. "Is he here?"

"I'd say there is a good chance of it." Papa stopped a waiter, and whispered something. "There are too many guests in the dining room to see if he's present."

Nick and Hawksworth pulled chairs up, and a few moments later, a bottle of claret was set in their midst.

Rupert checked his pocket watch. This was becoming ridiculous. "I am not going to hunt him down. I have nothing to say to the man. The only reason I came was to ascertain if there was any talk. Which there appears to be. If we don't leave soon, we'll be late escorting the ladies."

Two gentlemen Rupert knew only by name sauntered, brandies in hand, to the book. "Too bad for Stanstead, looks like Tewkesbury is going to have the lady."

Rupert's hands clenched. He was not going to react. He reached for his glass.

"Stanstead, didn't see you there." The words were slurred, as if the man had already imbibed a great deal. "Sorry about your luck."

He raised his glass. "Things will turn out as they should."

"Always maintain your countenance. Good man. Young yet. Plenty of time to get a leg-shackle."

The drunk and his friend wandered off. Several minutes later, a stocky man, not much above medium height, who reminded Rupert of his local squire, strolled in. "Stanstead?"

"I'm afraid you have the advantage, sir."

"Should've known it was nothing but a hum."

"I beg your pardon?" He set his drink back down.

"Damn me if you don't look like old Lord Beaumont when you look like that. Don't see much of Stanstead in you though."

Next to Rupert his father stiffened.

"I'm said to favor my mother."

"That happens. Some of mine look like their mothers as well." The man tucked his thumbs into the top of his breeches, leaning back like a strutting rooster.

"And you are?" This could only be Lord Tewkesbury. Still, the question had to be asked.

"Viscount Tewkesbury. Thought you might remember me. Then again, you were just a pup at the time."

Rupert reclaimed his glass and took a healthy draw. "You must excuse me, I do not remember. Have you just returned to Town?"

"No returned about it, my lad. Don't like the place. I'm only here to collect a new bitch."

The room had become quiet, and Tewkesbury's voice seemed to echo through it.

"Indeed." Rupert held up his goblet as if admiring the color of the wine. "I seem to remember you are famous for your dogs. I wasn't aware anyone was keeping them in Town."

"Not a hunting dog. Got all of them I need right now. I'm talking about Lord Brackford's daughter, Lady Beresford."

Something in Rupert shifted and he was closer to calling a man out than he'd ever been before. That, though, would not help Vivian.

"Here, here, man. Shouldn't be referring to a lady as a female dog," a gentleman said.

"No insult meant." Tewkesbury swayed back, and Rupert wondered if the man was in his altitudes. "All females serve the same purpose, breeding and companionship."

Rupert started forward, but Hawksworth placed a hand on Rupert's shoulder. "You are insulting, sir." Hawksworth's tone was deadly calm. "I do not yet have a wife, but I assure you I would not stand by and listen to anyone call her a bitch. I think you might wish to leave before someone takes offense."

At that point, the porter, followed by two footmen, approached Tewkesbury. "My lord, unless you apologize, I must ask you to depart the club. One of our board members has complained."

For a moment, Rupert thought the cur would resist, but after some coaxing from one of the other gentlemen, Tewkesbury left.

"Thank you."

Hawksworth shrugged. "Someday you might do the same for me. If you need help in a fight though, Beresford's your man." He tossed off his brandy. "I'll see you at the ball."

"You shall."

CHAPTER TWENTY-NINE

Vivian glanced at the clock and began to pace. "What could be keeping them?"

"Any number of things." Freddy patted the seat next to her. "Wearing yourself out with worry won't help."

"Very true." Serena pressed a glass of sherry into Vivian's trembling hands. "Sherry will help calm you. Robert and Edward are with him."

A few moments later the sounds of male voices floated in from the hall.

She drank half of the glass in one long draw. "They are back."

"See." Freddy smiled, and Vivian knew how lucky she was to be gaining such a wonderful mother-in-law. "Finish your wine and we'll go. The last thing we want is for them to settle in."

Rupert strolled into the drawing room, and his gaze went directly to her. Vivian still could not believe her luck; in the morning she would be his wife.

He didn't bother with the regular greetings, but simply placed her hand on his arm. "It is time to show the world we are betrothed."

"I agree."

Edward glanced at her. "How long do you wish to remain?"

"Clara suggested we remain about an hour."

"Perfect." Freddy took her husband's arm. "We have a busy day to-morrow."

"And an early one," Serena agreed.

Shortly after they arrived at Lady Jersey's ball, Rupert bent his head, his breath caressing her ear. "Dance with me in the garden."

That sounded wonderful, and romantic, and scandalous. "Won't we shock the other guests?"

"We're betrothed. We'll set a new fashion."

Vivian wasn't prepared to go that far yet. Perhaps when they were husband and wife she would have the courage. "I'll meet you out there."

"As you wish, but the next time we dance in the garden, we'll go out together." He glanced at a corridor leading off the ballroom. "Go that way, you'll find the second room has access to the terrace." He raised her hand and kissed it. "Don't be long."

Vivian gazed after him as he strolled away. A few moments later, she excused herself, found the corridor and the room. Just as Rupert had said, a French window led to the terrace. He was already there when she arrived. The strains of a violin began as he escorted her down the stairs and put his palm on her waist.

Nightingales sang and the scent of night-blooming jasmine filled the air. "I think I am falling even more in love with you."

"I know I'm more in love with you." His lips grazed her forehead. "Morning can't come soon enough."

"Nor for me."

"It is so wonderful to have Hector home!" Emily gushed.

Cressida had been happy to see her brother as well, but Emily had been gushing so much, Cressida was practically sick with it. "He said he was bringing me a present, but I haven't seen it yet."

Emily gave a sly smile. "He will be here shortly, and you shall see it. I promise you'll be vastly pleased."

The only thing that *vastly* pleased her was that Lord Stanstead was finally here, and this might be her only chance to make him marry her. "I'm sure I will. Hector always knows what I like."

Emily glanced around. "What can be keeping them?"

"Papa is most likely talking about politics to him."

Lord Stanstead had been talking with that Lady Beresford again, but now he was making his way toward the French doors that made up one wall of the massive ballroom. Cressida prayed with all her might that he would go into the garden. "I must go to the ladies' retiring room."

Emily bit her bottom lip, glancing around again. "I should accompany you."

"I'll not be long." Cressida tried for a carefree manner. "You wait for Hector. In any event, Mama is with that group of ladies not far from the corridor."

"Very well, but do not be long."

"I won't." And perhaps Cressida would have her own surprise when she returned.

Keeping her eye on Lord Stanstead, she skirted groups of ladies and gentlemen until she reached the end of the ballroom. Although he appeared to be in no hurry, stopping and exchanging greetings with his friends, he definitely seemed to be focused on the terrace. She must get there before anyone else met him, or her entire life would be ruined.

Lord Stanstead finally reached the French doors and ambled through them. Now was her chance. Keeping her pace slower than she wanted to, Cressida strolled onto the terrace, but he wasn't there. A sound drew her gaze to the garden, and she quickened her steps. Just as she was about to descend the stairs, an arm came around her waist, pulling her back.

It had better not be Hector. "Let me go. What do you think you're doing?"

"Stopping you from making the biggest mistake of your life," a man whose voice she didn't recognize said.

Whirling around, she was surprised to be facing nothing but a waistcoat and the ends of a neckcloth. She raised her gaze from the gold thread in his waistcoat to the snowy cravat, to a deeply tanned and incredibly stern face. "Who are you, and what right do you have to interfere with me?"

Without a by-your-leave, he turned her around and pointed. In the garden, Lord Stanstead and Lady Beresford were waltzing. "They are betrothed."

Cressida could have cried with frustration. "You've ruined everything!"

An amused smirk appeared on his face. "I doubt that."

"There you are." Hector's voice caught her attention. What was going on? He glanced at the man holding her. "Oh, I see you found her."

"Indeed I did." The gentleman's tone held no humor at all. "Doing exactly what Miss Woolerton thought she was up to. I am not at all sure this was a good idea after all."

"An infatuation, nothing more. Probably due to the stress of the

Season. She has had her queer starts, but in general she is a level-headed girl. You'll see."

Cressida closed her eyes, trying to make sense of their conversation. "Are you referring to me?"

"Forgive me, Cressy. I almost forgot you were there," Hector said in a voice that told her he was more put out with her than sorry, and had not forgot for a moment she was present. "Allow me to introduce you to Lord Kenington."

Her stomach sank, and a sick feeling rose into her throat. "The gentleman you met up with who has been traveling with you?"

"The very same." Hector gave her a warning look. "After I showed him the miniature I carry of you and some of your letters, he decided he would very much like to meet you."

Oh. Dear. God. This must be the "present" her brother had brought back. The Marquis of Kenington. No wonder Papa had been so set against Lord Stanstead, and Mama had not been concerned when he'd not shown Cressida much attention.

Emily had been right. Cressida should have been more careful. She held out her hand. "A pleasure, my lord."

He dutifully bowed over her hand. "At long last, Miss Banks."

As they reentered the ballroom and he glanced down at her, disapproval filled his green eyes. "As your brother mentioned, from his description and your letters, I thought I'd be meeting a woman, not a little girl bent on ruining the lives of others for her own pleasure."

He'd pitched his voice so low only she could hear him. For that she was thankful. Her cheeks burned with shame. No one had ever spoken to her like that. The problem was, despite being warned, she had been heedless and deserved to have a peal rung over her head. "I'm sorry."

Hector glanced back. "I know you two will have a great deal to discuss."

"We will indeed," Lord Kenington responded.

Cressida wanted to go home and hide in her bed. If she ruined this, her parents and brother would never forgive her. She would accept responsibility for her mistake and go on as if it was in the past. "I look forward to our conversations, my lord."

He glanced down, one black brow rising slowly. "I doubt that very much."

* * *

Rupert took his parents home before driving to Mount Street with Vivian.

"Will you come in and have a glass of brandy or tea?"

His arm snaked around her waist. "I have something to do, but it won't take long. Wait for me?"

She cupped his cheek in her palm. "Forever."

A half hour later, Vivian heard the front door open, and rushed into the hall. "Rupert, Nick is here. He told us what happened." She took his hands, holding them against her face. "I am so proud of you for not calling that dreadful man out."

They reached the door to the drawing room, but before she could open it, Rupert was kissing her. "I won't say I didn't consider it, but it would have harmed your reputation, and I could not have that."

"Thank you." She gazed into his eyes and saw all the love she now knew she had been missing, not only in her marriage but her whole life. "He must have been horrible. Even Nick had to dance around what was said."

"In a few hours it won't matter."

Vivian smiled at Rupert, and a peace settled over her. "It doesn't matter now. If only we didn't have to wait until morning to wed."

"Vivian, my love, I need to be with you."

They couldn't go to Hill Street, but she did have a wing of this house to herself. Clara had put Silvia and Nick at the opposite end of her wing. The only question was, how scandalized would Clara be if she discovered Rupert in Vivian's bedchamber? They were going to be married soon. "You must come in for a while; everyone is expecting you. But later, my maid will meet you at the garden gate."

Concern lurked in his eyes. "Come home with me, where I can keep you safe."

Oh, she wanted to, but that would upset her cousin. "You know I cannot, and it is not fair to ask it of me."

"You're right." He kissed her forehead. "Promise me you won't even step outside the house after I leave. Not even with a footman."

"That I can vow." She stroked his jaw. The light growth of his beard made it rougher than usual. "The next time I enter the wider world it will be as your wife."

"Thank you."

He bent his head to her again, and the door opened. Silvia's eyes rounded. "I'm sorry. It's just that you were taking so . . ."

"It's fine." Vivian almost laughed at her friend's expression. "We'll come in now."

"Sweetheart." Nick smirked. "I did suggest you leave them alone." This time, Silvia didn't rise to his bait. "And you were correct."

As they entered the drawing room, Lady Telford called for more wine. "After what Beresford told us, I am inclined to move the wedding up by an hour or more. Normally your father would have to come here to Telford House in order to discover my whereabouts, but with Tewkesbury"—she raised her lips in a sneer—"around, they might already know. I can't think they will come before ten o'clock, but one is better safe than sorry."

"If Mr. Trevor can be here by then, I agree." Vivian glanced at Rupert. "What do you think?"

"I'll send a message to my parents and cousins. They wish to attend the ceremony and won't care what time we have it."

"Stanstead." Clara looked more troubled than she had previously. "You should spend the night here. Your valet may bring your clothing over, and I'll have my housekeeper make up the rooms."

Vivian showed him to the writing desk, and in short order the notes had been sent by messenger.

"Clara, thank you for being so understanding."

"I'm merely attempting to keep any fighting that may occur to a minimum." Her tone was as proper as could be, but her gaze slid to Rupert. "On the other hand, I wouldn't blame Stanstead at all if he planted someone a well-deserved facer."

Later that evening, after everyone had gone to bed, Vivian took her bedside candle and walked to Rupert's chamber.

He was still awake, naked, and so wonderfully handsome. "I was coming to you."

She placed the candle holder on a table. "I thought you might, but it is easier for me to be wandering around than it is for you."

Rupert gathered her into his arms. "I missed holding you."

She leaned against him, giving him her weight, enjoying his strong arms and muscular body. "I know. This will be the last night we must sneak around."

The palm of his hand stroked her from the nape of her neck to her derrière, sparking a fire down her back.

"Umm." Vivian teased his lips with her tongue. "Make love to me, my lord."

"Gladly, my lady." Holding her hand, Rupert led her to the bed and slowly untied the ribbons of Vivian's nightgown. Opening the neck, he kissed each bit of her skin as he exposed it. By the time he reached her breasts, she was about to expire with unadulterated lust.

"Rupert, please, I can't wait."

"No?" His lips curved. "I thought you might want a sample of what I have planned for you to-morrow."

"This will kill me." She lay down on the bed, pulling him on top of her. "Someday I shall learn how to drive you to distraction."

"You already do."

Vivian held him tightly as he kissed her again. Wrapping her legs around his slim waist, she urged him to join with her. Before long, she was shuddering with completion, and Rupert plunged more deeply than he ever had before, wringing the most out of her pleasure before collapsing off to her side. For a few minutes, he cuddled her in his arms as their breathing slowed.

"Vivian, how did you know about the Hill Street house?"

She rolled over, lying half on his chest. "I had asked for a list of estates, and it had mistakenly been added."

"I find that extremely odd. Who were the property agents?"

"Jones."

"My love. I have a feeling"—his chest rumbled with laughter—"your cousin has been conspiring to help us."

"I think you may be right. I found it strange that she would put me in a separate wing."

"And when you didn't oblige her by taking advantage of it, the house appeared."

"How . . . how devious of her. Although, I don't understand why she did it."

Rupert covered her lips with his, kissing her sweetly. "She reminds me of my grandmother. They were raised in an earthier time. Yet I think she knew you needed to find a gentleman to love you."

CHAPTER THIRTY

A soft tapping at the door woke Vivian. Rupert's arms were around her and she was curled up next to him.

"My lady?" Punt said softly as she opened the door. "I must get you ready."

Rupert kissed Vivian. "I'll send her out in a moment." As Punt withdrew, he threw the covers off them. "My love, you need to dress for our wedding."

She went to grab the sheets back, but couldn't find them. "What time is it?"

"Almost six."

Vivian sat up, rubbing her eyes. "Two hours."

Getting up from his side of the bed, Rupert came around and pulled her up. "Less than that. You'll soon be mine forever."

"And you'll be mine." Vivian wrapped her arms around him, seeking his warmth. "I'd better go."

She broke her fast while the tub was being readied. Punt insisted on washing Vivian's hair, which had to then be dried. She'd never be ready in time. It was not until shortly before eight that she was finally at the dressing table having her hair dressed.

"I've never known you to fidget like this," Punt scolded. "But I suppose all brides get a case of the nerves."

Vivian hadn't been at all anxious about her first wedding. She had been too innocent to know better. Yet even now, her unease was not about marrying Rupert but that something or someone would stop her from doing so. "I'll try to be still."

Punt slipped light blue, apatite-tipped pins into her hair.

"Where did those come from?"

"Miss Silvia."

Vivian should have known. "New and blue, or borrowed?"

"New. Her ladyship sent a comb that's old and borrowed." Punt stepped back. "You'll do."

Vivian glanced into the mirror. Her curls shone like they had never done before. "What did you use in my hair?"

"A bit of oil her ladyship gave me. Do you like it?"

"It makes a great deal of difference."

The clock struck eight and Vivian almost came off the bench. "I'm late."

"Has no one told you the bride is never late?" Clara stood in the doorway. "Unless she doesn't appear at all." She stepped off to the side. "Stanstead's family is here, and he is champing at the bit."

Vivian expected to feel her heart pounding with nerves, but nothing but calm came over her. No matter her fears, neither Rupert, or Clara, or any of the others would allow anything to stop the wedding. "I'm ready."

Rupert couldn't tear his gaze from Vivian as she glided into the drawing room, a vision in a gauzy white gown with silver netting, which set off her perfect complexion. Her cheeks were a delicate pink.

Robert punched him in the shoulder. "You're a lucky man."

"I am." As Vivian came up next to Rupert, he held out his hand, waiting until she placed her fingers in his palm, where he would keep them for the rest of their lives. "Two hours has never before seemed like an eternity."

Vivian graced him with a brilliant smile.

Mr. Octavius Trevor opened his prayer book. "Shall we begin?"

"Yes." Rupert was more than ready to have the deed done.

"Who will give her ladyship away?"

"I will." Nick strode to the makeshift altar. "As the head of Lady Beresford's soon-to-be former family, I'd like to do it." He glanced at Vivian. "If it's all right with you?"

"I'd be honored."

Rupert held Vivian's gaze and she held his as they promised to love, honor, and cherish one another. A stifled sob came from one of their guests as the rector pronounced them man and wife.

Once they signed the register, Lady Telford announced an early breakfast. "It will still be a few hours until the wedding breakfast, and I imagine everyone is hungry. Lord and Lady Stanstead may lead the way."

Vivian turned to face their families, and stopped. "Mama, when did you arrive?" She looked around in panic. "Is Father—"

"No." Her mother rushed forward and hugged her. "No. I came straight here." Lady Brackford held Vivian by the shoulders, tears streaming down the older woman's cheeks. "How beautiful you look, and happy. I can't remember when I've seen you so radiant."

"I'm glad you're here." Rupert let go of Vivian's arm long enough for her to embrace her mother. "I really do not wish to see Father though."

"I can't blame you. A more addlebrained idea he never had. You'd think he'd been reared in a cow byre."

"May we," Nick cut in, "insult him in the dining room? I'm famished."

"Indeed we may," Lady Telford pronounced. "Cook has outdone herself."

The sideboard was laden with dishes, everything from ham and beef to kedgeree. Pots of jam and butter that had been molded into flowers and fruits were on the table, as well as cakes and biscuits normally served for tea. Footmen scurried back and forth with pots of coffee and tea.

"We won't have to worry about eating at the wedding breakfast." Rupert leaned back in his chair at the foot of the table, replete.

Vivian turned her hand that was under his and gently squeezed his fingers. "Considering how many guests we shall have, that might be for the best."

Rupert had been concerned about the condition of his house, but his servants had scrubbed and polished the ballroom and other reception areas so that they sparkled. There had been no time to change the hangings, but all else would be ready. Vivian would have nothing to be ashamed of in her new home.

A loud rapping came from the front of the house, and a few minutes later Barnes entered the dining room and bowed. "My lady, Lords Brackford and Tewkesbury wish to speak with Lady Stanstead alone."

"Not a chance." Rupert rose. "I shall go to the hall."

"Stanstead, I have too many breakables there." Lady Telford calmly poured another cup of tea. "If you are afraid they may make off with

Vivian, the gentlemen may join us here. Barnes, escort their lordships to me with two extra footmen in the event they require assistance making their departure."

All the gentlemen around the table had pushed their chairs back and focused on the door. A few moments later, Tewkesbury and Vivian's father stood just inside the room, waiting.

Lord Brackford bowed to Lady Telford, then to the company at large. "I didn't realize you had company." His gaze focused on Vivian. "Let's go, my girl. You'll move home until the wedding."

She paled, but remained seated and raised her determined chin. "I'm sorry to disappoint you, Father, but the only place I shall remove to is my new house."

He glanced at Tewkesbury and smiled. "See, I told you she'd go along. Always has been a biddable puss." Brackford directed his attention back to Vivian. "No need for that. If you wish Tewkesbury here . . ." Vivian's father screwed up his face. "I didn't tell you who you'd be marrying."

"Father, I am already re-married. We shall shortly be leaving for the wedding breakfast."

A flush rose in the older man's face, mottling his already florid complexion. "Nonsense. No one has written me asking for your hand. I refuse to allow you to wed anyone else but Lord Tewkesbury. You will do as I say. His lordship and I have settled the business."

Rupert had had enough. Just how thickheaded was his new father-in-law? "My lord." Rupert waited until Brackford realized he'd been spoken to. "Vivian and I wed two hours ago." The other man stared at Rupert, his eyes glazing over as if he didn't understand. "She is now the Countess of Stanstead."

"But . . . but . . . I made a promise to Lord Tewkesbury."

At the other end of the table, Lady Telford looked down her nose at Vivian's father. "Lord Brackford, has it escaped your notice that Vivian was not only past her age of majority, but a widow as well? You had no business, indeed no right, to promise her to another without her consent."

The man stood stock still, jaw hanging as if in shock.

For the love of God. Rupert squeezed Vivian's hand. "Sweetheart, I know he's your father, but he must either give up this foolish notion and congratulate us on our marriage, or leave. I will not have him upsetting you in any way. Not to-day or in the future."

Tewkesbury, who had been surveying the room as he bounced on his toes, suddenly seemed to take notice. "You mean it's already done? You're leg-shackled?"

"Christ almighty," Nick swore. "What the devil do you think Stanstead has been saying? Are the both of you deaf and dumb?"

Tewkesbury turned red enough to have apoplexy and roared, "Brackford, you promised one bitch for another!"

This time, Rupert had no hesitation. Before the cur could spew another vile word, he punched the man in his stomach and then his nose. Tewkesbury swayed, then dropped to the ground, holding his cravat to his nose. "You struck me."

"Call my wife vulgar names again and I'll do worse than that. I've had enough of your offensive analogies. If you utter another insult concerning her, you may choose your second."

The older man propped himself up on his elbows. "See here, young man."

"I'd stop if I were you." Hawksworth, who had accompanied his brother Octavius, grinned wickedly. "Stanstead has one of the steadiest tempers I've ever seen, but I wouldn't count on his patience lasting. He may never have fought a duel, but I've never seen him lose, be it in the ring, pistols, or sword."

Lady Brackford, who also appeared to have had enough, rose from the table. "Henry Brackford, stop acting like a knock-in-the-cradle, rubbishing commoner. Be a man and get rid of this poor excuse for excrement. You may also congratulate your daughter on making a better match by herself than you could ever have made for her."

Not knowing what else Tewkesbury was capable of, Rupert stood over the man as he struggled to stand. "Barnes."

"Yes, my lord."

"Have his lordship escorted out."

"It would be my pleasure, my lord."

Barnes snapped his fingers and two burly footmen grabbed Tewkesbury's arms. "The *ton* will hear about this, my lord," Tewkesbury shouted down the corridor.

"Good." Rupert was proud he kept his voice even. "Then they will know not to ever insult my wife."

There was a screech and the sound of a door slamming shut. Had Barnes actually had the man thrown out of the house? If so, good for him.

Narrowing his eyes, Rupert stalked over to Lord Brackford. "What is it to be, my lord? Do you wish to maintain relations with my wife"—that fact seemed to bear repeating—"or not?"

Lord Brackford searched those present, his gaze locking on his wife. "Miriam, you would allow me to be thrown out?"

She placed her hands on her hips. "I would do it myself."

He turned toward Vivian. "Vivian, you owe a duty to your father."

She rose from the table, moved to stand next to Rupert, and took his hand. "I owe a greater obligation to my husband."

The breakfast room became as quiet as a church during prayers. Finally, Vivian's father looked at Rupert. "I'm sorry for the trouble I caused. I wish you happy on your marriage to my daughter."

Rupert stuck his hand out. "We thank you. Now the rest of us are going to my house for a wedding breakfast. You are welcome to join us if you wish."

"I'd like that. You're very generous."

"That must have been some dog," Nick muttered, most likely speaking to himself.

"Oh, she was." Vivian's father took out his handkerchief and for a moment Rupert thought he'd weep.

"Nicholas Beresford." Silvia took him by the ear. "Do you not know when to be quiet?"

"There will be no more talk of dogs." Lady Brackford took her husband by the arm and led him out of the room. "Honestly, you'd think you were a bunch of little boys instead of grown men."

"One time my brothers and I tried to trade my eldest sister for a horse," Hawksworth said, earning him furious glares from all the ladies. "Fortunately, my father discovered the plan. We couldn't sit for a week and were on short rations for a month."

"I'm surprised Susan didn't hit you," Mr. Trevor added.

Hawksworth grinned ruefully. "Oh, she did. Papa had two footmen hold each of us while she took a shot. Made me wish I'd never taught her to punch."

Vivian began to giggle, then laugh, and finally tears ran down her cheeks, and she was holding her stomach, gasping for breath.

"You've given our poor daughter the vapors, Henry."

She waved a hand in front of her face as she tried to speak. "No . . . not vapors," she managed to get out between whoops of laughter.

Rupert held her, trying not to laugh himself. Eventually, she recovered her countenance enough to say, "Rupert, my love, I've never seen anything like this before. You were wonderful. The perfect knight in shining armor. Thank you from the bottom of my heart."

Damn everyone. He kissed her for all they were both worth, which was quite a lot, as it happened.

"All's well that ends well," Freddy chimed in. "My son, I have frequently been proud of you, but never more so than today."

"Yes indeed." Vivian dropped her arms. "Now we have a wedding breakfast to attend."

Standing in the hall of her new home, Vivian was overwhelmed at the number of guests who had arrived. "I had no idea there would be so many people. However did you manage it in such a short time?"

"Mama, Grandmamma, and Cousin Clara arranged it. I merely loaned them my staff."

Even Lord and Lady Banks were present; however, their daughter was apparently suffering from an indisposition and could not attend.

In addition to those of Rupert's friends whom Vivian had already met, the Huntleys, Wivenlys, and Feathertons had also arrived. Vivian had heard of them all, but never before met the other ladies. They were, to a woman, strong and resilient. She couldn't believe her luck in finding not only a wonderful husband but such good friends as well.

"It is time to join our guests, my lady." Rupert grinned as he took her arm.

She stared up into her husband's eyes. "I am the most fortunate of ladies to have found you."

"And I the most fortunate gentleman." Drawing her into his arms, he kissed her lightly. "I love you."

"I know." It had taken her so long to believe she was worth loving. Now his love sank into her bones, her very being. "I love you too. Forever."

"And ever."

CHAPTER THIRTY-ONE

Three hours later, only Vivian's and Rupert's friends and a small collection of other guests were left at Stanstead House. The weather was warm and dry as they gathered at a table near one of the terrace doors.

"Well, this is the end of it." Huntley glanced at each couple in turn. "Who would have thought that this would be the outcome of our wager at Beaumont's wedding?" He touched his glass of champagne to Serena's. "We have all married extremely well."

"I give credit to Marcus for starting this off. If it wasn't for him and Phoebe deciding they'd suit, I would not have met Serena." Robert Beaumont raised his glass. "A toast to finding the right mate."

"And children," Will Wively added, gazing besottedly at his wife, Eugénie.

"Absolutely, children." Kit Featherton grinned at Mary. "We must get together often, as our sons and daughters will be of an age."

"To the wager." Rupert raised his glass. "For some reason I think it helped us."

Nick and Silvia had joined them. He grinned down at his wife. "I don't know anything about a wager, but I think there might be one more wedding before the New Year."

"Who would that be?" Kit asked, his arm around Mary.

Nick motioned with his head to the other side of the room. "Who is that with Hawksworth?"

They all glanced over, but Kit said, "My sister? Hmm, that would be a good match."

Mary punched him playfully on the arm. "I forbid you to say a word to your grandmother. Besides, they do not look as if they are having a pleasant conversation."

"I think it might be too late." Phoebe pulled a face, directing their attention to another group of guests.

Sitting not far from where Miss Featherton and Lord Hawksworth appeared to be having a heated conversation, Kit and Mary's grandmothers, Lady Beaumont, Lady Bellamny, and Clara alternated between sipping wine, glancing at the young couple, and talking.

"Surely they wouldn't." Kit drained his glass and poured another.

Mary groaned. "They are in for it now."

Made in the USA
Lexington, KY
25 May 2019